# Five of Ash

## Gvonni Avner

Cover artwork by Sarah Wiener
Cover design by corvin.bookdesign

ISBN: HB: 979-8-9891476-3-2; PB: 979-8-9891476-4-9; e-book: 979-8-9891476-5-6 *for those who carry hope like a blade*

Aros is forced back to his home realm, a home he hated because of his unpleasant and abusive upbringing. People think the realm is beautiful—and it mostly is—but it isn't without the dark waiting to devour those who tread too close.

# The Continent of Cameleair
## Arteyva

# FIVE OF ASH

# CHAPTER 1

## ALCOHOL, DUST, COMEUPPANCE, AND MONSTERS

**Aros Caelum Hayes**

*The fifth smack to my face sent me to the ground again.*

*I withstood the first three, but the fourth felt like a sting of pain slicing through me. My body shuddered after I fell. Shivers of pain rippled through me as I lay on the ground, small, jagged pebbles stabbing into my knees. I thought that would have been it. I slowly brought my body up again, still on my knees. I looked up. I was shaking. He glowered down at me, his eyes still and full of malice. They felt dark as night, despite being an easy blue. Ever since I could speak, he would make sure to remind me that I was repulsive, worthless, and would always be rejected; that in his and my mother's eyes, I was a disgrace, and that they were mortified that such a monster could have been born. After he hit me for the fifth time, my father reminded me once more.*

*But I wasn't a monster. I was normal. I looked like everyone else. I looked just like any other five-year-old.*

My grip around the edges of the sink tightens. I could break this if I wanted to. I wouldn't even need to use magic; I'd do it with my bare hands. At twenty-four, I'm more than strong enough now. But no, this isn't the place. There is no need.

I look up into the grimy mirror. I see myself through the permanent haze of filth that glazes over it. My dark hair of loose curls and wavy strands begins to fall out of place. Unlike my father, my eyes are also dark. My light olive skin tone pairs well. Most people have no clue where I'm from. Several countries have been guessed as to where I was born, where my parents come from. No one has ever guessed right. I don't blame anyone for that, though, since I'm not even from Earth. After ten years of being here, I know how to go unnoticed.

I wash my hands quickly and return to the bar where Nick is sitting. I've considered him my best friend for the past five years, though recently I haven't been so sure.

"What took you so long? Were you banging a dude in there?" he asks. Nick is nearly half a foot shorter than me. I miss six feet by just a hair.

I answer by shooting him a glare.

"Jeez," he says. "Fine, sucking some dick. Whatever you're into." He gets up and walks toward a couple of girls who are chatting at one of the small, square tables pushed against the brick wall.

At first, his comments annoyed me. Mostly because I've never even done anything like that—not that it would matter much. I've met all sorts of people on Earth and have gotten along well with them. The rule applies to everyone; it doesn't matter who you are or who you are into. What matters is what you do, how you act, and how you treat others. It's been months of this now, and his words make me feel numb. But worse than that, they make me feel lonely. And then more of those memories come back.

*My first day at a new school. I was transferred when it was discovered that I possessed a "lower order" of Maleficium. Anyone possessing any sort of Magis would attend a school dedicated to teaching and honing their powers. I was a late bloomer, so I spent my first years at a normal learning* center. Even after my powers developed, my parents still believed I was unworthy. They had adopted a newborn shortly after the previous incident. They named him "Joshua" so that he would have a strong and typical name—a name that indicated he was worthy. Joshua was blessed by one of the Fae. My parents said that he would grow to possess extraordinary magical abilities of strength and willpower. Eventually, Joshua would be sent to a prestigious school in my homeland of Soulstice. They sent me to a boarding school in Voltar, a mountainous region closed off from the rest of the world.

I was ten when they transferred me. My first months there felt like heaven, despite the dangerous land around me. The school was a safe place in what was otherwise considered to be a land of hell. But after half a year, my parents caught wind that I was making friends, so they warned all the other parents of my dark disposition and volatile nature, which caused the other kids to fear me. So, I studied alone, I played alone, I roomed alone, until I was fourteen. Still, ostracized and feared, it wasn't enough for my parents. They wanted me dead. So, they spread rumors of my fate—how I was doomed to be possessed by a demon that would force me to kill them all.

One night, five of the final-year students decided they would destroy the threat to their lives. I was asleep, and their sneak attack left me nearly defenseless. Stripped down and tied to a lamppost in the front courtyard, frost covering all surfaces of the land and snow blowing in the light storm, they took turns casting their powers at me. And once again, it was like I was back with my abusive parents, being tortured over and over and over. One of them pulled out a sword, a blade made of fire and imbued with poison. The slightest touch to it would feel like a cut deeper than any ordinary sword could manage. Delicately, the blade caressed the right side of my chest. I yelled louder than I ever thought I could. The sensation of burning, the feel of blood spilling down my torso, and the spasm-inducing poison that crept into my veins—

And that's when it happened. A pulse of energy escaped from my body.

*They were seventeen, and all five of them flew back. The one holding the sword was impaled by it; the sword, being as powerful as it was, killed him instantly. Another kid didn't survive the impact with the ground, but the other three did. There was a twelve-foot radius around me of barren dirt. Flames licked the edges, melting the snow around, before being drowned by the water it created. My restraints broke, and I fell to the ground.*

*I looked up as I stood. The three survivors stared at me, eyes wide with fear. I could tell they wanted to run, but they were frozen in terror. I took a step toward them but then remembered that this wasn't their fault. They were fed lies by their parents, who got them from mine. I looked at the school. The fortress looked almost like a castle, though it didn't stand tall nor have towers. It only had three floors.*

*I ran into the woods. There was no future at the school. There was no future in the world. I had to escape somehow.*

I turn my ear to listen to what Nick is saying. I can't hear him. The girls are speaking, though. They don't sound interested. He probably doesn't notice. Or care. But he comes back quickly enough. I don't mention anything to him.

"Smile," he barks. "You look miserable, and I don't want miserable friends."

"Hard not to be miserable when your company sucks," I say without thinking.

He jerks his head and glares at me. "Hanging out with you isn't fun. You're a loser, dude. No wonder your parents didn't want you."

I clench my jaw. He's drunk, I know it. All those years being around him, I thought it would be safe to tell him bits of my past. Funny how when you're so desperate for someone to talk to, you end up with the worst kind of people.

The bartender comes up and slides a shot toward me.

"On the house," she tells me, loud enough to make her intention clear. She barely gives me a smile before walking away to attend to other customers.

"Even she feels bad for you," Nick snickers, his jealousy plain as day.

Some days my mind feels as if it were my worst enemy. Flooding me with the memories I so desperately try to escape from. No matter how far the past travels, my mind brings it back as if it all happened yesterday. But fourteen years of suffering doesn't happen in just one day. It happens over *fourteen damned years*. Simple math that my mind just refuses to comprehend.

"Don't worry," he says. There is something in his voice that I don't like. He's more drunk than when I saw him last, which hasn't been that long. "Since you won't, I'll fuck her for you."

I punch him in the nose, turning my head to look at him after I make contact. He topples backward onto the ground and hits his head. He falls unconscious. *No, you're not getting off that easy.*

I kneel and place my hand on his head. This isn't something I can do to someone like me, but to an ordinary, it isn't much of a problem. I heal the trauma he endured but leave the pain of my blow. His eyes open. I stand up and tower over him until he picks himself off the floor. I know that he knows he can't beat me. I have been physically stronger than him since we met.

He doesn't say anything. Nick throws his body at me. I dodge. He charges again. I dodge, but he throws his arm out to catch me. I catch it and flip him over, throwing him back on the ground.

A crowd of people comes by to watch. Nick starts to get up, but I kick him down again.

A hand touches my shoulder and tries to pull me back. I break free from it. The man behind me wraps his arms around my torso. I look up at his round, red face and nearly bald head. He's probably a bouncer, but he wasn't out front when I arrived. The man is just doing his job. He doesn't deserve it, but I don't have a choice. As he begins to drag me away, I kick his shin with the back of my foot. It doesn't do anything. I don't even think he felt it.

Fine.

I grab his arms. It takes seconds before he releases me, his arms suffering near-second-degree burns.

A quick glance around the dive bar tells me that the chaos is just beginning. People pull out their phones, most likely calling the police. Nick still lies on the ground, but I can tell he's planning to come after me. The large bouncer, confused and in pain, spots me and charges.

I take a step back. Everything around me disappears. First, a gray haze, and then a black nothingness. Then the spotlight comes. I've been here before. Commonly known as the Shadow Realm, one of the seven realms of this universe, the place serves as both a resting place for the dead and a passage between the realms—or at least I think it does.

I sigh and take a seat on the ground.

"I would apologize for making you wait for so long, but I was cleaning up your mess. Again."

The voice is unaccompanied. Kreavlos exists in the darkness behind the shadows, and he serves as the Overlord of the Shadow Realm, though I am certain it's a self-imposed name. Some say that he is the shadows. I say the prick is too ugly to want to show his face.

All jokes aside, he has rescued me from some unpleasant situations. He is also the only one who never cared about the rumors or even believed them. For that, I hold him in high regard.

"I'm sorry," I say, hanging my head.

"No, you're not," he tells me. "You hold in so much rage, so much anger and hatred, and wait for the moment for someone—anyone—to push you over the edge so you can let it all out." He stops. I don't say anything. "Maybe you just wait until you find an excuse to justify unleashing your power. But you use your power on the ordinary."

"Well, if there were more people like me on Earth, I'd happily fight them."

I get the idea that Kreavlos sits back in his chair, even though I am certain he truly has no physical form.

"That's your problem. You want to pick fights. Most people in your situation would find light in their dark past and pave a path away from it."

"Well, I guess I'm just not like other people."

Kreavlos huffs.

"You don't think you're the only one who has ever lived a life like yours, do you? There isn't even a named number today that can count the number of lives that people have lived. You are not nearly as unique as you imagine yourself to be."

I laugh. "My parents have already told me that I'm nothing special."

"That's where they are wrong. You have no idea how special you are—how powerful you are," he says. "You have only a small inkling of your strength. But it has been years since you've done anything like you did that night."

"Yeah, well..." I say, trailing off.

*The frozen air numbed my body. I could no longer feel the pain, though a dark ooze leaked out of the gash across my chest. I tripped over a branch and my face fell right into the snow. I was still naked, and it surely wouldn't be long until the outer, most exposed parts of my body fell off.*

*I got up and kept running. I didn't think anyone followed me. No one would be stupid enough to do so. Not after what I had just done.*

*As I ran through the trees, along the faint path rarely traveled, I heard rustling in the distance. I ran faster. It could have been a pack of wolves. It could have been something far more dangerous.*

*I never found out. Fog rolled in quickly. The wind picked up. Night was deepening, growing darker. The moon disappeared behind a shadow. Darkness began to swallow the trees. Whatever had been rustling in the distance stopped. I tried, but I couldn't escape it. The Dark Wind overcame me.*

*And that was the first time I ended up in the Shadow Realm, the first time that I met Kreavlos. The Dark Wind brought me there. I thought it was just a myth. Most people still do. But I know better now.*

*Back then—and even now—Kreavlos refuses to tell me anything more of the Dark Wind. His corporeal shadows, the ones he used to pluck me out of the bar, feel similar to the Wind, but they are much less terrifying.*

*I haven't seen the Dark Wind since that night.*


"It might be time for you to return to Arteyva."

The silence between us is loud. He knows I hate that place. I don't answer.

He remains as silent as ever. Without him, I am stuck here, some place in between all other realms, and I can't go far beyond the light. I've tried before, but no matter what direction I walk in, I end up walking back into the spotlight each time I make for the dark.

He leaves me no choice, even though he knows exactly what I am going to say.

"I intend never to go back there again."

He lets my words echo in the nothingness.

"I know, but soon, that choice may no longer be a choice."

"That sounds like a half-baked riddle," I retort.

"Hm. Well, you'll soon see."

I hear a loud snap, thunderous—as if it came from a giant's fingers. Suddenly, I'm back in the bar. It looks like no time has passed. Nick is still lying on the ground. The bouncer is there, his arm fully healed. But instead of chasing after me, he lifts Nick to his feet and forcefully escorts him out.

Confused, I look around slowly. People stare at me, their eyes wide with awe. Each time I catch someone's gaze, they quickly look away. I sit back at the bar. The same bartender who gave me a free shot slides another one over. I look up at her. Her skin is darker than mine, and her long, curly hair is a lighter shade of brown.

"Last call happened while you were in the bathroom," she says. "But I saved this for you. And," she says slowly and leans on the counter, "if you want, I can get you another drink while you wait for me to close up."

I chuckle softly. Kreavlos saw everything. That's why he put me right back where I was, though he made some memory adjustments for the ordinary. Whatever he did, everyone now thinks that Nick attacked me and that I put him down in self-defense. It also explains why their sense of time is off.

"Yeah, sure," I say. She smiles and walks away.

She's forward. I don't even know her name. I almost walk out, not caring to find out where she wants to take me. I don't, though. I stay put.

The bar closes. I drink only half the glass she left me while I wait for her to get off work. When she's done, the bartender nods to the front door. I get up and follow.

Other than the noise of the last customers leaving, the night is quiet. Two main roads are nearby, but no cars are about. Streetlights are plenty, a nice white along the roads, and orange at the intersection.

The bartender walks toward the neighborhood.

"Where are we going?" I call after her. I haven't followed yet.

She turns. "My place. I don't live far," she says. She smiles and keeps walking, knowing I'll follow. I do.

We turn a corner and then walk up a few steps into an apartment complex. She buzzes the pad to let us in.

"Do you mind stairs?" she asks.

"No," I tell her. I begin to get a weird vibe from her. But I've already come this far—it would be a waste to leave now.

"Didn't think so."

She jogs up the stairs to the fifth floor. I follow.

Soon enough, we're inside her apartment. A two-bedroom. She puts a finger to her mouth, telling me to keep quiet. We pass what I assume is her roommate's room. Once inside her room, she gently closes her door and runs at me, shoving me until I fall back onto her bed in the corner. She presses her mouth against mine.

Quickly she moves to my neck before sitting up. Something dances in her eyes. She grabs the collar of my shirt and pulls. She pulls again. And again. That's when I gather that she's trying to tear it off.

I laugh. "Are you trying to rip my shirt off?"

She bows her head. "I thought it would be dramatic."

"You like drama in the bedroom?" I ask, genuinely curious—maybe concerned.

Now she laughs. "No, not like that. I meant...passionate. Primal. You know, like the movies."

I raise an eyebrow. "The movies? You mean, like po—"

"No! Don't say it." She laughs.

I tilt her chin up to meet her gaze. I take my shirt off and push her back. She's wearing a crop top with some band on it that I don't recognize. I hope she isn't very fond of the shirt. I tug on it, tearing it in two.

"Of course," she says, chuckling. She quickly sits upright and places her hand on my chest. Gently, she pushes me back. When I lie down, she moves her head toward my waist. She tugs at my jeans, pulling them off, and then grabs me through my boxers. She takes me in her mouth. I close my eyes while she goes at it for a while.

I sit up and gently pull back her hair. I look into her eyes, kiss her, and then spin her around. I rip the straps off her bra and then close my hands around her neck. She lets out a gasp.

All she wants is to fulfill her fantasy. Maybe she reads books or is addicted to some other form of media. Either way, I give it to her.

When we're done, I tell her that I need to get going.

"Oh, but..." she trails off into silence.

I get up and start dressing.

"You sure you can't stay? We can go another round if you like."

I smile, holding my shirt in my hands.

"I'm tired," I tell her. I put on my shirt and gather my shoes.

As I'm about to leave, she says, "I never got your name."

"And I didn't get yours."

She sits on the bed, her blanket barely covering her. "I'm Jasmine."

I let out a quiet sigh. After some thought, I tell her, "My name is Aros."

The quiet between us keeps me there, even though I really want to leave.

"Do you want my number or something?"

"No." I say it too quickly. I sigh again and look at her. "I mean, I'm not on social media." I used to be, but it was always such a waste of time.

She looks up at me, her eyes wide. Knowing she'll feel disappointed and sad, not to mention whatever else, even if this was her idea, I know I have to do something. I walk to her and gently place my hand on her forehead. She looks at me again and smiles. I smile back. "Now. Sleep."

Her eyes close and her head falls, but I catch it and gently lay it on her pillow. The ordinary are too easy. Just like how I healed Nick, I could never do something like that to someone from my world.

It's half past four in the morning, and I'm still pissed about what happened with Nick and terrified of the possibility of having to return to Arteyva. I leave the bedroom.

Her roommate is in the kitchen, which is by the front door.

"Did you have a fun night?" she asks coyly. She has thin blonde hair and brown eyes. She is also topless, but I can't see much in the dim lighting. Not that I want to.

"Sure," I say, making for the door. She steps in front of it, blocking my way.

"We can have fun now," she whispers. "More fun than you can imagine. But I want you to be vocal." She leans in closer. Her breath smells so strongly of cheap vodka that I can almost taste it. I take a small step back, saying nothing.

She leans in again, but I turn my face away.

"I'm prettier than she is, you'll enjoy me much more, I promise you that." Her lips brush my cheek.

God, this chick is unbearable. And clearly has self-esteem issues.

I turn to face her. She's nearly as tall as I am. I look her dead in the eye. "You are so far from my type. Thanks, but, not really." I put my hand on her shoulder and gently move her out of my way. I don't need to look back to see the stunned look on her face; I can imagine it well enough.

To avoid any other interactions with her in case she comes chasing me, I jump off the stairwell into the bushes below, using magic to pulse energy from my hands to slow my descent when I'm near the ground.

The street remains quiet. I need to get back home so I can think. I need to get there fast. Kreavlos warned that I would not have a choice but to return to Arteyva. Why? What would force me to go back?

If I weren't so tired, I'd take a shot at teleportation, but that kind of magic is incredibly dangerous, and even those who are gifted with that power use it sparingly.

Even though I can do more on Earth than I can in the realm of Arteyva, I won't try it. Last time I did, Kreavlos saved my life. I vowed to never attempt it again, especially not when I'm this tired.

I let out a sigh. If only I had taken my car to the bar.

Then I remember: Nick has his truck. I got a ride with him to the bar since it was his idea to go out. I head back, hoping that for some reason he's still there. Knowing him and his constant, desperate attempts at getting attention, he still is.

When the bar comes into view, it looks deserted, but there are two cars in the lot right next to it. Spotting his beat-up white pickup isn't hard. I used to find something to admire about it: the constant damage and irresponsible driving it took, and to come out working after a shoddy repair. I walk up to it. Nick is sleeping in the driver's seat, face against the window and mouth wide open.

I touch my finger to the keyhole to unlock it. I open the door. Nick falls out, but I catch him. I don't need him waking up now. But if he does, I'll just put him back to sleep. Gently, I move him over to the other side. He's still snoring. I start up the truck and head home.

The drive, usually around forty minutes, is only twenty, and I didn't even have to use magic to make sure all the traffic lights stayed green, and the freeways were pleasantly empty. Usually packed, North Hollywood is quite lonely this early Sunday morning.

I park a ten-minute walk from my place. I don't need Nick outside where I live, though he will know that, somehow, his truck got me home because he lives ten minutes from the bar, but in the opposite direction. In the morning he'll remember what happened, even if everyone else at the bar would remember it differently. I'll get some rude texts when he wakes, maybe even some thoroughly ineffective threats. Or he'll take the hour-long drive back to his house in silence, except for the thoughts that will haunt his mind for years.

The 101, the 134, and just off the 210. Something about that drive instills peace of mind in me, useful for whenever I feel like lashing out. The roadways, vehicles, and all the mechanics of travel—Earth surely is different from Arteyva. The humans—the ordinary—of Earth live such sad lives. Magic runs deep within their world, but they have all but destroyed it, or they sat back and watched people destroy it. They are otherwise blind to what is right in front of them.

Reaching my building, I walk into the foyer and head up to the top floor. The penthouse overlooks Old Pasadena. The lights of the nightlife are mostly off. Most people out and about are probably starting their usual early day rather than ending their late night.

The head of my bed rests against a wall. Windows line two sides of the room since the bedroom is situated at the corner of the building. I lay down, pondering where to go from here. Starting over would be easy. But is it warranted? Is that even something I want to do? I've started my life over plenty, moving across the country and back. Always picking up new friends, new hobbies, only to watch them dissolve or break apart.

Sleep overcomes me quickly. I feel stuck in the same spot, my bed, but it is surrounded by darkness, with the unseen light shining down on it. I climb out of it, and I am standing in the heart of Downtown Los Angeles. The afternoon sun is hot. I look around the packed roads. Then the shadows close in. The wind picks up. It's as if the clouds moved overhead, but the sky is as blue as ever. The day soon feels like night.

And then I hear the screams.

I jolt awake and sit up. Beads of sweat fall from my hair onto my lap. My shirt is sticky, and my jeans are uncomfortable and tight. I don't usually sweat in my sleep. Even with the nightmares of my childhood tormenting my dreams, I don't. Usually, I either wake up immediately or ride out the nightmare unfazed. There's something unusual going on.

I remove my jeans and shirt. I had taken my shoes off last night but kept the socks on. I toss those into a hamper. I walk to the window and look out at the city. The sun is bright. A quick glance at my watch tells me that it is past ten.

After a quick shower, I head outside. It's a short walk to a coffee shop I frequent.

"Good morning, Aros," Olivia says as she sees me walk in out of the corner of her eye. She's putting together a cup for another customer. Around my age, Olivia aspires to be a photographer. We've hung out a few times, but only as friends. I've never made any moves on her. After having been a regular for a bit, we talked more and more, and our relationship evolved into one of those friendships that feel more like we're just casual friends that see each other every once in a while. But now, I realize that I might cherish our relationship more than I thought I had.

Her deep, fiery auburn hair whips around as she turns. Its layered waves go down to the middle of her back. She works six days out of the week to keep up with her bills while still finding time to put in at least five hours of dance a week and then countless hours into photography. I've offered for her to stay with me for free. I have the space. But she always declines.

When she's done servicing her customer, she calls me up.

"What will it be today?" she asks, smiling wide with her pearly teeth. Her eyes are a deep blue, their color popping out against the red of her hair. She's pretty, and I am sure a lot of the male customers come here because of her.

"Uh, I'll just do a black coffee."

"No problem," she says, tapping onto her screen. Double-checking to make sure I didn't misspeak, she asks, "Any syrup?" She knows my usual.

I shake my head.

"What kind of milk?" Olivia bites her lip, wondering if I truly want just a black coffee.

I shake my head again.

"I see," she says softly. "It was one of those nights."

Black coffee isn't my go-to. In reality, I despise it. But when I want to try to clear my head and arrange my thoughts, I usually drink a cup. It's like the monotonous, bitter, and near-painless torture helps me think clearly.

It doesn't take long for her to make it. She walks up to the counter. I reach out my hand, but she doesn't give it to me.

"Tiffany, I'm gonna take five!" she calls back to the blonde girl. Tiffany turns around and nods her head. She gives me a warm wave, smiles, and gets back to cleaning down the back counter.

Olivia leads me to a table by the window. I sit across from her. She then pushes the coffee toward me.

"What happened?"

I take a sip of the coffee. Olivia chuckles silently at me as I swallow the disgusting drink. Maybe I do this to punish myself. When I don't answer, she asks again.

I can't tell her about Kreavlos or anything about the Shadow Realm. Looking into her eyes, there's no way I'd tell her about the girl from last night, not when I am feeling guilty about it, despite there being no reason to be. It's just that the one-nights are all I've ever known.

So, with a sigh, I tell her about Nick and the fight we had. I tell her the details as most of the people there would remember just in case she hears the story from someone else. I'm not worried about any footage of the fight as Kreavlos would have seen that all of it got erased.

She only asked for five minutes, but I take my time telling her, sipping on the pungent coffee while in the back of my mind imagining all the reasons that would force me to return to my home world.

"Well, that sounds shitty," Olivia tells me. "But fuck Nick. I never liked him much anyway, and I only met him twice."

Twice? Nick and I got coffee here once almost a year ago, but he lives on the other side of LA, and he even told me that he didn't like the coffee from here.

Olivia knows I'm confused and tells me, "He came in a couple of months after you brought him here to ask me out."

I raise an eyebrow at her.

"Of course, I said no to him," she tells me. "I haven't been on a date in two years because I'm focusing on my dream. I wasn't going to make time for a date, especially not with someone like Nick."

"Is there someone you would make time for?"

The words run from my mouth before I can think better than to ask her something like that.

Olivia looks away for a second, pondering. She breathes in. For a moment, I think she's going to answer, and I wait with bated breath, both hoping and fearing that she says she would go out with me.

"If the right guy came along and asked—" she says, stopping abruptly. "Well, that remains to be seen."

I blink at her. She gets up and puts a soft hand on my shoulder. She'd hug me if she could, but her manager wouldn't like that. I've met him before. He's a decent, respectable guy, but he likes his employees to be professional with the customers.

"Again, screw Nick. People will come along and try to use you or put you down because they know that there isn't anything that you can't accomplish. I'm not sure what it is exactly, but you are amazing, Aros. So let the Nicks live out their lives in the pity they wallow in. You don't need that."

She walks away without giving me time to answer. I know she wants to say more on that subject, but it's clear she feels she almost said too much. I can feel it now between us, this tension building up. In these last twenty minutes, I've developed feelings for her. Maybe she already had them for me.

All I can do right now is hope I'm not just imagining things. Making a move if all she wants between us is a friendship would make things awkward. I can't risk that.

I gulp down the last half of the coffee and get up to leave. I look back at the coffee bar, but Olivia isn't there. I head out. I take an hour walk to a long bridge near the freeway that passes by the city. Tall lampposts standing in pairs line both sides. I look out at the landscape below. This bridge is brilliant at night and one of the prettiest sights in the entire county. I wonder why Olivia hasn't done any shoots out here. I should ask her about it next time I see her.

I stand here for hours. Cars pass behind me, but only one person walks by.

I want to speak with Kreavlos again, but I have no way of getting to the Shadow Realm by myself. I can call out for him and hope he answers, but I have a feeling he is unlikely to.

The sun begins to really blaze down. I look up at the sky. A few birds fly over. Two of them land on the bridge, only to quickly fly away when a car comes by.

An explosion tears through the atmosphere, followed by a loud roar. I look toward the city, but I can't see anything. The quiet that follows unnerves me.

I run back toward Old Pasadena. To make it there quickly, I wave my arms in the air until I flag down a car, run over to the driver, put him to sleep, and race over. When I turn onto the main street that runs through Old Town, I can see most of the city. I notice a cloud of dust in the distance. I hop out, leaving the owner in the passenger seat as I did Nick last night.

Then I hear the roar again. I pray that whatever the cloud of dust is, that Olivia is safe.

Screams erupt around me. Part of a building collapses as a winged beast flies straight into it. The beast soars into the air again. Something jumps off. I run toward it.

A scaly, bony creature lands in the middle of the road, stopping a car in its tracks with its bare hands. It has long, pointed ears and antlers sticking out of its head. With red, glowering eyes and a pointed nose, the creature looks around, sniffing the air, searching for food. There isn't anything alive that it wouldn't eat.

The cursed, demonic imps live in the darkest places on Arteyva, places forbidden for even someone like me to enter. As such, the ordinary on Earth are unable to see them—though if the humans were in my realm, they would definitely be able to.

The imp isn't loud, so they probably can't even hear it. The paralyz-ing fear that must be coursing through their blood is something I can't even begin to imagine. All around them, there is destruction, but no noticeable reason for it. It's as if their world is just blowing up. I imagine the horror it would be to see someone fly into the air and then see chunks of them disappear as an invisible monster eats them.

A monster. This is what my parents called me. I am nothing like this creature.

I am usually extremely careful about my use of magic, but the people around here are too distracted to notice someone like me.

The winged beast circles the sky over the imp, who is crawling on top of a vehicle. The driver of the car is unconscious. His head probably slammed into the steering wheel when the vehicle collided with the imp's hand. The imp only stands at five feet, but its scales and bones are stronger than most materials on Earth.

The imp punches the windshield to break in. I run along the sidewalk. When I am close enough, I send out a pulse of energy from my palm. The imp flies off the car and into the road. All the other vehicles in the immediate area had stopped driving, but beyond this ring of commotion, people are scrambling to get away from where the blast was.

I look down the street. Olivia seems to be safe, but the coffee shop is just two blocks away.

The imp snaps its head toward me. Its eyes flash before it charges, running on all fours. When it gets close, I take a sidestep, dodging its grasp. My eyes widen as it scoots to a stop, tumbling into the remaining bits of the side of the building its ride crashed through. I don't see any dead bodies. At least for now.

The imp lunges at me. I swipe at it, releasing a wave of energy. The imp flies again into the demolished wall.

Looking like a madman just standing there, I can feel several pairs of eyes on me. Of course, everyone can see me, but they can't see the creature whose attacks I keep dodging and deflecting. Soon enough, people will see me as the threat.

Knowing that this is going to be even harder, I run into the building, jumping over the low edge of the remaining outer wall. Three bodies are sprawled on the ground, two of them crushed by chunks of concrete. I was wrong. People have already died. Even though Kreavlos can erase this moment from everyone's minds, he can't bring people back from the dead.

With a shriek, the imp flies across the room, launching itself from the ground, and tackles me. It claws at me and tries to clamp down on my neck with its numerous short and pointed teeth.

I grab its head with both hands. It struggles violently, and I strain my arms trying to keep it in my grasp. I send out another pulse from my palms. The recoil from my magic vibrates through my hands, but I was ready for it. The imp, on the other hand, cries out as its skull is crushed. I look into its dark eyes as water fills them.

I toss the imp across the room. It tumbles across the floor, crashing into chairs and tables, then smacking into a large cabinet that must have fallen through the gaping hole in the ceiling. The imp shakes from the pain but does its best to stand back up.

Taking in a deep breath, I let out a jet of fire from my hands. I can smell its burning scales and bones in the air. I keep at it until its body is crispy, overcooked, and undoubtedly dead. I then blast it with energy, blowing it up into ash.

A loud roar rumbles through the air, followed by a chorus of screams that tell me the ordinaries can hear the beast, even if they can't see it. I dash back outside and look around. People are running, hands over their heads, as they try to escape whatever it is that they heard.

The beast lands on the road and swipes at someone with its tail. The person flies through the air and into a brick building, dead on impact.

"Aros!"

My heart stops. I turn my head. Olivia is running toward me, her eyes full of fear. "What was that sound?" She's still running. She has no idea that she's about to be parallel to the beast's path.

Just our luck, the winged creature turns its head curiously. Olivia slows to a walk just as she passes the beast's left hind leg.

Thinking fast and hoping it works, I look past Olivia. When she tries to catch my eye, she follows my gaze and turns her head back, just as I'd hoped. I reach out my hand, turn to face across the street, snap my fingers, and make an abandoned vehicle rise into the air, swirls of my energy manipulation holding its weight, and crash back down.

The creature snaps its head back to look at the noise and flies off toward it. A new wave of screaming and commotion erupts from the people. Olivia looks around in confusion, her hair blowing in the wind. I run toward her, pulling her with me as I pass, trying to get her as far away as possible, but I can't leave the area completely. Not with all the ordinary still in danger.

"What happened here?" she asks, breathing out. She looks around, panicked. To her, it must look like a bomb went off. "I heard the blast, but the roar?"

I turn my head back to peek at the beast. It's moving its head wildly, but it doesn't attack. With any hope, the beast was forcefully bonded to the imp and is slowly dying without its life source. Not likely, though.

"Olivia, listen to me," I plead, looking into her eyes. Even now, I can't help but notice how stunning they are. The fear that builds inside me makes my heart break. "I need you to run away, back to the coffee shop, and beyond. I don't have time to explain."

"What do you mean?"

I duck, pushing Olivia down by her shoulders as the beast roars again.

"What is it? It sounds like a monster!"

The creature has turned around and is taking slow steps toward us. Its strides are long, so it will soon be close enough to lower its head and swallow us whole. I have no clue how I am going to stop that thing.

"Please, get out of here. You might not see me for a while—"

Another roar. The ground shakes.

"What do you mean?" she shouts. Tears are pooling in her eyes. There's more than just fear—she almost looks hurt. When I don't answer, she shouts again, "What do you mean?"

"Go! Now!" My voice cracks with urgency.

Olivia doesn't move.

Then I hear a whistling in the air, followed by a howling wind. I look up over Olivia's shoulder. A darkening storm of wind rushes toward me from behind her. It's been a decade since I've seen it.

"Shit."

# Chapter 2

## Family Matters to Rule a Kingdom

**Aros Caelum Hayes**

There is nothing but darkness at first. The howls of the wind blend into a sound like a passing train. When this happened the first time, I was disoriented. Back then, I was so young, already afraid... and naked. Now... well, now I'm just pissed.

Soon enough, the darkness will fade, and I'll be standing in front of Kreavlos. Or rather, I imagine myself standing in front of him. I take deep breaths to calm myself.

If, for any reason, he hasn't already handled the situation back on Earth, I will have to go back immediately. But even thinking this causes me to worry. What if Olivia isn't safe? What if that monster is still terrorizing the city? I couldn't get a good enough look at it to know what it was. But I will have to ask Kreavlos how it got there in the first place. Everything that passes through the realms must go through the Shadow Realm. Kreavlos keeps things where they should be.

Technically, I am an exception.

Light blinks in the total black. The sounds die out. After a moment of silence, I hear footsteps on what sounds like stone. I don't remember this. Maybe the Dark Wind carried more than just me to the Shadow

Realm?

In what feels like a blinding flash, I am returned to solid ground. My eyes widen as I look around, my vision quickly coming to me. I am not in the Shadow Realm.

All around me, towering bookcases stand as still as ever, perfectly and neatly packed with books of all sizes. Flames of light float in the air close to the ceiling, their fire magically trapped in an everlasting spell, so that even if the conjurer were to perish, the lights would still exist.

The floor is lined with travertine. Columns of stone decorate the edges of the wide room, leading to the back where the walls curve into a crescent. The arched window covers most of the back wall, revealing a night of rain and the hint of a forest.

Footsteps approach from behind a bookcase.

"Oh!" She drops her books in surprise. As she bends down to pick them up, her glasses fall off. At least they land on a book and don't break. I walk over to help her pick them up. I gather the books in my hands.

"Get your glasses," I tell her. She does. She stands back up to her full height, which is about a head shorter than I am.

"Thanks, dear," she says, holding out her hands to grab the books. "I'll take those."

"No," I say, then smile. "I'll help. Where were you taking them?"

The wrinkles in her forehead crease, and she purses her thin lips, eyes narrowing in confusion.

"You don't seem like the servant type," she tells me. She reaches her hands out again, but this time they're shaking. "Now, if you would be so kind, my liege." She bows her head slightly.

My liege?

"What are you doing here?" The noise from behind startles me. I turn around quickly. I feel someone brush against me. The older lady snatches the books from my grasp.

"Princess Mattias," the lady whispers loudly. I suspect she's out of breath. "I am just closing up for the night."

Princess Mattias is easily more than a foot shorter than me. She has tan skin like mine, long dark hair, and matching eyes. She walks toward us. The way she carries herself almost makes me bow.

"No, I meant him."

Her voice sounds cold, unyielding, and unforgiving. I get the feeling that I've done something wrong.

"I—I—"

I stop myself and gather my composure. I'm not about to stutter.

"Did you say something?" There is a hint of amusement in her voice now. Out of the corner of my eye, I notice the nice lady's legs shaking.

"I was just offering my help," I tell her, my voice deeper than usual.

"Do you not know that it is illegal for a servant to let a nobleman or guest assist in their work?" Princess Mattias steps closer.

What kind of place is this?

I then remind myself I am probably not on Earth. Unfortunately, I get a good idea of where I am. The Magis in the air is heavy, unlike on Earth.

"Where do you hail from?" she asks.

"Soulstice."

"My, my, aren't you the bad liar."

I look down at my t-shirt. I know what she means. My shirt is off-white; you can nearly see the color of my skin through it. My jeans are, well, jeans. And I am wearing running shoes. I probably look like an alien. Meanwhile, the princess and the librarian are wearing linen gowns, though the princess wears color, while the servant's gown is thin and a translucent brown.

"Grace, leave," Princess Mattias commands. Grace takes a step, but the princess holds out her arm. She turns to face the older lady, smiles warmly, and says, "Leave the books."

If anything, the older lady looks more scared. "B—but Princess…"

"I want to read them tonight, so I will be taking them from you."

I know the princess is lying. She's just saving the lady from working too hard. I don't even know how late it is, but with the feeling of quiet all around, I imagine most people are in bed. And the servant librarian has probably had an extremely long day.

Then again, I am in a library, and it might be just past dinner.

Grace places the books gently on a table. She bows in thanks to her princess, her eyes filling with tears, before scurrying out of the library.

When the footsteps disappear, the princess shoots me a look.

"We're going for a walk," she says, picking up the books and walking toward the doorway. She doesn't wait for me to follow. The library leads right out into a straight corridor.

I need to know exactly where the hell I am. Why am I not in the Shadow Realm? What happened? If I think too much, the questions will eat me up. But still, I can't help but wonder if Olivia is safe. There is also the possibility that, without knowing why I am wherever here is, and with no way to get to the Shadow Realm, I may never see Olivia again. I may never see Earth again.

"First, we need to get you out of that ridiculous outfit," she snaps, laughing at me.

"First, I think I should know your name."

"You heard it," she retorts. "If anything, I should know yours."

Walking beside her now, I turn my head to face her and raise an eyebrow.

"Fine, I'll admit I'm curious enough," she says. "My name is Cami-la."

I nod my head. "Aros."

The corridor we walk down is wider than some apartment living rooms back on Earth. Over two typical stories tall and made of smooth stone, the corridor feels like a musty road that leads to a swamp. It reminds me of the corridors back at the school on Voltar, just bigger.

We pass by a long table lined against the wall. There is a quill and a piece of blank parchment lying on it. The quill surprises me, as surely they must have pens here. The boarding school in Voltar did.

Camila places the books on the table, barely slowing down her walk.

"So, where are you really from?" she asks again.

I let out a chuckle. "Really, I'm from Soulstice." I worry that she doesn't know where that is, but she should if she indeed is a princess.

I let the silence fill her mind with a thousand questions. We walk up a long flight of stairs that curves to the right in a spiral. We only go up one floor.

"I fled to Earth ten years ago," I tell her, though it isn't entirely true. "I really don't feel like getting into the details."

"You don't have to," she tells me quickly. "I know who you are."

I stop. Camila turns back to look at me.

"How do you know who I am?" I ask her, my voice nearly cracking. My parents would recognize me, eventually, that is, and then immediately try to kill me. My existence would threaten the life they've lied about for years.

"Edlyn rules over the land of Voltar, since Voltar is wholly unpopulated and is in our backyard."

I had my guesses, but I wasn't sure until now. I am back on Arteyva. Edlyn does indeed have claim over Voltar. I wouldn't say that Voltar is in their backyard. A wide river divides the two lands, and Voltar is full of rivers, dense forests, and a steep mountain in the north with almost no passable path. Edlyn, however, is mostly forested, with a gentle climb from the south up to the north, except for the mountains in the east.

"I was ten when the incident happened at school," she goes on. "You didn't know me then, but I knew about you." Camila stops by a wood and iron door. She unlocks it with a wave of her hand and steps inside. I can't do that here. The castle is protected with Magis that prevent unauthorized people from using their powers to access it. I follow Camila through the doorway.

What appears to be a bedroom closely resembles a closet. Trunks lie about, their contents spilling onto the cold floor. A bed in the corner is suffocated by piles of clothing, while one wall has a built-in shelf of books and cobwebs.

Camila snaps her fingers, and the lights from the chandelier above turn on. She points to a pair of woolen trousers and a thin silk shirt hanging off the bed before grabbing them. She tosses them to me. The silk is woven with threads of *fanglac*, a plant that grows only under the uninterrupted light of a full moon. These are the clothes of the wealthy.

"This room used to be my brother's," she says. "But he was killed before I was born. I am the youngest of four, five if you count Davide."

"How old was he?" I ask, keeping my voice soft.

"Three. He was the youngest, but when he died, my parents attempted to have another son. All of my siblings—my living siblings—are women."

I don't know what to say.

"In other words, I'm cursed to be a princess forever. Not that I want the throne my mother sits upon, but still, my sisters tease me daily about it."

Again, I don't know what to say. I let out a low cough, letting her know that I still need to change.

"Right," she says quietly and turns around. I change into the clothes she gave me. I then find a pair of boots that fit. When Camila turns around, she looks over me, as if determining whether what I'm wearing now is enough.

"I feel fine. It's not like I haven't worn clothes like these."

"Well, you haven't worn clothes like these," she replies. "Knowing your family, you couldn't afford the socks that would go with those boots."

I laugh. "Maybe they couldn't. But I would be able to."

"How? Your Earth money is worthless here," she points out.

She is right. Camila sifts through the pile of clothes on the bed. I know she's looking for something. Finally, she lifts out a thick coat made from griffin down.

"You'll want something like this," she says, handing it to me. "Winter is near, so the air outside has been getting very cold."

I put the coat on. It fits me pretty well, though I wonder why it's in here if this room was meant to be her late brother's, who definitely wasn't big enough for this to fit him.

"It's kinda sad. My parents fight over the use of this room. My mom wanted a place to remember him by, and my dad wanted another storage closet."

The bedroom is much too large to be called a closet.

I chuckle internally at the change in her words. Before, when she caught me inside the library, she sounded more proper, if not purposefully attempting to downplay her royalty a bit. But now that we're here with no one else around, she doesn't seem to care about her status, or my lack of.

Still, I need to find a way out of here. I should be in the Shadow Realm or back on Earth. Whatever, or whoever, the Dark Wind is, I don't get what they're playing at.

Camila walks out of the room and leads me back downstairs. Further down, we enter a grand atrium. I feel a draft blowing in from the cracks of the large double doors leading into the castle on both sides. She's right; it is cold outside. I don't understand how she deals with it, wearing only that gown.

The floors are marble, dark gray, and otherwise plain, if not perfectly polished. A chandelier of slowly rotating balls of flame lights the atrium in a warm ambiance. So long as the wind doesn't blow too hard, I can feel the warmth of the fires on my face.

Up a majestic flight of stairs, I begin to wonder how much of my home world I have yet to see.

Of course, I can blame my parents for that.

On the third floor, Camila leads me down a hall. We arrive at a solid iron door with a carving of a sun embedded in it and a trim of intertwining vines with a small flower hanging off every few centimeters.

"Wait here," she tells me. She goes into her room. I get a quick peek at what's inside, but I only see a tiny sliver of the massive room.

She's gone for less than a minute. Camila is now dressed in a coat, pearly white with a hint of blue, and, of course, adorned with gold cuffs.

"Where to now?" I ask her as she leads me back toward the stairs.

"We still have that walk we're going for."

I sigh and roll my eyes. I knew that much. But I want to know where I'm going. I want to know why I'm here.

Most of all, though, I want to speak with Kreavlos.

I've been secretly casing the castle so that I can escape. At least, I've been attempting to. Back on Earth, I could just use magic to get out of tough situations. And back at school, I got good at sneaking around and quickly finding secret areas or escape routes. But with Camila keeping a close watch on me, I don't have much of a chance to get out of here.

And even if I did, where would I go?

An idea comes to mind.

It's stupid. It's confoundedly idiotic.

It's also the only idea that has even the slimmest chance of working out in my favor. If we get close enough to the river that divides Edlyn and Voltar, I could cross it. We might just not be going near the river at all.

The atrium leads out into a courtyard. Four statues of winged lions spit water into a shallow pool with a dark bottom. The brisk air stings my face. The trees beyond the castle grounds are still brimming with green, though some of them will start to lose their color and eventually go into abscission. But beyond the raging river that runs behind the trees, most of the mountainous forest will stay green, despite the harsh winter.

"So, what's your story?" she asks.

"Don't you already know?" I retort.

"I only know the stories that I've heard," she says slowly. "Most of which, I should say, I never believed."

There's a distinctly quiet silence between us. She's holding back. Or she's trying to carefully word what she says next. Whatever she asks me, I'm likely to tell her. But I'm not going to tell her anything she doesn't ask about.

We walk down three shallow steps and onto the cut grasses beyond the courtyard. The forest isn't far, but the river that divides Edlyn and Voltar is much farther. I suspect the castle was built as close to Voltar as people were willing to go.

We pass through the first thicket of trees. Camila easily ducks behind most of the straggling branches, barely tilting her head when needed. I walk into the first few branches that I don't notice. One of them pricks my face. I put my hand up to my cheek. There is some blood.

I don't care much about the cut, but I push away any other branches I see.

I look behind. The castle is out of sight. Camila has a dim light coming from her hands, but it is hardly enough.

"You possess Magis," I say.

"Yes." She keeps moving forward. After a bit, she adds, "Tavtka."

Tavtka—a branch of Magis that deals mostly with the elements. Most people are restricted to just water or fire, while others can tap into air or earth. But the strongest can find their way with light, dark, and even sound. Lower orders of the Tavtka Magis deal with the mind, such as mind reading, pulling out memories, or sensing what one is feeling. But the mind is so complex that those who can work with it are limited to the infinite potential of another person's mind, and they aren't always right about what they see.

"I heard that you are a Maleficium."

She states it, but I know she's asking.

"Yes, a lower order," I tell her, just as my parents told me.

Camila lets out a breath. I'm not sure if she's just cold or nervous about whatever she wants to ask me next. To be honest, so am I. Kreavlos is the only person I've spoken to about what happened that night, and he doesn't count as a person.

Anxiety builds inside me. Part of me wants to tell someone—someone real, someone I can see. The other part of me believes that my answer will terrify her and that she'll attack me, forcing me to defend myself, at which point I'd probably kill her.

"What about that night?" she blurts out.

I don't say anything. She's going to have to be more specific.

She doesn't seem to catch on at first. Her steps are slow, and soon she comes to a stop. The dim light in her hand does little to illuminate her face, and I know she can barely see mine.

"That night when you ran away," she says. "When you killed those students."

I breathe in sharply. The air suddenly feels much colder. I didn't mean to kill them, but part of me doesn't even feel bad. I didn't know I could do what I did. And it was me or them.

"I don't believe you possess a low order of Maleficium."

No, of course I don't. I know that now. It took me years of self-training and riddled instructions from Kreavlos to be able to use my powers to the degree that I can. I've spent hours and hours in the Shadow Realm, lashing out at nothing with my Magis. Several nights, I would head out into the deserts on Earth, away from everything, just to practice. I know what I can do now, and I know that I haven't even reached the full extent of my abilities.

"No," I say.

Camila stares at me.

I form my hands into a ball and release a burst of light. The bubble floats above us, lighting everything in our immediate vicinity.

Camila scoffs.

"Show off." She keeps walking deeper into the forest.

"Where are we going?" I ask her. She responds by holding a finger up. Oh, it's her middle finger. Fallen branches crunch beneath my feet. Then I hear crackling as if there is a fire.

Camila suddenly stops and turns around to face me. I don't stop fast enough and walk into her, knocking her back. I reach out to grab her, my hand just between her shoulder blades, and she doesn't fall to the ground.

"I would say thanks, but you were the one who almost tackled me," she whispers.

"You just stopped walking!" I blurt out. Camila quickly hushes me.

"Don't speak unless spoken to," she says. "And I mean spoken to, not spoken of."

What the hell is she talking about?

"And turn that off!" she snaps, pointing up at the ball of light.

I do so. Camila grabs my hand and leads me forward. There is a clearing not far ahead. The red and orange light of a fire flickers back and forth. I hear voices.

Another crack beneath my feet, and we step into an open space. Several people sit around a small bonfire.

"Ooh, Camila, is this the sacrifice you brought us?"

Sacrifice?

Before I can comprehend anything, Camila is shoved aside, and two people flank me. One of them puts her arm through mine. "He's making me hungry." I slip out of her grasp.

Remembering what Camila said, I say nothing.

"Darling," I hear another woman's voice call out, but this time it sounds quieter and lacks the girlish excitement of a teenager. "Why have you brought an outsider here?"

Camila moves closer to the fire.

"He is a Maleficium, mother," Camila says. "He might be able to help us."

Queen Mattias shrieks with laughter. "It does not matter what he is; it matters what he can do! And what has he done to prove his loyalty? After all, he is not from Edlyn. That much I can tell."

Camila shifts uncomfortably. I am still flanked by two girls, and the fourth sister eyes them with resentment.

The Queen lets out a tsk. "Nothing. I see. Well, I am hardly surprised."

"It's a good thing little Camila is the youngest," the girl to my left says, thankfully leaving my side. "It would be such a tragedy if our kingdom were in her bungling hands."

I can sense Camila tensing, but she ignores her sister.

"If he is of no use, dispose of him," the Queen says. "And remember." She turns to face her two daughters who jumped up when they saw me. "I will not condone necrophilia within my walls again."

*Holy fuck.*

"I don't need to be of use to you," I spit out. "I need to be on my way back home." I don't mean Soulstice.

"How dare you speak out of line." The King stands up straight. He is nearly double Camila's height, who is barely shorter than her other siblings.

I let out a laugh. "I don't actually care who you are." I take a step closer to him. "I will be leaving now."

I turn and walk away. I shoot a glance at Camila. What a bitch. I don't know what she was trying to do, but clearly, I fell for it.

The Queen lets out her mirth again. "And where exactly will you go? All I need to do is send the order, and all the guards will be after you, right on your tail. There is nowhere you can run. And even if you cross the river and survive Voltar, it is illegal to travel into those lands. We will catch you eventually."

I stop in my tracks and turn my head back just a bit. They don't deserve the etiquette of facing them when I speak.

"Earth."

Gasps fill the air.

Then silence. Something in my mind keeps me rooted to the spot.

"How did you cross into another realm?" Queen Mattias asks.

"How else do you think? The Shadow Realm." I start walking away.

I'm not surprised by their silence. Everyone knows about the Shadow Realm. Few ever see it. And those that do, if they get there while still alive, usually don't live to tell the tale.

"Well, then," the King says. I hear him walk closer to me. Something in his voice has changed. "You must stay. I promise you in the morning I will tell you why."

It's my turn to scoff.

"That's not good enough for me." I don't turn back. I give him a second to respond, and when he doesn't, I keep making my way deeper into the forest.

"You must stay," the King commands. "The Azure Fox has made an appearance."

I retract my next step, stopping between two trees. The Azure Fox is a fairy tale. Well, technically, so is the Dark Wind.

"Did she say anything?" I ask curiously. Questions flood my mind. But these people have no answers for me. I need to speak with Kreavlos. Why hasn't he taken me back to the Shadow Realm yet?

"N—nothing," the King stutters. He lies.

The silence between us is loud. I'll admit, I am curious.

"I will stay until morning," I say, walking back to them. "I will not be guarded; I will not be watched."

"Of course," the King replies.

I nod. I look over to Camila. I swear I can see a hint of a smile on her lips. She's probably enjoying all of this.

"What was it that I could help with?" I ask, remembering what Camila had last said.

"It doesn't matt—"

"I was speaking to her," I say, cutting off the Queen and pointing to Camila.

Camila's eyes widen, and her mouth opens slightly. She looks uncomfortable, almost like she follows that same rule she told me about: not speaking until spoken to. I get the idea she is the least favorite child. That's something I can understand.

"The lower kingdom of Soulstice has been growing impatient and contentious. The Thorne family feels they are getting less than they give," Camila tells me. "And there are...rumors that they are gearing up for an invasion."

On a map, Soulstice covers just over half of this continent, while Edlyn spreads across the rest, except for the small portion at the top occupied by Voltar. Due to their location, it is likely Soulstice is a major agricultural provider. I learned a little about our world in school, but in Voltar, I only cared about learning how to protect myself. But I do have one question.

"Why did you call it the lower kingdom?"

Camila lets out a sigh. The Queen opens her mouth to answer, but I shut her down with a look.

"Three years ago, Soulstice agreed to terms with Edlyn to cede their kingdom to ours provisionally. A year ago, the Thorne family abandoned the agreement, claiming independence."

"Gorgrein had been launching attacks on Soulstice, so our army fought for them against Gorgrein. The coasts of Soulstice are far easier to reach than the ones we have, and no one dares get too close to Voltar."

The Queen speaks assertively, as if there is more to the story that I'm not hearing. I'll find out eventually what she isn't telling me, but for the time being, I don't care much.

"Well, if you know the Gorgrein people, who are known for being terrified of most Magis, especially Maleficium, then you know that Soulstice shouldn't be your concern," I say. "Not when their desire to rid themselves of the source of their fear becomes more powerful than the fear itself."

The King bellows a laugh.

"You think you know how to rule a kingdom better than I? We have united this entire continent. No other country has the army we do; no other kingdom is as strong as we are."

To me, it sounds like the King of Edlyn still considers Soulstice under his reign, while Soulstice's King and Queen, Marcus and Yvette Thorne, believe that they are once again independent.

"That may be," I say in a low voice, speaking slowly. "But it is clear that you are failing to keep your kingdom together."

The King shoots daggers at me with his eyes. I can see his arm shake. Unlike everyone else in his family, his skin is light. His eyes are a muted brown, and his thinning hair is gray. I don't suspect he is as old as he looks.

"We should probably get moving back to the castle," the Queen says, shattering the frigid silence that has nothing to do with the temperature.

Queen Mattias takes her husband's hand and begins to walk away. She picks up a torch, snaps her fingers, and ignites it. The torch was likely designed for her, to light at her command. The two twin sisters follow, with the other one behind her. Camila waits for them to walk a bit farther away before tilting her head, indicating to follow.

"You've got quite the family there," I say to Camila in a whisper.

"I know," she replies. "And you probably didn't pick up on this, but my quiet sister, she's the oldest."

I think about that for a moment. She looked reserved, somewhat fearful, and never spoke a word the entire time. I guess I can see it.

"Well, at least those twin sisters of yours aren't the next ones in line for the throne," I say. "But, thinking about it, I could probably work out something with them to gain their favor." I smile, though Camila probably can't see it.

"Don't flatter yourself," Camila replies, her voice devoid of emotion. "One time they seduced a half-ogre because it had a penis. They'd screw just about anything."

# CHAPTER 3

## THE FOX AND THE LADY

**Aros Caelum Hayes**

As promised, there were no guards outside my quarters. The room they left me in is on the fifth floor of the castle. Originally, they wanted to give me a room on the south side, overlooking the valley that eventually blends into Soulstice, though the kingdom of Soulstice is much too far to see from the castle. I told them I wanted windows looking out at the forest. Even though Voltar is forbidden land, and my time at the school there was unpleasant, it's the closest thing I have that feels like home in this world.

I'm not sure what exactly triggered their change of heart, but the King and Queen treated me like their royal guest; the bedroom is large, and they assigned a servant to be around if I need anything. I still don't understand why.

Sleep takes forever to come. While I arrived on Arteyva in the middle of the night, it was barely noon back on Earth, so I still feel wide awake. I search through the closets in the room. All kinds of clothes are packed inside, both for women and men. There is a bath. Not all homes or villages have that luxury. My family shared a bath with four other families at one point. They hated that they didn't have money, and when they took in Joshua, they hoped he would bring them riches with his promise of great strength. The school in Voltar had running water, but the bathrooms were shared, and I always had to bathe in the middle of the night to avoid unwanted interactions.

I stare out the window for an hour after washing myself. I catch my reflection in the glass. I used to be self-conscious about the scar across my chest, but I learned that most people don't notice it. And of those that do, even fewer mention it.

The peak of the mountain is covered in snow. It almost always is. The school is near the base of the mountain, nestled in a dense and somewhat secluded forest. The rest of the mountain is a sprawling land of nature and beasts. A few times wild animals visited the school, but none were as threatening as what we were warned of.

Just as the first rays of sunlight appear in the north, I begin to get tired. The peak of Voltar is still shrouded in night, but soon the sky above it will turn to a light blue. I lie on the bed. It's bigger than mine back on Earth. I close my eyes to rest, knowing that sleep will soon come for me.

*"It's never enough to just want something."*

*The words of the professor rang in my head. I knew he was right. He didn't need to tell me. But damn, it was hard always wanting something while feeling as if everything was constantly standing in your way. I wanted my friends back. I didn't want them to fear me. I thought, for the first time, that I knew what happiness was. But in the blink of an eye, everything changed.*

*"I just want my life back," I told him.*

*The professor sighed. He was quite young compared to the other teachers. His hair was still dark. He had deep blue eyes, fair, tanned skin, and kept a shaven face, his jawline easily noticeable. Most of the girls at school had a crush on him. Hell, even I thought he was handsome.*

*"That... may not be possible," he told me slowly. I could hear the pain in his voice. After the rumors about me spread across the school, everyone treated me differently. Professor Liams never did. Of course, he never had*

*much of a chance to.*

*Half a year later, he was gone. I never saw or heard of him again. The other professors wouldn't say much. And just like that, I sat in the back corner of every class. I learned to deal with the mutters and whispers about me, and the silence that followed when no one was around.*

*Both fortunately and unfortunately, it only took me a few days to get over losing my last and only person that came close to a friend. Life had never been fair to me up to that point. Why would it start to then?*

A bright light wakes me up suddenly. Somehow, from lying on the bed, I am now standing up. With that realization, I topple over.

"I apologize for the unusual method," the voice of Kreavlos says. He speaks more softly than normal.

"Where the hell have you been?" I say, picking myself back up. It takes me a moment to orient myself. To be honest, I don't even know if I am still asleep or not.

"Is that really a question you need to ask me?"

"Yeah! It is! Because hours ago, my city was attacked by two creatures of this world! How the fuck did they get there? Why didn't you take me out of there earlier? Why has it taken you this long to bring me here?"

My shouts reverberate in the open air. I know he does this to encourage me to quiet down. It works. Most of the time.

"Actually, I don't care. All I want to know is if Olivia is safe." I mean it. I speak with a lower voice, quieter, with hints of plea.

Any sound in the Shadow Realm is diminished while I await an answer.

"Yes," Kreavlos said. "The Dark Wind removed everything that didn't belong there."

"Well, it took me away. So, I guess I don't belong there," I snap back. "You were nowhere to be found."

"When the Dark Wind first took you years ago, it brought you to me.

I was tasked to watch over you," Kreavlos says, going into an explanation that I didn't know I needed. "All these years I've been making sure you didn't cause trouble on Earth. And clearly, since you need to know, I did not let those creatures through."

I didn't think so. I never did. But that means there is a much bigger issue at hand. The Mattias family is floundering with their kingdom, trying to reign over the whole continent, while something sinister is happening between the realms.

"I won't have much time to explain," Kreavlos says. "While you are on Arteyva, I cannot easily pluck you out of the world. You can call for me and, depending on where you are, I might be able to answer." He pauses. "Arteyva isn't Earth. The magic on Arteyva runs deep, you know this. Your power is stronger in Arteyva, but more limited in scope. Now, listen quickly, and listen closely."

Kreavlos doesn't give me any time to answer. I tilt my head down slightly, ready to catch every word.

"Olivia and Earth are safe. I altered the memories of all witnesses so that they would not remember what happened. Not completely, however. I could not repair all the damage in time, so they think there was a gas leak that caused an explosion. Other than those who perished, the ordinary are safe."

I nod.

"The Dark Wind called you back to Arteyva for a reason. I have yet to know all the details of why what's about to happen is, but it is not my place to tell you anymore." He stops speaking. I want to say something, but I know better. Something has changed. He can feel it. I can feel it. "You are about to be subjected to the test of your life. Remember this: do not give in to your demons."

*My demons?*

My eyes snap open again, but this time I am lying on my back. My forehead is wet with sweat. Brilliant sunlight penetrates the windows. I get out of bed quickly and dress in something light since the day is warm compared to last night.

I leave the sleeping quarters and wander around. I want to find Camila. I can remember where her quarters are—I just don't know how to get there. Everything up here was so dark last night that I can barely remember the layout of the upper floors.

There aren't any wide staircases nearby. The one I took last night was spiraling, positioned somewhere I take to be at one of the ends of the castle. Common sense dictates my path until I can see something I recognize.

When I see a corridor like the one where Camila's quarters are, I begin to feel relieved, only to realize that this floor looks the same as the one below me.

"Stop."

I freeze. I don't recognize the voice, but it is familiar. I turn around. Camila's oldest sister walks toward me, her back straight and eyes narrow.

"What are you doing?" she asks.

I shrug and glance to the side. "Looking for food."

"Breakfast was an hour ago," she says quickly.

I raise an eyebrow. "I'm not accustomed to my meals being restricted to a time of day," I tell her. "If you would please be so kind as to show me where I can get food, I would appreciate that. If not, then I will be on my way."

The thought of giving her an option to respond crosses my mind briefly, but I decide against it; there is no way someone from the Mattias family would offer such benevolence. I turn back and keep walking where I was heading—wherever that is.

To my surprise, Miss Next-in-Line catches up to me. She throws me a quick, emotionless glance and nods her head slightly, telling me to follow her.

Still, the corridors remain the same; large bricks of stone make up the walls, and the floor is made of slabs of rock. As there are rooms on both sides, there are no windows until we leave the sleeping wing. There is an overpass that serves as a skybridge of sorts, though each floor has the same hallway, and I presume we are right over the middle part of the castle. One side overlooks the central courtyard, while the other faces those mountains that I am increasingly feeling homesick for.

The eldest sister says nothing as she leads. I don't even know her name yet, not that I care much to.

We pass by a wide staircase, which is one of many in the castle.

"There will be food in the dungeons," she tells me. The tone in her voice is ominous, making those words sound threatening.

She must feel me tense slightly as she adds, "All of our food is prepped in the kitchens, which are located beneath the castle." Princess Mattias sighs. "My parents have granted you the privilege of being a royal guest. So, I legally cannot harm you."

I nod, even though I'm walking behind her, and she won't see it.

"What about illegally?" I ask.

"What a moronic question," she answers. "Illegally, I can do any-thing. I won't, though. As it is, I deal with enough pressure as the next queen of Edlyn. I can't afford the consequences of killing you."

Her words, I feel, don't deserve much of a response, so all I say is, "Okay."

The princess's stride slows for a moment, and I hear a faint huff, but she doesn't say anything. Finally, she pushes open a door, one that looks like every other. There are narrow stairs that we walk down; the entire staircase is unlit, making it hard to see. I don't understand how anyone would be able to distinguish that door as a passage compared to the other doors that lead into bedrooms. But I suppose that's the point.

As we go down, I can see light pass through the edges of some doors, but we don't go through them. I conjure a light in my hands, but she hisses at me, telling me to put it out.

At the bottom, we go through another door that leads into the dungeons. Fire crackles inside torches that protrude from the walls. These don't seem to be lit by Magis. To my right, there are empty cells, all closed with their own iron gates. These appear to be mostly unused, but I wouldn't put it past the royal family to let their enemies rot here.

If I had a castle like this, I'd probably do the same.

We pass through a pair of saloon-like doors into the kitchen. Long tables of wood and iron are sprawled across it. There are three large pits used for cooking, while many more black cauldrons sit above small fires. One of the tables is covered with small bites of food: cheese, fruit, and squares of what I take to be meat.

"I told you, breakfast is over, but feel free to help yourself to anything on this table."

I do. I shove anything that I can recognize into my mouth. It wasn't until I smelled the food that I realized just how hungry I actually was. When I am over my initial hunger, but not quite satisfied, I slow down and ask some questions.

"What's your name?"

She smiles. "How about you ask a different question?"

It's clear that she isn't asking. Fine. I'll get straight to what I actually want to know.

"Is it true the Azure Fox arrived in Edlyn?"

She nods.

"What did she say?" I ask. I lean against the table expectantly.

"Like my father told you: nothing," she responds. She's lying, just like King Mattias did last night.

"I don't believe you," I tell her. I pick some grapes off their vine, eating them along with balls of cheese.

She shrugs. "You don't need to."

"You know it's likely I'll find out whether you tell me or not," I say, standing up straight.

The princess eyes me, but I can't tell what she's thinking about.

I sigh. "When did she arrive?"

Another question with no answer.

I hear the swinging doors fly open and slam against the wall. My favorite princess of Edlyn walks in, though I still don't know how much I can trust her.

"The Azure Fox arrived over two months ago," Camila tells me, walking right up to her sister. She eyes her with a quick look of disgust before looking at me. "She told us to prepare for the Ash Trials. After that night, she made her way down the continent, visiting every town and village from here to the Coast of Ibari. Weeks later, the first of them arrived." Camila lets out a long breath. "And we now have two and a half hundred people willing to offer themselves to the Trials."

A subtle half-smile creeps onto my lips. I can tell that the eldest princess hates me for it, and that thought only makes my smile wider.

"The Ash Trials haven't taken place in centuries," I say, looking at Camila. "For all we knew, they were just a children's tale." I keep a straight face and unblinking eyes as I ask my next question. "How do I know I can trust you?"

Camila holds my gaze. "Because the King and Queen have ordered me to partake in them."

Understanding begins to dawn on me. The way Camila rarely, if ever, refers to her parents as her mother or father but almost always by their titles. Her display of kindness to the kingdom's subjects, and the ease with which she was able to welcome an outsider, me, tells me just how much she is unlike the rest of her family.

It also makes sense why the rest of her family was so hostile to me. Camila was never their favorite child. If anything, she seems almost neglected by them. Her twin sisters should be about my age, though I don't remember them at the school. Camila was probably sent there because her parents didn't have time to deal with her. They would have been too busy teaching and preparing the older sisters for the throne.

But there is one thing I am unsure of. Do the King and Queen want their youngest to prevail in the Trials? Or would they rather her perish? If they want her to win, then I might be just another obstacle in her path—in their path. That depends on how many victors are wanted.

"They're hoping she dies," the oldest says. The jealousy in her voice is strong, undeniable, and I don't understand why.

Camila lets out what sounds like a forced laugh.

"All my life the King and Queen have never given a shit about what I do or don't do," Camila says, her voice cracking just slightly. "And I don't even blame them. There is no way the throne would end up with me, not when I have three older sisters to sit upon it first. Plus, whatever boy they end up marrying. But now they have a chance for an increase in power, a chance to have something most of the world will be without. An Ash Lord."

According to legend, the Ashen Pit holds the ash of five souls; the souls of those who not only overcame the trials set forth to them but were then chosen by the Pit itself. It is said that by burning one's soul into the Pit as an offering, one would become immensely powerful, their Magis increased more than ten-fold, and they would become nearly immortal. But if one were to be killed as an Ash Lord, their soul would forever be burned to ash, condemned to an eternity of being material, as the soul itself should exist as something beyond physics.

Anyone whose ashes reside in the Pit is at risk of being torn apart by the removal of their ash. But no one knows where the Pit is, and it is impossible to tell anyone's ash from another, so those who are one of the Five would never dare remove any of the ash, for fear of killing themselves.

"Of course, the Trials are extremely dangerous, and I am the expendable one," Camila says. "Just as I was the only one to attend a school away from here, I am the only one to be subjected to the Trials."

"You don't have to participate in the Trials if you don't want to," I tell her. "Actually, according to the tales, you can't participate in them unless you willingly offer yourself up."

Camila shrugs. "The King and Queen have spoken," she says. "At any rate, who is to say that I don't want to be there?"

"Regardless, my family is sworn to protect all contestants," the eldest sister says. "And the Azure Fox told us that there would be a participant from Earth, and here you are, so, yeah." She doesn't sound happy about it. I can't quite put my finger on why.

But now I know this is why the Dark Wind called me back to Arteyva. This is why Kreavlos, no matter how much I may beg, will not return me to Earth. My being here has been a calculated effort.

*How fun.*

"When do they start?" I ask.

Camila looks at her sister briefly. "In two days."

When I am finished eating, Camila takes over my "tour" and shows me around the castle and its grounds. On the other side, closer to the valley, the land is covered in tents. Camila tells me that those tents are for the families of people who came to Edlyn Castle for the Trials. Only the volunteers are allowed to stay in the castle, something the King and Queen grudgingly offered. If any of the volunteers were to die before the Trials, the Azure Fox would not take kindly to those responsible. Of course, some of the wealthier families stay in the village, Aeilvow, that's situated at the base of the valley nearby.

An outside field used for sport training had been converted into an arena for practicing Magis. Simple rules have been laid out, such as not killing anyone and keeping the destruction within the perimeter of the arena. As we pass, I can see that the bare minimum has been done to provide the space for the participants. There's a short wall of stone to mark out the arena, most of which has already been damaged or broken through. Large scarecrows stand tattered, their straw splintered and mostly fallen out. Singes of grass lie scattered, and in the time it takes us to walk by, the small decorative pond was frozen and thawed back to water no less than four times. I see several people sneak back into the woods, outside the castle's territory.

It takes us just over three hours to walk across all of the castle grounds and the first two floors of the castle itself. Camila tells me that the third floor is used explicitly for the royal family, and the fourth floor is used as open rooms. The floor my quarters are on is for guests and royalty of other kingdoms. She doesn't tell me what the sixth floor is, and, though not technically a floor, there are four towers that rest at what would be the seventh floor, though I am sure the towers hold multiple floors themselves. She also doesn't tell me what's in the towers.

When it is lunchtime, Camila takes me to the Grand Room. Normally used to host special events, the Grand Room has been repurposed for the time being to feed all the participants of the Ash Trials. Again, just like their sleeping quarters, only the volunteers get to eat here.

On the north side of the Grand Room, arched windows line the entire wall and are the only windows in the room. On the south side, there are doors that lead to somewhere I can't see, but I think there are stairs behind the doors that go down to the kitchens.

"The King and Queen had every volunteer sign an oath that states they promise to participate in the Trials," Camila tells me. "Only those who signed stay in the castle, and all those who reside within these walls will be forced to participate, even if they lied."

"Do you think anyone lied?"

"Maybe. But I think that once the Trials are about to begin, there will be those who are no longer so sure about their choice."

"And what happens to them?"

Camila answers without expression. The way she does it is almost like it was something she was taught, not a way she normally would behave. "They signed an oath with the King. They either keep it or are sentenced to death."

While I'm not surprised, it wasn't what I was expecting.

The Grand Room smells delicious. There must be over a hundred people in here of all ages. Most look to be in their late teens to late twenties, but I see two who must be around fourteen and a few dozen or so who are much older than I am.

Someone shoves Camila as they walk by her, but she holds her ground.

"Oh, uh," the guy says, looking down at Camila, eyeing her. "Sorry, I guess." A lock of hair hangs over his pale forehead. He has light brown eyes and a natural red to his lips. Taller than me, he practically towers over Camila.

"Just watch where you're going," Camila tells him. The guy nods and walks on.

"He doesn't know who you are, does he?" I ask her as she leads me to the buffet.

"No, most people here don't," she says. "I prefer it that way."

I grab myself a plate of chicken on greens and a grain that looks like orange rice. Camila heads over to a nearly empty table and sits down. When I am settled across from her, something catches my attention. I look up. Glaring at me from across the hall is Joshua.

I smirk and look away. I can't wait to see how strong he thinks he's become. Part of him must be terrified of me.

"That's your brother, right?" Camila asks in a hushed tone.

"He's not my brother," I reply plainly.

"Well, your parents kinda made him your brother by adopting him."

I look down at my food before stabbing off a piece of chicken to eat. "Well, they aren't much of my parents either. If they can choose who their son is, I can choose who are not my parents."

"I see," Camila says. "I used to think I had it bad, but my family is nothing compared to how you must feel about yours."

"Again, I don't feel anything toward my family, because I don't have one." I keep my voice as polite as I can.

She lets out a long sigh. "Okay. Well, there's no easy way to tell you this. They're here."

I look up at her. I can tell she chooses her next words carefully.

"Joshua's parents are here to watch him enter the Trials."

The rest of lunch is eaten in silence. Camila lets me wander on my own afterward. She tells me that the meals for the Trial volunteers are an hour after the royalty eats. When she leaves, I make my way back outside. I don't feel like practicing with the others. Part of me is worried that they will recognize who I am. But that's a pretentious thought. My parents did their best to hide the fact that I even existed. Only those I went to school with would know me, and only a very few of them would recognize me by my face alone.

If I use my power and they notice that I am a Maleficium, they might connect the dots. While it would help me pass the Trials, I cannot train with the others.

I make my way through the woods. I keep going until I reach the river at the end. It is over a hundred feet wide, and the other side is drastically different from where I stand. Due to the coming winter, the ground across is covered in a light frost. Most of the foliage that grows near the riverbank is gone. The base of the mountain lies just another thirty feet away, but the side is too steep to climb. To travel up it, one would need to follow the river for over a mile before they could trudge a path up the mountain.

The fast-flowing water roars with the sharp wind. It must be about twenty degrees colder on the other side. I don't see any animals across the river, but birds and squirrels chirp and chatter behind me in the trees.

"Voltar is intimidating, isn't it?"

I see someone walk up beside me. I turn to get a good look at him. Green eyes and long, slicked-back brown hair. He has some stubble growing on his boyish face, but he must be around my age. He is just shorter than I am. When he turns to face me and speak, I notice his thin lips and planted smile, as if he is always happy about something.

Or is always high on something.

"Not really."

I don't feel much like making conversation with him.

"No, not really," he echoes.

He just stands there. He's a bit awkward and, as such, is making me feel awkward. He takes a sip of something out of a flask that I did not realize he was holding. He points out across the river.

"That's where I think the Ash Trials are gonna happen."

Yeah, I figured as much too.

"Are you drinking?" I blurt out, letting my curiosity win.

He lets out a nervous laugh. "Yeah, I, uh, it helps calm the nerves."

Something tells me that he is more of an alcoholic than a social drinker.

"Well, uh," I say, looking down and smiling. "I guess I'll be seeing you around." I look up at him. "Good luck with the Trials."

He ponders for a moment. "You too."

I leave the place I sought out for peace. I don't know what his name is and, while he seems innocent enough, there's something about him that makes me feel a bit uneasy. I take my time walking back to the castle. That's pretty much all I have now. Time. Two days until the Trials begin. The fairytales about the Trials are full of adventure. There are so many stories about them, all with varying outcomes and settings. There are stories about the Ashen Pit losing just one Ash Lord, and so Trials were held; those ones were mostly bloodbaths, according to legend. Everyone was fighting to become the next Ash Lord. But then there are the stories of the first Trials. Those, though dangerous, were a test of power and loyalty. I can't help but wonder, since there are five, maybe just four, spots open, if these Trials would be the same test of loyalty. Or if the

Trials will feel like I'm at school all over again.

I step out of the trees and onto the grassy field. Someone charges and tackles me. As we fall, I take one look and immediately know who it is. His short, dark hair, dark eyes, and pale skin give him away. His face is slightly red, just like it always has been. Nothing like a blush—more like a permanent sunburn. Joshua.

I flip him around and he lands on his back. I push out, sending a pulse at his chest. The ground beneath him cracks. It's just grass and dirt, nothing to be proud of. I get up to my feet, waiting for him.

"Mom and Dad will be so proud when I kill you."

This guy must be about nineteen now.

"You're still trying to get your parents' approval?" I ask him tauntingly.

He picks himself up. He shows me his right hand. Flames appear around it. He's a Fae-Blessed. A fire Fae loaned some of its power to him. The Fae are an unusual people—powerful, but odd. They usually keep to themselves in their own realm, but some like to interact with humans. We all look the same, for the most part.

"Since they never wanted you, they chose me," he replies, sneering. "I already have their approval."

I put on a look of confusion. "Why would your parents want me?"

"They don't!"

"Okay, so what? Your parents don't want me. They don't even know me! Why would they want me?"

"They're your parents too!" He lunges a ball of fire at me. I dodge it. It lands somewhere in the fields, lighting up the grass.

I laugh. "You're crazy. If they were my parents, you would be my brother. But I don't even know you."

Joshua's face turns even redder. He shouts and throws more fire at me. Again, I dodge it. I can feel the heat of the flames as they eat up the grass behind me.

"How do you not recognize me?" He's still shouting.

"Probably because you're weak, and I usually don't pay attention to people like you," I say just to rile him up.

He screams again, his voice cracking. He's trying to be tough; I get it. But I don't understand why he thinks he has to prove himself to me, to prove he's stronger. He's not. He probably never will be. Fae-Blessed are usually the weakest of all Magis since they wholly depend on the Fae that granted them power.

Steam rises from his head. He sends a jet of blazing flame at me with both hands. I put my hands out, one right behind the other. The fire hits the wall of energy I made and spreads out before me. I twitch my fingers, and the fire flies back toward Joshua. He can't dodge it and is knocked to the ground. His own fire won't injure him much, but it will hurt his pride.

My counterattack proves to be the most devastating to the field, however. Fires burn out of control everywhere.

"What are you doing?" someone shouts. I turn to look at her. She's blonde with piercing blue eyes, and just to match, she has a strip of blue hair falling down one side of her face. And, of course, she has that Earth-English accent. Her eyes flash, and she raises her hands to the sky. She closes her hands, as if grabbing something, and pulls down. As if a plug has been pulled in the sky, a shower of rain falls across the field.

The fires die out quickly.

"We're not supposed to fight each other!" She's shouting at me.

I point to Joshua, who is still on the ground, seething. "He started it."

"You can't attack other volunteers!" the blonde girl yells at him. She walks toward him as if she's about to kick the shit out of him.

"His name isn't on the wall!" His voice cracks again. "He's not a volunteer! He's a demonic Maleficium!"

My body tenses. It's the one thing I was trying to avoid. That's why

I kept to using only one type of Magis—sending out pulses of energy, levitating things. Seven-books-of-magic-school type stuff, nothing too crazy. Make them think I'm just a Tavtka. But now the word's out. Maybe people won't believe him.

I can feel people turning to look at me. With each passing second, the crowd around us grows.

"Actually," Camila says. Relief floods me when I see her walking up. She's accompanied by her eldest sister and the King and Queen behind them. "His name is on the wall." She walks right up to Joshua. "Get up." Her voice is unusually deep and commanding. Clearly, her parents didn't teach her nothing, even if it's just the crude basics of what it takes to rule a kingdom.

Joshua stands. He glares at me but then looks like he's about to shit himself when he notices the King.

"You are banned from practicing," Camila tells him. "You are to stay in your assigned quarters. You are not allowed to leave. You may eat lunch and dinner, but only when accompanied by one of our knights. If you break these rules, if you try to escape, if you attack anyone, we will hold you in the cells until the Trials begin, at which point we will let the Azure Fox know exactly what you've done, and she can deal with you as she sees fit." Damn. Camila can be a bit scary. There's something in her voice; the way she talks as if she's holding back, like she's trying not to shout, trying not to physically hit him, that makes her sound powerful.

Joshua doesn't respond.

"Did. You. Hear. Me?"

Joshua gulps, nodding slightly.

"Take him."

I didn't realize that a knight had shown up, let alone three. Two of them grab Joshua by his arms and walk him away, the third following.

"The same goes for Aros." King Mattias glares at me.

For a second, my heart sinks. Not that it would matter. With what's been revealed to everyone, I want to stay in my quarters anyway.

"No." Camila's voice. She turns around and walks up to her father. She looks up at him and calmly says, "Aros was attacked. He defended himself, and with little harm to the volunteer."

"But what about the harm to our fields? He's a Maleficium!" There it is, that word. That curse. "He is dangerous."

"Yes, he is," Camila says in the most matter-of-fact voice I've ever heard. "He is very dangerous. He also is innocent, which is why he will not be punished."

King Mattias glares at his daughter. I can tell that he wants to retort, but he doesn't. All he does is turn around dramatically, his long cape brushing against Camila, and walks away. Camila's mother and sister follow.

I look at her, breathing normally now. "Thank you."

"I knew at some point something like that would happen. I'm just glad I was here when it did."

I nod. "What wall were you guys talking about?"

"Oh, the wall with all our names carved into it?" It isn't Camila who answers. It's the blonde girl who caused it to rain. "It's in the atrium."

"My family wanted something to show off the supposed power of having hosted the Ash Trials," says Camila.

"But it's unlikely the actual Trials are being held here," I say.

Camila shrugs. "I know that. But you've met them, so you know what they're like."

I roll my eyes. "When is it time for dinner?"

"Soon, but we can head there now," she says. "I'll show you the wall on our way."

"I'll come along too!" the blonde girl says. I need to start getting people's names. As if reading my mind, or just being polite like normal people, the blonde girl says, "My name is Abigail. Abigail Coriffer, that is."

I nod. "Aros."

Camila starts walking away. Abigail and I walk behind her. Without looking back, Camila says, "Princess Mattias."

"Cool," Abigail breathes out.

As we walk toward the castle, I wonder about the extent of her powers. If she can only summon rain, it's likely that she is Fae-Blessed. If she can summon and control storms, she's either a Fae or an extremely powerful Tavtka. But some people think it's rude to ask what kind of Magis they possess.

"So, is it true? Are you really a Maleficium?" Apparently, she doesn't mind asking someone about it.

"Yeah."

"That's so cool," she says. "I'm a Tavtka, and rain isn't the only thing I can do."

Good to know. Part of me wants to ask her what else she can do, but I don't. If she wants, she can tell me. But I won't push it, just like she isn't prying me on what it's like to be a Maleficium.

"Back in Carroldore, I was always asked to make it rain so they could grow their crops," she tells us. Well, me. I don't think Camila is paying attention. "But when the Azure Fox came, I just knew I—"

A loud shriek from the skies interrupts her. Almost paralyzing, the shriek reverberates through the air. I look up. The darkening sky seems clear; Abigail's rain clouds long gone. We're almost at the castle gate. The three of us wait another moment. The dusk is silent. One by one, people go on with what they were doing, most of us heading to the castle for our dinner. Since the Trials are so close to starting, and Voltar is so near to the castle, we don't discuss the sound.

We walk into the atrium. Camila leads me toward a wall that a dark-skinned man is leaning against. Upon a closer look, I can see him etching a name right under mine with flicks of his finger.

"You're a Rogvey," I say. Rogvey possess Magis that primarily deals with art. They can create all sorts of things depending on how their powers align with themselves. Most people consider them weaker than Fae-Blessed, so much so that it is hardly considered a form of Magis by some. I, on the other hand, very well understand that if this guy can carve a name into a stone wall, he can do the same to my body. And more than just tattoos; if he were strong enough, he could carve right through me, essentially slicing me in half.

"Aye, I am," he says, standing up and proudly admiring his work. He's taller than me and lanky. I read the name below mine: Sefryn Loste Ambers. "I've done all the names on this wall."

It sounds like it's his first big job. We all got to start somewhere. I don't know him, but I am happy for him.

"I'm Peter," he says.

I give him a small smile. It would be rude not to introduce myself.

"I'm—uh." I scratch my eye. "I'm Aros."

As expected, his eyes widen. "Like the Aros Caelum Hayes!" He's so excited.

*The?*

"Yes," I tell him.

"I did your name not an hour ago! See, right here!" He points to it.

"It, uh, looks great," I say with the biggest smile I can muster up.

"Good work, Peter," Camila says. Peter regains his composure and bows. Camila returns a curt, short bow and walks away. Abigail and I follow her.

Dinner is quick. Abigail joins some of the friends she's made, while Camila and I eat mostly alone. At the other end of the table sits the guy who approached me by the river earlier. He takes a large sip from a goblet, and I wonder what's inside it.

When we're done, Camila shows me to my room again. Not that I needed it, but now I know exactly where I am in the castle, and I won't be getting lost tomorrow morning. I spend hours in my room reading through some of the books that lie around. I could spend time outside, but I don't feel like socializing with anybody. Plus, apparently, I'm not the best at choosing friends, just based on my time on Earth. Though Olivia is an exception.

I close my eyes to sleep, and my nightmarish dreams seep in. I know I'm dreaming, but it all feels so real. There are a hundred imps attacking me. Olivia is there, but she turns into an imp too. A winged beast flies over me.

Suddenly, I'm back in Edlyn. The castle is eerily quiet. The moon is high in the sky, but the sun hasn't fully set. Then I hear that shriek. This time, a winged monster accompanies the shriek. It ignites the tents on fire. This isn't the same beast that I saw on Earth. This is something different, but it is too far away to clearly see it, though I can tell it has a slender body.

People are crying out, shouting in fear. I hear windows break. Tall figures jump in. With human-like bodies and heads with seven eye sockets, the creatures scurry through the castle, lunging at any man they find and devouring them. But the women, no. When they find a woman, they snatch her and pin her to the ground. She screams, but no one is around. I can't do anything. I must still be dreaming. But it all feels so real.

They forcefully tear off her clothes. A black, slimy, and slender tail creeps toward her, and I know what they plan to do with it—

My eyes snap open. The night is quiet. I don't get out of bed. Again, I can feel the sweat on my body, drenching the sheets.

I don't sleep for the rest of the night.

Morning arrives, and I force myself to shower and go downstairs for breakfast. There are a variety of juices, but there is also tea—and coffee. Camila isn't around. Abigail waves merrily at me but doesn't join me at my lone table. Even the guy with the flask isn't here, but I am thankful for that. There are more people here than there were last night, though. I briefly lock eyes with some girl across the room, but she quickly goes about her business.

When I'm done, I head back to my room. Passing by the wall of carved names tells me that more people arrived last night. At this rate, there could be over three hundred participants in the Trials.

Camila pays me a visit, asking if I want to spend some time outside. I decline, telling her that I'd rather just stay in. She nods in understanding and leaves.

I spend the day reading through books in the library. Most of the stuff I read I already know, but it doesn't hurt to refresh my mind about this world—my world. It isn't until after dinner that I find a book on what monsters exist here, but since I don't read about what I dreamed of, I know the book is incomplete. Maybe I missed something in the other books that sit on the top shelf of the bookcase in my quarters.

The Trials are to start an hour before noon tomorrow morning. That's plenty of time after breakfast to do any last-minute preparations. I just wish I knew what I needed to prepare for the Trials. The trouble is, even after reading through countless stories of the Trials, all of them are different and are never done in the same place. According to the tales, no one ever knew what they were getting into until the Trials started.

Before heading to my room for my last night here, I check the names on the wall. There must be over twenty more names than I last saw.

When I get to bed for the night, I pray to Kreavlos (him being the closest thing to a god I know) that I won't have any nightmares. I don't need a repeat of last night. I still feel uneasy about it. The way the nightmare blended from my real-life experience into...that.

My prayer was answered. I wake peacefully, but I can tell there is something different about this morning. The castle is unusually busy yet feels quieter than usual. I head to the Grand Room for a quick, large breakfast. Camila is absent again, but I suppose she is doing some sort of private royal send-off.

I get back to my chambers. I don't even know why I came here.

Nothing here is mine, though the clothes are mine for the taking if I wish. I dress in something a bit warmer. I have a feeling that the Trials will take place in Voltar, just like that guy said. It would be a shame to die from hypothermia of all things.

The fields that the other volunteers practiced in underwent another change. Tall posts were erected, all bearing the different flags of the continent, with the Edlyn Royal Flag being the largest and tallest.

The royal family stands upon a low wooden stage facing the gathering crowd. Many of the volunteers are accompanied by others. Having barely seen them, I don't know if they are friends, family, or people they met here. Abigail waves at me. Two people are with her, most likely her mother and her younger sister. There are others that I recognize, though I have never interacted with them, walking along with loved ones. In the crowd, I spot the river guy. He, too, is wearing a large coat. There is no one with him. Feeling bad for the guy, I walk up to him.

"So, this is it," I say.

He lets out a low, booming laugh. "Yup. Are you ready?"

I shrug. "Probably."

"Me too."

We walk toward the stage. There are no chairs to sit on. As we wait, the crowd grows quite large, probably close to a thousand people.

The sun continues to rise in the sky. Most people mutter among themselves. The river guy and I talk a bit. That's when I learn his name is Arthur Theodore. Not that it matters, but he tells me his full name, his middle name being Drew.

I tell him my name. He's heard the rumors of me being a Maleficium. When I tell him I am, something glints in his eye.

"Oh yeah? That's so cool!" His voice sounds strained. "Like, I've only heard of them, but I never thought someone like you actually existed. I mean, yeah, a lower order, but you're like the full deal!"

Something feels off to me about him, but he remains seemingly harmless, so I don't dwell on it. He also might just be awkward around people, despite how hard he tries not to be.

A fog creeps in from the north. The royal family looks to their left, the rest of us looking to our right. I can't see anything except the fog. Then, on the stage, a young woman appears. She has fair skin, ash and white hair, and gray eyes. Next to her, a large animal materializes from the fog. With pointed ears, a large snout, and silver-blue hair, I know that she is the Azure Fox.

The royal family steps off the stage. Camila looks around at her sisters, clearly thinking they are making fools out of themselves, as the three of them trip over each other, almost toppling to the ground.

"On behalf of the Ashen Pit, I present to you the Azure Fox," the woman says, and I can't help but notice how perfect her skin looks. She must be around my age. Heck, she might be younger than me. She's absolutely beautiful.

I shake my head, knowing that after this, I'll never see her again. A quick look at Arthur tells me he is just as captivated.

The large fox, so large she almost looks like a wolf, steps forward. She opens her mouth. Without further movement, she speaks.

"Welcome to the Ash Trials. Those of you who volunteer, I praise your courage. I praise your power. But be warned, those of you who seek power in the name of greed, you will fail. Even if the Trials are not to kill you, you will not be chosen."

There is a moment of silence.

"The Supreme Ash, alongside the Ashen Pit, will choose four of you who make it through the Trials. Yes, that is correct. Four. The Pit has spent the last decade preparing for these Trials. The Supreme Ash has been the sole Ash Lord for years. He will choose the next four, as he sits upon the throne that is the Pit.

"Beyond the river await your Trials. One by one, the volunteers will step upon this stage. You will place your right hand on my head, and I will transport you to the Voltar Academy."

Shit. This is not just like my days at school all over again. This will be exactly like my days back at that school. Part of me wants to leave. I never signed an oath with the King. I don't have to be here. But Kreavlos' words ring in my head. He's right. I know he is. The Dark Wind brought me back to Arteyva. While the Trials can only be participated in by those who volunteer, once again, I am an exception.

But it's not that I don't want to. I mostly just don't want to go back to that school.

It is just a small part of me that wants to return. I'm not the same fourteen-year-old boy I was back then. I am much, much stronger now. I am a completely different person.

"Do not rush, as the Trials will not begin until all the volunteers are present. Once there, the Supreme Ash will greet all of you. He will tell you what awaits you in the Trials."

The Azure Fox bows her head. No one moves.

"Well, then," the girl next to the fox says. "I guess I'll go first." She gently places her hand on the fox and disappears.

Gasps erupt from the crowd.

Slowly, those of us who volunteer make our way to the stage. Camila is sent off by her family and is the second to go.

Step by step, I get closer to the fox. Out of the corner of my eye, I spot Joshua and my parents. Well, his parents. I turn my head slightly so that they can't see my face. I don't need to deal with them. I certainly don't need them to see me and then do whatever fucked-up thing that comes to their mind. Of course, now they can't hurt me. But they can try. It wouldn't be a good start to the Trials. With any luck, they'll walk with their chosen son to the stage, say their goodbyes, and never notice me.

I don't care what happens to Joshua. Once we've started the Trials, I won't seek him out for any revenge. But if he attacks me again, I won't have to hold myself back.

Arthur and I walk on stage. A line has formed. We walk up to the fox. Arthur gestures for me to go. I can feel his anticipation.

"You go ahead, I'll be right behind," I tell him. He nods and gives me that unnecessary smile of his. He places his hand on the fox. He vanishes.

I take a step closer. The Azure Fox looks up at me. Our eyes meet. She doesn't blink, but she gives me a knowing look. She bows her head again, ready for me. I gently place my hand on her head, and I am swept off my feet into darkness.

# Chapter 4

# A Court of Memory and Blood

**Aros Caelum Hayes**

Of all the times that I have traveled by means beyond my understanding of Magis, this is by far the most comfortable. The darkness fades into an easy light. I can hear water as if it were plummeting down a mountain, splashing into a basin below. The air is warm but gradually becomes cold. As the sound of falling water dies, the light around me increases. Silently, I now stand outside. My surroundings come into view—familiar, yet different.

In the middle of the courtyard stands a statue of a hippogriff on its hind legs. It towers over me, nearly as tall as the school itself. Looking around, the lampposts I remember are gone. Instead, there are four glowing tiles at each corner of the pavement, with tall pillars behind them. The tiles are new, but the pillars I remember. Seeing the light frost on the ground, I can vividly recall that night—the blood-soaked snow, the ring of fire, and the three survivors. I can also remember my screams.

A number of volunteers are already here, and in seconds, the next one arrives. There doesn't seem to be any sort of organization as to where we appear since Arthur is nowhere in sight.

"You made it," Camila says from behind me. I turn around.

"Of course, there—it was easy," I say, confused. "We're all going to make it."

She does her small shrug, head tilt, and slight eye roll. "For now. The Trials may not be a deadly tournament, but we are still in Voltar, and something tells me that they aren't going to be restricted to the school grounds."

I look back at the school. Somewhere on the third floor is my old room. If we have the time, I want to go see it.

"We don't know that," I say, though I agree with her.

"Yeah, you do." She walks away.

I notice Joshua glaring at me from the other side of the courtyard. When I look at him, he turns away. I let out a small chuckle. He arrived before I did but seems to be all alone. I'm not surprised that no one likes him.

Most people wander around a bit. Some have clearly made friends or came here with friends, while others look like they feel entirely out of place. I see an older man using a cane to walk. He eyes the other volunteers as if wishing he were with them, but no one pays him any attention. He slowly turns his head toward me, but I look away before he can catch me looking at him. It might be a bit sad to see him there so lonely, but I don't need to be the one to keep him company.

It doesn't take long for the courtyard to become overcrowded. Some people head into the school, while others wander off the courtyard, though they don't stray far from the stone pavement.

Someone brushes past me. I see a rose fall to the ground. I bend over to pick it up. So does that someone else. Her hand looks so soft. Even though my fingers touch it, I let her pick it up. I stand back to my full height. I open my mouth, too stunned to say anything.

It's her—the woman who spoke alongside the Azure Fox.

She blinks at me and smiles shyly. Holding the rose in one hand, she uses the other to brush back her hair.

"Uh, hi," she says. I raise an eyebrow, trying to speak, but still say nothing. "Sorry about that."

Still, I say nothing. She bows her head slightly, just a bit awkward, but only because I still stand there, looking like an idiot.

"Well, then," she says and begins to turn away.

"I'm Aros," I force out, my words a little too fast.

She turns back to face me again. "Sefryn." She smiles again.

It's like the rest of the world around me has disappeared, other than the sun's glow that creeps around the mountain, lighting her face. Sefryn Loste Ambers. I remember reading that name just last night.

"Well, uh, are you here for the Trials?"

It's been a long time since I've been this stupid with a girl.

"I think we all are."

"Right, of course," I say. My hands are sweating, despite it being quite cold outside.

"Um, but I thought you were—"

"Not now," she says, cutting me off. "But I can explain later, okay? I just want to first make it through whatever this is."

I look around. The crowd must be at least three hundred people. We're all just gathered here, not knowing what to do next. The Azure Fox said that the Supreme Ash would welcome us. And then a thought dawns on me. Maybe Sefryn was asked by the Azure Fox to speak to everyone, but she was just another volunteer. I understand why. As far as people go, it's hard not to notice Sefryn.

But even so, the Azure Fox surely can command attention easier than Sefryn.

A warm breeze washes over the brisk air. The atmosphere begins to glow. Nearly everyone turns to look at what's happening.

A man appears in front of the hippogriff, accompanied by a dark mist that quickly vanishes. He looks to be a bit taller than me, probably about six feet. With brown hair speckled with hints of blonde and hazel eyes, there is something magnetic about him. I find myself taking small steps closer. Sefryn follows me.

"Oh, sorry, I didn't mean..." I say, hyper-aware that our fingers touched. Again. What are the odds?

She smiles again. "No, it's totally okay." She moves to stand next to me. There are two thin steps on all sides of the hippogriff. The man stands on the top step, the statue's belly over his head.

He catches my eye for a moment. I swear I can see a small smile tug at his lips. He looks away and out over the crowd.

"Welcome, my fellow Magis."

His voice is deep and resounding. He smiles out at the crowd.

"Let's cut to the chase, shall we? You are all gathered here for a chance to become something greater, to become part of something that others far less brave than you could ever hope to achieve. The Ashen Pit has been void for too long. Three disciples, in the form of animals like our Azure Fox, have been roaming our world, keeping the darkness at bay, keeping us as safe as they can.

"As you've heard in fairy tales, our world is composed of a Magis so strong at its core that we still have been unable to uncover all of its secrets. But we have seen these powers manifest. Among us, many stand, their powers varied and perhaps formidable. You would be wise not to underestimate them, and wise to know what they are capable of. It could be the most important element in these trials.

"Here among us stand the Tavtka; those born with the power to manipulate the elements. Then we have the Rogvey, two of whom we have with us today, who can create wonders of beauty out of their bare hands." He smiles again with that wide grin, teeth glinting in the sunlight. "But do not look down on them as you've been taught to do," the man warns. "Their powers are stronger than you know."

After a short pause, he goes on. "And then we have the long-lived Fae. Four have joined us on this fateful afternoon. Their powers are quite...diverse. Each born with a specific gift, these powers only grow stronger with age.

"And then there are those who are chosen at birth and blessed by the Fae. Their powers grow stronger in concert with one another. There are many in this crowd. You consider yourself lucky, as you should."

He doesn't mention anything about the dangers of being Fae-Blessed. If the Fae that chose you dies, your powers disappear. There is no way around it. The toll on your body is tough, but not lethal. It's the idea that you've lost who you are as a person that kills you. There hasn't been a Fae-Blessed who lost their power that didn't end up taking their own life within weeks. It wasn't that they couldn't live without it. It was that they didn't want to.

"And then there are the...Maleficium. A rare Magis indeed, and to be of the high order is even rarer. Many of you have been taught that they are evil. This isn't necessarily true. Some countries in our world teach that the Maleficium are dangerous, are deadly. In that regard, they are not wrong. It is true that a Maleficium may never learn his full potential."

I tense at his change of pronouns. He had been speaking generally, but this time, I feel like he's talking about me. Unless there is another Maleficium among us?

"Maleficium, historically, have been hunted down. It's a shame, really," he says before pausing for a moment to look down. "The Maleficium are powerful, yet to what extent is unknown. Lower orders of Maleficium will display within the first few years of life. The stronger ones... Well, some say that their power may never emerge."

Again, the man looks in my direction. He's definitely talking about me. I can feel Sefryn's eyes on me. The side of my head feels warm, but I don't look at her.

"We have here, among us, five Maleficium of the lower order, and two of the higher." He steps forward, one step down. "My name is Claudius DeGhore. I am a Maleficium of the high order." He steps down again. "And the other with us is Aros Hayes."

Claudius looks around at us. "But you already knew that. The rumors spread fast." He walks back up the two steps again. "I, like all of you, do not know what the Trials will entail. That is up to the disciples to decide. What I can tell you is this: these Trials are not meant to be a war against each other. You must work together. You must protect one another. The four Ash Lords will be chosen as those who prove to be the greatest leaders. The strongest fighter belongs in the barracks, on the front lines, fighting the enemy. Powerful, yes, but true strength lies with the leader, the one who will do everything to protect those under him, for the leader is nothing more, at his core, a servant of the people."

Something tells me that Camila agrees with him, which is why she silently disagrees with how her family rules their kingdom.

Claudius opens his arms wide.

"This will be the last time you see me until the Trials are over. Remember, it is desired that you all survive. But be careful; be vigilant. The land of Voltar is home to some of the most despicable and terrifying monsters. Do not become one of them. Tomorrow, as the first light shines upon this statue, the Trials will begin. Step off the courtyard and into the woods. Your tasks will reveal themselves to you. You may work alone or you may work together. It is your choice. These are meant to test your greatest weaknesses and see if you can overcome them.

"As there is no turning back, if you do not feel like participating in these Trials any longer, then wait here until dusk tomorrow. The disciples may grant you leave. Either way, this school, long since abandoned, is furnished with sleeping quarters and food. But after sunrise tomorrow, those amenities will no longer exist."

He remains silent for a while. There are murmurs among the crowd. I wasn't sure what to expect, but these Trials don't seem so far-fetched. I just don't understand how the tasks will present themselves to us.

I also don't understand what he meant by the school being long since abandoned. Why would they close it?

"Good luck. If the Ashen Pit sees you fit, it will call upon you."

A blast of wind billows through the courtyard. Darkness surrounds us. The loud roaring pierces my eardrums. For a moment, I think it to be some trick, but when the wind clears, all is the same, except Claudius DeGhore is gone.

"Well, that was... enlightening," comes Camila's voice from behind me.

I turn around. "What did he mean by the school being long abandoned?"

Camila laughs. She looks up at me, and her smile falters. "Oh, you really don't know? Well, uh, after that night you... escaped, it was decided that there would no longer be a school here. We finished most of the year, but the transporting Fae came early, taking us all back to Edlyn. From there, it was a bit chaotic, seeing that all the students got back to their actual homes."

By "decided," she means by her parents. Which means they most likely remembered who I was when they first saw me a few days ago. They remembered what I did. It explains their attitude.

"So, it was because of me," I say quietly. I look down at the ground and shake my head. I turn to look at Sefryn, but she is no longer there.

"Hey, hey! You guys ready for the big day tomorrow?" says Arthur. He walks up to us, a wide grin on his face. Is he really always this happy? There's still something about him that doesn't sit right with me.

"Yeah, I think we are," Camila answers. "Are you?"

"I was born ready!" I notice now that there is a drink in his hand. I don't even know where he got it from. The cup is disposable, a translucent green, which means it probably was made from some large leaves and treated by a Rogvey to be used as a cup.

"So, what's your plan for the Trials?"

Arthur doesn't say anything. He just looks at us, his smile unfading, probably waiting for Camila to answer.

"I think it would be best to go through the Trials as a small group,"

Camila says. "Of course, that leaves the possibility of only one person being chosen."

"Yeah, but on the bright side, you would probably survive the Trials," I say. I don't know much about the extent of Camila's powers. If being chosen depends solely on strength, I don't think she would be, unless I just haven't seen what she's capable of. But Claudius told us that the Ashen Pit wants leaders, which means she's most definitely in the running. As for me, well, I had been hoping that power would have been enough.

"Eh, I usually do things alone," he says, taking a swig from his cup. He then *eats* it. Technically, it is edible.

Camila turns to face me. "So, is there anything you want to do today?"

I sigh. Before I answer, Arthur walks away.

"Yeah, I want to see my old room."

"Of course. To say goodbye, or to remind yourself of all the pain you've endured?"

"Both," I tell her, but I get the idea she already knew that.

Camila heads toward the school. Taking a moment to prepare myself mentally, I take a long look at the fortress-like structure. Above the first floor, there is a terrace. Tattered flags bearing the Edlyn crest—a white horse upon a setting sun—hang from its corners. But in the middle, the flag of Voltar billowed in the wind, whole and pristine, as if it were newly made. The Voltar crest is of the mountain of Voltar, placed inside a majestic shield, ornately carved, with a sword behind it. The school lies at the base of the mountains, the forest leading to its entrance. If you walk out of the school's main entrance, you can see the higher elevations of the mountain.

I used to spend a lot of time on the roof. From there, facing the other side, you could look out over the mountain land and see the vast ocean beyond. At the perfect angle, you can see the river that separates Edlyn from Voltar.

"Come on," Camila calls out to me. I jog up to her.

The entrance hall is made of jagged stone walls like the inside of a cave, and the floor is unpolished. It never was kept like the Edlyn castle, but there is something about the cold, damp feel to it that holds a nostalgia I didn't know I had.

We go up a helical staircase not far from the entrance. We pass the second floor, going right up to the third. There is no terrace on this floor. All the rooms up here served as dorms for the boys, as well as all of the teachers. The second floor was dorms for the girls, and it also had bathrooms on both ends. The first floor held our classes, dining hall, and an infirmary.

All the way down the hall, we make it to my old room. I'm not sure how Camila knew this is where I stayed, but I suppose I became quite popular after I left.

"Careful," she says, a hint of sarcasm in her voice. "It's said that if you stay too long in here, the demons will possess you and throw you into a homicidal fit of rage."

I raise an eyebrow. "Was that the rumor?"

She laughs. "For some, yeah," she says. "But it didn't really stick. Most of the students started to realize how badly you were treated, and eventually those three that saw the whole thing became very unpopular for what they did to you."

I don't know what to say. Hearing that doesn't bring me any joy or sense of revenge. Again, I feel bad for them, for everyone who went here and had to listen to the lies that my parents so carefully made sure were heard.

"It didn't matter for them," Camila says, still talking about those who survived my outburst. "The school practically closed within a week. So even when we stayed to finish the year, there was too much else going on for anyone to bother them."

Part of me is sad about the school closing, but another part of me thinks it was for the best. I don't think children should be this far away from home, especially when this place is so dangerous. In my time here, four kids died. Or rather, they were presumed dead. Technically speaking, they disappeared. But each time it happened, it was because they left the school, venturing out into the mountain.

Maybe the school really is a fortress, a haven from what lurks out there. Or maybe it was the professors who kept it safe. Or both.

I push open the wooden door. It is much smaller and lighter than those in Edlyn Castle. A single bed stands in the corner. I probably wouldn't fit comfortably in it anymore. A broken desk lies across the room. A small window overlooks the forest's trees. You can almost see the sea and the horizon. I used to imagine flying out of here, sending bolts of lightning down on those who hurt me. But I can't fly, and I can't control lightning.

Kreavlos was right. I know I am powerful. I just don't know to what extent. Even if I don't get picked as an Ash Lord, I hope to at least understand myself and what I can do. If I got just that, I would be sort of happy.

I may not tell anyone this, but I fully intend to become an Ash Lord. There's no way around it. A small voice in my head tells me that I have already been chosen.

"This is... depressing," Camila says. I know what she means. This room is smaller than the others, made for just a single person. Most of the students shared dorms with others, their rooms holding four or six.

"Taking a tour?" The voice startles me. I jump slightly, but I do my best to not move. I turn around. Sefryn stands in the doorway, leaning on one side.

"Visiting... memories," I say, the words slowly leaving my mouth.

"I see," Sefryn says and joins us in the room. "I have a new friend who would like to join us."

"What do you mean?" I ask, wondering if Sefryn took the time to meet as many people as she could.

"We're going to work together during the Trials," she says, as if I should have already known that. "Word is spreading quick that loners are likely to die within the first week."

The first week. I knew that the Trials would take place over some time, but I had hoped it wouldn't be weeks. Fast-paced and straight to the point. That's what I would have liked.

"She says she already knows you, though," Sefryn tells us. "Abigail?"

As though practiced and on cue, Abigail Coriffer walks in.

"Did you miss me?"

Oh no. Surely, she's going to have multiple opinions about everything during the Trials. I had enough of her when she butted in after my fight with Joshua.

"But you can't do that here!" I mock her in my head, imagining one of the many things she might say.

"No," Camila answers, laughing. "I can't say that I did."

Abigail strides through the room to the window. She leans against it and looks back at us. "I think that you'll find me to be a perfect mate."

I step backward, putting my hand up. "Whoa. What do you mean?" I ask her.

"Like a teammate. We're heading out into the Trials in groups, right? I'll be the perfect teammate."

I shoot a look at Camila, then at Sefryn. They both look amused, but they don't say anything, as if the choice is mine.

"Oh, yeah," I say, not knowing what else to say. "Sure."

After standing there in silence, Sefryn suggests we make our way to the kitchens to grab a last meal. She leads us out and downstairs. Most of the volunteers are inside now; the outside is getting cold as the afternoon blends into night. I then get a horrible thought—the thought that half of these people won't even survive the first week of the Trials. It won't be a monster that kills them. It will be the cold.

The dining hall is much bigger than I remember. I would think the opposite would have happened. But feeling so small and alone, I probably never noticed the grandness of where I ate, trying to avoid seeing anything beyond my plate.

I don't know who made or provided the food, but I sure as hell appreciate them. An animal like chicken exists on Arteyva, but it has bigger bones and less meat. Lots of skin, though, but minimal feathers. Like a chicken, it too can't really fly.

But served on a large, oval-shaped silver platter is chicken. There is even a decorative and handwritten parchment that says it is an Earth delicacy.

Not entirely true, but I suppose to the people of Arteyva, it would be, since they don't have ordinary chickens here. I think the Fae Realm does, though.

"This here is for the freak," I hear someone say to my right. Ignoring him, I serve myself some chicken onto my plate. He then shoves me slightly.

"Oh, sorry," he starts to say before looking at me, his eyes widening. He is easily half a foot taller than I am.

I stare him down. He doesn't know what to say. He stutters something I can't understand before quickly walking away. His friend glares at me and echoes back to me, "Freak," before walking away.

Some people never grow up, do they?

I head back to the table Sefryn chose for us. As I eat, I notice someone sit down next to me. I turn my head. It's Arthur.

He ignores me, shoving food into his mouth. I shrug to myself and keep eating. Sefryn and Camila are chatting on, mainly about Camila's life in the castle, though Sefryn seems more interested in Camila's side of her story rather than the sugarcoated and socially acceptable story I'm sure her parents force her to tell.

Abigail had gone off right before I got back to the table. She returns now with a friend. Out of the corner of my eye, I notice Arthur grab his plate and lick it completely clean.

"Hey, uh, Aros."

I turn to look at Abigail and her new friend, who is also blonde, but with shades of light brown.

"Hey," I say back to her.

"This is Clarissa. She wants to stick with you—I mean," Abigail stutters, shaking her head. "She wants to be with us." Clarissa looks uncomfortable—possibly just shy.

"Okay, why?" I ask.

"Because everyone here knows, whether they like it or not, that being with you is likely their best bet to survive." I look up at the newcomer who just walked up after Clarissa. He is about Arthur's height, also has brown hair, but has matching eyes rather than green. He is noticeably the oldest out of all of us, probably in his late thirties.

"I mean," the guy says, laughing to himself. "If I could stay here through the morning and just get back to Edlyn, I'd do that. But something tells me I already made the choice, and the Ashen Pit isn't about to let me, or anyone, turn back."

Honestly, I think it's funny that so many people believe the Ashen Pit to be this living, breathing, and thinking thing. From what I understand, it's just that—a pit. I do believe the stories of the Ash Lords and how burning their souls into the Pit made them nearly immortal and incredibly powerful, but the Pit itself isn't dictating anything. No, there must be something, something like Kreavlos that is behind it all.

The man is right that he isn't going to be allowed to just turn back; that much I can feel. There is something in the air that's changing as the night draws close. This meal, the sanctuary provided for us—all of this was done to give us just one last day where we didn't have to worry. But once the Trials start, well, only the best will make it.

"Bernando, by the way," he says, holding out his hand for me to shake. I take it.

"Aros."

Like he didn't already know that.

"That's why I'm here."

My head jerks to my right, stunned at the sudden voice from the somewhat quiet and awkward, except when eating, Arthur. Alcohol was not something I found that was provided, though I suppose there are stashes somewhere. Considering it took this long to say something, I don't think Arthur found any. Whatever he drank earlier, it wasn't his first choice.

"I want to head into the Trials with you guys."

Camila, who is sitting across the table from Sefryn, who sits by me, leans over and says, "But I thought you were a 'I usually do things alone' kind of guy."

"Well, I've never been the best at making friends," he says, seemingly with some trouble. "And I've heard that the Trials will be impossible to survive alone. I thought that this was probably a good time to make friends."

"And what do you offer us?" Camila asks him. Her voice sounds accusing, as if he isn't worth her time. But I don't blame her. I am totally okay with helping anyone out, but from someone who insisted he do things alone, there's still something not quite right about his attitude.

"I am a Maleficium," he says. Then quickly he adds, "A lower order, of course. But still, I'm strong. My brother is stronger, though. But he isn't here."

One way to think about it is that there is safety in numbers. Another way is that the more there are, the more I might be burdened down.

Camila looks at me, waiting for my answer.

"You're the royalty here, not me," I say in a low voice. If they want me to keep them all alive, someone else can at least make the decisions.

"Yeah, but you're the one everyone's talking about," she says. "But fine, I'll decide. Arthur and Bernando can join us."

"Yes," Bernando says a little too enthusiastically. He coughs into his fist and hurries away.

I look around the table. Including myself, we have seven in our group now. That's not a bad number. But I'm still trying to work out how exactly we're all going to provide ourselves with the necessities, such as food, water, and shelter, while we're out in the wilds of Voltar. Honestly, what we need on our team is a Rogvey. That or a Fae who can work with nature. I want to ask what Clarissa and Bernando can do, but something tells me neither of them are Fae.

"Well, to celebrate, we should find those barrels of vodka and rum that I'm sure the professors at this school used to sneak off to," Sefryn says, smiling widely at all of us.

She grabs my hand and leads us out of the dining hall. The way she walks, full of purpose and confidence, I get the feeling that she's already found those barrels.

Sefryn pushes open a door and heads right in. She's moving fast and still grabbing onto my hand. I almost tumble down the stairs. I let her hand go and make my way down at my own pace. Behind me, Camila lights up her hands so we can see better.

The stairs don't lead down far. The room is almost like a small basement. The walls feel damp to the touch, and the smell of wood and rum lingers in the air.

Abigail shuffles through a cabinet that sits under the stairs. She tosses us glasses. Arthur doesn't catch his and it shatters on the floor.

"Oh, fuck," he says.

"Here!" Abigail calls out, throwing him another one. Arthur catches it this time.

"C'mon, everyone, let's fill up!"

Sefryn takes off the lid of one of the barrels. She scoops out the dark amber liquid from inside. We follow her game plan.

"To overcoming the Trials!" Camila declares loudly, raising her glass up. The others cheer, and I chime in. I'm pretty sure I hear Arthur mumble something to himself about surviving.

We drink. And drink. And drink. We end up trading spots on the floor, leaning against the wall or the single wooden post that seems to serve no purpose.

I don't really know these people. I trust Camila, and I trust Sefryn, though I'm not entirely sure that isn't only because I'm attracted to her. Knowing that, I try to keep my distance. The Trials are not the time to be chasing romantic relationships. Or seeking out a single night of pleasure.

Arthur becomes quite vocal after a few drinks. He tells us of his brother mostly, someone who he claims to be proud of and be his idol. At the same time, he sounds like he's doing everything he can to prove that he can be better at something. Better at anything.

Clarissa and Abigail seem like they are already close and end up sharing a moment, laughing about it right afterward, and accidentally spitting in each other's faces. I'm not sure why they kissed, but I know I missed something while Arthur was telling me how cool it is that I'm a powerful Maleficium.

He's beginning to grow on me. Maybe he just felt left out as a child, always trying to be someone his family can be proud of. I can understand that, even if I don't relate. I can't remember a time I wanted my family to be proud of me. It's hard to want to make someone proud when the first lesson they taught you was how to feel a complete absence of love.

Later, most of us end up passing out, Clarissa and Arthur the first to do so. Camila followed after, and then Abigail, leaving just Sefryn and me awake.

Still, I make sure that I'm more than an arm's length from her. She looks at me, her pale eyes slightly glazed over. She holds a half-smile.

"Are you ever going to explain?" I ask, my words trailing off as if I didn't finish a sentence.

She giggles. "Explain what?"

*Explain how you're so fucking beautiful.*

"Why you're a volunteer," I answer, my head dropping down slightly. "When I first saw you up there, I thought you were..." I can't finish that sentence with the words that come to my head. I close my eyes, praying she'll just answer.

"The Azure Fox approached me as I made it to Edlyn," she says. "I had only just made it from Sarstoka." I actually don't know where Sarstoka is. "She just asked me to say a few words."

"But why you?"

That came out sounding rude, too rude. I didn't even mean it like that. Luckily, it doesn't faze her.

Instead, Sefryn laughs. "That's what I asked it—her," she answers. "The Azure Fox told me that humans were more likely to listen to someone they can relate to."

She sighs, though I think she's just tired. I am too. I can feel the weight of my eyelids. I'm struggling to keep my eyes open.

"She said that if I said a few things, she would be able to take over, and that everyone would be able to hear her better."

I don't understand. I don't want to be awake. I open my mouth to ask her another question, but nothing comes out, except perhaps some drool.

I wish she were next to me. She could lay her head on my chest, and I could lay my head on the top of hers. The desire for her warmth makes me feel cold. I move closer. Well, in my head I do. I can't move. Too tired. I didn't realize it until just now, but my eyes are closed. They still feel heavy. They hurt just a bit, like they were open for too long.

Back on Earth, so long as I wasn't around Nick, the person who would, without fail, cockblock me, I'd go for her. I don't let myself think those dirty thoughts.

But am I really that drunk?

If Sefryn were with me, my arms around her, I'd feel better.

Just keep dreaming.

Shrieks.

More shrieks.

Screeching cries fill my ears. They're so loud. They're so annoying.

But then I hear people screaming. Somehow, their screams sound so much louder.

My eyes snap open. I hear blasts of stone. Roars reverberate through the corridor above. More screams. The others wake too. I run up the stairs and push open the door. Something then rips it off its hinges, and it flies down the corridor.

A large beast flies past me. Its momentum kicks speed into the air that nearly knocks me off my feet.

A body is thrown at me. It hits the wall and falls to the floor. Looking down, I notice that it's the older guy I saw alone yesterday.

The hairs on the back of my neck rise. I don't know how, but I can feel it about to happen. I turn back to the others, duck slightly, and throw out my arms to my sides. A force field of energy surrounds us. The lower wall in the basement is blasted apart. Stones are reflected off my shield. The black, scaly beast is knocked away by its own force colliding with my energy.

The ground outside is revealed to us. The entire wall was demolished. Looking out to the right, the courtyard stands. I release the shield.

"Let's go," I say in a low breath. I jump down the stairs and out into the open. The others follow me. I take a quick count. Everyone is here. They're all fine. For now.

The sun is barely coming up. But there is enough light to see what's happening.

I lead them up to the courtyard. Several of those same winged beasts fly in the air. Most of them are too large to go into the school, but they do their best to knock down its walls. Smaller beasts swoop in and out, almost always carrying a body in their jaws.

It snowed last night. Where there should be white all over the ground, there is red. Too much red.

I was going to get us back to the courtyard, but that seems to be where most of the commotion is happening.

There is a scream behind me. I turn back and look. Camila throws something into the air—three discs of light. They slice through a beast that was flying down. The discs don't kill it, but knock it off course enough for us to move out of the way.

"The forest!" I shout.

Arthur steps forward, moving away some light debris on the ground with energy, just like I can. Half of a body drops from the sky, landing in front of Abigail. She freezes, her eyes wide. I get it. This half of the body is the top.

Not only that. It's Bernando.

Most of his hair had been torn out, and his face is marred with fang marks. There's red in what should be the whites of his eyes. Wherever he was, however it got him, the guy never stood a chance. I can only hope that he had an instant death rather than being alive before getting ripped apart.

I grab Abigail and lead her forward. She moves, her legs complying with my speed. But she doesn't notice anything. Her eyes stay fixed in one direction, even though she's no longer physically seeing what she just saw.

"Duck!" I hear Camila's voice ring through the air.

We all do. I have to push Abigail's head down. For whatever reason, I close my eyes too. There's a bright flash. I hear roars and shrieks from those creatures.

"C'mon, run!"

I look out to the forest. Camila is sprinting toward the trees. Most of the ones that are close to the courtyard have already been torn down. Stealing a glance, I look up. The creatures are swinging their tails, wildly moving their heads side to side. Camila has temporarily blinded them.

Abigail falls to the ground. I bend down to pick her up. A beast cries out. I look back. It's coming right at us.

I send out a pulse of energy at it. It recoils, but just a bit. A jet of flames erupts from my fist. Shrieking, the beast flies out of its way. For a moment, it looks suspended in the air, flapping its enormous wings. It charges again.

A bolt of lightning strikes down. All I can see is white. My eyes burn, but not like last night when I was tired. No, this is fiery, stinging. When my sight returns, I see the beast lying on the ground. I didn't even feel its impact when it hit. It's dead. I'm sure it is.

I look around, confused and grateful. Abigail. She stood up. There's something in her eyes, a cold look of anger. She struck it down. Abigail isn't just able to make it rain. She can call down storms.

I hear a high-pitched cry behind me. I turn. An imp. A freaking imp. The ugly small creature runs at us, holding an axe small enough for its size. This one is nothing like what I saw on Earth. I snap my fingers. A beat passes. Then another. The imp explodes.

The others have made it to the cover of the trees. I shout at them, waving my hands wildly, telling them to go further.

Abigail and I run as fast as we can. Most of the chaos is still tethered to the school. Before we make it to the trees, I take a quick look back.

Less than a quarter of the school remains intact. The courtyard has been demolished. Even from here, I can see the piles of dead bodies, all human, sprawled across the school grounds. The smaller creatures touch ground near them, lowering their heads so they can feast on their meals, while several more of the tiny imps run to the feast, picking out small body parts to play with. I was worried hypothermia would kill half the volunteers. If only. Those that died today would have been lucky if it had just been the cold.

# CHAPTER 5

## SNOWFALL

**Aros Caelum Hayes**

Trees shoot up to the sky before leaning over to attach themselves to the adjacent tree. All I can see now when I look up are the leafy branches that bind together. It feels like we are walking down a tunnel. Behind us, there is a thick wall of wood. Small flowers sprout from it in pink, white, and purple. Camila holds two orbs of light in her hands, something that seemed to surprise her when she first did it. Arthur and Clarissa walk in front of me, with Camila ahead of them, and Sefryn leading us, waving her arms over her head and creating a natural barrier to protect us. Abigail walks with me, her eyes still set forward, but now there's only anger in them.

No one says anything. Who would? What would any of us say? No matter how much I felt I had mentally prepared myself for the Trials, nothing would have prepared me for this. A voice inside my head wonders if that had even been part of the Trials at all.

Other than the reeling of my mind, I feel fine. Nothing beats a possible hangover like being hunted down by murderous, winged monsters.

After walking for a bit, Sefryn ceases her Magis that had been creating the walls of trees around us. She doesn't put any back in their original spots, leaving all the trees connected in the shape of a tunnel. For us, that's a good thing.

While I knew we were walking uphill, I wasn't sure how far we were going. I still don't know. We walk along what looks to be an intended path, though I don't know why there are any man-made paths in Voltar since no one ever wants to go here. Varying degrees of elevation surround us. We're so deep into the mountain that I can't see the ocean. I'm sure if I were to walk far enough in one direction, I would reach a cliff that plummeted down to where the school stood, or even further. But I also might hit a cliff that dropped right into the sea.

One thing is for sure, the temperature is dropping. I look around at the others. Clarissa's clothes won't keep her warm enough. That's okay, I think to myself. I can give her my coat. I can make a fire to keep us warm. I can think of something.

We keep walking. The sun has already passed high noon and is beginning to set behind us, indicating that we're headed north.

Then dusk comes. It isn't long after that when the eerie dark of night sets upon us. Still, not a word from anyone. But I can tell some of us are getting tired.

"Hey, guys," I call to everyone, having to clear my throat to get my words out. "Let's take a break. We need to find somewhere safe to stay the night."

For whatever reason, Arthur walks off the path. The others follow him.

"Right here is fine," I say slowly, wondering why we're walking into the thick of the trees.

The others nod and sit down. Arthur stares at me before walking back to join the rest of us.

"Here," I say as I put my coat around Clarissa. I immediately regret it. I don't know how she's been dealing with the cold.

I join them on the ground, and the six of us sit in a circle. Sefryn calls over some branches and twigs and stacks them. I touch them with my finger, sending out a small flame to light a fire. No one says anything.

As I look at them seated around the fire, tired and scared, it hits me that keeping everybody alive might be harder than I thought.

"Clearly, these Trials are nothing to joke about," I say, rolling my eyes at myself for even saying it. "I hate to say it, but those creatures are probably not the worst thing out here, and we need to be ready to face whatever is next."

"H-h-honestly," Clarissa says, shivering. "I just want to make it out of here alive."

God, I wish she hadn't said that. It almost feels like a death wish. That was exactly what Bernando said. But even more so, everyone here entered the Trials willingly, except perhaps me and Camila. But who am I kidding? She has personal reasons to be here, just like I do.

"After being raised in that orphanage, I thought that entering the Trials would prove to the world that I am not broken," Clarissa says quietly. "Not worthless," she adds, her voice barely even a whisper.

Abigail gently puts her hand on Clarissa's back.

"You don't have to say it," she tells Clarissa. "Not if you aren't ready."

I hold my breath. Judging by the lack of sound from the others, I can tell the rest do the same, waiting to see if Clarissa is about to open up. We may all have just met each other, but I know we're already bound for the rest of our lives.

"I was taken in by Helena, one of the wardens at Miss Maribels," Clarissa says. "She found me out in the streets at night in the middle of winter. My father always blamed himself for my mother's death, and he couldn't handle it well. Sometimes he'd take it out on me."

After I look up, I wish I hadn't. There are just a few tears coming down Clarissa's face, which tells me she's holding them back as best as she can. Whatever happened to her, and all that's happened now, something changed inside her mind. Now she might be full of a regret purely driven by fear.

"Miss Maribels took in young girls who lost their homes or couldn't stay home for one reason or another," Abigail informs us. "It's a hidden place, away from most people but is close enough to my hometown of Carroldore for a morning walk."

"I remember looking back and seeing my blood instead of my footsteps," Clarissa says in a hush. Her eyes stare out into the dark, seeing nothing but the night she speaks of. "All the blood at the school. It's just--it reminded me of it."

After a moment of silence, Camila leans forward and says, "I would never see you as broken or worthless. Even though we met only yesterday, I could see it in your eyes. You are a fighter." Clarissa nods, not quite smiling, but her frown is much less pronounced.

"And a survivor," Abigail chimes in.

I nod, smiling at Clarissa, hoping she can hear the words I can't find to say. But that's because everything Clarissa said reminds me of something unrelated but is very much real at the moment. I don't think the point of the Trials is only to survive.

"I just want everyone to make it out of here alive," I say, hoping my words find agreement within Clarissa. Still, I curse at myself for saying it. Death sentence. "And we can do that. All of us can."

"I think so too," Arthur says.

"Me too," Abigail adds. She even stands up. The others follow.

I sigh to myself. "Well, I guess we're done resting. But we need to find a place where we can make camp. Something a bit more permanent, preferably."

"How permanent are you talking?" Arthur asks. A waft of booze floats through the air. I wonder if he packed alcohol somewhere in his coat before we fled the school since he said that it calms his nerves. The friendly Arthur from before is gone, almost like the guy beside me is a completely different person. If he did bring along alcohol, he's going to have to drink more to get back to his usual self.

"Just until these Trials are over."

Abigail then asks the question that's been burning in the back of my mind, the one I don't know the answer to.

"And when will that be?" Abigail sounds like a scared child. I can see how much she's begun to trust me by the look in her eyes. It's almost like hope. It makes me uncomfortable. My knee-jerk reaction is to just turn away and ignore her, but I stop myself.

I turn back and look her in the eye.

"Honestly, I have no idea."

I see hope fade in Clarissa's eyes, and that bothers me even more. For so long, I got used to treating people that way—purposefully keeping them at arm's length, or even further. I feel like, for all that I've been through and the pain I've endured from trusting others, it's become so hard to let myself build trust with anyone. That's probably why most people I met back on Earth were not the best company; I chose to be around them knowing that I'd never fully trust them. In a way, that was easier. I didn't have to rely on them, and they didn't have to rely on me. Now these people are starting to trust me. I can't keep them away. If I keep them away, they'll die for sure. And I know that I'm going to have to start trusting them too.

Olivia crosses my mind. She always had a good heart, and she always knew I had one too. It's been just a few days since I've seen her.

I look back at Sefryn. A few days ago feels like another lifetime.

Sefryn catches up. I'm not sure if she saw me look at her. There's something inside me that just feels... different. There's more than just physical attraction to her. It's almost like I've known her for a long time. But I know that's because I want to know her for a long time. Sefryn catches my eye. She gives me a small smile. I smile back, though I cringe mentally because I know that my face probably looks like I'm holding in gas.

*There's no way she knows what I'm thinking*, I tell myself.

Camila conjures two orbs of light in her palms. She's gotten stronger already. Her light is sufficient that I don't need to do anything to complement it. I'd also rather not attract too much attention just in case something finds us.

Other than the thinner, yet fresher air, I wouldn't know that we were in the mountains. I don't even think we're that high up yet, but all the foliage makes it hard to tell. It stopped snowing, and the ground is wet but otherwise uncovered. Bats pass by over our heads. Luckily, they're just tiny, normal bats.

We walk on. We've been at it for probably eighteen hours. It feels longer. My throat is dry, and my stomach growls. I'm surprised everyone is keeping their cool, even though they're likely just as hungry as I am. It's possible the shock of this morning hasn't fully worn off.

"Oh, hey, check it out!" Arthur calls out loudly. He was walking in the back by himself. He's pointing to the left. I walk back and look. At first, all I see are more trees. I look deeper into the woods. Though far, it is there, clear as ever now that I see it. In the mountain face, which I didn't know we were so close to, there is a tunnel.

"Let's check it out," I tell him.

"I'll wait here with the others," Sefryn tells me, her breath cutting through the brisk breeze, warming my right ear and cheek.

"But what if something happens?" I look at her.

"We'll be fine out here," she says. "That cave, there's no telling how far it goes or what's inside there. Just don't be long."

I look over at Arthur. He shrugs, that same happy smile again planted on his face. I really don't understand him.

"Okay, let's do this," Arthur says.

I follow Arthur through the trees. He almost trips on three separate occasions. I'm not sure if he's excited or just clumsy.

He might just be drunk, but he doesn't smell like it anymore.

It takes us a bit over five minutes, even at a jog. The mountain isn't too steep, and trees grow from it, so there's no way I would have seen it back on the path with the forest trees being as tall as they are.

The cave opening is barely taller than me. I flick my finger and send a ball of light into it. When it gets a bit further from us, it expands. The cave doesn't go too deep. Other than some lonely stones, it is empty. It's large enough to hold the six of us comfortably, but it isn't much bigger than that.

"Oh, this is gonna be perfect!"

"Good find, Arthur."

He looks up at me, his smile wider than usual. "Thanks, man!"

I nod. "C'mon, let's grab the others."

We run out of there, almost cackling to ourselves. My throat is still parched, and my stomach is in pain from hunger, but at least we have somewhere safe to stay.

I let Arthur tell the others the good news, and I can tell he enjoys feeling like a hero when they all smile with relief. Then we lead them back to the cave. Once we're all inside, I realize it's slightly smaller than I thought, but still big enough that we can lie down without being pressed against each other. The ground is surprisingly soft with dirt. It almost feels fluffy to the touch.

Tonight we can sleep in peace. Even though we're starving and dehydrated, we've made it a full day. I put up an energy barrier at the entrance, and I enchant it to last even while I sleep. The energy of pulling that off, though, knocks me out quickly.

I am in the coffee shop. Olivia has her back facing me while she prepares a cup of coffee. She turns around. It isn't Olivia. It's Sefryn. My heart doesn't sink. If anything, I'm happy. I'm excited.

It doesn't last. My eyes snap open. Sunlight seeps through my energy wall, the rays of light spreading out.

Half of my face is covered in dirt. I must have been tired. I almost never drool, but there it is, spilling majestically out of my mouth. I wipe it into my shirt. Clarissa still has my coat. I still wear a thin cardigan, and it provides some warmth. Still, I'm fucking cold.

I stand up slowly. I need to pee, so I take down the shield and run out. I go far enough where I feel no one will accidentally come across me doing my business.

Remembering how dangerous Voltar can be, I remind myself that I need to be careful. Maybe it's because I'm back on Arteyva and all my memories are slowly and subtly flooding my head that everything around me seems like a threat. Maybe it's because of what happened yesterday that I'm scared shitless, not knowing what these Trials are supposed to bring. Some of my recent dreams haven't helped either. But also, even with the others around, I feel more alone than ever. I always had Kreavlos I could count on if I got into anything too sticky. Here, though, nothing is the same. I'm now back in a world I have spent nearly half my life avoiding, back in one of the most dangerous parts of it. To top it off, I am apparently insanely attracted to someone I just met, and it feels like that attraction is beyond physical. Hell, if I let myself, I could probably imagine a future with her.

That might be the scariest thought of them all.

"You okay?"

I jump and realize I was so lost in my thoughts that I haven't covered up yet. I lift my trousers, struggling to button them like a nervous kid. I spin around when I've gotten my pants back on. Sefryn stares at me.

Of course.

I now immensely regret having anything that important exposed for so long.

"You scared me," I say. I can see my breath in the air.

"You scared us," she tells me. "We woke up. You were gone. The shield was gone."

"I had to take a piss," I explain.

Sefryn shakes her head and walks closer. "That's not what it looked like from where I was standing."

I raise an eyebrow. "What did it look like?"

She shrugs.

I hold my gaze on her. She walks around me now. When she looks away, I'm sure I can see the glint of white in her smile.

"We're hungry and thirsty," she tells me. "We need a plan on how we're going to survive, because I will be cursed if we die because we starved."

We lock eyes for a moment. I can't help it. I burst into laughter. Sefryn looks at me incredulously.

"Yeah, you're right, that would be absolutely," I lower my voice, pausing for a moment to find the right word, "disappointing."

Sefryn clicks her tongue. "That's the nicest way you could put it."

I chuckle. "What are the others doing now?"

"They're waiting for me to get you back," she says. "But if I don't return in half an hour, they'll send someone else to look for us."

I let out a sigh. "Okay."

I take a few steps toward the cavern, passing Sefryn. I don't know what makes me do it, but I look back at her. With a small smile on my face, I reach out my hand to grab hers. She takes it. I gently pull her closer before leading us toward the others.

My eyes widen. I don't understand why I'm so nervous. Maybe, for once, she's someone I care for, someone I have feelings for, and not just another body count. Too many times I've been with a woman, and it didn't mean anything; it has never left me feeling like I'd made some great conquest, as Nick would proclaim. I just end up feeling empty.

I've never been in a relationship before. It never seemed right.

When these Trials are over, I'm going to properly ask her out.

The sound of rushing water hits my ears. I abruptly stop walking. My hand releases Sefryn's. I turn around. Lowering my head slightly, I close my eyes, trying to concentrate.

"What is it?" Sefryn asks in a whisper.

I hold a finger up to her. It sounds like it's coming from all around. The twigs and natural mulch crack beneath my feet with each step I take. The flow of water is louder. It sounds like it's crashing from up high.

I tilt my head up and look at the sky. Light gray clouds conceal any blue that exists beyond them. Then I sense it.

The path that we walked on all day yesterday was quite thin. Barely a path at all, it was the most marked, but marked only by a distinct line that wove between the trees. Unlike most of the forest ground, the path was composed mainly of dirt. On the other side, there are just as many trees as there are on the side I currently stand on. All of them are full of deep and verdant foliage. Just like I can't see the cave behind me, I can't see what's on the other side.

But now I can smell it. I don't know how to describe that feeling. I start running. Sefryn doesn't hesitate to follow.

Darting through the trees and hopping over displaced boulders, I make my way as fast as I can. The trees thin out, welcoming me to a wide view overlooking a valley. A river runs quickly through the forest, and all of its water cascades down the massive waterfall that flows deep into the valley below. The water has no idea just how beautiful it is, how precious. I fall to my knees and dunk my head, swallowing gulps of water until it goes up my nose.

I cough and splutter onto the ground. My nose stings like there's still water in it, but I felt it spill out. Sefryn laughs at me. She's much more graceful than I was as she cups her hands and sips water from them.

"I could stay here for hours," I say. "But we need to get the others."

The walk back seems to take forever. When we're back, the others take no time in telling me off for wandering away without letting anyone know.

I stand there, shivering, because my head is so cold. The river was refreshing, but its waters were icy.

"I won't do it again," I blurt out. I barely heard any of what was said. "But listen, I found a river."

"Aros! The man!" Arthur exclaims. He pats me on the back. "Show us!"

I smile. I turn around and start leading them. I light a fire in my hands, providing myself with some heat. If anything, walking with everyone to the river feels even longer than it did when I was walking back from it with just Sefryn.

Everyone has the same reaction of joy as I did, but Arthur takes it to another level when he jumps in. I don't know how deep the river is. Arthur surfaces. He moves quickly toward the waterfall. He swims against the current, but he isn't strong enough. I can see his eyes widen as he realizes what he's done.

Hundreds of feet. That's how far down the valley is. I jump into the river. I still don't know how deep it is. I swim toward Arthur. I reach out my hand for him to grab. Right before he does, I try to plant my feet into the pebbles below. I can't reach them. My face is submerged for a moment. I kick up, spitting out water. Arthur grabs me. I do my best to hold his weight against the current. I want to believe that I've caught him, that he's no longer flowing with the water, about to fall over the edge.

Taking a gamble, I use my free hand and blast fire forward, aiming it away from Arthur. The force of the blast keeps us from moving closer to the edge. Good thing. Arthur is less than ten feet away from it.

Branches crawl toward the riverbank. Thick ones slink into the river. More branches and vines rise out of the water. They tie themselves around Arthur's arms, but they retract quickly.

"Aros!" shouts Sefryn.

I look over at the others. Sefryn has her hands outstretched toward us. She tilts her head toward Arthur. I see it now. My fire is too close for the branches on that side. It seems that they don't want to be burned.

Or Sefryn is smart enough not to drive them into my flames.

I catch Sefryn's eye. Something in it tells me I can trust her. I release my blast of fire. The river immediately overcomes me, and I rush toward Arthur. I feel vines wrap around my ankles. I then hit something at my waist. It prevents me from moving with the water. I press my legs against it, being careful not to topple over. There is a small wall of trunks and branches that stops either of us from getting caught in the strongest part of the current. Vines creep out and grip me.

Arthur is pulled out first. He is gently dropped on the riverbank. I feel the tug of the vines on my arms. Sefryn struggles as she pulls at the air, willing the vines to move toward her.

I see her mouth move. She's saying something, but I don't know what.

All of a sudden, the strength of the vines increases, and I am pulled out of the water. My drop to safety isn't as gentle as Arthur's was. When I hit the ground, Sefryn lets out a quiet scream of relief and collapses to her knees.

My body shivers. I cough, though there isn't any water in my lungs. I lie on my back, one knee raised. I look over at Arthur. He's shaking violently. Abigail and Clarissa stare at him, not knowing what to do. Camila looks at me, wondering what I'll do.

"Everyone, step back," I say as strongly as I can through chattering teeth. Everyone moves a step back. I guess my voice wasn't strong enough. "More!" They move back further. My jaw begins to hurt from the constant force of my teeth.

I light flames in a circle around Arthur and me. Ten feet high, the flames flicker dangerously, but I don't let them go out of my control.

"Strip your clothes."

Arthur doesn't hear me. How can he? He's shivering so much. He was in the river longer than I was. I do it for him. Right before I fully expose him, I look away. When I'm done, I walk away from him. I put up another wall of fire between us, and I do the same for myself. At first, I'm cold, the fire seemingly doing nothing to ease the threat of freezing to death. I step closer to the fires, and finally, the flames start to keep my body warm.

Minutes pass. I squat, keeping still. I let the warmth of the fire fill me. My clothes dry quickly. When I feel it's safe enough, I put them back on. I try calling out to Arthur. The roar of the fires is too loud. Slowly, I lower the wall between us. He's dressed. He stands there, his nostrils flaring. His mouth is thinner than ever.

Arthur walks up to me.

"Don't ever do that again," he growls.

"Do what?" I ask, not breaking eye contact.

"Remove my clothes without my permission."

"You were hypothermic. You didn't give me much choice."

I lower the flames around us. The others rush forward. The air is so much fresher now.

"Then you should have let me die!" Arthur shouts.

The others turn to look at him, clearly confused.

"I'm not that type of person," I answer, keeping my voice even.

"Oh, what do you mean? Because from where I stand, I think you just wanted to see me naked!"

I can feel the others wondering what happened.

"I didn't see anything! I asked you first, but you couldn't hear me, and I had the flames around us too so that you and I wouldn't be exposed for everyone to see. I also made a wall between us."

"Yeah, well, I can see right through you," he seethes.

"Hey!" Camila steps forward. "I don't know what the hell is going on, but from where all of us stood, it looked like Aros saved your life. We knew what was happening when we saw the fire. It doesn't take a genius to figure it out."

"Yeah, Arthur, be more grateful," Clarissa says, keeping her stare for a moment before quickly looking away. She steps backward slowly before walking toward the river to drink more water.

"It was your dumb ass that jumped into the river," says Abigail. "Aros risked his life to save you, and Sefryn didn't have an easy time either, trying to pull you both out. But it sounds like it would have been better for all of us if we had just let you drown." Abigail rolls her eyes, and she too walks away.

I look at Sefryn. She keeps quiet.

Arthur looks pissed, but he doesn't say anything. He just keeps glaring at me, like everything is my fault.

"I'm ready to go back to the cavern," I say. Camila and Sefryn nod, and we make our way back.

Abigail and Clarissa return shortly afterward. I light a fire in the middle, contained by swirling energy. It keeps the cave warm. When Arthur returns, if he even does, I'll put up the energy barrier again, and that will likely keep in the heat.

I turn my head to look outside. Snow begins to fall, making patterns on the forest floor where the trees don't cover. I let out a sigh. Though it is pretty, it's only going to make things harder. And none of us even know what these Trials are. Have they already started? Are we still waiting for someone or something to tell us? Or is it up to us to find out, and are we wasting our time being unprepared for the land?

No matter the answer, I have a feeling we'll be finding out soon.

# Chapter 6

# Fae and Bone

**Aros Caelum Hayes**

After settling in, the five of us sit around the fire. It's been over an hour. The temperature quickly drops as the snow picks up. I put up my energy shield, blocking the cave entrance, even with Arthur still somewhere on the other side. Now hydrated, we still have the issue of finding food. But we're all too exhausted to do anything about that right now.

"So, Sefryn," Abigail says, looking over. "How exactly did you do that back at the river?"

Sefryn looks around at us. She lowers her head and shakes it slightly. The locks of her ash-white hair fall over her face.

"I might as well tell you now, since you'll eventually figure it out," she answers. She takes a deep breath and lets it out slowly. "I'm Fae."

A silence falls between us, but not like the kind Sefryn thought there would be.

"And?" Camila says, as if she's still waiting for the reveal. While the Fae primarily live in their own realm, almost a quarter of the population of Arteyva is made up of the Fae people. But in Praellen, otherwise known as the Fae Realm, only Fae live there, with possibly an occasional visitor. If a Fae and human were to wed, the Fae would move to Arteyva. They are also an integral part of the magic that runs deep in our world, so the two realms are heavily connected. There is another realm I have heard of, also intimately connected to Arteyva, but like most people, I don't know what it is.

"That's it," Sefryn says. "That's how I was able to do that."

"So, you're bonded with nature?" I ask her.

She shakes her head. "Not quite, as I don't have any control over animals." She pauses, thinking. "If I were truly bonded to nature, I would be able to communicate with all animals, even get them to work for me."

"That sounds like it would be dangerous," Abigail says.

"Not any more dangerous than an untested Maleficium," Sefryn retorts.

"True," I say in a lower voice.

Now there's an awkward silence between us.

"Why were you so worried to tell us?" Clarissa asks.

"Yeah, it was almost like you were embarrassed," Abigail chimes in. "We know that there are four Fae with us, and it was pretty clear from that morning that you were one of them."

That morning. It was only yesterday, but calling it that doesn't feel right. It doesn't feel like yesterday. It feels like something else, like some alternate universe.

"Well, I don't know. Before I came to Arteyva, I was told to keep my heritage—my race—a secret. At least at first. They were worried that I'd get a lot of attention if people knew I was a Fae so soon."

I laugh. The others look at me.

"Sorry, it's just that I understand. I did my best to hide what I am. It didn't work, though. People knew who I was before the Trials even began."

"Yeah, but for you, other people are scared of you," Sefryn says. "They're not scared of me. They just might want to use me."

"Maybe. I don't think they all are, though," I answer. "Sure, there are those like Joshua who came after me in the open, whether out of fear or something else. And I'm sure there are others who are waiting for the right moment, maybe when I'm vulnerable. But not everyone is scared of me."

The fire crackles, embers spitting out. I lower my energy wall so that the smoke can escape out of the top of the cave opening. Some of the cold air from outside seeps in, but it was getting too warm in here anyway.

"Sure, usually that's smarter, but in your case, it is dumb," Sefryn says. "We should remind everyone of your story, of what happened when people tried to attack you while you were vulnerable. They treated you horribly just because you were different."

"No, please don't," I say, looking down. It's hard to put together my next words. I didn't know that Sefryn knew about me. Did the tales of my time at school make it to the Fae Realm? "I wouldn't mind if everyone forgot about that night." I don't need to be reminded of that again and again by others. My memory doesn't let me forget.

Sefryn eyes me curiously. "Are you scared of your power?"

All of a sudden, my face feels very hot, warmth from the fire aside. I look up. Everyone's eyes are on me.

"I—maybe. I don't know what I can do. I've never pushed myself to my limits." Part of me doesn't want to. But Camila says that exact thought runs through my head.

"You know, the Trials might just force you to."

"I know."

"When that time comes," Sefryn says, "you must embrace it. It could mean a matter of life or death."

"I know."

A somber tone surrounds us. Or maybe it just surrounds me. No one says anything. We sit there by the fire, lost in our own thoughts. I know that I can trust everyone around me. That much is clear. What we're supposed to be doing in these Trials, that isn't clear. Why I was called to my home, that isn't clear either. There's still so much at play that I don't understand.

But I imagine being alone with Sefryn. She could be lying in my arms, asking me these questions, and I'd answer them. I'd open up to her. It's hard not to let those thoughts cross my mind. Of course, I can't do any of that right now. Not with everyone else around.

I see a figure outside. I turn my head to look. It's Arthur. He doesn't quite fall into the category of those I trust. But I think he acts out of insecurity, which is another thing that is clear to me and that was made clear after his recent outrage.

I lower the shield. He steps inside. I raise my hand. Arthur waves. I wasn't waving at him; I was putting the shield back up.

In one hand, Arthur carries a dead animal. It kind of looks like a raccoon, but it doesn't have that mask over its eyes.

"It's all I was able to catch," he says, raising the animal into the air. "But hopefully it will be enough for now."

The girls look at him with disgust.

"Sure, just... put it over there," I say, pointing to somewhere near the front of the cave. He does. He comes back, standing with his arms at his sides. No one says anything to him. Arthur sits. The girls move a bit closer together, increasing their distance from him.

"Look, I'm sorry," he says, his voice unfaltering, but he can't look anyone in the eye. "I overreacted. I've been hungry—"

"We're all hungry," Abigail says, almost standing up. "But none of us have acted like you did."

Arthur looks down for a second. "I know. It's no excuse. I was just embarrassed. And I'm sorry."

"It's fine," I say after some time. "If you want to eat the... food you found, be my guest, but I'm going to decline."

Everyone else does too.

Arthur doesn't touch the animal, and the poor guy lies by the edge of the cave, unwanted and killed for nothing.

After a few minutes, Sefryn gets up and announces that she's going to find food. I tell her that I'll go too. I start to get up.

"No, please don't—" Abgail says, cutting herself off abruptly. She stands, looking over at me, her eyes flickering toward Arthur.

*Please don't leave us with him.*

I get it. And now I like him less. I can forgive him for acting out. Hell, I've been through so much worse. But making the others uncomfortable enough that they don't want to be alone with him is so much worse. Especially since it's taking an opportunity for me to be alone with Sefryn away.

"I—I'll go with Sefryn," Abigail says. Camila catches my eye. I sit back, relaxing my body.

"Okay," I say, my word barely louder than a whisper.

Clarissa moves closer to me. Camila doesn't do anything. Arthur does his best to look interested in something in his lap, though there is nothing.

Sefryn and Abigail leave. Arthur doesn't say anything, but his usual smile is gone. The four of us don't speak. I lie on my back. I have to move a small pebble out of the way so it doesn't jab into me. I stare up at the ceiling.

Camila and Clarissa start whispering to each other. I can hear what they say; they don't talk about anything interesting. I don't think Clarissa liked it being so quiet. I didn't mind, but I also don't mind hearing them in the background. I peek over at Arthur. He was looking over at me but quickly looks down into his lap again when I catch his eye.

High afternoon hits us, but it's blanketed by even more snow. The wind picks up. Just as I begin to worry about Sefryn and Abigail, they return. When I let down the shield, snow blows in and quickly melts in the warm air.

Berries and nuts. That's what Sefryn and Abigail found.

"We're back!" Abigail announces as if we hadn't noticed. She nestles down where she was sitting before. Sefryn sits next to me, with Arthur on her other side, though he is still distanced from the rest of us.

"I also have eggs, though I'm not sure they were worth it," Sefryn says, taking out eight small, quarter-sized eggs from one of her pockets.

"Well, they are now," Camila says. "The birds that laid them won't touch the eggs since you took them."

"I don't even understand how birds are laying eggs out there in that weather," Clarissa says.

"Maybe they're old eggs?" Sefryn suggests. "I only found them because they fell out of a tree I was harvesting."

"We'll know if they're bad once we open them," I tell the others. "If only we had a way to cook them."

"Ah!" Sefryn pulls out a small wooden plate from her coat. I can tell she just made it. Being made from the wood of a tree, it would ordinarily burn in the fire.

Sefryn creates a lip around the edge of the plate. The eggs are cracked and dropped inside. Using my powers to raise the plate into the air, I hover it over the fire, creating a small shield beneath it to prevent the flames from burning through. The eggs cook quickly. There isn't much of it, but we divide the contents into our hands and eat.

A small taste of food and my stomach growls louder. The berries and nuts they gathered are unbelievably tasty, and I eat as much as I can without feeling bad about taking too much. Arthur refuses the berries but eats some of the nuts.

Now I'm wishing I had water to wash it down.

"We need to get more organized about this," Sefryn says. Camila nods in agreement.

"Does anyone want water?" I ask. The others nod. We get up and head toward the river. As we walk, Sefryn weaves her hands around. She creates small cups and hands them out one by one as they're made.

Bended and molded bark make up their outsides, while a blend of leaves sits inside so that the liquid doesn't leak out.

The trip to the river is uneventful. We all scoop water into our cups and drink. Arthur doesn't jump inside or do anything drastic. He's still a bit farther away from us but seems to slowly get closer. Before we leave, Sefryn asks us to wait. With more complicated motions of her hands, she intertwines vines and wood together to create a large bowl.

She hands the bowl to me. I fill it with water from the river and carry it back. When the wind and snow pick up, Clarissa pushes wind from her hands in an arc above us, protecting us from the worst of the weather as best as she can.

When the cave comes into view, I see something inside. I look closer, picking up my pace. Flourishing her tail, her blue glow lighting up the cave, the Azure Fox stands on all fours, seemingly waiting for us. Her ears perk up when she sees us, and she turns her head to look into my eyes. She spits out the carcass that we left there. It looks like she tried eating it but decided that it didn't taste good enough.

She lets us pass her when we enter the cavern. I set the large bowl of water toward the back. We stand, staring at her, unsure of what happens next.

"You may sit."

At almost four feet tall, she's bigger than the average wolf. From afar, one might mistake her for one, but up close, you can see her bushy tail, long pointed ears, and narrow snout. Though like a wolf, the Azure Fox would easily be able to tear apart human flesh. It's unlikely the Azure Fox would have to resort to such measures, though, as she could probably do away with someone with just a blink of an eye.

Arthur sits first, with Abigail and Clarissa following right after him. Sefryn, Camila, and I exchange looks. The Azure Fox lowers her head, her eyes looking directly at me again. The rest of us sit down.

"Welcome to the Ash Trials," she says, just opening her mouth, her words ringing through the cavern. "Voltar is your test."

She lets us sit there with those words. I had already surmised as much. But there is something that is missing. Something I'm not sure of.

"You will find that there are safer places for you to rest, such as this cave or small paths that you may walk, avoiding the dangers of the deep forest and mountain. I created these to ease your journey. But do not let your guard down. You haven't even seen the true horrors of what lives here."

"Was that morning at the school part of the Trials? The monsters, I mean," Clarissa asks, raising her hand for some reason. I take her to be the youngest of us.

"Everything that happens here is part of the Trials," the Azure Fox answers. "You were told that the Trials were to start yesterday morning. They did. Once dawn came, I let down my magic guards around the school."

"So it was you?" Clarissa asks, but she looks down quickly. "I just mean, t—the monsters were part of the Trials."

"I did not know that was going to happen," the Azure Fox answers. "As I told you, you haven't seen the worst of Voltar. People should not have slept in that morning. But they did. And they paid dearly for it. Note that you must be careful in your choices. I won't be here to protect you. I need to see who can make it. The Ashen Pit will have it no other way."

"How long do we have to survive here?" I ask. "Weeks? Months?" I just want to know what I'm—what we're up against.

"You must find the Ashen Pit."

"The Ashen Pit is here?" I ask, standing up. The Azure Fox growls slightly, but I don't sit back down.

"Yes, the Ashen Pit is in Voltar, hidden from everything so that it will remain untouched. You will have three clues to help you find it. If you succeed, I will meet you at the Ashen Pit and return you to Edlyn. Once the Trials are over, the Ashen Pit will choose the next Ash Lords."

"When are the Trials over?" Clarissa asks.

"When no one is left," the Azure Fox answers. "The volunteers will either find the Ashen Pit, or they will die trying."

No one says anything. Compared to two days ago, there are probably only half of us left. The first morning was nothing short of a massacre. Now that I think of it, there was probably enough food provided to those creatures for days. We should get moving soon. I don't want the monsters to catch up to us.

"Your first clue is this: Locate the Ivory Skeleton." The Azure Fox takes a step closer to us. She paws the dirt. "I hope one of you knows the tale."

In a dust of frost, she disappears.

I look down at the ground. I've read the fairytale. In fact, I read it just a few days ago. Lucky me.

"Does anybody know what she's talking about?" Clarissa asks.

"I do," Camila says. "I've heard the tale."

I look up at her and smile. "Do you want to do the honors?"

"Sure," Camila says, shifting slightly. "The Ivory Skeleton was once a mammoth. So massive in size, he was feared by the other creatures of the mountain. Rightfully so, as the mammoth had the power to move mountains. But the mammoth never hurt anyone. He was a gentle creature, despite his great strength.

"So, what happened to our mammoth? One day, a creature known as the Serpent wanted the mammoth gone. He was large, too, but the mammoth scared him. He projected that fear onto the other animals."

Camila tells the story like it's a children's tale. She probably heard it from her parents, possibly one of her older sisters. She seems excited to be the storyteller now.

"One day, entirely unprovoked, the Serpent coiled and lashed out at the mammoth. Confused and not wanting to hurt the creature, the mammoth jumped back. Thinking he was attacking the poor snake, the other animals charged at the mammoth. In a panic, the mammoth quickly backed up. Unfortunately, the mammoth stepped too close to the cliff's edge, and the rocks gave way, causing him to plummet into the valley below. When he hit the ground, the impact created a massive crater. Alive but unable to move, the mammoth lay there for weeks, roaring out, but no one came to help. Eventually, the mammoth passed, and its flesh soon rotted away, leaving behind only its bones."

I hear a sniff. I look up to see Clarissa wipe her eye with her—my—jacket.

"That's so sad," she says. "He was probably one of the nicest animals ever."

"They say that's how the horrors of Voltar were born," I say. "Darker fairy tales tell stories of how those animals, deranged and haunted by their conscience, became vicious monsters so that they could take down the Serpent. They hated the Serpent for tricking them, but all the Serpent did was amplify their fear. Eventually, the animals lost their minds and never returned to their old selves."

"Is the Serpent still alive?" Arthur asks.

"Some stories say that Voltar, as in this entire mountain, is the Serpent. The Serpent could read into one's mind, targeting their fears and using those against them," I reply with a shrug. "Of course, I don't believe that. But a giant serpent lurking in the mountain, preying on fear? That's believable."

I don't mean to scare them, but I couldn't help telling that story. It fascinated me when I read it. Of course, part of me feels like it is real. I know Voltar is a terrifying place, with even more terrifying monsters. But there is something that I feel is lurking in the back of my mind, trying to claw its way to the front. If it's fear, surely it is the work of the Serpent.

It's like the longer a person is here, the more they succumb to their fears. Finding the Ashen Pit has to be a quick journey for us. Because if we're here for long enough, and the monsters of Voltar don't kill us first, then the darkest of our fears will. Serpent or not, even the strongest of us will lose our minds. I look over to Arthur, knowing that he will lose his mind far sooner than I will. But does that pose a threat to the others?

"Hey, look!"

I jerk my head toward the front of the cavern where the sound came from. There are nine people looking inside. The guy who spoke points at us with a long stick narrowed at its tip.

"If it isn't the Maleficium, Aros," he says mockingly, taking heavy steps toward us. "I think I'll just get this over with."

I then realize that my shield isn't up. It hasn't been since we got back because the Azure Fox distracted me. I forgot to protect us. I forgot to protect them.

He flashes a wide grin. He has straight brown hair. Parts of it go over his eyebrows, but it isn't much longer than that. He must be barely twenty-one. His green eyes flash with hatred. "It's time to avenge my brother."

A jet of fire blasts from both his hands into the cave. I throw out my hand, and it dies out before it reaches us. If he's just a Tavtka with fire powers, or even a Fae-Blessed like Joshua, then this will be easy. If he is a Maleficium, even if a low-order one, or a Fae, it could be more challenging. It also doesn't help that there are eight other people backing him up.

Ready on their mark, they charge. The guy blasts more fire. With my palms facing toward them, I create another shield that deflects their attacks. Three of them keep running and fly back when they hit the shield.

Roots from beneath the trees erupt from the ground. Four of them are pulled down by the roots, which then wrap around their bodies. Another blast of fire heads my way, but it's deflected by a strong wind from behind me. I turn to look. Clarissa's fingers are interlocked, her palms facing outward.

Arthur jumps in front of me. He fires off blasts of energy.

The fire guy lunges at me. His arms are covered in fire, but the flames don't harm him. I run at him. Using my powers, I grab his arms. The flames don't hurt me, but I can feel the heat of the fire. His eyes widen, not understanding why I can withstand his fire.

We begin to wrestle. He throws my grip off him and tries to punch me. I dodge it. He punches again, I dodge, but I don't see his other fist, and it collides into my head, just missing my ear. I stumble. I throw out my arm, sending a pulse of energy at him. When it hits, the guy staggers backward. I rise back up to my full height.

A bolt of lightning strikes nearby. The noise rings in my ears. There is another flash of light, and I'm momentarily blinded. When I can see again, I notice Camila and Abigail stepping out of the cavern. They walk next to each other, their hands ready for battle, stretched out to their sides.

The snow picks up and begins to storm around. Abigail and Clarissa work together, sending small shards of ice dust at our attackers, nicking them in their faces.

The pyro dude shouts out angrily and punches the ground. A wave of fire rises up and crashes down. I reach out to grab it. My friends behind me fall. The flames scorch dangerously close, threatening to burn anything in their path. I tighten my fist as if the fire were in my hand. Slowly, the flames die out. All seems silent for a moment. I can't even see the snow fall anymore. The guy stares at me, his chest rising and falling quickly. I take him to be their leader.

I throw out both my arms, sending a slice of fire at the others, knocking them to the ground, just as the fire guy did to my friends, but I don't let the fire rage on.

"Sefryn!" I call out. I shoot a quick look at her. She nods.

I walk up to the guy, lifting him off the ground and shoving him into a tree. Sefryn dances her arms around, calling up more roots to trap the others.

"What the hell are you doing?" I ask him, refraining from shouting.

He spits in my face. Classic. I don't move. I barely give him the satisfaction of blinking.

"You killed my brother," he says.

"I don't even know you," I reply. "And it's been a long time since I've been on Arteyva."

"Yeah, because you had to run away from the scene of your crime."

That's it. His brother must have been one of the guys I killed that night. Of course I didn't mean to. But it isn't like they didn't deserve it.

"They attacked me. All of them attacked me," I tell him, seething. "There was nothing else I could have done."

"They didn't deserve to die," he says. "I watched as the teachers found them, found him, and removed the bodies before the other students could see." He pauses, then whispers, a sad pain in his cracking voice, "He didn't deserve to die."

I look away for a moment and let out a small chuckle. "I think we have different opinions about that."

Physically, I let him go, but I hold him to the tree with ropes of energy. Serfyn walks up. The tree begins to deform, opening up and swallowing most of the guy. When he is sufficiently trapped, Sefryn releases her hold on the tree.

"Don't come after us again," I tell him. I walk over to Camila. "Blind him for me, would you?"

Camila smiles. "Temporarily or permanently?"

I shrug. "You choose."

I don't look when Camila does it, but I can hear the guy roar in pain. The others remain trapped on the ground, lying down and pinned by the roots.

"I suppose we can't stay here," Clarissa says. I put my arm around her—half for comfort, but also because I am starting to feel cold, and she still has my coat.

"No, we can't," I tell her. "But we'll find someplace even better."

The six of us walk away, continuing on the thin path the Azure Fox made. Somewhere in this mountain is an enormous crater nestled in a valley. With any luck, we'll come across it soon, along with another place to rest for a while. But even once we find the Ivory Skeleton, it is likely to send us on another scavenger hunt, which means there is no place we can set up a true camp. I suppose that's the point of it. The Trials are about surviving Voltar and all that dwells here, along with some unfriendly faces. We aren't to make a home here.

I feel bad about killing his brother. Nevertheless, in the end, I would have been the one dead if my powers hadn't broken free. And I don't think I deserved what they did to me. I don't think I deserved the childhood I had. But here I am, and I can't change what was done.

"Chase," Camila says to me, hurrying to catch up. "That's his name. He was in my year back at school."

"Hm," I say, still slightly lost in my thoughts. "Hopefully, we don't run into him again."

"What would you do?"

I look at Camila. "Honestly, I don't know."

"Why didn't you just kill him back there?" Arthur asks. "You know he was going for it."

"Because I'm not here to kill anyone," I say.

"So what? You just want to become an Ash Lord? And just fuck it with everything else?"

I shoot a look at Arthur. "No, I care about people. I want us—I want everyone to make it through the Trials alive." I shake my head. The mountain trail gets steeper. "And yes, I want to become one of the next Ash Lords."

# CHAPTER 7

## GRASS AND LEAF

**Aros Caelum Hayes**

The sun begins to set, and it really sucks that it's happening. We haven't found a new place to rest for the night, and there has been no sign of the Ivory Skeleton, which means it doesn't look like we're stopping anytime soon. But something biting at the back of my mind tells me that our luck is going to run out if we don't leave the dark of the night. It gets even colder. I have to hold fires in both my hands to keep myself warm. Despite my exhaustion and how uncomfortable I feel, I don't want to stop just anywhere. I feel we are too exposed out in the open, so I mention nothing about taking a break. As we trudge on, I can hear distant howls in the night.

I notice that the trees seem larger than earlier—taller, thicker, and some have a moss that must thrive in the frosty weather. Roots spring out of the ground and back in again. We have to be careful as we walk over them so we don't trip.

We walk through a narrow valley; the cliffs of the mountain flank us, and the rise of the ground steepens. The number of trees thins, and other plant life becomes sparser, though we still walk over thick roots. Moths fly around, though they don't seem to know where to go. Unfortunately for both me and Camila, they swarm our hands after night settles in, circling the light sources in our palms. Even with the fire burning against my hands, the heat barely keeps me warm.

Camila holds rings of light. They are an easy blue. She's getting more creative with her powers, but I still sense uncertainty. Growing up in her family, I have a feeling she was always made to feel less than. I don't think she knows how powerful she is. As such, I have a hunch that this is only the tip of her capabilities, and the Trials will force her to discover just how strong she truly is.

"Hey, put those out."

Shivers run down my spine. She spoke slowly, in just a whisper. I can feel her behind me, her lips near my ear. In the near-freezing temperature, I can feel her hot breath on my neck. I hadn't noticed she was behind me or anything she was doing while I walked on, lost in my thoughts.

Obeying, I put out the fires in my hands. It gets darker. It also immediately gets colder. I guess the fires did more than I thought.

Something is placed on my shoulders. It feels like a blanket. I grab it, reaching my hand back. Sefryn touches my hand and guides it. She's a bit clumsy, but eventually, I find the sleeves. It's some sort of coat. It feels warm and soft to the touch, but something about it feels brittle.

The moon hides behind the peaks of the mountains. The canopy of trees makes it darker still. The only light we have right now is Camila's. I light up rings just like hers. I didn't know I could shape them like that. I guess I never thought to.

"Look at it," Sefryn says, her voice louder and lighter.

I look down at the coat. It's woven out of the detritus of the flora around us, deep green with random bursts of dark brown. The coat does an impressive job of keeping me warm.

"This is amazing," I breathe out.

My lights barely let me see her face, but Sefryn smiles. I smile too. We lock eyes for a few moments. Unless I read it wrong, I can feel the connection between us grow stronger. I could kiss her right now. I almost do. But Arthur turns his head back for a second. He looks away quickly, but it's enough for me not to make a move.

We reach the crest of the trail, and our walking path goes downhill. The light of the moon becomes unimpeded, and I can see a valley of giant trees below. Off-center, one of the trees stands taller than the rest and looks wide enough to drive a large pickup through.

Faster than I anticipated, we reach the base of the valley. The closer we get to the giant tree, the more we need to squeeze through the spaces between the other trees. That's when I notice that many of the trees are connected to each other, as if they are growing as one.

A howl pierces the night. Abigail and Clarissa cover their ears. My head jerks toward the source of the noise. A towering werewolf stands just ten yards from us, growling viciously, drool dripping from its mouth. It must be at least three heads taller than I am. It has a chipped fang, which, if anything, makes it the sharpest tooth it has. Its claws are overgrown, and they all curl. With thinning gray hair, it looks sick. But that doesn't stop it from eyeing us as its dinner.

Werewolves, cursed creatures that used to be human, are not allowed in Edlyn or Soulstice. They are mostly banned from other parts of the world. So, of course, they would be in Voltar. I've only read about them. They don't turn on the full moon; they are always stuck in their wolf-like form. Even though I knew they were real, I didn't truly believe in them. Now I definitely do.

The werewolf leaps at us. Clarissa shrieks, stumbling out of the way. I send out a blast of energy. It hits it midair. The werewolf falls to the ground but gets up quickly. Shaking its head, it leaps again. I send out another pulse. Roots shoot up from the ground. They wrap around its hind legs and yank it backward. The werewolf falls to the ground. It frees itself from their grasp, tearing the roots apart as it does so.

Clouds move overhead. I shoot a look at Abigail. It's too risky to call down lightning. If it were hot enough and strong enough, she'd set the valley on fire.

Arthur sends out waves of energy, but they do little to the werewolf. As a creature of Magis, any Magis weaker than it is ineffective.

The werewolf runs toward a tree and quickly scales it. It turns around and launches itself with its powerful legs. I get ready to fry it. An orb of flame gathers in my hands, shifting from red and orange to a burning blue.

"Get down!" I hear Camila shout.

A slice of light flies in front of me. It arches upwards and cuts straight through the werewolf. It collapses on the forest floor, severed at its stomach. I turn back, letting the flames in my hands die out. Camila stands there, looking up at where the werewolf stood, and breathes heavily. Her eyes are hard and certain. She's beginning to understand that she is capable of far more than she was brought up to believe. I look back toward the creature. Something catches my eye, but I can't see it clearly.

I shoot out discs of light, but they aren't meant to attack. The thickest of the trees comes into view. Searing red, I can see the deep gash in its trunk from Camila's attack.

Something else comes into view. A hollow sits at the base of the largest tree. The opening is only about five feet tall, but I can't make out how deep it goes.

"Camila," I call out, a thousand thoughts racing in my mind. But I'm happy. "You're awesome."

"Thanks," she says, walking up to me. "I didn't even know I could do that."

"Well, if the Ash Trials don't bring out the best in you, Voltar surely will," Sefryn says.

"I always thought that my powers were almost useless," Camila says. "No one ever said that to me outright, but I believed it."

"Nonsense," Abigail says. "You have the power of light. Light is one of the strongest elements ever."

Clarissa and Arthur chime in with their praise. I don't think Camila really hears it. I can tell she's surprised but proud of herself. I'd be proud too. I am proud.

"Well, let's take a rest for the night, shall we?" I call out, pointing to the hollow in the tree. Arthur cheers loudly and makes his way over.

"Did I do that?" Camila asks, confused.

"I don't think so," I tell her. "But you helped us find it."

Camila nods. The rest of us catch up to Arthur, who walks toward us after wandering deep into the tree.

"I couldn't find out how far it goes," Arthur tells us. "But it feels like the ground goes downward."

"Like it goes beneath the ground?" Clarissa asks.

"I guess so," Arthur says. "But I'm not sure."

I look up. It is taller inside than the opening. The "ceiling" of the tree must be over ten feet high. I don't know what I expected to see, but I can barely see anything because it's so dark.

"Well, either way, keeping up two energy barriers might be a bit much for me," I say. I can feel my strength decreasing. With the fights, all the walking, and lack of consistent food, I don't know how much longer I can go. We also need to find a new source of water.

"So, then what? We can't stay here for the night?" Arthur asks. Something in his tone sounds more than irate. It almost sounds accusatory, as if *I'm* the problem.

"I never said that," I answer, my voice flat. I walk past him and look into the cavity. "But it will probably be safe if we take watches."

"Fine, I'll take the first watch. Who wants to take it with me?" Arthur looks around, his eyes landing on Abigail and Clarissa.

"No," I say. I try to choose my next words carefully.

"Aros and I can take the first watch," Sefryn says, saving me from having to say anything. She looks over to Camila. Camila nods, knowing that she is going to be paired with Arthur. "Abigail and Clarissa can go after us."

"And I will watch the sunrise with Arthur," Camila says. "We'll wake everyone up when it feels like a good time to get going again."

Arthur holds his breath. "Fine. But we should find some food now. And water. I'd rather know we have those before heading off to sleep."

"I have the food solved," Sefryn says, calling large fruits into the cavern, strung on vines. She must have found them when we first entered the shallow valley.

"I don't want to keep eating that crap," Arthur complains. "I'm a man, and I can't live off fruit and other shit." He walks outside. "I'll find my own food."

"Arthur!" Camila shouts. I can tell she's done with him. We all are. "We can find meat in the morning. For now, eat what Sefryn brought in. We're all tired, so if you go out there to hunt, you're going to be on your own. We won't follow. Your Magis barely did anything against the werewolf. Do you really think you're going to survive what else is out there?"

Camila's words are harsh but needed. I've wanted to say the same thing. I've wanted to say worse. But I keep stopping myself because I don't want to give him more reasons to dislike me. Not that I care. Not anymore. The guy is a complete dick-fuck.

Arthur tenses, but he turns around. Humbled, Arthur does his best to play off anger. His eyes are narrowed as he walks past the rest of us, refusing to look at anyone.

The rest of us thank Sefryn for the food and eat the fruit. I don't even know what it is. It feels like a peach but is bright green. But it does taste pretty good. I eat five of them. They also hold water, helping us hydrate as well as feel full.

Arthur sleeps somewhere out of sight. Clarissa and Abigail move a bit deeper into the hollow to sleep. Sefryn weaves together fallen foliage to make pillows for them. Grateful, they take the pillows and lie down, closing their eyes. Arthur didn't wait around long enough for Sefryn to make him one.

Camila, Sefryn, and I sit against the walls of the tree. We don't say anything. We know what each other is thinking. Arthur might have to go. If he keeps at it, he's likely to put us in real danger. But even as much as I would want to, I won't let us toss him aside. He'd surely die out there.

When Camila starts to yawn, Sefryn makes her a pillow too. Camila thanks her and heads somewhere a bit away to get her sleep. It's not until about half an hour later, when we can hear the low, quiet snores from the others, that Sefryn and I speak.

"So, you want to watch the front or the back?" she asks me.

I shrug. "The back, I guess. If anything happens, you can use the trees outside to defend us."

"Technically, I can use the tree we're inside to defend us," she replies.

"Oh, that is true."

She gets up from leaning against the wall. "Come here."

I do. She sits on the ground, facing outside. I sit, facing deeper into the hollow. Our backs are leaning against each other. She feels a bit cold, but I'm sure I feel warm to her.

"I can light a fire if you like," I say.

"No, it's okay. Save your energy. We might need it."

I nod.

Luckily, sitting on the bare ground isn't comfortable, so the urge to fall asleep doesn't hit me, even though I'm quite tired.

"What do you think was wrong with it?"

"What, Arthur? Probably self-esteem issues," I respond.

The silence I hear is the loudest it's ever been. Then Sefryn starts giggling into her hands, trying to cover up the racket she's making. She even snorts.

I turn my head back. The back of her head smacks into my nose. I recoil in pain and put my hand up to it, the stinging still strong.

"Oh, sorry!" she cries out, twisting her body around. She grabs my face to turn it to hers. I look down at my fingers. There's no blood, but it still hurts.

"What was so funny, anyway?" I ask.

She starts laughing again, but she does better at controlling herself.

"When I asked you what was wrong with it, I meant the werewolf."

"Oh." I let my head fall. I suppose I'm way more tired than I thought I was.

"Still, you're probably right."

I let out a chuckle.

"Well, the werewolf was alone," I say, trying to change the subject because I'm a bit embarrassed. I'm not embarrassed about how I answered. I'm embarrassed because I'm letting Arthur's attitude get to me.

"Yes, at least we hope."

Sefryn and I shift back to our previous positions, leaning against each other's backs.

"So either it was kicked out of its pack, or..." I trail off, pondering the possibilities. "Well, maybe it was sick. If it was, it was probably rejected by the others."

"What would make it sick?"

I shrug. "Could be anything. But most likely the curse that afflicted it. I mean, it is Voltar, and the werewolf is far from the strongest thing out here. In fact, it's probably one of the weakest."

"I guess for the werewolves, the best thing to do is kick out the weakest of their pack."

So many unspoken words are exchanged between us. She's right. I know she is. But we aren't cursed creatures. We aren't animals or beasts of the night. So, no matter how irritating Arthur gets, I'm not about to abandon him. If he ends up putting us in danger, though, that's a different story. I may not have killed Chase, but we did leave him and his group there to die. Whether they survive or not is up to them.

"How did you make this?" I ask her, patting the coat she made for me. I am curious to know, but I also want to change the subject.

"It took some time—I am no Rogvey—but there were enough leaves and grasses around that I figured I could work them in together somehow. I knew you were cold, even if you tried to hide it," she answers. "By the way, that was quite thoughtful of you to give Clarissa your jacket. She should have been more prepared, though."

I don't blush. I don't.

"Yeah, well…" What am I saying? "I figured that I could make fire and keep myself warm. She couldn't."

"I'm just saying, I know a hero when I see one."

Are these just compliments, or is she flirting? I can't tell. I want to punch myself for not knowing, for being so flustered around her. During normal interactions—well, normal for participating in Trials on Voltar—I'm fine. I'm comfortable around her. But when we're alone, something gets at my nerves.

Throughout the night, we hear howls and bird cries in the distance, but we never see anything. Despite Sefryn saying that we might need my energy, I light a fire. It's off to the other side of the tree's cavern, but not close enough that it could risk burning the tree.

Looking outside, I notice that the snow on the ground steadily rises. It's hard to see much, but the flickering flames of my fire help.

The night goes on. Lost in my thoughts, I don't notice Abigail waking Clarissa. When I sense them nearing, I look up.

"Hey, guys," Abigail says. Her hair looks a bit messy, and I can see the tiredness in her sharp blue eyes. But she also has a determination in them that tells me I'm not about to talk her out of taking her shift. Not that I would want to, but I'd do it.

And for that, I respect her so much more. The seemingly annoying and possibly prissy person I thought she was before doesn't seem to exist. Maybe it was our horrifying entrance to the Trials, or maybe she was always like this. Either way, Abigail seems very down-to-earth and responsible. I couldn't be more appreciative that she is here with the rest of us.

"It's our turn now," Clarissa says. She, on the other hand, still seems a bit uncertain, but I know her heart is in the right place. "I don't know how long it has been, but I was clearly rested enough to wake."

"Okay. Don't hesitate to wake me if anything happens," I tell them.

"What, you don't think we can handle it?" Abigail asks. With a sudden vision of the time when she struck down a monster with a bolt of lightning, I know she can handle things.

"Not at all," I reply with a smile. "I know the two of you got this. But I'd rather be careful than sorry." I make eye contact with both of them. "So, please, if anything happens, just wake me."

Abigail smiles. "Of course. Now get some sleep. You deserve it."

Sefryn and I walk over to where Abigail and Clarissa were. They took their leaf pillows, but Sefryn makes us two more. I lie down near Camila. Sefryn isn't far from me. Arthur snores in his sleep. I look around the cavern. Clarissa and Abigail have already started talking. Sefryn catches my eye, gives me a smile, and then turns around, ready to fall asleep.

I close my eyes. Sometimes it takes me a while to fall asleep. I hope that this isn't the case tonight.

I must have knocked out quickly into a deep sleep. I'm startled when Camila shakes me awake. At first, I think something's happened, but the sun has simply lit up the world outside. I don't see Arthur. Camila walks to the others and gently wakes them too.

My fire died. Camila tells me that Arthur didn't like it much, so he put it out, claiming that it would burn down the tree. I step outside, noticing how unusual the landscape is with the descending land but giant roots that make the ground look like an illusion. Trees tower above me, stray leaves falling down. Most of the trees here are still green, but some have become bare. There's nearly half a foot of snow on the ground. It is also a good thing I wore boots.

"There should be some kind of water nearby," I say, more to myself than anyone else. When I turn around to suggest we look for some, I catch Arthur in my peripheral vision. He's carrying a decent-sized boar in his arms. It's clearly dead; I can tell from the multiple gashes across its body.

He walks by me without a word. Arthur dumps the boar inside the tree. The girls back away quickly, most of them visibly disgusted.

"I got us some real food," he says. He starts throwing out slices of energy at the animal. When he realizes that all he does is cut deeper into the carcass, he stops and starts trying to rip out pieces of it. He finally gets a chunk.

"Ugh," I say quietly to myself. Abigail and Clarissa make their way outside and stand near me. I wonder if he just has an obsession with killing animals.

Arthur turns to look back at me. "We could use that fire now, to cook this up and eat."

I shake my head. My stomach feels a bit uneasy. I'm hungry. I would normally eat it, especially since this would be the first meat I've had since we began the Trials—that is, if he hadn't mutilated it so badly that it looks diseased.

"I'll light you a fire, but I'm not touching that."

Arthur looks at the others, surveying their faces. "It's fine. I'll eat it myself, raw. When I'm done, we can head out of here. I'll find us a source of water."

Camila walks over and says quietly, only to me, "Yeah, and are you going to jump inside again?"

I let out a small laugh.

I light a fire anyway. It crackles just outside the opening into the tree. Arthur ignores it. He stuffs the raw boar into his mouth. Abigail gags immediately. I know it tastes worse than it looks; Arthur's eyes give him away. He keeps at it. It's disgusting, revolting to even hear. Sefryn can't stand it and leaves the tree. It probably died slowly, being cut up again and again because Arthur couldn't just make a clean kill.

Just before I'm ready to turn away, Arthur stands up. He looks over at us before heading our way. I can see a slimy goo dripping from his mouth. He wipes it with his arm but doesn't get it all. An off-colored blood stains his stubble, which has grown a bit thicker over the past few days.

"I'm full," he lies, clearing his throat. "So, we should head down that way." Arthur points toward the tree, indicating that we should go around it. It's so massive, though, that I feel like we may not get anywhere. Again, I notice how the landscape is so weird, almost unnatural. I can't tell what's around us, beyond what we can see. Only when I look up do I really understand how massive the tree is, and I realize I underestimated its size last night. I can't see a way around it. But that tunnel... It must lead somewhere. "We'll probably find wherever the trees are getting water over there."

No one moves.

"I think we should head through the tree," I counter. "It could be a dead end, but something tells me that's the way to go from here."

Arthur stares at me with dagger eyes.

"I agree," Sefryn says.

"Me too," Camila adds. Abigail and Clarissa clearly agree too. Arthur makes an audible scoff and turns away without saying anything.

Knowing where to go from here, even if not knowing where we're going, I take the first steps toward the tree. I have to hold my breath when I walk by the boar. The thought that he found it already dead crosses my mind.

I can hear Clarissa's disgust behind me as she passes the animal. If I were looking at him, I'm sure I would have seen Arthur roll his eyes at her.

When we get far enough, Camila and I have to light up our path so we can see where we're going. The ground indeed goes down, and the further we go, the steeper the trail becomes. Though mildly concerning, it is a pleasant change from the mostly uphill path we traveled yesterday.

We don't say much as we make our way. Like me, I think the others are listening intently for anything out of the ordinary.

Our road narrows, and the ground becomes bumpy with roots. I keep moving on, despite the thought that we might be hitting a dead end soon.

But then I see it. The distant light that grows bigger with each step. Up ahead is our exit from the tree. I just hope that whatever is on the other side doesn't try to kill us.

# Chapter 8

## The Lake of Mourning

**Aros Caelum Hayes**

Blinding—way too bright for a moment. If I didn't know any better, I'd think Camila went rogue and is trying to kill us with her light.

Once my eyes adjust, I am welcomed to a breathtaking view of a large valley. I can see at least three waterfalls pouring down into the depths below. Looking up behind me, I see a tall, vertical rock face, though most of it is actually the giant tree we just walked through. The bark is petrified from this side, as if it is trying to blend in with the mountain. Arthur was wrong. There was no way we could have gone around the trees; if we did, then we would have come face to face with a drop of a hundred feet.

Arthur was wrong. I shouldn't be surprised.

The fading morning haze obscures the base of the valley below, and I can only hope it's what we're looking for.

Our path is narrow but even, descending at an easy pace. Good thing, too, because one slip or a wrong step would lead to falling into the chasm.

Above us is mostly open sky, but the overgrown canopy of trees on the land above hovers over the edge, creating a shade where rays of sunlight filter through. It amazes me that this place exists in Voltar, especially when winter is near, and the mountain is largely covered in snow.

Abigail walks up beside me, just slightly behind because the road isn't wide enough for two people to comfortably walk side by side.

"This is amazing," she breathes out.

"It is," I say, a bit wary of why she made her way past the others to talk to me.

She says nothing for a minute, but I don't think she's said all that she has to say.

"I just wanted to apologize," she says.

"For what?" I ask, not having the slightest clue what she's referring to.

"Just...for everything."

My forehead crinkles slightly, something she obviously doesn't see.

"You're going to have to be more specific," I tell her. "I'm pretty certain that *everything* isn't your fault."

She lets out a small laugh. "No, but I judged you unfairly back when we met at Edlyn Castle. I didn't know who you were, and even when I found out, I didn't understand everything that you went through. That's what I meant when I said I was sorry about everything."

I clench my jaw, not understanding why she thinks she has anything to apologize for. She wasn't there. She can't undo what was done to me.

"Well, you weren't there, so there really isn't anything for you to be sorry about." She's sweet, though.

"No, but if I were, I would have struck down the other kids who treated you badly."

I laugh. "It wasn't long after I arrived at the school that it was all of the kids who treated me badly," I tell her. "My parents did everything they could, and more, to make sure that everyone was scared of me. They were always ashamed of me, thinking I had no powers, but when I showed some promise, they wanted to make sure that their shame wasn't unfounded. It was like they couldn't accept that maybe they were wrong about me."

"That sounds horrible."

"My parents are horrible people," I say. I don't think I've ever said that out loud to someone, even though I always knew it. Before arriving back in Arteyva, I wished so many times that I had other parents, better parents. Loving parents. But after these past few days, I don't care anymore. It was what it was, but they didn't raise me. They don't define me.

*There was that time shortly before I turned eight. My parents never had any Magis. They were ordinary. They always knew that they wouldn't have any power over others. That's why I had been such a disappointment to them. They thought I had no powers too. A Fae never came to bless me when I was born. My father liked collecting all sorts of weapons. He never learned how to use them in combat. Every time he went to learn, he'd give up in a week. But I could be used as practice.*

*He crafted a weapon from an old oar. It was a murky brown, stained from whatever waters it had been in. But my father attached small spikes to it. They weren't large enough to cut deeply or through something, but they were still sharp. My stomach was apparently the perfect place to swing it at. The pain left me breathless, all the air pushed out of my lungs. The spikes cut my stomach, and I bled from four places. The cuts didn't go deep at all, but the pain stung. He swung again, hitting me in the ribcage.*

*Light-headed and out of breath, I ran outside. The home was small, just like the other ones that neighbored us. What could be used as farmland was left untouched and uncared for. It was muddy. The sky still rained down, though it wasn't pouring like it had an hour ago.*

*A young woman saw me. She ran toward me and pleaded that I follow her to her home. I agreed. She had a husband, and I didn't understand then, but from what I remember, she must have been about four months pregnant.*

*She was able to heal me. She was a Fae-Blessed. My cuts sealed up, leaving not a scar or even a bruise. I was still shaking from the pain, but I could breathe again. I didn't understand how I had never seen her or her husband before. I never got the chance to.*

*When I returned home after dark, my father was furious. He wasn't able to get it out of me. I never told him who healed me. But somehow, he knew. Two days later, the woman and her husband were found dead, beaten brutally, tortured.*

*They tried to find who did it, but my father had quickly gotten rid of all his weapons. He acted like he was shocked, saddened, and scared for his family. I wanted to tell, but the investigators didn't stay long enough. When they came back for more questions, my father beat me unconscious so that I wouldn't be able to say anything.*

*So much of my life when I was that young was spent knocked out.*

"Are you okay?"

Abigail surprises me when she puts her hand on my arm.

"Yeah, I'm good," I say, my eyes widening when I see how far we've traveled. The morning fog has dissipated. We're halfway down, and as clear as day, the bones of a giant skeleton lie at the bottom. There is a large crater surrounding it. I can see the tusks of what used to be the mammoth that lived here. Like me, it was feared by others because of a lie that was told. "The Ivory Skeleton. We did it," I say.

"Yeah, that's what I was trying to point out to you."

"Oh, I'm sorry," I say, looking back at her. "I must have spaced out."

"I'm sorry for talking about your past," she tells me. "I won't do it again if it reminds you of how terrible it was."

I laugh in my head. She needs to work on her wording. I know my childhood was terrible; I don't need her to say it. But it doesn't bother me either.

"It's all good. Honestly, everyone back then is dead to me. Just nobodies that I used to know." *Of course, some of them are actually dead.*

"If this place had enough rain, you could probably help the plants grow. Flowers could rise from the ground, covering the skeleton," I say, still in awe of the skeleton.

I turn my head back again, then face forward immediately. Arthur has caught up to us and is walking behind Abigail, like how she walks behind me.

"You could do it," he tells her, having heard what I said. "That's how amazing you are."

Is he trying to hit on her?

"Uh, thanks. But I think I'd rather leave nature to do its thing," Abigail responds. "Plus, it's Sefryn who can literally call up the flowers from the ground."

"Yeah, but she's not you." Arthur speaks in a deeper voice, like he's trying to sound different. I can feel Abigail's discomfort with him so close to her.

"Hey, let's just enjoy the view," I say loudly, gesturing to the valley with my arm.

A small moment passes. But then Arthur says it.

"I am enjoying the view."

Abigail and I both know he isn't talking about the valley. I move to the side. Abigail takes the chance and walks past me. Arthur tries to do the same, but I walk back in line.

"Me too," I say, smiling and looking out.

Arthur doesn't say anything. Anger boils from his body. He can't hide it. I'm sure that everyone can feel it.

Unfortunately for him, I spent so much of my life being attacked that I can feel one coming. I duck. Arthur tries punching the back of my head. I look back. He bends, arms ready to shove me toward the ledge. I quickly punch him in the face. He stumbles back. Clarissa shifts her feet backward, avoiding Arthur.

Before he moves too far back, I grab his coat and shove him against the rock face. His head slams back into it. That must have hurt. I didn't mean to do it.

Abigail watches, though she keeps her distance. There's something about her, though, something in the way she stands. I think she's readying herself to attack if she needs to.

"You need to stop."

I don't ask him what his problem is. I don't ask him what's going on. My hand pushes him just below his neck. If he wanted, he could easily counter, but I keep myself ready in case he does. Part of me, though, wants to just toss him off the ledge now. Odds are I'll be saving us a lot of trouble if I do so.

No one says anything. I wonder what they're thinking.

"Fine," Arthur growls.

I keep my hand on him, but I ease the pressure a bit. I jerk my head toward Abigail.

"You walk in front," I tell him.

Abigail presses her back against the rocky wall. I release my grip on Arthur. Without a word, he takes his spot in the front and keeps walking.

I turn back to see Clarissa wide-eyed, probably memories of her father's angry outbreaks flitting through her mind. Camila just holds her gaze, her eyes falling on mine for a second. Sefryn seems annoyed.

"Let's keep moving," I say. I walk past Abigail, putting myself between her and Arthur again, though Arthur has walked ahead of us. I keep the distance the same.

I don't know why I don't just let Arthur die. Any one of us could kill him easily. Sefryn could crush him under the weight of a tree, trip him with a stray root, or suffocate him with a vine. Abigail could simply strike him down. Though I wonder how much power she uses when she does that and if it tires her quickly. Clarissa could create winds that just blow him off the ledge. Camila, even using the most basic of her power, could blind him, causing him to stumble and take that wrong step right off the cliff. That is, if she doesn't just slice him in half with her light. But

I don't think Camila can easily make her light into a weapon like that just yet—only when she's in danger.

We walk at a leisurely pace, which is a hundred percent on me since I'm in front. Arthur has already walked off farther than I can see, but every now and then I catch a glimpse of him when the path turns back, climbing down the wall, and he's there. He never looks up. From what I can tell, he doesn't look back either.

Maybe we'll find another group that will take him in. Being a turdy prick doesn't qualify one for a death sentence. I tsk to myself. Unfortunate.

My stomach growls. As if she heard it, Sefryn pushes past Abigail and hands me a fruit. I look back. They're all eating.

"Thanks," I say. Then an idea comes to my mind. "Hey, give me another one, will you?"

Sefryn does.

"Let's hope he's hungry," I say, levitating the apple-like fruit in front of me, suspending it with my energy flows. The five minutes that pass feel like forever, but finally I see him. I look down. There isn't a path just below us. Instead, it turns back and forth at shorter distances up ahead. No problem.

Hoping my timing is correct, I fling the fruit at Arthur. When it gets close, I slow it. I let the fruit hover for a few seconds and then release my grip when Arthur walks underneath. It misses his head, but I think it nicks him in the nose.

I turn back, acting like I'm talking to Sefryn. I can't see what Arthur does, but I hope he's looking up, confused.

Giggles from Abigail and Clarissa tell me that I may have been successful.

I turn to face forward again. Arthur is walking as if nothing happened.

"It hit him," Sefryn says. "Barely, but he felt it."

Abigail laughs. "He looked up as if he'd see where it had fallen from," she tells me. "But then he tried going after it while it rolled, but he didn't make it in time."

"What do you mean?" I ask.

"It just fell down the cliff," Clarissa chimes in.

"Well, yeah, but couldn't he just summon it back? It isn't very heavy."

"We all know that even if Arthur has that power, he isn't very smart."

I snort and choke down my laughter. Camila's right. The guy isn't smart. There's something about him that makes it too easy for me to trash-talk him. It's been a while since I've met someone like that. But it's been barely a week since I've known someone like that. It's like Arthur replaced the Nick in my life.

We keep at it. The afternoon swells high and dies down. The sunlight fades out earlier than it normally would since the sun is behind multiple ranges. Still, even though it gets a bit chilly, it doesn't snow, and it isn't nearly as cold as it was last night.

It feels like hours walking down the path, turning around, back and forth, tracing the edges of the road. Closer to the bottom, the path is more jagged. I'd just jump down, but we aren't that close, unfortunately. But being this far down, the bones of the mammoth tower over us. It didn't look quite this big when we were at the peak.

It's hard to keep track of time. It's earlier than it feels, which means I'm more tired than I should be. My legs ache, and my core feels empty.

We near the bottom. Arthur is staring at the skeleton. Perhaps he's found something because he's standing so close to it, inspecting it.

Just a few hundred more steps. No biggie.

Walking up to Arthur brings both a joyful relief because we've made it and a sense of dread because he's there. How long until he says or does something that gets on everybody's nerves?

"They beat us here," he says, his voice barely cracking. "We shouldn't have been resting for so long."

He doesn't point anywhere, but I look at where his eyes stare. Carved into one of the mammoth's ribs, in a sloppy form of pyrography, you can see that Chase left his name there.

"Good for him," I say, walking away. I don't understand how he beat us here, but I don't let my mind dwell on it.

I was distracted before, but now I notice that there is a massive lake just ahead. I had seen it while we were walking down, but it didn't have its magnificence from way up there, nor was it as inviting as it is now. I head over, hoping to get a long drink of water.

Something hits my back, and I stumble forward. I almost trip and fall to the ground. I spin around. With his right hand out, carrying a bubble of energy, Arthur charges at me. He throws it. I deflect it with a swipe of my hand.

"You suck!" he shouts. "You're a terrible leader! You can't even make sure we're the first to make it out of here!"

He tosses more energy at me, but it's too easy to fend off his attacks.

"It's not a race!" I shout back at him. He stops, planting his feet on the ground.

Seething, he finally opens his mouth. "When I take you out, I'm going to take over and get everyone out of here. Then they'll see that I was always better than you."

I don't say anything. I don't laugh. I don't sneer.

I don't react.

Two thoughts bounce in my mind. Clearly, if Voltar truly does bring out your deepest fears, then Arthur is feeling those effects. But just as clearly, if Arthur doesn't check his attitude, I will have to get rid of him. I keep telling myself the same things over and over: "Don't kill Arthur." "Make sure Arthur dies." My head turns slightly to the side, the lake visible out of the corner of my eye.

*I could drown him.*

"Knock it off, both of you!" Clarissa shouts at us. To make her point, she blasts forceful winds at us. Arthur takes a step forward, fighting against the strength of the wind. The others come toward us.

I lock eyes with her for a moment. She releases her force, and the dusk becomes still once more. I put out my hand, urging the others to stop coming nearer. Knowing what I mean, Sefryn steps forward slightly, reaches her arm out, and tells the others to stay back.

Arthur looks back, noticing the others. He sneers.

"When they see me beat you, they'll know who's the better man."

*Don't kill Arthur. Make sure Arthur dies.*

"That won't happen," I reply. "You can't beat me."

It feels right, facing off against Arthur like this. The banter between us means nothing to me. I could end him here, right now, but I want him to attack first.

"Maybe if the others butt in to save you."

I scoff. "That won't happen either."

"We shouldn't be fighting each other!" Abigail's voice makes Arthur turn his head back. He stares at her for a moment before turning his eyes back to me.

Arthur steps closer, distancing himself from the others.

"You know," I say slowly, "she will never see you as anything more than the weirdo who couldn't even flirt with her."

Arthur's eyes narrow.

"She thinks you're pathetic."

Arthur lunges, shooting beams of energy at me. I dodge them all. He sends out another one, though this time it's a blast of fire. Small. But still, it's fire.

I counter it with energy shots of my own. I can see the others nearby, but they don't move. Not yet. I can sense they want to, though. I can't let that happen.

Like I did before when I saved his life, I light up a ring of fire around us. It blazes strong, the heat burning my eyes. Arthur punches out, more balls of fire spitting from his knuckles. I don't know what makes me do it, but I move my arms behind me and swing them over my back. Water jets out from the lake, drowning his fire and smacking him in the face.

Realizing what I've done, I shift the wall of fire I made. I bring it closer, forcing Arthur to move toward me. I take steps back and open the rear part of the wall, revealing the lake behind me.

Strong gusts blast through, threatening to carry the flames beyond my reach. I hold them down with all my focus. Arthur seizes the moment to blast energy at me. I'm shoved off my feet and fly back, easing myself into a clean landing as I splash into the lake.

I swirl around in the water and send a thin wave at Arthur. I'm careful not to disrupt my fire walls more than they already have been.

*Don't kill Arthur. Make sure Arthur dies.*

The urge to kill him rises within me. I can't, though, because if I did, I would be the monster my parents claimed I was.

I send out a force of energy toward him. Arthur tries to catch it to weaken its power, but he can't quite manage it and is knocked back, almost landing in the flames.

If he were to burn to death, that would be fine too.

He shouts, eyes wide and saliva spitting from his mouth. The roar of the fire drowns out all other noise. Arthur continues to shout, but if he's saying anything, I can't hear him.

I pull the wall closer. Arthur runs forward, blasting me with more energy. The waves are deflected back with licks of the fire I pull from the walls. I push out my left arm, and the wall of fire extends back, giving us more space.

Now circling each other, I just need to get him closer to the water. Arthur lunges at me, forgetting to use any magic in his attack. With my logical senses leaving me, I don't move until the last second. I curl my hand into a fist and hit him dead center in the face. That wasn't without sacrifice. Arthur manages to deck me in the ear. But while I stumble, my head dizzy for a second, Arthur falls back, flat on his ass.

When I can see straight again, I take threatening steps toward Arthur. Still on the ground, he blasts out small discs of his power, but they're so weak I can practically flick them away.

He's bleeding from his nose. I can feel his blood crusting on my hand as it dries quickly in this heat. I put my palm on his forehead and force him onto his back.

The hairs on my neck rise. Something isn't right. The air around us changes. I look up. Rain starts to fall heavily. The fires die out, barely even sizzling as they drown. This happens too fast. It isn't natural. I look over and see Abigail raising her arm.

Once again, I look to the sky. Heavy pellets of rain splash onto my face. Lightning. She's summoning lightning. Is she about to strike me down? Or him?

Maybe she's just warning us to stop fighting.

Or not.

I feel it just before it happens. Not knowing why I do it, but knowing it feels right in the moment, I reach up to the sky with one arm and point toward the lake with my other. The bolt strikes down. It wasn't going to hit me. It wasn't going to hit Arthur. It was going to strike nearby, but my outstretched arm channels it toward me as if it were a lightning rod.

The burning heat fills my body. I smell smoke and fried meat for a moment. I'm blinded by the flashing of white and blue. Incessant cracking fills my ears. But the rush of power moves through me. I turn my head back to the lake. From my finger, the power from the lightning shoots out into the lake. I can almost see it in slow motion. It makes contact with the water and spreads out. It sounds as if a thousand things fall into the water, and then everything is silent once again. Even the rain is gone.

I'm breathing heavily. I'm not quite sure what just happened. I am drenched in water. So is Arthur. He's still on the ground, now covering his nose, trying to stop the bleeding.

"Oh my gosh," Abigail says, running over to me. "I'm so sorry! I thought I felt where you were! I didn't mean to!" She throws her arms around me and sobs into my shoulder. I hug her back, trying to tell her it's okay, but she can't hear me.

"Guys! Look!"

I hear Camila's cry and look around for her. She's running toward the lake. She lets out a large sphere of light to make it easier. I hadn't noticed it had gotten so dark.

Splashing into the water, Camila and Clarissa run into the lake. They shove their arms into the water. When they're done, they come back carrying something in their arms.

Abigail releases me. I assure her that I'm fine, and we head over to see what their excitement is about.

Fish. It's fish. All dead, ready to cook, though already slightly fried.

"The electricity must have zapped them dead," Sefryn says. "While that was... shocking, to say the least," she adds, looking around for any of us to roll our eyes. "At least now we have food for dinner."

"That's amazing," I say, imagining drool spilling from my mouth. The thought of eating fish is probably the best thing that's happened to me since arriving back on Arteyva.

"You channeled my lightning, and this happened?" Abigail says, still in shock.

"I did. And I didn't even mean to," I tell her.

"I didn't either," she says. "I was just trying to break the both of you up. The lightning was supposed to strike near the fires, which I figured was far enough away from both of you," Abigail explains. "I swear, I would never mean to hurt you."

I let out a sigh, but I'm more amused than anything. I take a quick peek toward Arthur. He's starting to get up.

"I think your aim was fine. But somehow, I called the lightning toward me before redirecting it to the lake," I tell her. "If anything, the whole thing was my fault."

"Aros, explain later!" Camila shouts at me. "Light up a fire and let's get cooking!"

I look back at Abigail. She looks into my eyes, and we burst into laughter. I'm not sure how I know this, but I just understand that we're going to work well together. She might still be a bit prim deep down, but her heart is in the right place, and she cares for others in a way that is lacking in so many people.

Arthur comes up to us, but he keeps his distance. It's just a bit awkward, knowing that I was set on killing him not five minutes ago. But once again, dumb luck has saved his sorry ass. With the discovery of new strengths in my powers and a full dinner just minutes away, I'm feeling good, so when Arthur looks at me with apologetic and pleading eyes, I jerk my head for him to follow us.

We sit under the skeleton. It's tall enough that I could put anyone here on my shoulders, and they still wouldn't be able to touch the top. I light three fires so that we can cook multiple fish at a time. When needed, I call small waves from the lake toward us, yielding a couple more fish when I do. I can't quite get the water to us, though, meaning I'll need more practice with this ability.

All in all, even with Arthur sulking just feet from us, I can't help but smile to myself as I lie down on the quasi-sand of the crater carved at the bottom of this valley.

"You know," Camila says out loud. We are all lying down, ready to sleep for the night. "The stories that are told explain how the lake came to be."

"Oh?" Clarissa says. "Do tell."

"The regretful animals that helped slay the mammoth filled the rivers above with their tears. The tears poured into the valley and filled part of the crater. Some call this the Lake of Mourning."

"But I thought that the mammoth would rest in the center of the crater?" Sefryn says. "So how come there isn't water here?"

Good question. I hadn't even thought of that.

"I don't know," Camila says. "This is just one of the many stories I was told as a child. But now I think I understand what the tales are trying to tell us, even if they are slightly different."

I hear Arthur shift. His back is facing all of us, but I get the idea that he hasn't fallen asleep yet.

"No matter how dark life can get, there will always be light at the end to dawn on a new beginning."

# CHAPTER 9

---

# PYROGRAPHY AND THE ART OF CARVING BODIES

**Aros Caelum Hayes**

I t's still dim out when I wake again. The sudden need to relieve myself woke me in the middle of the night. It was perfect timing, with everyone else asleep.

My eyes adjust slowly. My view of the sky is wholly obscured by the bones of the mammoth. Parts of its belly lie on the floor, while a lot of its underside is now buried in the sand. I stare up at the ceiling presented to me. It's silent, and all I can see are the bones right above me. Either the others are up and about, or they haven't woken yet.

I gaze over the gashes and other cuts in the bones. Whatever parts of the stories about the mammoth, it must be true that it suffered, even after its death. As I scan over all the etchings, I can see something I make myself imagine is an eight. I wonder if I can find other number-like wounds in the skeleton. I look around, searching. Nothing else stands out.

Finally, I notice something that looks like a mountain. I inspect it closely. Now that I see it more, it doesn't seem coincidental. And thinking about it, the eight doesn't seem to be just a result of the attacks. But the mountain looks sideways compared to the eight. If someone did carve these into the skeleton, why would they be so close together but not drawn from the same angle?

The mountain begins to move, swaying back and forth. I squint my eyes. Is it really moving? Am I that tired?

It erupts into flames, flickering back and forth. It was no mountain. It was a fire carved into the hard bone. My world fades to black around me. It isn't quite like when Kreavlos calls me or when the Dark Wind takes me somewhere. I don't feel like I'm moving through space. But it feels like my mind is. Amidst the darkness, I see a small fire, burning on and on. Wind blows through. It never stops. Even when the rain comes, the fire crackles on. It isn't very big. There's a blue tint at its base that blends into the orangey-red flames at the top.

"Aros."

My eyes snap open. I didn't even know they were closed. My breathing remains normal, calm, just like it had been moments before. All I see now are the same two carvings I noticed earlier. It's not an eight. It's an infinity symbol next to a fire. Both are large enough to see even when they are so high up. Sefryn comes into view. Her eyes are unmoving. She stands over me, leaning over slightly. Her light hair falls forward.

"Look."

Sefryn turns her head up.

"There are these etchings in the bone mass," I tell her. "I was staring at them, and then I must have fallen asleep. I dreamt about a fire, a fire that burned no matter the circumstance. Even when the rain came, the fire lived on."

"I see them," Sefryn says.

"Sounds like the Eternal Flame," says Camila.

My body flinches at her voice. I didn't hear her coming. Camila walks up to Sefryn, sparing me a short look before staring up at the carvings.

"Another one of your fairytales?" I ask her, sitting up.

"Yes, actually," Camila says. "I used to read a lot when I was younger.

Why do you think the first place you saw me was in the library?"

I nod to myself. "Makes sense," I say, wishing I had read more while I was in Edlyn than I did. The day or two of reading I had doesn't make up for years of lack of study.

"The Eternal Flame was always said to be somewhere in the mountains, though the stories aren't all the same. Some of them say the flame burns in the middle of a lake or somewhere deep in a cave. One even says it burns in the sky."

"Well, I think we can say that the Eternal Flame isn't in a lake. At least, not this one," I say.

Camila turns back and looks at me. "I don't know why I didn't think of it before. But I think there's a good chance it's somewhere here in Voltar."

"It wouldn't be fair to expect you to remember everything," Sefryn says, turning back as well. "With everything that's happened so far, it's not like this place is designed to bring a sense of calm to you."

"No, it's not," Camila says gravely. "It's actually designed to bring out the worst in you."

"Yeah, well," I say, looking past Camila and Sefryn toward the lake, near where Arthur was sleeping. He's sitting up like me, staring at us. His eyes are unmoving, his face almost expressionless. But what is it that I see? Anger? Hatred? Resentment? "It works faster on some than it does on others."

"Right," Camila answers. I know she knows who I'm referring to. "So, we should get moving again. The Eternal Flame is our next clue. That's what we need to find."

Sefryn walks closer to the lake. I get up and follow. "Maybe it'll be the last," she says hopefully. "It would be great to get out of here. And maybe the Eternal Flame is what burns our souls—that is, if we are picked to be the next Ash Lord."

"If so," Camila says, walking with us. Abigail comes over from the cliffs we traveled down yesterday. "Then finding the Eternal Flame is probably going to be the hardest part. The deeper we head into Voltar, the more dangerous it'll be."

"And the harder it will get on our minds," Sefryn says.

"But the Azure Fox told us that there would be three clues. This is only the second." Camila looks at me, then to Sefryn.

"I'm hoping that all Voltar does is bring out the worst in us," I say, immediately regretting it. A sense of fear overwhelms me. I have to stop walking for a moment. My heart beats faster. I can feel the sweat on my palms. I had lied. I sure as hell hope that Voltar doesn't bring out the worst in us, because that wouldn't mean anything good if the worst parts of me became uncovered.

"People can change, you know," Abigail says.

Camila shrugs in agreement. "She's right."

I know they're referring to me. But they don't know me. Camila does, a little. But the others weren't there that night. They haven't seen what I'm capable of when I lose control.

Clarissa joins us as we look out over the water.

"Anyone hungry?" I ask.

"No," Camila answers quickly. "But we should eat. Or maybe somehow bring food with us."

"That's probably not very practical," Sefryn says. "But still, we should think of something. While it isn't freezing here, when we leave, I don't think the warmth is going to follow us."

"Okay, but how do we get out of here?" Abigail asks. "I'm going to kill myself if we have to walk back up the mountain."

She has a good point. It took us all day to get down it. It's going to take much longer to go all the way back up. Plus, it'll only lead us back to where we started, and I didn't see anywhere else to go then. I look around, hoping to see something that indicates there's another path. The whole valley is surrounded by those same cliffsides that are also part of the tree near the top. The waterfalls, five that I can count now, all seem to lead into the lake, which covers more than half of the valley. But wouldn't the crater that we stand in be fully filled with water? It would make sense if the water had nowhere else to go, but there must be something I'm not seeing.

"There!" Clarissa points out toward the lake.

"Yeah, I see it too."

Hearing Arthur's voice startles me. I had forgotten he was even here.

"See what?" Abigail asks him. She otherwise doesn't acknowledge his presence.

"Under the lake, there's a tunnel. That must be where the water flows through. We'll have to swim through it."

I look across the lake. Yeah, I can kind of see something that looks like it could be a tunnel. But even then, where does it lead? How far does it go while still fully being underwater?

"I don't think we'll be able to make it," I say. "There's no way to know where it leads. We all could drown."

"Chase made it here, and he's gone now," Arthur says. "He wasn't scared to do what was needed."

"No, there!" Clarissa shouts, interrupting my internal fight of self-control and lashing out. "Behind the waterfall!"

I don't know how she saw it. Behind the furthest waterfall from us, all the way on the other side of the lake, there is a large cave. That must be where our exit is.

"Good job, Clarissa," I say. I walk along the shore to find the best way to get across.

"So, do we all fancy a swim?" Abigail asks. Her voice is just a bit flirty, but I enjoy how it lightens the mood. For a moment, it feels like we're just friends hanging out, spending a day at the lake. It's just a moment, though.

"Why not?" I answer. "I can help us all dry off afterwards."

"Sounds fun!" Clarissa says, skipping along the side of the lake. We follow her, trying to get to a part where the distance across seems the shortest.

Clarissa looks across for a moment, and then at all of us, her lip in a small, thoughtful pout. "I think I can get most of our clothes across the lake with my wind," she tells us. "Our coats, I mean. I don't think we want those weighing us down while we swim."

She has a good point. Plus, mine might not make it after being subjected to that much water and movement. Sefryn could always make me a new one, but I'd rather keep what I have now. It must have taken her hours to put it together the other night.

"Let's try it out," I say, removing my leafy coat from my body.

"Is that all?" Sefryn asks, eyeing me playfully. She removes her coat. And her shirt. And her pants. For a second, I think she's going to strip completely naked, but she doesn't. She doesn't expose anything indecent.

Sefryn walks up to me and leans close to my ear. "If Arthur wasn't here, I'd lose my top too."

That brings a smile to my face, and I feel like an idiot with my grin, but I can't help it.

Wait.

*That was definitely her flirting with me.*

"Okay, let's see!" Clarissa says, keeping her bright disposition. Sefryn holds up her clothes. Clarissa waves her arms around. When the wind picks up, she blasts Sefryn's clothes across the lake. One piece almost doesn't make it, but Clarissa shoots a strong gust at it, sending it flying off near the rest of the clothes.

She does the same with my coat, shirt, and pants, along with my socks and boots.

The others do the same. Camila keeps her shirt on, but she removes her bottoms. When Arthur holds out his clothes for Clarissa, he glares at me. I ignore it. When I see Clarissa hesitate, I give her a small nod. She obliges and sends his clothes over the river, though half of his coat lands in the water.

Once again, Arthur distances himself from us. I keep getting the sense of self-loathing that lies behind his outward, unfriendly feelings.

Our swim across takes some time. The lake is wide, though it doesn't go very deep. Still, toward the heart of the lake, my feet can't touch the bottom. The water is cool, but there's something pleasant about it. It's like the first shower I've taken since we've been here, other than being submerged in that freezing river while trying to save Arthur. I don't count that. The water here isn't nearly as cold.

When we're about halfway across, I can feel a light current. My guess is that it leads to that underwater cave. Something I'm glad we don't have to go through, but I wonder where it leads.

Sefryn splashes water into my face. I splash back, and soon the five of us are swimming around, throwing water at each other. Arthur quietly makes his way to the shore.

It's a small relief, just having fun. We don't stay long, though. The rising sun reminds us that we're running out of time. It doesn't matter to me if Chase makes it to the Ashen Pit first, but I hope that we don't end up being the last ones.

We get to shore. Arthur is fully dressed again, but water drips from his wet clothes. The others gather near me, and we dry off by a fire I make. I'd be willing to help Arthur too, but I'm not going to offer it. And I know he has an illogical sense of pride that makes it so that he won't ask.

"Shall we get moving?" Abigail asks brightly.

"Lead the way," I say.

She smiles and nods to Clarissa, who takes the lead. We slip behind the waterfall and enter a narrow cave. The stone is a bit wet, so we have to be careful with our steps. It feels cooler in here, just a tiny bit.

Up ahead, we have to jump down a drop into a shallow river. The water flows beneath the path we took, probably right from the lake. But the opening that the water flows through isn't very big. The average ten-year-old wouldn't be able to fit through.

"Glad we didn't take the underwater tunnel," Camila comments.

I hear a soft huff from Arthur, but he doesn't say anything.

The tunnel drops again, leaving us another obstacle to jump down. My feet splash as I land. The water runs more quickly here. Up ahead, it curves out of sight.

We keep going, following the turning path. We end up coming to a short rock face. It's flat, so there isn't much to help us climb up. The water runs off beneath it, through another opening that is too small to fit through.

"Do we seriously want me to climb up that thing?" Camila asks.

I turn to look at Camila. She's the shortest of us all.

"I can help you climb up it," I tell her. I walk up to the cliff, find a place to hold at the top, and pull myself up. The walls of the cave are slightly wet, so using my legs to help push myself up doesn't work well. I let out a small grunt as my leg slips. I pull harder, getting my arms over the top. After a short pause, I heave the rest of my body above the ledge.

I turn around and look down at the others.

"Who wants to go next?"

Arthur steps forward.

"I don't need your help."

I step away from the ledge, giving him room. After nearly five minutes, it's clear that he, in fact, does need my help.

I don't help him. I'm going to stick with my decision to not offer that anymore. But I can't have him holding everyone else up.

"Hey, shouldn't we be moving as fast as we can?" I ask him.

"We'd be far from here if you would help me," he retorts.

I let out a chuckle.

"But you said you don't need my help," I say, loud enough for everyone to hear.

Arthur turns around, only to see four women staring at him, their arms crossed. He turns to look back at me. I just hold my gaze, my half-smile struggling not to turn into a grin that I would only be able to describe as dickish.

He knows he can't win.

"Could you help me?" he asks, knowing that I was waiting for him to. I move, just slightly. Yeah, nah. He's gonna have to do better than that. "Please?"

I squat down and hold out my arm. He grabs my hand, places his other one on the ledge, and I help pull him up. He quickly lets go when he's got a leg over and does his best to stand up quickly.

Camila is next, and I pull her up, my hands over her wrists and hers over mine. Sefryn nearly makes it up herself. I do the same with Clarissa as I did with Camila, though I struggle a bit more with her.

Arthur tries to help when it's Abigail's turn, but she doesn't grab his hand when he reaches down for her.

"I'd rather not," she tells him after a minute of him hanging down. He storms off, walking away from the rest of us.

It isn't long before we're on our way again. It's colder here, though. That is very noticeable. Camila comments on it.

"Yeah, I feel it too," Sefryn says. "Maybe we're close to the end of the cave."

"How far have we gone? Because I can still see pretty well," Clarissa says.

The cave, while dim compared to the world outside, is illuminated well enough that I don't have any trouble seeing. With the multiple drops and changes in elevation, I'd think it eventually would have gotten dark.

I look up. The ceiling doesn't have any noticeable openings, but it's shaped weird and covered in ridges and varying shades of stone.

"Maybe light seeps through somewhere up there," I point out.

"It also could just be Voltar being a magical and mysterious place," Sefryn says. She makes a valid point.

We keep going. We have to scale up another cliff, but this one is much easier as there are small plateaus that serve as steps, and everyone is able to get up on their own.

Once we reach the top, a cold, freezing breeze slashes against our faces. The light changes from a warm, sun-like temperature to a cold, covered-in-snow kind of light. We've made it back into the mountains of Voltar. A river runs outside just beyond us. I'm surprised it hasn't frozen over yet.

"Okay, is it just me, or is it way more freezing than it was before?" Abigail asks.

"It's colder for sure," Arthur replies, taking his coat off. He offers it out to her.

Abigail does her best to not look disgusted. I notice it. Arthur doesn't.

"Don't be stupid, you'll freeze without it," she says as politely as she can, turning away. "It's cold, but I'll be fine."

The snow crunches beneath my feet. None is currently falling from the sky, but I'm sure that will change soon. Having left the cave tunnels, we are now confronted with a steep hill. We could follow the river downstream, but somehow, I get the idea that's not where we should go.

Slipping becomes a theme between us. It's hard to tell just how deep our foot will go with our next step. The ground here is made of dips, ridges, and mounds. We just can't see any of it.

Sefryn, Camila, and I clue in the others with our findings about the Eternal Flame. Clarissa and Abigail seem intently interested, while Arthur remains silent, almost as if he's sulking. But I know he's carefully listening to every word.

My foot hits something hard and unyielding, though the light layer of snow on top is soft and slick. Purely from an instinctive curiosity, I use my foot to wipe away the snow. I look down.

I wish I hadn't.

It would have been so much worse if his eyes were open. He looks like he was somewhere in his fifties, but that might be due to the glazed and frozen nature of the body. I hear a loud gasp.

Looking over, I see Abigail staring down at something. I look up. The crest of the hill lies not far from us, but the hills roll, so we'll be climbing up the mountain soon enough.

"There's a lot of them," Camila states in her flat tone.

"Let's keep moving," I say. "Watch your step. Try to not look down."

Of course, I then notice Arthur kneeling down, using his hand to wipe snow off one of the bodies' faces.

"What are you doing?" I blurt out.

"Checking to see if it's anyone I recognize." Arthur stands up again. "Some of the volunteers looked like real nasty people. We're better off without them."

Yeah, *no kidding*.

"Okay, let's get a move on," Abigail says, struggling to keep her composure, but she does it. I can see her shaking, though. "The creepy vibes of this...frozen graveyard just..." She shakes her head and makes her way toward the top of the hill.

Clarissa is silent, almost stiff, except she keeps up. I don't want to imagine what seeing the dead bodies reminded her of.

Many possibilities of what happened run through my mind. It looks like they froze to death while sleeping, but that wouldn't make sense unless the cold became freezing overnight. Or maybe they just weren't prepared at all, and eventually, the freezing temperatures killed them. Most of the bodies remain covered beneath the surface of the snow; their heads being the main part we see except for stray hands with missing fingers.

From what I can see, they weren't killed by anything or anyone.

Unfortunately, they just didn't survive the harsh conditions of Voltar.

Reaching the peak of the steep hill provides brief relief, but at the bottom of the hill's descent on this side, just before the land rises again, are four people. One stands out, clear as day.

Chase.

They don't notice us.

Never mind. They do.

One in the group points toward us. Chase jerks his head in our direction. He blasts fire at us. We're a bit far for his reach, but I can still feel the warmth of the flames splash against my face.

"Slide down," I tell the others. I kneel, keeping my feet planted in the snow, and push myself down the hill. Everyone follows.

As we're sliding, Chase runs toward us. Using both hands, he sends a wave of fire. I blast out a larger wave of energy. My defensive attack collides with his fire. The two energies shoot toward the sky in strands, blue and red, before dying out. We're almost at the bottom. Chase plants his feet in the snow. A spear of fire forms in his hand, and he throws it toward me. Clarissa blasts wind at it, dispersing the blaze before it reaches me.

We reach the bottom. Arthur charges at Chase and tackles him.

Fuck. I really wanted to punch him.

One of the girls from Chase's group picks up snow with her powers and shapes it into a spear, just like Chase did, but hers is made of ice. Her dark skin and darker hair stand out in the white of the landscape, and I can't understand how I didn't notice her before.

Before she has a chance to throw her icicle, the girl is tossed into the air. Whatever happened, it wasn't Clarissa, but Clarissa uses her wind to toss the girl even further away.

A giant of a man roars into the air. He's bald, likely almost double Chase's age, and has green eyes like Arthur. Well damn, Arthur, Chase, and this guy could all be related, especially with their shared anger issues.

His roar turns into screams of agony. I don't understand why. For a moment, I'm frozen by my confusion. The man tears off his jacket, and the one beneath it, revealing a tattered white shirt that becomes more and more bloody with each passing second. He rips his shirt off too. Gashes are being carved into his tattooed chest, deeper and deeper. Then his face gets cut up, as if there were an invisible blade slicing through him.

With enough blood lost, the giant drops to his knees, falls forward onto his face, and makes no movement, no sound. I look around.

"Ah, he was weak too! Just like the others I killed."

I turn my head just in time to dodge a jet of fire from Chase. I fall to the ground. As I'm getting up, Chase is blasted off his feet, just like the other girl was. I look around.

A group larger than Chase's makes their way toward us at a sprint. Leading them is someone who looks familiar, but I don't think I know him. Behind him, another guy waves his arms around. He's the one who's been blasting wind.

"The fighting stops now," the guy in front says. His voice is deep and bold. With incredibly tight, coiled hair, easy dark eyes, and a perfectly shaped beard, he commands a presence unlike any other. His skin is much darker than mine.

Chase walks back to us, but he doesn't seem poised for battle.

"Whatever, Elder," Chase says, spitting on the ground.

Elder raises his head slightly. "Where's the rest of your crew?"

Chase's lips curve into a sick smile. "They were too weak to be with me, so I killed them." He turns to look at me. "Of course, Aros here and his guys made it all too easy. With everyone trapped beneath the roots, struggling to move, once I broke free, it was easy to bash their heads in."

I exchange a look with Sefryn. Of course, it wasn't our fault, but we didn't think they'd die at the hands of the person they looked up to.

"You know more than half of the volunteers died that first morning, right?" Elder says, walking up to Chase. Elder is slightly taller than Chase, who is about my height. "We can't be killing each other just because we want to."

"Yes, we can," Chase replies. "There are four spots open, so I intend to make sure all my guys take one of those seats at the Pit."

Elder sneers. "I just killed one of yours," he says. "Including yourself, there are only three of you."

The third person comes into view. He's not as big as the guy that Elder killed, but he's also bald, though his head is heavily scarred.

And I now understand who Elder is. He's a Rogvey. And there's something about him that makes me think he's related to that guy who carved our names into the wall back at Edlyn Castle.

"Yeah, well, you're an asshole," Chase says. "And a hypocrite."

Elder nods. "You're right," he says. "But I'm going to give you a chance now. Leave. Get you and your two friends to the Ashen Pit in one piece. But if I see you attack someone again, I will take all of you out."

Chase steps back. He looks toward the last two members of his crew. "Let's go," he calls out. They follow him as he walks away. It's hard to tell where anything is. There is a distinct lack of trees here, and the white hills all look the same. Chase looks back at us. He stares at someone. I turn to see where his line of sight is. He's locked eyes with Arthur. "Well, we do have an open spot now if anyone wants to join me. Peace and other bullshit won't win you anything, even if you do make it out of here."

No one moves. There's tension all around us. Would it not be better if Arthur just left us now by joining Chase? It would be. So why is there a part of me that hopes it doesn't happen? That might just be the fear of not being enough creeping into me. I'm old enough to know better now, though.

Perhaps Voltar is slowly but surely taking a toll on me.

Arthur folds his arms, silently declining Chase's offer. Without expression, Chase and the remaining members of his crew leave and disappear out of sight.

"Aros," Elder says, turning to me and extending his hand forward. I take it. "Pleasure to meet you. I'm Elder."

"And you're a Rogvey," I say. "A powerful one, too."

He looks down and smiles, perfect teeth, perfect lips. A quick glance at the girls tells me that they admire his looks.

"Yeah, but I'll tell you, carving into that big one from that far away wasn't easy."

The large man still lies face down in the snow not far from us. Snow has started to fall, and I can't see any blood around his body.

"Are you related to that other Rogvey back at the castle?" I blurt out.

"Yeah, the young man carving names into the tribute?" Elder asks. "He's my son, Peter."

"Yes, that was his name," I say out loud, even though it was mainly to myself.

"He's not fond of fighting. He likes the true nature of the Rogvey, making art. So, he didn't want to participate in the Trials. But I've always had a disposition to defend people. It felt like this was the right thing to do."

I nod.

"Of course, this wasn't what I was expecting."

"No kidding," Sefryn says, placing her hand on my shoulder. I tense but do my best not to show it.

Abigail and the others stand nearby. Elder and the wind guy stand next to each other. They have about five people behind them.

"Well, I don't mean to leave you after...well, that," Elder says. "But I should get my guys somewhere safe for the night. And I don't think your crew needs my help."

Arthur scoffs. He mumbles something to himself. Elder gives him a look of disbelief but doesn't say anything about it.

"Be safe out there, Aros," Elder says. He turns back. As he walks away, he waves his arm for the others to follow him.

Arthur shoves between Sefryn and me, breathing into my ear. Irritation prickles my skin. "We should be following him. He clearly knows what he's doing."

"You're more than welcome to follow him," I retort. Arthur doesn't move. He doesn't reply either.

I head toward the tallest hill. That seems like the best place to go. I'm not sure what it is, but I have this feeling like there's a compass in me, one that is pointing me in the direction of the Eternal Flame.

As the day gets later, I start wishing that we had brought some of that fish with us. But I know that it likely would not have survived the fight. We keep at it. I have to remind Arthur not to eat the snow around here as a substitute for water.

The hills keep going on and on. It becomes harder to not lose faith in our path. The constant snowscape makes it hard to believe we're getting anywhere and not just going in circles. We must be high up on the mountain because the sun seems to be high in the sky longer than it usually seems. We're no longer so low in elevation that the mountain and trees obscure the view of the sky. Now, the heavens above are wide open.

A single tree, lush with green leaves, stands out in the distance. The mountain slopes downward. As we get closer, I can see the horizon sitting above the sea. We've traveled to one side of the mountain. It's impossible to know exactly what side. Valleys of forests sprawl at the depths of the mountain.

I notice that Arthur talks with Clarissa. She seems to be polite, giving curt answers and small smiles. As long as he isn't being himself, I'm sure she's fine. I know Clarissa can handle herself. And I know if she needed help, she'd ask for it. But it's somewhat nice to see that for once, Arthur doesn't seem to be pissing everybody off. But I keep an eye out all the same. I know Clarissa is fighting her demons, pushing through her fears as best as she can.

Other than the tree itself being the only one around for miles, there is nothing special about it. The mountain ground rounds slightly, sloping down more before steeply shooting up. It rounds a peak of Voltar. Something tells me this might be the highest point of the mountain. And that's when I can feel it—pure intuition, but somewhere up there, the Eternal Flame burns. It will either give us our next clue or, in some way, be the end of the Trials.

# CHAPTER 10

## THE TUNNEL OF ARCHIVES

**Aros Caelum Hayes**

"Any food?" Arthur asks quietly. He turns his eyes to Sefryn for a moment. She raises an eyebrow at him. *Yeah, now he wants her help with food.*

"No, sorry," she says, talking to all of us. "There's one tree around, and it doesn't bear anything edible. Even its leaves are toxic to people."

"Can't you just make fruit appear out of nowhere?"

Abigail and Clarissa look at Arthur like he's the dumbest thing to walk the planet. Sefryn doesn't even answer him. She just sighs and places her hand on the tree. I look around. It is tempting to head back down the mountain, find the valleys and flowing rivers of clear, clean water. We might even be able to cross the waters that separate Voltar from the rest of the continent. But I know we can't really do that. There's no leaving Voltar right now. It's complete the Trials or die.

I look up toward the peak, trying to discern anything that hints there's something up there. It's not going to be a hard path to walk. It looks like the road curves alongside the mountain, rising higher and higher at a gradual slope. But the freezing temperatures and lack of sustenance are what's going to get us. Maybe there's something on the other side, out of sight only for the time being.

"We need to keep moving," I say. "If we stay here too long, we'll end up like the others." My mind brings forth a picture of the other volunteers who froze to death, unable to find a safe place to stay. I refuse to let that happen to any of us.

We shuffle along the road, leaving behind the sole tree, the one thing that makes the environment not look like a frozen death sentence.

Surprisingly, it doesn't feel long before the tree is out of sight, and we're on another side of the mountain. Our path is flanked by the rock faces of Voltar's highest peak. Occasionally, a random lump of snow will fall down, sometimes rolling into a ball and traveling downhill. None of them are very big, though.

The sun lowers beneath the sky. When it's near the bottom, it quickly drops out of sight. Minutes later, we're surrounded by darkness, but the moon is quite bright from this high up. Still, Camila and I help guide everyone with discs of light.

Bats fly overhead. I keep an eye on them, unsure if they're something else in disguise. For where we're located, it feels eerily quiet, like we're being watched. Like we're being hunted.

We don't talk much for the first several hours. It would be too exhausting. I know all of us want to stop for the night, but there is nowhere that seems like a good place. A cave, a large tree, or even just an inlet into the mountain face would suffice. But there's nothing.

We make it all the way around the mountain, back to the side where we can see the land below. That single tree is visible, looking quite small from up here.

"We've come a long way," Sefryn says. "Maybe I'm beyond exhausted, but it doesn't feel like we've walked that much."

"No, it doesn't," I reply, staring out at the tree. The others stop with us. This small moment of rest won't do much for us, but it's better than nothing. "The road must be pretty steep if we're this much higher already, even if it didn't look like it."

"Yeah, that's what I was thinking," Sefryn replies. I turn to look at her. She is staring out too, but when she feels my eyes on her, she turns her head and looks into them. "But still, I feel like I could go on for hours if we need to."

"Let's hope we don't have to," I say. It was just two days ago when I felt like we almost kissed. Even with everyone around us, not watching but aware, I'd do it.

She smiles slightly and lets out a tiny sigh. "Let's keep moving." She breaks our eye contact, walking away up the path.

Few words are exchanged between us all. Arthur talks too, but he now makes more conversation attempts with Clarissa. I suppose he gave up on Abigail. Or he's just desperate for whoever he can get. I wonder what he's trying to prove to himself.

It takes a lot for me to constantly think the worst of someone. Arthur managed to get there in less than a week.

Step by step. And then another step. And more, and more, and more. Snow falls lightly over our heads. The coat Sefryn made me keeps me warm, but my unyielding hunger makes my core feel cold. At this point, it feels like I'm working off fumes. If I stop moving, I might not be able to get going again.

The path is long. And it goes on and on. That lonely tree disappears from our view again, but now, higher than we were before, when we're traveling on the other side of the mountain, we can see a wide plain, sloping down slightly. We can also see the path we'd taken some hours ago below us. Our footprints have already been covered up by snow.

"Nhuya!"

With no worldly clue as to what the sound is supposed to mean, I turn to look at the source of the odd noise. It's Clarissa. She's hopping, up and down, up and down, at a rapid pace, and pointing out toward the peak of the mountain. *Yes, that's where we're headed*, I think to myself. But it's still a long way up.

But then I notice it. It's a cave. I'm so happy that Clarissa has a knack for seeing things that the rest of us miss.

"Finally," I breathe out.

Somehow, despite our total lack of energy, we move faster, almost running toward the cave. It's smaller than the first one we stayed in, but it's something, and it's slightly nestled out of the way, so that it isn't easily noticeable from the path.

I rest my hand on the wall of the cave. It feels wet. I look. Water runs down from somewhere above. It trails off into the snow, probably freezing soon after it gets outside. I press my hand against the rocks, letting water fill my cupped hand. Sefryn and Camila do the same. When we've had our drink, which wasn't enough for me, we step aside and let the others go.

Of course, Arthur has to ruin it by licking the wall itself.

Luckily, I know I can move water with my powers. I sit at the other end of the flowing water. I light a fire inside and set up an energy field at the cave's entrance. With my finger, I pull over a strand of water, pool it in my hands, and drink. I help the others get their fill too. Unfortunately, there still aren't any trees around, so Sefryn can't make us anything like a cup or pillow. The stony walls and floor will have to do.

"So, we rest here for the night?" I ask.

"We should keep moving," Arthur says as everyone else nods their heads, agreeing to get some sleep for the rest of the night.

"You can, if you want," Camila says, her tone almost threatening. "We're not going to stop you."

Arthur ponders this. He looks out into the night. Luckily, the moon provides enough light to see well enough, so he could do it if he wanted to.

Just when I think he's about to walk away, and I ready myself to lower the energy barrier, Clarissa speaks up.

"Arthur, just stay," she says. She looks up at him, too much kindness in her eyes, but then again, she might just be really tired. But I know

Arthur will see whatever he wants to. He'll believe whatever suits his motives best.

"Okay," Arthur replies. He comes over and sits much too close to the rest of us. Sefryn and Camila exchange looks with me. Abigail sucks in a deep breath. The only one who doesn't have a small reaction is Clarissa, who fell asleep before Arthur sat down. He looks at her, a weird glint in his eye, accompanied by an odd smirk.

"How romantic," Camila jokes with me, rolling her eyes. Sefryn and Abigail giggle. If Arthur heard her, he doesn't show it.

I wake up with Sefryn's head nestled on my chest, on that part just by my shoulder. I look down. I had fallen asleep leaning against the cavern's wall. She fell asleep close to me, and part of her body lies on my torso. It is now that I notice just how bad we all probably smell. Still, I smile.

I then realize that she's been awake this whole time. She chose to stay here. She chose to stay with me. Something in my heart warms, and I get the idea that this really could be something.

"Hey," I say quietly because the others still seem to be sleeping.

She doesn't look up at me. "Hey."

I shift a bit.

"Do you want me to move?" she asks.

I hesitate for a moment. "Not really," I tell her.

"Good," she says. I can see her smile. "Because I'm comfortable here."

I smile again. "Good."

We don't say anything more. I turn my head slightly to look out of the cavern. The snow glistens in the sunlight. It's probably much later than it ought to be, if I think about how we should keep searching for the Eternal Flame. But I think it's good for us to get enough rest. I don't know when we'll get the chance again.

I take down my barrier, making it easier to enjoy the view outside. The distance, dropping down the mountain and eventually to the sea, blends into the background of snow outside. I'm not sure how long we sit there for. But if I had to stay here forever, I could be okay with that.

Fuck, I just wish we were alone.

To make it worse, Arthur gets up. He takes a quick glance outside.

"What the hell!" He storms out of the cave and then back in. I exchange an eye roll with Sefryn, and we get up. "Everyone, wake up!" he shouts, as if he didn't already wake the others.

"What's going on?" Clarissa asks sleepily. She sits up from what must have been the most uncomfortable position I've ever seen someone in while lying on the ground. If my fire hadn't been burning all night, she would have been very, very cold.

Arthur walks over to her and kneels. He takes her hands into his as if to comfort her. She must still be tired because she doesn't seem to notice at first. Then Clarissa looks up at him, grimaces, and pulls her hands away. She stands up.

"We should have woken hours ago," he says, standing. He looks around at us. "If they weren't so selfish, enjoying their little *moment* together, then we could have been on our way. For all we know, we could have found the Eternal Flame by now."

Camila stands, rolling her eyes. "I doubt it," she says. "And I think we all needed to get some extra sleep."

"I agree," Abigail says. "The sleep was good for us. That includes you too, Arthur. But it doesn't seem to have done much for your shitty attitude." She walks outside, looking up at the sky and breathing in, stretching her arms to her sides.

"What did you just say to me?" Arthur chases after her and reaches out to grab her.

Camila snaps her fingers, sparking a small ball of light that flicks his hand away before he can touch Abigail. He spins around, nearly growling.

"She said it how it is," Camila says. "Check your attitude. Otherwise,

I'll toss you off this mountain myself." There is an eerie calm on her face that says her threats are not empty.

Arthur glares at her, mulling over his choices.

"Stand down," I tell him, then quickly turn to the others. "Let's drink up," I say to them. The need to piss overwhelms me. I had gone in the lake in that valley, unintentionally, but that was the last time. I get my fill of water and help the others too, since no one wants to touch the cave wall after Arthur defiled it.

I head outside. I walk a bit away from the others, telling them I'll be back in a minute. They give me the space I need, but there really isn't any privacy out here. So, I just go out in the open, barely attempting to hide myself. It isn't like there's anyone around to see me.

We get going again. Apparently, the girls didn't have an issue doing their business close together, though they had Arthur walk far away. It appears that they are so done with him that, even after the incident, none of them seem shaken.

The peak of the mountain looks much closer to us today than it did yesterday. I can see cliff edges and smaller mountainside landings that carry trees on their backs, but they are out of reach. Hopefully, our path takes us there, and hopefully, we can find some food. I didn't want to mention it to anyone. It's been over a day now since we last ate.

To make it worse, the sun, as blazing as it is, does little to warm us. My face is cold. I can feel my lips chapping. The frozen air stings my eyes when the wind blows.

My mind wanders as we climb up the rest of the mountain. I stop noticing the scenery—that is, what little scenery is around. A small smile passes over my lips as I remember those lonely days back at the school. Sometimes it really wasn't all that bad. It didn't have a massive library, but most of the students never used it, so its emptiness made it feel big when I was in there alone. There was a book I read at least three times. It was a story about a war between immortal creatures and witches who used dark magic to bind people's minds with spells that utilized blood and fire.

But I think one of the professors saw how into the book I was, and they must have had it removed from the library because I never saw it again.

The story itself was fantastical, even knowing the kind of world I lived in. I've heard multiple stories about creatures and other beings that seemed to be immortal, and only when I saw the Azure Fox did I start to think they might all be real. But I never thought about the blood witches, about how they might have been real. What if they still exist?

Our path thins. We've reached the spiral that leads straight up to the peak. Upon our arrival, we let out a sigh of disappointment. There isn't anything here but a tunnel. It looks like it goes deep into the mountain we climbed for hours. Stepping into it would almost feel like we're going backward.

"I'm too tired to argue," Abigail says, her words all too relatable.

It's still bright out. We made good time. That, or we were way closer than we had thought. I wonder if anyone else slept in that cavern overnight like we did, or if they kept going up the mountain until they came here.

But there is the chance that we are the first to arrive here, which is either awesome or disheartening if this tunnel leads nowhere.

"I agree," Camila sighs.

With that, we walk into the tunnel. The light dies out quickly, so Camila and I have to provide it. The incline is steep. Somehow, the varying shades of brown in the winding tunnel are blander than the constant, pure white that we dealt with outside.

"Did you ever hear about the blood witches?" I ask Camila.

She laughs. "Blood witches? I haven't heard about those since I was like five."

I shrug. "I read about them while I was at school. Years ago," I explain. "For some reason, I just thought of them."

"Oh yeah, like that story about the war?"

"Yeah!"

"Um, sorry, the war?" Clarissa asks. She shuffles her feet. "I haven't heard anything about a war."

"This was a long, long time ago," Camila clarifies. "The blood witches were battling the immortal creatures. The immortal creatures have watched over our world since its inception, but the blood witches wanted more power."

"Who were these blood witches?"

We all turn and look at Arthur. It isn't like him to get involved in our conversations. And especially now, when everyone tolerates him—just barely—I don't think my patience with him will hold. He can take the ride with us to the Ashen Pit. That's it. But he otherwise isn't a part of our group.

Of course, Camila answers. I think that, for once, she's around people who appreciate all the things she's learned. And it isn't like the rest of us aren't curious to know either.

"The blood witches were composed of Fae, Fae-Blessed, Maleficium, and some Tavtka."

"The Fae were part of them?" Sefryn asks, both surprised and curious.

Camila nods. "It was a Fae, a mind one, that was able to develop the spell that allowed those with Magis to use the blood of their enemies to control their minds, thus controlling all their actions."

The silence between us makes our combined and discordant footsteps echo through the tunnel.

"Do you think they were real?" Arthur asks. I roll my eyes. I don't know if he's just trying to make conversation or if he's just a creep.

"Dude, just stop," I tell him, trying to keep my voice quiet. I don't try that hard.

Arthur makes a sound that reminds me of a hiss that a cat would make.

"They could have been," Camila answers. "But if they are still around, they're very good at hiding." We keep walking down the tunnel. "I can tell you one thing: if anyone found out that any were alive, they'd be hunted down quickly. People tend to dislike their minds being taken over."

"I know I wouldn't take too kindly if someone did that to me," Abigail chimes in, throwing a look at Arthur as she brushes past him.

The hard, uneven, and rocky surface beneath our feet becomes flat. The sounds our steps make are even. I look down. Stone has been laid, making a road for us to walk. Then I notice the unlit sconces jutting out of the walls.

"Hm." Camila eyes the walls thoughtfully, looking down as far as she can see. She guides her light ahead of us. She flicks her fingers and then curls them toward her. The lights fly into the sconces and bounce their way toward us, lighting each one. Camila then flings the lights down the tunnel, lighting the rest of the way.

"Impressive," I tell her, putting out my orbs of light.

"That was so pretty!" Clarissa says.

The lights from Camila burn like flames, but they remain the bright, white, and blue-tinted light that they always have been.

The tunnel widens, and we soon enter a massive, circular room. There are only two entrances. The walls are lined with curved bookshelves made of wood. There are at least seven sets of shelving, maybe eight, hanging off the walls in perfect rows.

"I could spend all day in here," I say, admiring the shelves packed with books.

"I was thinking the same thing," Sefryn says, walking close behind me.

"Well, we can't," Arthur tells us bluntly. "As you *should* know, we need to get out of here. So, let's keep moving." He storms off toward the other end, shaking his head. The rest of us look at each other. Abigail rolls her eyes. Clarissa doesn't say anything. I don't need to look at Camila to know what she's thinking.

We know we should keep moving. But we stay there for a moment. We don't pick any books off the shelves. We don't speak. We just wait.

When it's been long enough, and we feel that Arthur has gone sufficiently far that we won't hear from him for a while, we get going again. Surprisingly, the books and tomes don't end in the circular room. The tunnel is paved with the same stones, the walls are made of tan brick, and both sides have two long shelves running down as far as I can see, stocked with more books. These shelves are about waist-high for me, and the lights sit above them just like they did in the previous tunnel.

"You know," Camila starts saying, "if Arthur survives this—which he likely will because he's with us—when we get back to Edlyn, I can just have him detained and thrown in the dungeons."

"I like the way you think," Abigail responds, nudging Camila playfully with her shoulder. "For how long? A week? A month?"

"A year?" Clarissa adds excitedly, surprising me.

Camila chuckles. "Let's just say we can forget he's there once I throw him in. So, to answer your question, forever."

The girls laugh at this. Honestly, I'd think nothing of it if she actually went through with it. Maybe after years of silence, other than talking to himself, he'll realize how annoying he is.

We keep walking down the tunnel. It bothers me a bit that we climbed up the mountain just to walk through a tunnel, going back down it. The thought that we're going to just end up going in a circle crosses my mind, and I have to constantly push it out. There's no way we're going in the wrong direction. We worked too hard to get here. It can't all have been for nothing.

Hunger gnaws at me, my stomach threatening to eat itself. I don't know how much farther the tunnel goes. All of a sudden, I begin to feel trapped. We've gone too far in to turn back now. What if we're just about to get to the other side? The itch to leave here immediately runs down my body. I start to devise plans for an escape. Is my magic strong enough to bash through these walls and the rest of the mountain?

A calming hand touches my back and moves up to my shoulder. I turn to look at Sefryn. She gives me a small smile and a determined look. I'm not sure if she picked up on how I'm feeling or if she just heard the noises my stomach continues to make.

In contrast to the sconces that had been lit by Camila, there are four ahead, two on each side, that burn with fire inside them.

I walk a bit faster, wondering why these are lit with fire. Did Camila do this? Or maybe these were missed when she lit them, and Arthur took the liberty of lighting them himself? I look around. It really isn't hard to see, but it's easy not to notice if one were to walk right past it.

A doorway, shaped like an arch, of stone and marble, sits within the wall. Two of the fiery lights flank it. Another tunnel lies beyond, but unlike the one we came through, I can see its end, leading into a room. At the same time, looking down the path we were headed, I see rays of sunlight filtering through. We're close to the end. We've made it out.

But do we leave, or do we see what this room just steps away contains?

Without discussing it with the others, I take almost involuntary steps through the archway. There's something here. I can feel it.

Now inside the small chamber, I understand why I was so drawn here. Water flows down the back wall and into the room, though it is extremely shallow. My steps splash as I walk toward it. Somehow, the fire burns in the middle of the water, without fuel and without protection. The flames dance lightly on the surface, the reflections in the water racing wildly, accompanied by quiet crackles.

"That's it," Camila breathes out as she and the others catch up.

Arthur isn't here. "That's the Eternal Flame."

Arthur isn't here. "That's the Eternal Flame."

# CHAPTER 11

## THE ETERNAL FLAME

**Aros Caelum Hayes**

"What do you think?" Camila asks. She stares right at it without blinking.

"I think it's impressive," I tell her, although I'm not exactly sure what she's asking.

Clarissa hurries closer to it. "I think it's beautiful!"

"It is magical, alright," Abigail states.

"Yes, it's all of those things," Camila says, sighing slightly. "But I mean, what do you think happens next? Are we supposed to do something? Read a clue in the flames?"

"Maybe if we offer Arthur as a sacrifice, the fire will give us our next clue," Sefryn mumbles, close enough to me and Camila so that we are the only ones to hear it. I suppress a chuckle.

"I don't think that'll work," Camila says. "The Eternal Flame would know that it's doing us a favor, and therefore Arthur wouldn't count as a sacrifice."

Before I can laugh again, Clarissa asks us, "So, what do you guys think?"

I sigh and walk around the fire. Small splashes wash over my ankles. The water isn't freezing, but I'd still rather not be wet, so I take lighter, more careful steps.

"I'm not sure," I say, gathering my thoughts.

"Should someone tell Arthur?" Clarissa asks. None of us like the guy, but she's currently being the most patient with him. And the most thoughtful. Even if it is clear she doesn't like him. Maybe it's the fact she grew up in an orphanage that makes her not want him to feel like he's all alone.

"Yeah, if you want," I respond. "But I don't think it'll matter either way. We'll either figure out what to do next or be stuck here forever, with or without him."

Clarissa lets out a long sigh. "We should get him." She goes quiet for a moment and looks down. "But I don't want to be the one."

I look at the others. Their looks tell me the same thing. No one wants to bother with him, but I know Clarissa will bug me about it at some point if we leave him wherever he went off to. She's quickly come to have trust in me, even if her gut may have told her otherwise at first. I don't want to let her down.

"Okay, see what you can figure out," I tell the others. "I'll be back in a minute."

I head down the tunnel and turn right, walking out of the dim lighting into the bright light of the setting sun. Arthur stares out across the way, arms folded over his chest. This side of the tunnel leads to a wide plain. It looks as if there's a winter filter placed over the landscape, but unlike the mountain now high above us, the land isn't covered in several inches of snow. Instead, the grass grows peacefully, and only parts of it are buried beneath snow piles. Trees line the edge of the plain, with many more resting below. Far in the distance, I can see the vast ocean sparkling in the light. This must be the far north side of the mountain; I can't see the sun itself, which is setting in the opposite direction.

It's still cold out, but the chilly green landscape is far more pleasing to the eyes than the frosty, arctic hell that makes up most of Voltar.

"Arthur," I call out. He doesn't react. "We found it. The Eternal

Flame." This gets him to turn his head back.

"Where?"

I jerk my head toward the tunnel. "It's just back there, in a small chamber just down a hall."

He stares blankly at me.

"If you want, come see it," I say, getting annoyed. I turn back and head toward the others. I don't understand how Arthur missed it. I can't help but think that the rest of us are carrying him through the Trials. If he hadn't been with us that first morning, he probably would already be dead.

When I return, Camila looks up at me and shakes her head. Nothing. But I can't blame them. What is it exactly that we're supposed to do now?

"I'm gonna go get us some food," Sefryn says. "I could feel the trees and plant life outside the tunnel when we got close, so I'm sure I can get us something."

"I'll go with you," Camila offers.

I nod and resume my slow pace around the flames. As Arthur finally enters, Sefryn and Camila walk out of the chamber. Arthur spits out what he would like to call ideas. We ignore him. Until...

"Why don't we set fire to ourselves, and then maybe we'll become a part of the flame?" he says, his tone implying that he truly thinks he just solved it. "Because for all we know, this is the Ashen Pit."

"That's probably the worst idea I've heard," Abigail retorts. "Can't you feel it? There is a strong, powerful magic in this fire. But it isn't anything like what the Ashen Pit will be. I know that in my heart. Plus, this looks nothing like a pit."

"Maybe it's just a name, and there is no pit," Arthur says, not even trying to keep the anger out of his voice.

"Fair point," Abigail says, her words short and sharp. "But it got the name somehow. And now that we know it's real, I'm gonna bet that there *is* some kind of pit, or something that you could call a pit."

"I agree," Clarissa says. "This isn't it. But this Eternal Flame is something. We just need to figure out what."

Arthur kicks water toward the flames. The flames flicker momentarily, but the water evaporates, leaving the fire burning hot as ever.

"Why would you do that?" Abigail asks.

Arthur sneers. "Isn't it eternal?" He walks away, taking heavy, intentional steps to slosh around water. I move my fingers, creating a vine of water that wraps around Arthur's leg. I will my mind to freeze it. It does, barely, but enough so that for a moment Arthur is rooted to the spot. Fire burns from his hands, thawing it.

"That won't work on me," he seethes. "I can create fire now."

I realize then that if Arthur can create fire now, there must be a way I can learn to conjure or create water, or any other element for that matter. But now isn't the time to test it.

"Yeah, I know," I reply. "But even with that, you know that I am still much stronger than you, and quite honestly, I am losing my patience with you. So if you're going to be unhelpful," I walk up to him, staring right into his eyes, mine showing all the anger I have for him, "or if you're going to act like a dick-fuck, then leave us. Wait outside. Be anywhere else but here."

Arthur crosses his arms and sits right in the water, not caring that he's getting wet. Or he does, but he doesn't show it. It isn't out of the question that he forgot that there is water on the ground. I resume waiting near the fire with Clarissa and Abigail.

By the time Camila and Sefryn get back, all we've accomplished is losing a staring contest with the flames.

"I made us some small stools," Sefryn says, six woven stools floating behind her. Camila carries a similarly woven basket filled with berries and larger fruit. Sefryn passes us the stools by flicking her finger, sending one to each of us.

We all dig into the basket for food. Even Arthur does, and without complaining.

At this point, I'm so hungry that I almost feel nauseous as I eat. But I keep eating. It helps that the fruits are filled with water, which helps quench my extreme thirst too.

While we sit around the Eternal Flame, Camila tells us about Edlyn and how the kingdom came to be. "Or, at least, this is the version that has been passed down to me," she tells us, implying that it may not be an accurate telling.

"Long ago, Edlyn Castle—"

"I don't need a history lesson," Arthur says. "I don't fucking care if you're a princess. You're not the most important person in the world, not even close to it. No one wants to listen to you."

"Oh, and we're supposed to care what you have to say?" Sefryn snaps. "You sure talk a lot of shit like you're above everyone else, but really you're just a weak and bitter nobody." Sefryn sighs. "It must suck to be you."

Arthur purses his lips. He stands quickly and walks out of the chamber.

None of us say anything. Even Clarissa remains silent. But I know we're all glad he left. There's no need to go after him. With any luck, he'll never come back.

Eventually, Sefryn pipes up, speaking with a much lighter and friendlier voice. "Aros, tell us about Earth."

The three other girls look at me quickly, as if they've all been dying to ask me.

"What do you want to know?" I ask. "I promise you, Earth is nothing compared to Arteyva."

"That doesn't matter," Sefryn says. "We just want to know about it. You might be the only person alive from here who's been to Earth. Typically, we're all forbidden to enter that realm."

"Well, I don't know why I was sent there," I say. "But it isn't like

Praellen was going to accept me."

Sefryn lets out a laugh. "No, we're not usually accepting of unwelcome outsiders. But for a Maleficium like you, I think the Fae Empress would have made an exception."

"I don't think I would have fit in with all the Fae," I tell her.

"Trust me, I think you would have done just fine."

My head feels hot, completely unrelated to the fire.

"Well, uh," I say, clearing my throat. "Earth is just a bit like Arteyva, but without the magic and the terrifying creatures, and most of the people there are boring. Um, the sun rises in the east and sets in the west, but our days and nights are about the same length."

I'm struggling to describe to the others a realm that I've lived in for so long.

"Is there really no Magis there?" Camila asks.

I shrug. "None. They do have technology, though. Not like the steam-powered elevators in Naierkor," I say, speaking of the largest city on the whole continent. It's the most technologically advanced, even if the steam is powered by Fire-Fae-Blessed and Tavtka. "Imagine having access to all the information on Atreyva in your pocket in a little glass rectangle." I'd show them my phone, but Kreavlos would never have let any of my Earth artifacts into Arteyva.

"Wow," Camila says.

"That sounds like Magis to me," Clarissa chimes in.

I shrug. "It doesn't feel like it most of the time."

As we talk, we snack on the leftover berries from Sefryn and Camila's foraging adventure. All the nuts and seeds that Sefryn and Camila gathered fell to the bottom of the basket, so I didn't see them before.

As night falls, the chamber seems like the safest place to rest—but we can't really sleep here. We could rest in the tunnel that leads in here instead. But I keep having this feeling that we should stay where we are. Arthur sulks back in and takes his seat, staring off at the wall with water running down it.

As the night goes on, the cool air from outside creeps in, but the fire keeps the worst of the cold out. I'm about ready to call it, ready to find a softer part of the stone ground, set up my defensive walls, and get some sleep. But still, something tells me to wait.

And wait.

Just a bit more.

Just. *Stay.*

The flames slow, the crackling ceases, and everything is silent until I hear a faint gong that reverberates throughout the tunnels. When the sound fades, so does my vision. The walls disappear. After a moment of silence, the sound of running water reaches my ears, until it too goes away, along with the rest of my vision.

It feels like I'm back with Kreavlos, like I'm in the Shadow Realm. But he isn't here.

The ground shakes. I don't know what's happening. I still can't see anything.

I'm standing on an uneven circle of a plateau, high, high up. Behind me is a small bridge that is connected to a large piece of land easily recognizable as Voltar. The highest peak sits in the distance, but where I stand now isn't much lower in elevation.

Ahead of me, there's another bridge, though this one spans a much greater distance. It's an old, wooden suspension bridge. Wooden poles stick up at various points; though if there had been any ropes to stabilize crossing the bridge, the ropes are long gone.

Looking down is a terrifying thing to do. Way, way down, there's a small and shallow creek running through various trees. Falling is a guaranteed death. The wind blows strongly here, and I have to fight against the currents to keep my balance. Across this bridge, there is a small temple.

The Ashen Pit. It must be inside.

I gulp, the buildup of saliva in my throat doesn't go down easily. Before I work up the nerve to cross, I hear a horrible shriek. I turn my head back. There's one of those creatures I saw in a dream. Standing like a human but over eight feet tall, the black and slimy-skinned creature cries out again. It brandishes its tail before charging toward me.

I run. The wooden planks of the bridge sway with each of my steps. I throw my hands to my sides to try to keep my balance. The bridge rocks side to side violently. When the creature runs over it, its long talons tear through the only support the bridge has, and the bridge collapses. I grab onto one of the planks as the bridge behind me flies toward the ground. Still connected to the other end, the bridge swings toward the rock face of the mesa. The creature plummets to the land below.

The jagged rocks look really close now as I dive closer to them.

My eyes snap open. I'm shaking, sweating, and disoriented. I don't know where I am. Trees are perched around me. I sit in the small clearing. The grass is soft, a colorful, bright, deep green. There are fireflies floating ominously.

There's a rustling beyond the trees. The moonlight shines perfectly over the clearing, but behind the trees, I can't see through the darkness.

The Azure Fox walks through. She looks down at me.

A screech pierces my ears. I look up. A giant owl lands next to the Azure Fox.

Then I hear the wind, but it doesn't pass through the trees. It's like a twirling breeze. Shadows form from the air, spinning around until they become just an indistinct shadowy mass moving quietly above me.

"Who are you?" I ask.

The owl steps forward. He must be over ten feet tall. He has spotty brown feathers and wide eyes, and a mean-looking beak. He lowers his head.

"I am Palvadore, or 'the Avian of the South' as I'm called on the other continents," he tells me.

"I am Grisla," the Azure Fox says. She lifts her head up slightly, a motion she's using to show trust. "But you know me as the Azure Fox."

Kreavlos grunts. I know him, though I have never seen him take form before. Not that these wispy shadows I see are much of a physical form, but at least they're something I can see, even if I am not able to touch.

"You've made it quite far in the Trials," Grisla says. "I praise your skill thus far. But I must warn you. The land of Voltar is becoming more and more dangerous."

"The Magis here is vast. It can fill a thousand oceans, and then some," the Avian of the South says. "But this Magis has grown unstable, which is dangerous, as it is quite literally the core of our world."

"The core?" I ask.

"Yes," Kreavlos answers quickly. "Arteyva was born from Voltar, and the Magis here shaped the world you know. It is otherwise untapped, uncontrollable, and ever-changing."

I stand up. The fox and the bird are too big already, and sitting down, their size makes me uncomfortable.

"What do you mean, Arteyva was born here?"

"Does it matter?" Kreavlos bellows. "It just was. And the Magis here is so powerful that not even we can control it."

I shake my head slightly. "Who are you?"

The owl sits straighter, somehow now taller than he was before.

"I believe we just told you that."

He didn't understand. "No, I mean, what are you?"

Kreavlos shifts toward me. The floating ball of wisps creeps me out, and I shuffle backward a bit.

"We are the Aeturnous Kitisma," Kreavlos answers. "We were born from the core Magis of this realm. You could say that we are essences of Voltar itself."

"But do not concern yourself with what we are," the Azure Fox snaps. "Concern yourself with surviving the Trials. More than half of the volunteers perished that terrible morning." She sounds genuinely upset, which gives me the idea that the attacks from those creatures were not intended as part of the Trials. But those creatures were of Voltar, and Voltar *is* the Trials. What did they expect? "Another quarter of the volunteers have already succumbed to the dangers that they faced."

"Why are you telling me this?"

"Because we have been watching you," she answers. "Though we cannot interfere with what happens here."

"So, what are you guys doing now?"

"We come to you as part of the visions the Eternal Flame grants you," the large owl answers, his voice almost like a constant sneer. "The Eternal Flame provides tiny clues, puzzle pieces, so that you may find the Ashen Pit. This is but one."

"Why are the Trials happening now?" I ask them. The question has been burning in my mind since I learned that they were happening.

"Something in the world is shifting," Grisla tells me. Something in her voice is ominous. There is a slight fear, like she knows that they alone won't be able to stop whatever may be coming. "We cannot figure out what it is. For the first time since our inception, we do not know what threat is headed our way. Whatever it is, the Ash Lords will be able to defend our world."

"And the Ash Lords are as strong as the seats are filled," the Avian says. "For too long, there has only been one Ash Lord, waiting unneeded. But our time of need draws upon us. We must be prepared."

"Make your way quickly to the Ashen Pit," the Azure Fox pleads. "But stay vigilant and safe as you do so. The number of volunteers is small compared to when the Trials began. We cannot afford to lose any more. Spilling the blood of any Magis was never intended, even if expected."

"But be warned," Kreavlos says, his voice even deeper than normal. "The Ashen Pit is designed to keep out anyone who is not an Ash Lord.

So, the perils you face there may be the deadliest yet."

"That is, if the land of Voltar doesn't cost you your life before then." The Azure Fox's words send chills down my spine.

And I'm back. The humming crackling of the flame goes on. The water runs down the wall in the back. The others still seem to be in a trance, learning whatever their visions have to say to them. Are the Aeturnous Kitisma going to speak to the others too?

Either way, I know where the Ashen Pit is. At least, enough that I'll know it when I see it. But I don't know where that temple is or how to find it. I hope that this is some sort of puzzle and that the others will have the pieces I'm missing.

I wish the others would wake up. Waiting here makes me feel un-comfortable. The anticipation starts to build, and I begin to feel slightly queasy. How much time do we have before we are in as much danger as I was warned about? How much more dangerous are things going to get?

I wonder if any of the others have been here, if Chase has already fought his way to the flame and is somewhere near the Ashen Pit. Now that I sit here, alone with my thoughts, the Trials feel more like a race. I hate myself for thinking it. But now Arthur has a point. What if it is a race?

It can't be. Not traditionally. But what if, when someone makes it out of the Trials, Voltar becomes more dangerous?

The Aeturnous Kitisma may be the most powerful beings in all the realms, but they aren't stronger than the core of Magis itself. What if Voltar considers that with each volunteer who passes, the need for others to make it is unimportant? But that wouldn't make sense. The Ashen Pit wants the strongest. It wants the leaders, according to Claudius. But what if he is wrong? Clearly, even the Supreme Ash is considered lesser than the immortal creatures. He may be the most powerful human in this world, in all of the realms even, but he isn't the core of Magis. And that's why he can't just pick out the Ash Lords. Not when there are four to pick. The Ashen Pit has to do that.

Arthur wakes up next.

"What happened? What did you see?" I ask him.

He looks at me coldly. "I fell asleep. What, you want to know my dreams? I didn't have any."

Yeah, we all fell asleep. Luckily, we slept where we sat, and none of us fell over into the water.

"None?" I ask him as nicely as I can, curious if he truly saw nothing.

He doesn't answer immediately. "I was on a beach. There was sand. That's all."

He's hiding something. Rage begins to boil inside me. How can he still be so selfish? We need each other to find the Ashen Pit and get out of here.

Before my anger tops off and I shout at Arthur, Abigail wakes up.

"The storms," she says. "We need to follow the eye of the storms."

Storms? As in more than one? Would they not all have their own eye?

Before I can ask her, Camila wakes up. She stares into the fire, her eyes unmoving. She has something. I know it. I want to ask her what she saw, but Clarissa wakes next. Her eyes are wide. She looks terrified. Looking closer, I can see her trembling. I move over to her.

"What is it?" I ask her as gently as I can, but my excitement is too much. I place my hand on her shoulder in an attempt to comfort her, which works slightly. Arthur shifts uncomfortably in his seat, scowls in my direction, but doesn't say anything.

"Beware of the still night," Clarissa says. That doesn't sound like a puzzle piece. That sounds like a warning. "If all gets still, then get out." Her lip trembles.

What does she mean? Most nights in Voltar feel still, especially when we're deep in the forests, and the trees beyond us have already blocked the path of the wind. Most of the animals here sleep through the night, except for those silent hunters and the monsters. But so far, the only creatures that are a threat to us are very, very loud. So, what is considered a still night?

The fear in her shaking voice does little to calm me. The chills running down my spine increase. In one moment, everything around me felt normal. Even our journey through Voltar as we made our way to the various clues felt normal. I felt safe. So far, nothing has changed. But these foreboding warnings feel like the realm has already shifted, just like they told me it would.

To make it all worse, Sefryn wakes up. Her piercing gray eyes freeze my body. Whatever she saw, it wasn't a clue either. Unlike Clarissa, Sefryn remains quite composed. She gathers herself and gets oriented to her surroundings. Camila looks over to her. Sefryn then looks right at me.

"One of us is about to die."

# Chapter 12

## The Calm Before the Still

**Aros Caelum Hayes**

The others shift uncomfortably in their seats. We wait with bated breath for Sefryn to tell us more, but she doesn't speak. She stares into the fire, just as Camila did. Arthur narrows his eyes, as if he is trying to act angry, but I can see right through it. He's scared.

"What do you mean?" I ask Sefryn. "What did you see in your visions?"

With how the others move and let out their breaths, I can tell they all had visions too. Arthur looks annoyed now. Maybe he was telling the truth. Maybe all he saw was a beach and sand. Is that part of the puzzle?

"I didn't see much," Sefryn says. She stands up and begins pacing. "But I heard the voice. It sounded like the Azure Fox. And she told me that one of us is going to die."

I get a sick feeling in my stomach. Even though I know it means that *one of us* is about to die, I hope that I am wrong and that the foretelling of death refers to some other volunteer. Even though I get the fleeting wish that it is Arthur who will be put into the ground, I can't bring myself to just get it over with—kill him myself, and thus possibly save the others.

The more I dwell on it, the stronger that urge builds up inside me.

"I asked why and if there was anything we could do to prevent it,"

Sefryn continues. "But I got no answer. Eventually, though, my vision came back to me. And we were standing at the peak of the mountain, just before we walked into that tunnel that led us here. All of us were standing. Next thing I knew, we were in some dark temple. But I couldn't see anyone, just shadows of people. I knew they were us, but there were only five."

"Okay, so, if we keep going, one of us will die. But if we turn back, we all can leave?" Clarissa asks, though I don't think she expects an answer that she would like.

"Well, that doesn't make sense. We can only leave Voltar if we get through the Trials. If we turn back, yeah, sure, we're all still alive. But then we spend the rest of our lives here," Camila says.

Everyone stares at me as if I have the answer. I feel like I'm running out of breath. I raise my voice slightly. I'm not mad at anyone. I'm just mad that that's the vision they gave Sefryn. It doesn't help us one bit. We already know that Voltar is dangerous.

"Even if we survive," I say, my voice level now, "we wouldn't make it a year. The Trials don't end until everyone has passed or died. The Ashen Pit would never let us off. It wants new Lords. I bet you it would do anything to make sure it got exactly that. So, if we turn back, if we survive but make no effort to complete the Trials, then the Ashen Pit itself will take us out."

"You speak of it like it's a living thing," Arthur says bitterly.

"Yeah, well, it is. Voltar itself is living. Voltar is the core of Magis that this world is built on."

The others look at each other. Some of them nod.

"It makes sense," Camila says. "In Edlyn and Soulstice, these stories aren't readily available or told, but on the other continents, they speak of Voltar being the most powerful source of Magis in this realm. That's why Gorgrein doesn't like us being so close to it. They want Voltar for themselves."

I laugh. "Well, I don't think it works like that."

"Yeah, obviously," Camila replies. "But they don't know that. They think Edlyn is the strongest kingdom because we get our power from Voltar. Really, it's because they're dumb enough that they believe things like that."

"So, what do we do?" Arthur snaps.

"We keep going. We look out for each other," Clarissa answers. "Aros is right. We have to finish what we've started."

Abigail stands up. "I'm not scared of the warning, or premonition, or whatever it is that we'd like to call it." Her English-like accent comes out even more. "We're strong, all of us. We got this. We can do this."

"I know we can," I say. "But we have to be careful. In my visions, I saw where the Ashen Pit is. I don't know how to get there, but when I see it, I'll know. But in my visions..." I pause for a moment. I don't want to tell them that I spoke to three of the immortal creatures. No. If anything, that would probably push Arthur off the edge. "In my visions, the Azure Fox spoke to me. She said that Voltar is changing and that the land itself is going to become much more dangerous."

Arthur brushes this off. "She said that before."

"This time it was different," I tell him. I don't know why I even bother. The others will listen. They'll heed the warnings. Arthur will do whatever makes him feel better.

If one of us has to die, it should be him. I can't help but think it again. There is no question about it.

"I can tell you what I saw," Camila says. "This tunnel, this chamber. All of this here is a gateway to a separate part of Voltar. It's like the valley with the mammoth. We're still in Voltar, but not the same Voltar we've been in. I think we're much closer to the Pit than we realize."

"The Azure Fox also told me that the Ashen Pit is designed to keep out anyone who isn't an Ash Lord," I tell them. "So, its Magis is likely something strong, something beyond anything we've imagined. We're not Ash Lords, so when we get near, it'll do something to keep us away."

"That doesn't make sense," Arthur says with a scowl. "We didn't cross anything. We just walked down a tunnel."

"It makes sense if you believe in Magis," I say, standing up. "Considering what we can do, I think it's safe to say that we all believe in it."

Arthur stands too. He did it so fast that if he had been holding a cup, all of its contents would have spilled out.

"Don't speak for me."

I stare at him incredulously.

"There is nothing supernatural about any of this. It's just who we are."

I look at the others, a half-smile of amusement on my face. "Even with our lives rich with Magis, there are things beyond our understanding. That's what we would call supernatural. Those are the things *we* call magic," I tell Arthur, speaking as someone from Arteyva—not Earth. "If you don't believe in any of it, then why the hell are you here?"

Arthur doesn't have a response to that.

That's what I thought.

"Let's sleep outside," I say, leading everyone out. Arthur hesitates but follows, almost silent except for his grumbles.

"Wouldn't it be safer inside?" Sefryn asks me quietly as we step out into the night. The fresh air is welcoming to my lungs. I breathe in deeply, slowly. Light, fluffy snow falls from the sky. The clouds are a light gray and thin, leaving plenty of space for the light of the moon to beam through. "You could make those walls that you normally do. It just feels so open out here. Like we're exposed."

I turn to look at her. Her face is close to mine. My eyes flick down to her mouth briefly. The others are wandering around, enjoying the change of scenery. I'm grateful that she speaks quietly, as if not wanting to put doubt in anyone's mind about my choice—not that anyone but Arthur would think anything of it. But it's better not to give fodder to his asinine personality.

"I think I can make a bubble around us," I tell her. "But if that fails, we can just take turns like we did a few nights ago. Either way, I was starting to feel trapped inside, and the thought of sleeping within those walls was just...not doing it for me."

"I understand," she says. "I didn't like being in there either. But I know what I saw." She speaks in a whisper now. "I don't think it's safe for us. Here, maybe it is. But once we leave this place, we're going to have to take on a different strategy."

If, or when, it comes to it, and it is clear that one of us is in mortal danger, I intend to use Arthur as a shield to protect anyone else. It's a fucked-up thought, I know. Quite frankly, Arthur's death to save one of us would mean he finally did something worthwhile. That he was finally not worthless.

"If what Camila said is true, then we're close to the Ashen Pit," I tell Sefryn. "We're not going to be in Voltar for much longer. With any luck, this will be our last night here." I give her a smile. "C'mon, let's just enjoy the view."

We walk toward the others, who are spread out, looking over the cliff at the land below. After a few minutes, we sit in a circle as usual. The grass is soft enough that we don't need anything else. I could lie on my back and be comfortable enough to sleep peacefully. I light a fire. Sefryn walks off, letting us know she isn't going far and will be back soon.

She didn't lie. In just a few minutes, Sefryn is back with apples. Good old-fashioned, normal, plain apples. She's run a long stick through them.

And with that, we roast our apples over the fire like they're marshmallows. Of course, no one here has had a marshmallow.

"Sounds sticky," Clarissa says when I tell them about the fluffy, white campfire treats. "But delicious."

Camila, Abigail, and I exchange a look and then burst out laughing. Immature, sure, but we could do with the distraction. Sefryn playfully slaps my arm and rolls her eyes at the other two girls who laughed with me. I even see Arthur crack a smile, but he doesn't join in.

"What? They do! And I bet they're really sweet," Clarissa adds. "I bet I could just heat one right up so that it's just perfect, then shove it in my mouth, poke at it with my tongue, and swallow."

I burst out laughing again along with Camila. Abigail contains her laughter with great difficulty and whispers to Clarissa, who then shrieks with laughter and a snort, claiming that she wasn't thinking anything like we were, that she truly was enjoying my description of marshmallows and the camping tradition of roasting them over a fire.

It's amazing that we can just enjoy each other's company and have fun while surrounded by a dangerous land that we're constantly reminded is trying to kill us. Even with our lack of resources and the constant moving wearing us down, we can just sit back and relax. With the exception of Arthur, everyone here feels like the family I never had, like the family I always wished I had. Clarissa tugs at her coat and pulls it so that it is tighter around her. I smile. If I had to give her a coat again, I'd do it. I'd do it for anyone here.

Well, maybe not.

But maybe so. I know that I tend to be soft when it comes to someone needing help. I don't think it's a bad trait, but with Arthur around so much, I fear that my willingness to help anyone might cost someone dearly in the end. I have to be careful about it.

Still, there's probably nothing that can change my mind about my plan for Arthur. His death won't be in vain. It won't be for nothing. It might not even come. I know we're close to the Ashen Pit's location. Ideally, all of us will be back in Edlyn before night falls tomorrow. But more and more, I just want it to happen.

"What do you think you'll do when we get back?" Abigail asks, pulling me out of the depths of my thoughts. She's looking at me. I hope someone else answers instead. Truthfully, I don't know what I'll do when

I get out of here.

"It depends if I'm an Ash Lord or not," Camila answers. "If I'm not one, I'll probably go back to my dreadful life, doomed to forever be a princess."

"Well, do you want to be a queen?" Abigail asks her.

Camila shrugs, but then quickly shakes her head. "No, I don't think so. I'd rather be able to live my own life without all the expectations of being royalty."

"Yeah, but being royalty comes with its own perks, right?" Sefryn says.

"Yup, it does. It's a give and take. There are pros and cons to both lives."

Camila turns to me.

"So, what about you, Aros?"

I chuckle. "Like you, it depends on whether I'm an Ash Lord. If I'm not, I'd probably go back to Earth." I steal a glance at Sefryn. "Well, maybe not. That depends on other things."

I don't say more. There's a huge part of me that knows I'll be an Ash Lord, but the seeds of doubt are constantly fighting to grow inside me. What if I'm not chosen? I'd prefer to go back to Earth. But with everything that Kreavlos said after the Dark Wind pulled me to this realm, I think that I've already been chosen. I must have been.

So, as an Ash Lord of Arteyva, what is it that I'll do?

My path forward is as uncertain as the changing world. There's not much I can do about that. But there are parts of my life I can control. And once we've made it out of here, I'm going to take my shot with Sefryn.

Of course, if things got serious with her, she'd have to consider leaving her own realm. Would she do that for me? Does she even feel the same way?

The snow falls harder, but the warmth of my fire is more than enough to keep us comfortable. We keep talking, not caring to sleep yet, even though it's probably well past midnight. Abigail tells us that she doesn't want to become an Ash Lord, to which Clarissa agrees.

"I didn't know what I was getting into," Abigail says. "And now that I've seen some of the horrors of our world, I'd rather not deal with them. Not like this, at least. Don't get me wrong, I'll fight to protect those in need. I will always do that. But the idea of burning my soul into that collective," she says, closing her eyes and shivering, shaking her head, "it just isn't for me."

"But I'd bet you'd make a badass general," Clarissa tells her. "With how you can call down lightning? And I'm sure that's not all you can do."

Abigail smiles. I know they've been close for a while. The thought makes me look over at Camila. She and I are just as close, at least I think we are. We don't share the same type of bond that Abigail and Clarissa do, but it's just as strong. If there is anything I can do for her when we get back to the castle, anything to make her life easier, I'll do it. I'll find a way. Camila deserves more than she gets. Just as sure as I am that I will be an Ash Lord, I am sure Camila will be too. She, at the very least, has a great destiny in front of her. I think she's ready. She's been ready.

Looking back at my life on Earth, I realize that I never really had any purpose. There was no meaning to my life. Friends came and went. I spent hours in solitude honing my powers but could never tell anyone who I was. It was lonely. And somehow, I didn't go completely mad. Kreavlos helped a lot. He kept me in check if I ever seemed like I was diving off the deep end.

The time I've spent here in Voltar is the most adventure I've ever had. Other than fighting those beasts on Earth just before I arrived, I've never been in a situation as dangerous as this. And that's because I belong in Arteyva. I've always known it. But at the same time, I've always felt like an outcast here. It was the same on Earth, though.

Thinking about how we're nearing the end of the Trials is almost saddening. Almost. But once we're out of here, I can start making my own choices. I won't be stuck with what's around me. So far, most people don't seem to care about the rumors my parents spread about me. Most people don't even believe them, not anymore, since it's now widely known that I'm a Maleficium. To them, that means there was never a demon that possessed me.

I have to wonder. If my parents never treated me the way they did, would I have discovered my powers? Or would they have remained dormant for years, possibly forever? It's impossible to know for sure, but they say that there are some people who are of a high order of Maleficium who never discover their true power.

Looking around me, I know it doesn't matter. If everything I've been through has led me here, I wouldn't change any of it. I know that I've met some of the best people there are, and I am extremely grateful for that.

The wind breezes through, going between the strands of my hair. The fire is making me feel a bit too warm, and the wind brings a pleasant chill to the back of my head. The flames of my fire blow around slightly, sparks flying off into the air before dissolving. We've eaten all the apples Sefryn brought us. Arthur is asleep, lying on his back. The others look ready for bed, too. I look up at the sky. The snowy clouds have cleared. Stars shine brightly. The moon sits there, large, majestic, and still as ever.

A knot ties in my stomach.

*Still as ever.*

I only now notice it. The wind that cooled me down has died out. The fire crackles in the otherwise silent night. The hairs on my neck rise. Suddenly, without a breeze or gust, my fire goes out. I don't even see smoke rise from where it burned. The stars stop twinkling. Each leaf on the trees looks frozen in time.

Seconds pass.

There's a pit in my stomach accompanied by butterflies. My heart beats faster. The others begin to notice it.

Seconds pass.

Something feels different.

Seconds pass.

Seconds pass.

Sefryn and I lock eyes. Everyone but Arthur, who is still asleep, is on high alert.

It's happening. The night is as still as ever.

*The night is still as ever.*

# Chapter 13

---

# Nightmare

**Aros Caelum Hayes**

The first thing I hear is the faint thumping. It isn't long before I can feel the vibrations in the ground. Something is heading toward us. The five of us stand up quickly, looking behind us, trying to see whatever is drawing close. I snap my fingers, sending a spark of energy that pops beneath Arthur's head, effectively waking him up.

"Something's here," I say out loud to Arthur, but I don't think he hears me.

The quiet jabbing at the ground continues. As it gets louder, the soft stomps on the ground are accompanied by high-pitched laughs, mischievous and terrifying. I can almost imagine a pack of animated dolls climbing over the cliff.

They're not dolls. Small creatures, barely taller than a foot, climb over the ledge. These guys must have had a hell of a time getting up. And they're carrying small weapons—makeshift crafts of sledgehammers, clubs, axes, and spears.

Looking like rabid and ugly babies, with mottled, loose skin and pointed ears that shoot out to the sides, it's clear these creatures were once dwarves who have been cursed by a dark Fae for one reason or another. Once just a made-up tale of creatures I read in books, I step back at the realization that most things I read about that I never believed in exist solely in Voltar.

Clarissa screams as one of them throws something at her. She ducks right into the projectile's way, and it knocks her in the head. Abigail rushes over to help her get up.

I blast a wave of energy at them. The dwarves hop high into the air, and I only manage to hit three, who fly back and out of sight.

Something jumps onto the back of my head. I thrash about, trying to throw it off, but it claws into my scalp. A fist-sized boulder slams into my left ear, causing my head to throb in pain. I grab the creature and pry it off me.

It wriggles about, shrieking as loud as it can. Using the hand I hold it in, I release fire from my palms and roast it until it's silent. I toss it at the others who are still jumping over the cliff.

"The tunnel!" Sefryn calls out, already making her way. The rest of us follow her. There must be a hundred of the creatures around. They're quite small and serve as a tripping hazard if we move quickly, except for when one of the dwarves gets a good shot and stabs or whacks our shins with something.

We never went far from the tunnel, so we make it in less than a minute, but only to find another swarm of manic dwarves running down the corridor. Several hop out of the tunnel that leads into the chamber with the Eternal Flame. We skid to a stop.

There's a loud bang. We cover our heads. Barely able to see, I try to usher the others out of the cave. I trip on something and hit grass. My face slams against the ground, and I can feel a spurt of blood from my nose.

I look back, my eyes watering from the pain. The tunnel has collapsed completely. I'm not sure how far the damage goes, but I know the lone chamber is buried underneath the rubble. Several of the dwarves lost their lives too. I know the flame is eternal, but even if it lived, I don't know that it'll ever be seen again. I can't help but think that it might work in our favor.

I also can't help but think it was a good idea we didn't stay the night in the chamber.

Clarissa and Abigail let out screams. I think the worst.

I look around, worry coursing through me. Thankfully, the others made it out. Camila and Sefryn help me to my feet. Hot liquid still spills from my nose. Salty sweat runs into my eyes and mixes with the tears, making it that much harder to see. Wind whips around my face, rustling the leaves of my coat.

When I can finally steal a glance, I notice the number of small dwarves must be close to half a thousand. They jump from trees, from the shattered boulders, through cracks in the collapsed tunnel. They. Just. Don't. Stop. Coming.

Arthur starts kicking them. Occasionally I hear a faint squeak as one flies backward. Then Arthur is stabbed in the ankles by three of them. He shouts in pain, cursing, and attempts to stomp on the creatures. But they aren't small enough to be stomped dead like bugs. The dwarves end up tripping Arthur, and he falls back, only to get pierced in the ass by another dwarf.

I roast the little guy until he crumbles to dust. Lucky for Arthur, most of the weapons are small, and none of their spears or spiked armaments are large enough to impale us; though used properly, they could still be lethal.

Rain pours from the sky, the drops hard pellets that feel almost like hail. Using the rain called down by Abigail, Clarissa pushes out gusts of wind, violently swinging her arms. From behind, the wind presses through. It's strong enough to make me need to stabilize my balance. Clarissa then bends her knees, squatting to the ground. A wave of wind blasts between our legs and at the dwarves. Most of them are thrown off their feet and fly into the air. Clarissa makes sure that her drafts carry them high up, where they then quickly drop to the ground, slamming into it so hard that their bodies leave small craters in the dirt.

But it isn't enough. Dwarves continue to come at us from all sides. Camila tries to disorient them with blinding light, but the dwarves never seem to have much of a plan of action. They move about without care for where they go, only fixating on one of us occasionally.

The air is filled with cackles, screams of pain, and the thuds of dwarves as Clarissa continues her onslaught.

I fold my arms over my chest. I place my palms on my biceps and lower my head. I close my eyes and take a deep breath. My eyes still sting, and my nose still runs with blood. I sense where the others are. We stand close to each other, pinned to the spot by the devilish creatures that surround us. I throw my arms straight out to my sides, turning my forearms and fingers toward the sky. A bubble of energy materializes just beyond Sefryn and Arthur, who stand at either end of our group. The energy bubble expands quickly, detonating like a bomb and tearing through anything in its path. More of the tunnel and mountain collapse. The tallest of the trees in the valley just below are hit like a hurricane, and branches and entire treetops are ripped off their trunks.

There's a moment of quiet. I can still hear the little fuckers rattling along the land. I open my eyes. A small sea of destruction lies beyond me, but it's mostly of dead dwarves.

Sefryn lets out a breath. She looks at me. Her eyes widen, and she hurries over. She puts her hand to my nose and wipes away blood, but more comes out. It's no longer spewing like it first did, but my head feels light. The sting from my nose runs to my eyes. Abigail eases the rain up, but water still falls from the sky.

"Here," Sefryn says, dropping to the ground. She pulls out grass and shapes it into thin wads. Before I realize what she's doing, she shoves two of them up my nostrils. Blood still runs from my nose, but it eases, getting partially soaked up by the grass. More effectively, the makeshift gauze acts like a bandage, hopefully soon stopping the bleeding completely. I am quick to learn that it doesn't.

"The flame," Clarissa says quietly. "Do you think it survived?"

"That doesn't matter right now," Abigail snaps. Clarissa looks hurt for a moment, but then something in her eyes turns to fear.

I don't tell the others my thoughts about it. Buried beneath all the rubble, it has little to no fuel to keep it alive, even if the only fuel it needed was oxygen. A part of me hopes that it truly is eternal, made from some form of Magis I still can't understand, and that it will burn again, like a phoenix coming back to life.

"Do you think they're gone?" Arthur asks. I turn my head to look at him. He barely did anything against the dwarves, and the little he did was to save himself. The rest of us tried getting rid of the small monsters despite what they did to us, so that we could save everyone. The urge to outright kill him boils within me.

The rattling and tapping continue. They're going to be back soon.

"You can't hear them?" Camila asks him, though she doesn't wait for an answer. Evidently, she's also upset that Arthur barely did anything to protect the rest of us. "I swear, if we make it out of this, I might kill you myself."

Arthur tackles Camila to the ground. It was so unexpected that none of us had time to react. Clarissa shrieks and covers her mouth. Sefryn and Abigail look stunned.

I throw my arms down, grab Arthur's jacket, and roll him over, off Camila. I punch him in the face, knocking his head back into the ground. Then, with the help of my Magis, though it's harder to use my version of telekinesis on a person, my streams of energy pull him to his feet. Disregarding my powers, I push him toward the collapsed tunnel. He stumbles back. Arthur throws out his arm, flames burning in his palm.

As if that's a threat.

I hear the scurrying of the dwarves. The little suckers hop down from the tunnel. Arthur is too focused on me to notice them. He throws his arm holding the fire. I run at him and grab his fist, extinguishing the flames. He looks at me, eyes wide in surprise.

Seeing the dwarves near us, readying their weapons, I use as much physical force as I can and shove him back. I use a spurt of energy to amplify my assault. Arthur falls back to the dwarves. While some are squashed under his weight, many of them do their best to catch him. They carry him slightly before letting him drop to the ground. Then they start hacking at him with their various weapons.

"Let's go," I say, turning back to the others. I help Camila stand fully. She looks mostly unharmed. I probably look worse than her. There's a cut above her brow and one on her lip, but those could have been from the cursed dwarves and not from when Arthur tackled her.

Still, anger rises in me, making my head very hot. I turn back and blast fire at the dwarves and Arthur. I hear their screams, and even, to my silent delight, I hear Arthur's roars. He blasts jets of fire from his flailing hands, killing some of the dwarves on him, but there are too many for him to defend himself against.

We run alongside the cliff. It's impossible to know where to go; it looks as if the small creatures are coming from every direction.

Now there are even fewer options. The tunnel is collapsed. The mountain it ran through stands taller and taller the farther we go from the exit.

Up ahead, I see a wave of the gremlin-like creatures charging toward us. I'm ready to make the jump off the cliff, but a terrible shrieking rips through the air, silencing everything else. I look around but can't see anything. The dwarves scurry away, though, as if their lives depend on it.

We turn and run in the opposite direction of where the dwarves went. Arthur is running toward us. There's just a small moment when his eyes are filled with hatred, a desire for revenge, but that look disappears as another shriek cuts through the air. When Arthur gets closer, I can see that his face is severely bruised and that blood leaks from several wounds. He deserves it.

Another shriek, though this one is more of a high-pitched howl. Whatever is near, it isn't something I want to find us.

I point and jerk my head toward the valley of trees. Hoping that the others noticed, I turn sharply, run toward the edge, and jump. As I fall, I realize that the drop is much farther than I thought. My stomach rises to my chest. My lungs feel full of air, and I can't breathe. The ground rushes toward me quickly. I do my best to land, bending my knees to ease the impact. When my feet hit the ground, the jolt of the sudden stop charges up my body. I fall as if I tripped and roll into a tree. I look back. The rest have jumped off too. Most of them make it fine. Camila topples hard when she hits the ground, but she stands quickly.

Realizing I'm still on the ground, I get up. Clarissa falls the hardest. Her leg takes the brunt of the impact. She cries out in pain, sliding slowly down the soft grass. I run over to help her. Arthur does too. He helps her and attempts to pick her up, but before he can stand straight with her body in his arms, he accidentally drops her to the ground. He scrambles to help her back up.

Something darts through the trees but is still out of sight.

Sefryn flicks her hand up, breaking a branch off a tree. She quickly shapes it into a javelin and throws it. I don't think it hits anything.

A low, deep hissing fills my ears. It's quick, erratic, and every time it goes silent, when I hear it again, it sounds louder. I can't tell where the sound is coming from. There's more rustling behind the trees, but I don't think the two noises are from the same thing.

Something crashes into my shoulder. It doesn't hurt. I turn my head quickly and see Arthur stomping toward the trees.

"I'll handle it," he calls out.

Something leaps from the darkness as Arthur moves toward it. It collides with Arthur and tackles him to the floor. A pulse of energy leaves both my palms, directed at the monster. The pulses don't do much, but I manage to distract the monster and turn its attention to me. It crawls over Arthur, leaving two gashes in his torso. I build up energy in both my hands as the monster walks toward me, standing up on its hind legs. A nasty, thin tail brandishes from behind it.

A jolt of terror spasms through me, flickering the energy I hold balled in my hands. This is one of the monsters from my dream—my dream back in Edlyn, where the monsters attacked the castle. If they're anything like what I saw in that nightmare, we're all dead. Most of us worse off.

I let out a yell, building more energy between my hands. When it takes another couple of steps toward me, I push out the ball of crackling energy. It hits the monster in the head, whipping it back and knocking it over. Arthur scurries out of the way, still on the forest floor.

Roots crawl up from beneath the ground, wrapping around the wrists and ankles of the monster. A breeze picks up, wind blowing in a large circle.

The drizzle that had been falling on us turns into frost, small shards of ice and snow raging about in the whirling wind. I walk slowly toward the thrashing monster. Each time it nearly breaks free from one of Sefryn's roots, she wraps another one around it.

Then a bubble of wind surrounds the monster. I can feel the rush of air blow toward me. The writhing monster's violent motions quickly die down to slow, sluggish movements. The circling wind rotates faster around the beast. That's when I realize what's happening.

Clarissa limps toward the monster. I turn to look at her. Her eyes are fixated on it, her fingers locked together and palms facing outward. She twitches her fingers slightly.

Then it's done. The beast has fallen, put down and asphyxiated by the ball that sucked out all its air.

I walk closer to get a good look at it. Other than its hoof-like hands, the anthropoid monster looks as if it could have, at one point, been human. But then I notice something that disgusts me—it's tail. Or what I thought was its tail.

Long, slender, and pointed at the end, what should be a tail is, in fact, a reproductive organ.

I take several steps back very quickly.

Clarissa stumbles next to me, holding her arm. She's bleeding through her torn pants and stands at an odd angle from the fall she endured earlier.

"That was amazing," I breathe out.

She nods in response.

I hate to remind her of the pain she's in, but... "How are you doing?" I ask.

"It hurts," she answers. "Bad."

I breathe out, stifling my sigh. I need to figure out where to go and how to get there as quickly as possible. The monster may be dead, but I know we're still in danger.

The snow continues to fall, heavier now. I look toward the sky, then up at the cliff we jumped down, and then down into the descending wooded landscape.

Arthur turns around and looks back at us. He starts walking over, but Camila steps in front, her arm pointed toward him.

"You don't take a step closer," Camila tells him, her voice dark and hushed. "Stay back."

Before Arthur can react, Camila tenses. We all do.

More of the hissing passes through the trees like a nefarious wind. We hear the crunch of leaves as something passes over them.

Tired of not being able to see well, I shoot out an orb of light into the trees, just to give us a moment to see what lurks behind them.

It's not just another dick-tailed monster. There are at least five. Their deep amber eyes glare at us, and drool spills from their mouths. Clarissa lets out a small cry.

We're fucked. *We're so fucked.*

And we all know it.

Ignoring Camila's warning, Arthur hurries toward us, putting distance between himself and the monsters. No, he hurries past us, leaving as far as he can.

My light goes out, and all we can see now are the faint glows of the eyes staring right at us. If my dream taught me anything, Arthur and I are their food, and the girls are their prize.

Without so much as a roar, one of them lunges. Clarissa cries out, slashing a blade of wind at it. I blast out fire, burning it as hot as I can. Clarissa's wind blades leave a gash in it while my fire makes it roar in pain, stopping it in its tracks.

Its friends don't like that. The other four leap at us. Abigail shouts into the wind. Thunder rumbles overhead. Flashing lightning burns through the sky. A howling wind picks up again. Sefryn pulls branches from the surrounding trees and catches the monsters, but they quickly break free.

I curl my hand into a fist and then extend my fingers quickly, facing my palm to the ground. The water beneath us freezes over. Clarissa and Sefryn keep the beasts at bay as best they can. Camila throws out discs of light, trying to slice through them like she did the werewolf, but these creatures are much stronger.

The ground beneath the monsters freezes too, and the beasts start to slip on the icy ground.

"Run!" I shout, pointing toward the downward slope. I let the ice beneath our feet melt so that we don't slip. I throw out balls of light to show our way and make sure there's nothing else in our path, but I let the orbs die out so that we aren't followed.

I'm tackled to the ground. A snarling fills my ears, and something wet and slimy runs down my face. I roar in agony as my shoulder is torn into. I turn my head back as much as I can. From their hoofed hands, they can release their retracted claws, making the monsters even more deadly.

I'm pinned to the ground. Half my face gets buried in the dirt. I see Camila not far in the distance. She, too, is knocked to the ground. I shout out for her as I see the monster move its tail closer to her.

No. I'm not going to let it happen.

I will not.

I jerk my head away from the monster's bite. It chomps down on the dirt. I can see its ugly eye stare at me as it spits out the mud. I blast fire into its open mouth. It recoils, slicing my shoulder again, and roars into the night. I blast more fire at it, so forcefully that I slide back. I don't wait to see if I've finished it off. I have to save her.

I run toward Camila, who does a good job at blinding the creature enough that it can't quite get to her. Not yet, at least. I scramble, crawling on the ground, fighting with dirt and twigs to gain traction. I fling my arm forward, sending waves of energy at the monster.

I hit it. I also hit Camila. They fly back, Camila catching more airtime than the scaly fiend. I knew I'd get them both, so I didn't send out a surge of energy. What I did was buy Camila and myself some time. Camila recovers quickly, but she doesn't stand up. The monster whips its head around and tries to shake off the shock of the impact.

I quickly get to my feet and run toward them, still slipping on the slick leaves, but I manage to keep from falling. The monster stands up. Taking my chance, I shoot a bullet-sized fireball at its head. It burns straight through, but it unfortunately doesn't kill it.

Camila scrambles back, but only far enough to put some distance between her and the creature. She isn't looking to run; she wants to fight. Clouds move quickly overhead again, and torrential rain pours down. I see flashes of lightning travel across the sky. I stick my arm up, hoping I can attract it.

I do. I feel the power rushing through me mere seconds before it comes down. I'm ready for it, and I aim it at the monster, which mistakes my commotion for meaning I'm its next target. It barely begins to charge at me before the lightning crawls out of my extended hand toward it, frying the monster instantly.

I hear another thunderclap. Abigail is around somewhere. I rush to Camila, check that she's alright, and we make our way through the trees. We both shoot out discs of light, moving them between the trees to light up our way and hopefully distract the monsters.

"What are they?" she asks me.

"I don't know," I say. I briefly tell her about the dream I had back in the castle. She lets out a long breath but doesn't get the chance to say anything. We hear the screams of terror somewhere near us. I can't tell who it is. We glance at each other for a quick moment before breaking into a run.

We're careful to move through the trees and not trip over the roots on the ground. Small acorns fall on us, but I get the feeling something is shooting them, taking aim at our heads. I don't take the time to look.

There are three people in the distance. I can't tell from here, but it must be the girls. Trees are pulled out from their roots and tossed aside, falling onto other trees, sometimes crushing them, sometimes leaning against them. Sefryn, Abigail, and Clarissa are fighting two of the monsters. Abigail whips her hands around, summoning rain and hail. Clarissa pushes the monsters away with blasts of wind, but they keep coming back.

Camila crosses her arms, sticking them forward, and creates a blade of light. Getting the sudden idea, I do the same. I blast mine out at the same time she does. The two crescent-shaped discs of light collide, ten-folding their velocity. The blinding light catches the eye of the two monsters. They look at it curiously before having their necks cleanly sliced off.

The air is silent for a moment, briefly broken by the sound of the two heads hitting the ground and rolling off into the distance.

Then I hear the screaming again. It never came from the girls. It's like a high-pitched shrieking. If I didn't know any better, I would say they were monkeys. I look up to the sky. Shadows jump from the trees, landing out of sight within the other trees.

Camila and I run over to the girls. Sefryn looks the worst. Ripping up whole trees from the ground must have been no easy feat. She did it, though, and she's still standing. She breathes heavily. Sefryn looks into my eyes and nods, letting me know that she's okay.

I notice that Clarissa is moving about fine, but that must be the adrenaline taking effect. Though she appears to walk without pain, she still has a limp, and her leg stands at a slight, odd angle.

Something plops onto the forest floor. I whip my head back. All I see is a small shadow. It isn't one of the dwarves. There's a hint of a curly tail behind it. It shoots back into the trees before I can get a better look.

As soon as it disappears, I feel like I never saw anything at all. I must be going crazy.

Replacing it is another monster, teeth snarling, drool oozing out. Its terrifying amber eyes sweep over everyone around me. I step forward, creating a whip of fire in my hands. I get its attention. I also get the attention of the four other beasts behind it.

How many of these things are there?

Abigail throws her hands in the air, whips them around her head, and throws them back up. The wind comes at us faster and faster. Twigs and branches snap off from the trees. Sefryn has to keep a close eye on them so that nothing hits us, moving any that come our way. The rain falls even harder, soaking us completely. Lightning flashes in the sky; thunderclaps sound overhead, almost in perfect sync with the flashing. Some of the smaller trees collapse, and the even smaller ones fly into the air. I hear a loud, thunderous roar, as if a thousand trains are upon us.

Then the wind dies down around us. The rain stops. It's still loud, but my immediate surroundings are quiet. Beyond our ring of safety, the winds rage on, coupled with streaks of lightning and pellets of water and ice. Abigail has called on a hurricane to get rid of the monsters.

Something lunges through the winds. It tackles Abigail. Camila is fast to react and sends the monster flying, with Clarissa and Sefryn working together to kill it. But it's too late. The time that Abigail was down was enough to ensure that the storm she conjured is no more. Instead, we have moderate rain and no wind. But only one beast remains. The rest either died or ran off.

I no longer hear the shrieking monkeys. If they were ever real, they're not here anymore. Most of the trees around us didn't make it. The land surrounding us looks like a battered, decrepit, and haunted site. Any trees that still stand are mostly jaggedly ripped apart, with only a very few as tall as they once were.

Now Clarissa screams, her voice higher and coarser than before. One of the beasts lunges seemingly from nowhere. While down, Clarissa blasts air from her palms. It's strong enough to send the monster flying.

I shoot out a small spurt of fire toward another monster that enters the clearing. I miss. The monster snatches Clarissa while she's still down and runs, dragging her by her bad leg. The screams that fill the night are the worst yet. The raw and guttural sounds of despair and horror reverberate in my bones. It takes me seconds to snap out of it, to release myself from being petrified, and chase after her.

I can't hear anything else. I can't see anything but what is directly in front of me. The monster is far in the distance. I need to shoot light toward it to make sure that I don't lose it. Even though I can barely see them, I know Clarissa is being battered as she's roughly dragged across the jagged terrain. I have to move quicker.

I leap over fallen tree trunks. I duck under wayward branches. I send fire out into the distance in anger. Why can't I run any faster?

Her screams continue. They're still all I can hear. There are pauses, small, silent spurts that sound like gasps for breath. I don't know how long she can endure it.

Something grabs me, and I'm thrown to the ground, the impact colliding with the force of my run knocks the air from my body. Whatever is on top of me feels impossibly heavy. I exhale, even though there's no oxygen in my lungs. My grunt is silent, and I have to close my eyes to stop my vision from reeling. It hurts. It all hurts.

"Aros! Aros!"

Clarissa's cries force my eyes open. Still dizzy, I punch and claw at the thing on top of me. It has hard skin, covered in something slick, with patchy spots of fur. Then I realize it has its teeth sunk into my right shoulder.

I place my free hand on its head. It feels almost human. There is no snout, no pointed ears. It reeks of sewage water and rotten fish. I press my hand down and pulse out energy, spurt after spurt after spurt. The constant impact to its skull makes it release its grip. Once my other arm is free, I grab its head in both my hands. Luckily, it's still hurting from my energy pulses, so it can't put up much of a fight, but it cries out, clearly in pain.

I grip it hard, my fingers digging into its head. This time, I shoot energy from both my hands. It struggles more. I tighten my grip, roaring with the force of it. Despite the monster's thrashing, I manage to hold it still, my muscles screaming in pain. I send out faster and stronger bursts of energy, quickly crushing its skull. Its amber eyes go still, its face slackens, and its... *tail,* falls to the ground. I take in deep, almost panicked breaths, the oxygen clearing my head.

I shove off the monster and quickly get up. Pain shoots down my right shoulder to the other side and then travels down my body. I shudder; the pain makes it feel like it's impossible to move. I clench my teeth, ignoring the agony as best as I can. With my other arm, I light up the world around me, not caring how bright it is. I want to attract attention if that's what it takes to get to Clarissa and save her. I see nothing.

I run toward where I last saw Clarissa. I don't know where the others are. All I can hope is that they have already saved her. But my heart sinks as I realize I no longer hear those agonizing screams. But the more I run, the more I can hear the snarling, the low growling, and the faint hissing. I run faster.

Throwing my arm out, I send a disc of light. It flies forward, cutting around the trees. Further they soar. Then I see something. The large, dark creature is on all fours. I can't see anything else because its face is low to the ground. I can't see its full tail.

The light dies out. My chest tightens. Somehow, I run faster. When I get close, I shoot out more light, setting my fists ablaze as well.

"AROS!"

The blood-curdling scream makes my entire body want to freeze, but I still charge between the trees. I can't feel my legs. I don't even know if I'm breathing. I don't even feel the teeth marks or gashes that probably cover my body.

*Just a little longer. Hang in there.*

Then everything comes into view. The monster is hovering over Clarissa, forcing itself on her with its disgusting tail with rapid movements. Clarissa turns her head. Her eyes widen as she sees me. Then she starts spasming. Her body violently shakes, her mouth open and spilling out bubbling saliva. Her eyes glaze over, tears of pain forming in them. I throw fire at the beast. It jumps back but doesn't release its tail. I punch out a fist-shaped surge at its head. It knocks it back a bit. I go blind with rage as it still doesn't release Clarissa.

I roar, conjuring up a blade of light that slices clean through its member. It falls to the grass and recoils like a dying snake. The monster howls in pain. I seize the moment and blast fire at it using both arms. I can't feel anything in my right shoulder except the warm blood crawling down it. I alternate between razors of light and searing flames. The beast endures the hits, but it has no time to retaliate.

With another howl into the night, calling out to the wilds, the monster jumps into the air, releasing its claws from both its hooves. I dive out of the way so that it doesn't hit me on its way down.

I spin around, spewing fire everywhere. The monster is distracted, eyeing the flames that threaten to swallow it. I begin building up energy, radiating unseen in my hands. My arms shake as the power of my Magis builds to a point where I may not be able to control it. The monster flails, jumping back and forth to avoid the fires that are quickly spreading. The energy continues to swell, only now becoming visible. It's almost there, a burning, deadly orb of power in my hands. If I do this wrong, it could backfire on me, but I don't care. I will kill this monster even if it kills me in the process.

The monster roars, lifting its head high, calling out into the sky once more. It leaps into the air, clearing the six feet of flames that rage on. With a roar that tears at my throat, I shoot out the orb of raw power, aiming just below the beast. It feels like everything moves in slow motion. With the flick of my finger, the bubble heads straight for its target.

My head explodes with pain as the radiating circle collides with the beast, shredding it apart in a detonation designed to kill instantly. The sudden power released from me throws my mind into excruciating pain that radiates throughout my body.

I've never used that power on anything even a quarter of the size of the monster. I collapse to my knees, catching my breath as quickly as I can. Ignoring the waves of pain threatening to knock me out, I scramble as fast as I can to Clarissa.

I find her sprawled in the same spot, her body bent unnaturally. I don't want to believe what I'm seeing. She doesn't move at all. She doesn't call out my name or scream in terror. Her clothes are torn, exposing most of her skin. One arm lies on the ground, outstretched toward me, in the same direction her face is.

When I get close enough, I can see the lifelessness of her eyes. Tears still trail down her cheeks. She looks like she was strangled—dark bruises cover her neck, with thin, scattered cuts all around it.

But none of that is the worst part.

Her torso is so mangled that it is impossible to tell inside from out, as if the monster couldn't tear into her enough. I try not to look where she wouldn't want me to—but it's impossible not to see. The portion of the lower end of the beast's tail still penetrates her, though it no longer moves. I catch the damage out of the corner of my eye, as if it were the sole target of something viciously wicked.

Mangled.

My vision goes white-hot with rage—

I shout at the stars, curling my hands, my fingernails digging into my palms. Tears spill from my eyes, and I lose control. Fire spews from my fists, blazing across the ground and toward the trees, building up the fires that I set already.

I can't feel the heat. All I can feel is the rage consuming me whole.

Flames erupt from my mouth, lighting up the sky in terrifying colors of red, yellow, and orange.

# CHAPTER 14

## INCUBI

**Aros Caelum Hayes**

*"Aros!"*

The call of my name sounds like the call of a ghost. The echoes of her cries reverberate in my head. The pleas to save her, the hope that she'd see the sun rise, only to be replaced by the look in her eyes when she knew that she was going to die.

When she knew that I would be unable to save her.

When she realized that I had failed her.

"Aros!"

I don't know how long it's been. Everything around me has been burned to a crisp—all the trees and bushes as far as I can see are charred. It takes me a moment to realize that the colors in the sky are from the sun and not the fire that ignited from my body. But the colors aren't even the same. The sunlight shines down, but it's impeded by the smooth, gray clouds tinged with blue.

The ash that falls is half snow. She doesn't place a hand on my shoulder. She looks at me and then to where I stare out. I never let my fire touch Clarissa's body, leaving it as untouched as I could allow.

But her body is torn. Broken. Lifeless. Her once-blonde hair is muddied and tangled.

Sefryn lets out a quiet gasp when she sees the body. She doesn't say anything, but I understand. What could she possibly say? I've had time. I've had the early hours of the morning to process what happened, and I'm still barely able to.

A horrible noise reaches my ears. I look up. Something bubbles inside Clarissa's body. Her stomach writhes, like something is trying to get out. I stand up and walk cautiously toward it, mesmerized by the horror of what I'm seeing. Her skin stretches as something moves inside, pushing up. Her stomach looks like it's about to tear.

It bursts, revealing a shrieking creature barely six inches tall. Blonde hair grows out of its head as the ugly gray of its skin turns light. Then it looks at me, those amber eyes turning a familiar shade of light brown. They're her eyes—Clarissa's.

As it transforms, it looks more and more like Clarissa while still remaining just as small.

The infant creature cries out, but it sounds more human than monster. It sounds like a baby. I take a few more steps toward it. Its hair begins to fall out at an alarming pace, and in just a couple of seconds, the creature is bald. It looks at me curiously, not making a sound.

A sharp-edged branch pierces its heart, and it dies instantly.

I whip my head toward Sefryn. She looks at me slowly, her eyes hiding pain.

"We need to get out of here."

She's right. I know she is. I let her lead me away from Clarissa. There isn't much I can do with her body, other than burn it, but something about doing that feels wrong. Leaving her like this feels worse. Sefryn can tell what I'm thinking, and she presses her hand on my back, urging me forward.

Then I see it—my jacket, tattered and torn into three pieces. I take a step toward it but stop myself. Even if it were intact, the jacket would be useless now.

Sefryn steels herself to do what I can't, and she picks up the pieces of my jacket and gently covers Clarissa. She then softly urges me forward again, leading me away from this cursed place.

The smoke from the recently perished fire rises around us like a fog eerily floating among graves. As we pass through it, it's as if we're seeing the gloomy and dreadful aura that has become part of who we are.

The trees thin out, and a brilliant skyline awaits us, revealing a region of Voltar unlike anything I've seen. But as we near it, I realize that this is the edge of the land, and that the ground ceases to exist. I look out at the vast openness, whatever lies below obscured by a sea of clouds that is probably designed to deter anyone from going over the edge.

Sefryn doesn't let us linger. I don't mind her leading us to wherever it is that we end up. I know she doesn't know where we're going, but she's trying. I can't stop thinking about Clarissa. At this point, I realize that Arthur was right. I can't keep everyone safe.

I don't even know if Camila and Abigail are still alive. Even if they survived the night, are they going to be able to survive the land? The longer we walk, the more the snow falls. I can make fire if needed. Camila and Abigail can't. But maybe Camila's powers of light will help them. I hope they're safe. But beyond that, I pray that they're alive.

Sefryn has to make us new clothing. I didn't notice it last night, but my coat fell apart, my pants were torn, and any garments I wore beneath the cloak have been shredded. I wore them like rags, not noticing and not caring how I looked.

If Sefryn hadn't taken me away from the site, I'd still be there, crouched over and staring at Clarissa, waiting for the worst of Voltar to claim me for itself.

She mutters something about being thankful that there are evergreen trees and plants around. By this time, our feet crunch in the packed snow below, a fresh layer turning the top stark white.

We coast along between the edge of the world and the thicket of trees. The sun looms over us, lighting up the world in a bright haze as it slowly begins to descend.

The longer we go, the more I come back to my senses. I do my best to squash the pain of sorrow and fury that burns inside me. Amidst everything that was going on, and after everything that happened, Sefryn somehow found me. However it happened, I am grateful. Now that I've begun to move on from the tragedies of the night, I wonder what those things were. I dreamt about them, saw their horrors up close. And now I need to know exactly how to kill them, so that when all of this is done, I can return to this place, hunt each one down, and end them forever.

"What were they?" I ask.

Sefryn turns an eye toward me but doesn't reply.

"I feel like it's something you know how to answer," I say, pressing her to say something.

She shakes her head. "You don't want to know, trust me," she tells me in a whisper.

"Probably not," I reply, contemplating it. "But I need to. I dreamt about creatures like that the night before the Trials."

"You dreamt about them?" she asks, turning her head to look at me.

I run my hand through my hair. "Yeah. It wasn't a pleasant dream. But I thought that's all it was."

"And now it feels like it was a premonition."

I shrug. "Sure. But that was, what, a week ago? If it was a premonition, then I need to know how they work."

Sefryn looks away from me. "Unfortunately, I can't answer that. Most of the world doesn't believe in being able to see the future. I don't think it's possible." She sneaks a concerned glance toward me again.

"I know," I say. "But you can tell me what those things were."

Sefryn lets out a breath. "Incubi."

I look at her curiously. "Those didn't look like the incubi that I've read about."

"No, that's because those incubi don't belong here. They belong in Praellen. I don't know how they got here," she says grimly. "But they are rare. Horrible creatures. Not cursed, though. At least, not in the normal sense. These creatures were made on purpose. There's a folktale about Illayana of Gorveight, a Fae-Witch who sought to rule Praellen, but after suffering multiple defeats from the Fae Empress, she receded into darkness for five years. When she finally reemerged, she unleashed monsters that nearly won her the war. But the story goes that she could not control them, that they attacked the women of Praellen, and not only the Empress as she had desired. The Fae Empress had to eradicate them herself. Illayana willingly gave herself up for imprisonment after that. I suppose now that it wasn't just a folktale."

Sefryn stares off for a moment, then continues, "They were twisted, twisted creatures. Illayana created them by giving physical form to the spirits of Earth called incubi by the ordinary. The incubi kill and feast on men, and then rape women to impregnate them. As you saw, they then give birth just hours later, and the female younglings of incubi some-times shapeshift to resemble their mother. All incubi grow to adulthood within three months, and, whether born as a boy or a girl, they always become male. That's why the stories always describe them as being so desperate for women, even going so far as to kidnap women in some versions of the story. Human or Fae women are their only hope for surviving."

My stomach twists. Once again, I learn of another creature that was believed to be a myth.

"That's why you killed it," I say.

"Without hesitation," Sefryn says. "I had never seen one in person, but knowing about them, I couldn't let it grow to adulthood."

It makes sense. These things are born monsters. If I had known, I would have done the same. But there was something about its eyes, the way they looked at me, and all I could see in them was Clarissa and the way she looked at me when she knew it was too late. She knew, just as I understand now, that all the visions we saw were true; one of us was going to die while the rest made it out of Voltar. But if I have anything to do with it, I'm going to change that.

"To make it worse, incubi can only live by consuming the soul of their parent."

I stop walking. That can't be. If it were true, that means Clarissa was removed from existence entirely.

"As a baby, I don't think the incubi feed on the entire soul," Sefryn goes on, sensing my worry. "It's likely that her soul is intact. It was barely alive for a minute."

"How certain are you?" I ask her, though I feel like I don't want to know the answer.

"Not much at all," she says slowly, knowing that I won't like the words. "It is impossible to tell. Incubi haven't been seen in Praellen for nearly a century."

A pain shoots down my arm from my shoulder. My fingers go numb, and my hand feels paralyzed for a second. I let out a hiss of breath, trying to subdue the pain, as if not crying out would help. It probably doesn't, but I feel like it does.

Until my knee gives out, and I collapse into the snow.

My mind is hazy. Everything around me feels like a blur. When I try to concentrate on anything, the pain exploding in my head gets worse. Trying to pick myself up, my left arm gives out too. I can feel the cold burn of the frost on my face, the heat of my body insufficient to melt the snow away. My body begins to shake, my insides turn cold. It feels like the core of my soul is empty, static, lifeless.

Even if I could move, I don't have the will.

If this existence after death means that I'll stay like this forever, a hurting pain that feels numb and the understanding that there is no moving from here, I'd be okay with that. Just so long as it's over.

A soft crunching sound enters my consciousness. I feel my ears as I hear it. I can feel my body, aware that I am not dead. Pretty sure I'm not dead. Despite the aching pain that hits me constantly like a dull axe, there is a thread of bliss in my veins.

Then I hear the crackling. There's a warmth radiating toward me. The wind screams, but I don't feel its touch.

I don't want to open my eyes. Whatever it is, wherever I am, for what feels like the first time in forever, I'm at peace. No, it isn't that good. But everything is okay. It feels like it will all be okay. I drift in and out of mindless, dull dreams. Each time I wake, I keep my eyes closed, but I take deep breaths. I can taste the winter air outside. I don't think my face moves, but I imagine a small smile creeping over my mouth.

*Time to nap again.*

There is a tightness in my chest when I wake. It feels like I might have rough coughs spewing from my mouth if I open it. Sweat leaks from my pores, making me feel damp. I shift around, but it's hard to move.

"Sorry about that."

I jolt awake, my eyes open, staring straight up, still unaware.

Thick woven wood makes up the sky, looking almost like straw. I see the shadow of sputtering flames dance across the wood. I move my head slightly, trying to look outward. Sefryn crawls over to me. I look down at my body. I'm wrapped in various foliage threaded together. I push outward a bit.

"Oh, you can definitely break those if you want," Sefryn says. "It's probably safe now. I had to do something, though, when you started having seizures."

I close my eyes and swallow a groan.

"Where are we?"

Sefryn sighs but gives me a genuine smile. She sits next to me, closer to my head. "We're still in Voltar," she tells me. "Not far from where you collapsed."

It comes back to me. All of it. Clarissa, the incubi, the story Sefryn told me about them. When I fell to the ground, I was in so much pain that I was almost hoping that it would have been my end.

"I built this out of what I could," she says.

I'm lying on my back, and I look around as best as I can. We're inside a hut, and I marvel at how sturdy it looks, despite being made purely from branches melded together.

"After you fell, it looked like you were going to die. I couldn't move you. When you calmed down, I was able to put this up around us. While you were blacked out, you had more seizures, but none as violent as the first. I had to walk for almost an hour to find the plants I needed to help save you. I almost got lost on my way back since everything turned white again after the snowstorm. I started the small fire, which wasn't easy, and hoped for the best."

Silence falls between us. After a while, even though I know she isn't looking for it, I say, "Thank you."

Sefryn smiles. She takes in a breath. "I care about you, Aros. I wasn't about to let anything happen to you. You would have done the same for any of us."

I nod, our eyes meeting for a fleeting moment.

I look down at my body again. Beneath the restraints, there is a blanket of leaves, similar to the coat she made me, keeping me snug inside it. And I realize that I'm completely naked underneath.

"Hey, uh, did you—?"

"Only for a moment," she quickly answers. "During your first seizure, you... burned everything that you were wearing. Once you calmed down and I enclosed you in this tent, I made you a blanket."

She looks around awkwardly. There's just a tinge of blush on her cheeks. It sounds like I was naked for longer than a moment, but I don't mention that.

"To say I didn't see anything would be a lie. But it was only for a few seconds!" She chances a quick look at me. "I swear, I only did what I had to do to make sure you'd survive."

I don't say anything. Part of me is amused.

"Please don't go all 'Arthur' on me."

A laugh escapes from my mouth, quickly choked down by coughs. I catch her eye, and we burst out laughing again. It may hurt, but I need this really badly. It takes several minutes for the laughter to die out. But then everything comes back, dragging me back into somber silence once more.

"Let me grab you some food and water," she says, crawling over near the fire. The hut she built is maybe six feet tall at its highest point, giving little overhead room for standing, even for someone of her size. Camila would also feel cramped inside here.

"How long was I out for?" I ask her. The dread of her answer settles in.

She turns back to look at me, a small cup of leaves, just like she made before, in her hands. Then I notice the wooden bucket and the basket filled with fruit. There's also some form of dead animal that she's been cooking. I don't know how I didn't smell it earlier.

If she collected all of that...

"Six days," she answers.

I stare back up at the ceiling. So much can happen in six days, especially in Voltar. For all I know, she and I are the last ones here.

"We can't stay here," I tell her. "We need to go."

She shakes her head.

"No, you need to heal," she says. "Your shoulder took a bad bite from the looks of it, and whatever you did to kill that monster that got Clarissa, I think it weakened you a lot."

I don't say anything.

"You might not want to admit it, and that's okay." She comes back over with water. "But you have to take it easy. We're safe here for now.

When you're better, we can get moving again."

Sefryn reveals a radiant orange berry that was in her hand. She squeezes the juice out of it and into the cup of water, then hands it to me.

"Drink this. It's going to help you heal faster. I couldn't force it down you earlier, but now that you're awake, you can take it."

"What is it?" I ask.

"Lorigh berries," she answers. "I thought that these existed only in Praellen, but I found some while I was looking for water. They are very rare, even in my realm. But they are one of the most powerful healing elements in the world. Ten of these hold enough healing fluids to bring a hippogriff back to life. The plant produces just one berry at a time, and they never grow right next to each other."

I drink all the water from the cup. There is a hint of a citrus taste, so soft that it is as if the water had been passed through the scent of an orange. Sefryn places three red apples by me so that I can grab them easily if I want.

"How come there seem to be so many things from your realm here?"

Sefryn shakes her head. "I wish I knew. I can only guess, but each time I do, the theories I think of are more unbelievable than the last."

"Maybe there's a connection between here and Praellen."

"Maybe." Sefryn looks around. She sighs at the fire, which looks like it is slowly dying out. Peeking outside, all I can see is snow. The trees in the immediate vicinity are bare. Sefryn probably had to use all their leaves for everything she made me. "I'm going to need to replenish the water. Hopefully I'll find more of those berries," she tells me. Sefryn begins to crawl to the front of the hut.

"You know the others could already have found the Ashen Pit," I call out. "We might be the last ones."

"I don't think so," Sefryn says with a shrug. "It's just a feeling I have, though."

She looks at me, waiting for an answer.

"You didn't have to save me," I tell her. "Even now, you can head off, finish the Trials, and get back home."

Sefryn crawls back to me. She looks into my eyes for half a second and kisses me on the forehead. She snaps the leafy ropes around me so that I can move freely.

"I'm not leaving you."

# CHAPTER 15

## THE CALL OF THE ASHEN PIT

**Aros Caelum Hayes**

Sefryn doesn't come back for several hours. Deep down, I wonder if she took my advice and went off to complete the Trials. I wouldn't blame her. That way, at least one of us will have made it. But I know in my heart she hasn't done that.

She carries in more water in a bucket she made. Sefryn holds up three of those orange berries. When she puts down everything in her arms, she immediately makes me another cup of water with the juice of the berry inside it. I drink it right as she hands it to me. While she was gone, I could still feel the pain as my body healed, but I wasn't blinded by it.

"How are you feeling?" she asks me. There's been something different about her. All her movements have been graceful and tender, but there's part of her that feels tense. Knowing her, she's probably keeping alert in case anything comes after us. And maybe she's worried about me.

The hut she made fully protects us from the weather, except for the bits of snow that are billowed into the front of the hut by the raging wind outside. I can see the snow continue to pile up. Sefryn's constant runs to get more food or water make a path through the snow, which is otherwise half a foot tall.

"I'm better," I tell her. "Thanks to you."

Sefryn kindles some new scraps of wood, reigniting the fire.

"I can probably help with that," I tell her. I sit up slightly, supporting most of my upper body with my forearms.

"I know, but I want you to get more rest," she says, looking over at me. "I think in two to three days you'll be back to normal. And I mean *normal*, with all your strength and energy back."

Something warms in my chest. I don't know if it's the idea I'll have all my strength back soon or if it's from the heat of the fire as it comes my way.

"That soon, really?" I ask her. I didn't think much of it, but I thought I would be down for the remainder of the Trials. Surviving the Trials now is something I've been unsure about.

"Yeah, that soon," she says. "And then we can be out of here, find the others hopefully, and leave Voltar." Sefryn takes a deep breath. "I hope I never have to come back to this place."

I nod my head, getting lost in thought. I feel like I let out the rawest part of my emotions regarding Clarissa. Those emotions are still here, but they are no longer a volatile, uncontrollable living thing inside me. Sefryn and I haven't talked about it since she told me about the incubi. I don't know how she's dealing with it. She may not have been there when it all went down, but she saw the aftermath. I just can't bring myself to ask her about it.

"How's it out there?" I ask.

"Just a lot of snow," Sefryn tells me. But she knows what I meant, so she adds, "But otherwise there's nothing." She pauses for a moment. "The incubi are probably the most fearsome things out here. They'd kill anything that isn't their goal. So any other monsters that have been in this area are either dead or have fled."

I nod, understanding why the dwarves had suddenly run away.

"So no sign of the incubi either, then?"

"No. I don't know how many people are left, but the incubi probably found enough women to do what they came for."

A silence of a thousand words falls between us. Neither of us is comfortable enough to open the chest of how we feel about that night, but I know we both would like to talk about it. At the same time, I'd be perfectly content to never mention it again.

Sefryn moves closer to me. She sits, leaning against the smooth wall of woven twigs and branches. I sit up slowly, leaning too. My body feels as if it hasn't moved in a week, which is unfortunately accurate. The soreness and pain I feel from moving, even just slightly, feels almost as unbearable as I felt after Sefryn found me.

"Still hurts?" she asks. She knows I do. But once the pain of creaking muscles subsides, I feel relaxed again.

"Just a bit, but I feel better and better with each hour."

I think I hear Sefryn give me a soft reply, but I can't make out what she says. My eyes feel heavy. The effort it took me to sit up exhausted me. I take deep breaths. I can hear Sefryn breathing next to me; I can hear the crackling of the fire and the whistles of the wind.

And now I am outside, standing in the snow. The blizzard rages on around me, but I am inside a bubble, safe from the elements. I don't even feel cold.

Emerging from beyond the bubble, the crease unfolding as he enters, like there's a break in the physical reality of existence, Palvadore steps in. He looks down on me, his eyes all-knowing and disapproving. So far, out of the three, he's the only one that I don't like.

"You should be dead."

I don't flinch. My eyes don't move. I hold my gaze, staring into his terrifying amber eyes.

"I'm not," I reply after some thought.

"I see." He ruffles his feathers.

I look around. Of course, none of this is real. I'm probably just passed out right now, doing the same thing I've done for the past several days.

"Why would you say something like that?" I ask.

The Avian of the South lowers his head to look at me more closely.

"It was a compliment of sorts."

I don't say anything.

"You should be dead," he repeats, but this time he continues to speak. "The incubi are incredible hunters. They can sense a woman up to nearly a kilometer away. But their senses aren't nearly as great as their ability to home in on fear. Their very presence near humans can cause fear to blossom, bringing it out. They can cause hallucinations and paralyze their prey. Those with weaker minds are particularly susceptible, and the closer they are to a weak-minded individual, the worse that person's fear will stink."

"So how did they find us?" I bite my tongue. I know the answer, and he knows I know.

"Do you even have to ask?" he says, as if I'm slow.

When I don't say anything, he goes on, "Even if the one scared of himself makes it through the Trials, the Ashen Pit would never pick him."

Palvadore isn't the politest person, or creature, but I like him more now. I'm also angrier with Arthur, but maybe more so at myself. His presence really did put us in danger. I should have killed him. There were too many chances to do so. And because I didn't, Clarissa is dead.

"Don't do that," Palvadore says, eyeing me intently, knowing I blame myself. "The incubi traveled across all of Voltar. They surely met others too."

"What about my friends?"

The word still feels alien to me.

"I'll show you," Palvadore says, reaching his giant wing out. I squint as the feathers cover my eyes. When I open them, I am brought back to that night. I can see it all immediately—the placement of the trees, the descending hill, and me running off after Clarissa.

The feeling is odd. Everything around me seems so real, like I am right back there, yet there I go, running off into the woods.

Abigail and Camila shout for me. They start to run, but two more of the incubi jump in front of them. Then Clarissa's screams pierce the air. The incubi turn to look and start running toward the sound of fear.

Instead of running away and saving themselves, Abigail and Camila chase after the beasts. Camila lights up the world around them. Streams of light chase the monsters. Abigail calls down lightning. It catches the attention of the incubi, who stop in their tracks. Momentarily distracted, they turn back to face Camila and Abigail.

While I was running, I never noticed the lightning. I wonder how close it was to me. I wonder how close the incubi got.

Camila grabs one of the monsters with a whip of light. The incubus screams into the air, its flesh burning as the whip sears through it. Abigail is quick to summon another lightning strike, this one lasting seconds, blazing white and blue as it fries the monster.

The other incubus tries to run away, but Camila whips her hand, commanding her leash to grab it. The monster roars, but seeing what happened to its friend, it fights through the pain of its flesh being roasted and lunges at Camila. It tackles her to the ground. Abigail pulls chunks of hail from the sky, launching them at the monster. It rears its head. Camila lets out a bright flash that blinds it, causing it to take several steps backward.

Abigail helps Camila scramble to her feet. I can see it in their eyes now—fiery determination replacing fear.

The incubus notices. It charges at them, and the two of them run. Camila blasts discs of light toward it, but they all miss, cutting through trees instead.

I'm not sure how long they run. I don't even know how they avoid running into anything. It's so dark. But then the sky lights up. At first, I think it's something the girls did, but it can't be. It's too far away.

My stomach drops as I realize that the light in the sky is because of me, meaning by this point, Clarissa has already died.

The incubus looks up too. Her senses returning, Abigail strikes it down. The thunderclap is so loud it feels as if the force of the sound could knock the trees over. The incubus drops dead.

And I am returned to the dome enclosing me, protecting me from the outside.

I blink. A lot. Abigail and Camila are alive.

And from what I just saw, those chicks are total badasses.

It's going to break my heart when I have to tell them what happened. But I also can't help but feel pride and warmth in my heart. Not only are they alive, but they also saved me. I don't know if I would have been able to fight off three incubi and the one that got Clarissa.

And then that pride is replaced with cold determination. Arthur wasn't around. He wasn't there. He ran off the first chance he got. He's alive. I know he is. But he won't stay that way for long.

I'm going to kill him.

"Do not go on a detour," the owl says. I get the idea he can read my mind. At the very least, he can sense how I feel. "The Ashen Pit is growing impatient. If it doesn't earn its Ash Lords soon, it will seek to end the Trials immediately."

"Meaning it's going to kill us all?"

Palvadore nods.

"So, no one has made it yet, then?"

There is a pause. "You and Sefryn *could be* considered to be the closest, but others are catching up."

Though I am not completely sure I understand what he means by that, I let it go.

"But how can anyone get here? That tunnel collapsed."

Palvadore chuckles. "The tunnel from the peak of Voltar leads into this place, a place that is a separate realm. The tunnel cannot be destroyed."

"Wait, we're in a different realm? Then where am I?"

"Voltar," he answers simply. "Voltar, as you know it, is a gateway to the *realm* of Voltar." I don't get the chance to tell him that what he said doesn't make sense. "That's why the laws of this land are so vastly different from Arteyva."

"How big is this realm?" I don't have time or the patience to argue or disbelieve what the stern owl tells me.

"It is constantly expanding and contracting," he says. "But like Arteyva, the core of its Magis is shifting. The incubi and other beasts just as terrible may very well find a way out of here. That is why I keep visiting you. That is why the others are watching you."

"So, you don't visit the others?" It wasn't really a question.

Palvadore waits a beat before answering, "No. Kreavlos told me that it would be enough to speak with you." He pauses again. "I'm not sure if I've made it clear enough, so I'm going to lay it out plainly. The Ash Trials must come to an end swiftly. The Ashen Pit is already influencing the Trials. The tunnel from Voltar into this realm? I said it cannot be destroyed, and that is because the Ashen Pit will not allow it. In fact, before that night ended, a new tunnel had already been carved." Another pause, this time the giant owl lowers his head even more, his face closer to mine. "Those incubi? Harmless peasants compared to what the Ashen Pit can bring into existence."

"Don't worry, I won't go hunting down Arthur," I tell him. "Not until after the Trials."

"I would expect you to do so eventually," Palvadore says. "As the Ashen Pit knew from the moment he entered Voltar, before the Trials even started, Arthur would under no circumstances become an Ash Lord. When you all sat by the Eternal Flame at midnight, Arthur was given no visions. He was in a trance, like the rest of you, but has no memory of anything that occurred during that time. Deep down, even

Arthur knows it himself."

And that was why Arthur never told us the clue he got from the Eternal Flame, why he was so silent when he first woke. He never had a clue to begin with. Hearing us tell each other about what we saw probably made him realize that he would never make it. He was no longer jealous of just me; he was jealous of everyone.

I used to feel bad for the guy. But knowing his insecurity and fear made it easy for the incubi to find us—well, I need to find a way to ensure Arthur meets the same fate Clarissa did. Letting him live for so long, how does that now reflect on me?

"Good luck," the Avian says, backing away toward the blizzard outside the bubble dome. "Don't die."

I wake up immediately and find my head resting on Sefryn's lap. Her fingertips are partially in my hair. She's sitting cross-legged. I stick my neck into the air, craning my head back so I can look at her. She's sleeping. Fuck, even with the cuts she has on her face, her hair tangled and dirty, and the bruises that change the fair color of her skin, she's still just so freaking beautiful.

Sefryn opens her eyes. I flinch, looking away quickly. I don't know why, but I sit up.

"I'm sorry," I say, breathless from my quick reaction. "I must have passed out."

Sefryn stares at me, and I can tell she's trying to put together what's happening.

"I know," she says. "And I thought you—it—was...cute."

I let a moment pass between us. I wonder if I should tell her about what happens in my dreams, when the Aeturnous Kitisma visit me. I've only met three, but surely there are more.

I want to tell her. But something holds me back.

"You think I'm cute?" I blurt out, dissipating my other thoughts.

Sefryn lets out a small laugh. "I think you're much more than that."

I turn my head to look at her. She hasn't looked away. Our eyes meet. Something swells inside me. My heart beats faster. I move my face closer to hers, unsure if this is happening or if the connection I feel is just in my head. All those thoughts I had about this moment, the times I imagined how it would be—how she would smell, how she would feel against my lips, how she would taste—those thoughts rise to the front of my mind, begging for answers.

After the last twenty-four hours, there shouldn't be any doubt in my mind about how she feels about me. With all the times she's flirted, thrown hints, and purposefully met my gaze—I should know better than this. I feel like a teenager, shaking because he's about to expose all his feelings, completely bare, to his first love. But I never felt that way before. I have never felt *this* way.

Sefryn goes for it, pressing her lips against mine, making it the softest, firmest, and sweetest kiss I've ever had. Beyond the scent of stale sweat, I can smell the frozen and dry pine on her—an undertone of amber and smoky earth. Her breath carries the citrusy taste of those berries, and I pull her in closer, parting her lips so I can get more. She lets me roll my tongue around. I forget to breathe while I try to silence all sounds but hers, listening intently so that I learn what she likes most.

I touch her cheek with my fingertips, drag them down her face, and gently place my hand around her neck before moving it to her hair, tugging slightly as I run my fingers through it.

Even in needing to catch our breaths, we don't stop. The blanket of leaves covering me falls a bit, exposing my upper body. She places her hand on my chest. I move my hand back to her chin, tilting it up before barely pulling away to meet her eyes.

Her gray eyes burn bright.

The sound of crackling lightning cuts through the moment, just as intense as the fire in her gaze.

We sit there, our mouths still so close that we share breaths. The storm rages on outside, thunder rumbling nonstop. But I don't hear any rain.

"I'm going to check," Sefryn says, looking away and getting up. She goes outside.

I sit there for a moment, calming my breathing. I thought that was going to go much further. I was ready for it. Still am.

"Aros, look at this," Sefryn calls to me, still looking outside. I can hardly see her in the dim light, but there is no longer a blizzard out there.

I get up, rearranging the blanket Sefryn made me so that I can cover myself properly. The morning is early. The outside air is biting. My bare feet get the worst of it. But luckily, the freezing temperatures of earlier have subsided.

I stand next to Sefryn, looking out beyond the hut she made. Way out in the distance, I can see swirling clouds in the sky, with one large eye in the midst of them all, looking like a black hole until bolts of lightning strike from within.

"That's where the Ashen Pit must be," she says.

"Yeah. Follow the eye of the storms," I chant, echoing the words Abigail said when she woke from her Eternal Flame visions.

"We should get going," Sefryn says. "I have a feeling that the Ashen Pit is calling for the Trials to end."

I don't think she knows just how right she is.

Turning to look at her, I nod, knowing that our moment, however brief, would be the last until we make it out of here. In those minutes, it felt like I was in another world, another realm, and that all the worries and threats of the Trials were behind us.

I've been forced back into the reality of the Ashen Pit's desires.

# CHAPTER 16

## SAINTS OF QUIRLEN

**Aros Caelum Hayes**

"I need to make you some proper clothes," Sefryn tells me. "But I don't think it's a good idea to wait for me to find more trees that I can use. We should get moving as soon as we can."

I nod and slowly unwrap the blanket from my body.

"Turn around!" Sefryn says, turning around herself.

For some reason, I hadn't thought of that.

I obey and hold out the blanket behind me, lighting a new fire with my free hand. When Sefryn takes it, I spin the flames around me, mostly to provide warmth. It takes her longer than I expect, but I don't say anything, realizing that what she's doing probably takes others much longer to do. Weaving together the brittle leaves, grass, and sticks that make up the blanket must be difficult, especially since the older the leaves get, the more they threaten to crumble.

When she's done, Sefryn asks me to put out the fire around me and places the coat over my shoulders. She used part of the hut material to make the jacket more comfortable. I can sense how close she gets to me, but I don't think she thinks anything of it. I push down those feelings, the desire and need for her, telling myself that there will be plenty of time once the Trials end.

"Do you feel ready?" she asks me.

I nod. The worst part will be getting used to walking again. When I turn around, I find that she's made me pants and shoes too. Sefryn gives me another cup of that berry water and then turns around, staring out of the hut and giving me my privacy.

When I am dressed, she leads me out into the open land. When we're far enough away, she snaps her fingers, and the woven, wicker-like material of the hut crumbles. I turn back. The two fires that were inside start burning through the flora. With a smirk, I snap my fingers too, and the fires burst into something fiercer, eating through what served as our temporary haven.

The storms in the distance seem so far away, but I feel like we're so close. So, so close. The crisp air no longer feels solely like a frosty winter; now it has that scent of freedom to it and the taste of victory.

Even without the blizzard, the land here is monotonous and never-changing. The ground is bare except for the snow that is still piled all over the landscape. Though my legs feel normal again, our path feels more exhausting than if we were climbing a mountain.

We walk for hours, not saying much. I just wish we could skip this part and get to the end. Get to where I know for sure Abigail and Camila are alive. They may have survived the night of the incubi, but it's been a week since, and Voltar is too dangerous to be certain of anything.

I don't even know how Sefryn and I survived the week. If anything threatening happened, Sefryn not only saved me but has kept quiet about it. Honestly, if anything did happen, I would want her to tell me. But I'd also feel bad that I couldn't help, which may be why she hasn't said anything, if there is anything to say.

There's a moment when I wish we could just fly. And then, with a pang of guilt and sorrow, I remember that Clarissa would probably have discovered that she had that kind of power. She could have been so amazing.

She was so amazing.

But that sadness feels numb. The guilt tears at my soul worse than what I think the Ashen Pit will actually do to it. Even so, the emotions I feel are lost and buried as if the reason for their existence happened decades ago, like that whole night is just a memory of a distant past.

I turn my head back. Other than our footprints in the remaining snow, nothing about the scenery behind us is different from where we're heading. Well, nothing but the footprints and the storming clouds still far out in the distance. And I know what's there.

Just as I am about to say something, it feels as if I walk through a thin wall. The sensation is like I've entered a pool; I can feel the pressure of the water, but I can still walk right through. Without so much as a ripple, the whole landscape changes. I can see the peak of Voltar again, off to the side. We are so close to the mountain face, but unlike when we climbed it, there doesn't seem to be a path up.

Any snow that was around us is mostly gone. A few patches remain, but the ground is mostly a dark green of short grass.

"What just happened?" Sefryn asks. She looks around, bewildered, a frantic worry in her eyes.

"It's Voltar," I say quietly. "It's changing."

Sefryn eyes me, her look knowing. Knowing that I'm not letting on as much as I know.

"I don't think anyone can ever fully understand this place. So, it must be Voltar, just doing its thing," I say, trying to explain away why I seem to know so much, but wincing at my choice of words.

Sefryn doesn't respond. She looks around, but her eyes are calmer.

"So, we keep going." She states it, but it also feels almost like a question.

I nod, indicating the storm clouds in the distance. Those don't seem to have come any closer, but I know we must be nearing them. As we move forward, there is another tug at my conscience. Abigail and Camila are probably still in the previous portion of Voltar. I can't tell if my belief that they are still okay is justified or just a hope clouding any sense of reality.

We walk alongside the mountain cliff, the early winter ambiance prevailing even now. I keep having this sense that the Ashen Pit is calling everyone closer together. The Trials are, in a simple word, a game. Winning is making it through the Trials, but some think that winning means they must be one of the next Ash Lords. I don't blame them. If I made it through the Trials and didn't become an Ash Lord, I'd feel like I had lost.

It isn't enough to just survive. You have to be chosen to truly win.

Guilt passes through me. Abigail doesn't care about being an Ash Lord. Clarissa didn't either, not after she saw what the Trials were like. All she wanted to do was make it through to the end.

I hear crackling in the distance, the splitting of wood shards as they burn in a fire. With how close we walk by the cliff wall and the way it rounds out of sight, I can't immediately spot where the fire is. It isn't long before we see its source.

Two figures sit by it. I tense up. It could be Chase. Having just one other by his side isn't out of the question, since he's proven that he doesn't care about killing those who follow him if they seem too weak.

One of the heads turns, noticing our approach. It isn't Chase. I can see him clearly now. Elder stands, his tall figure a reassuring sight. He has a scar across his right eye now, but his eye otherwise seems fine. He and the other walk toward us.

"Aros," he says with a smile as we approach, his arms out, ready for a hug. I hug him quickly. I barely know him, but even when we first met, he felt like someone I could trust. He gives Sefryn a hug too. The other person walks up to us. She's frail-looking, with long and thin hair. Her brown eyes suit her, just like Elder's suit him, but her eyes, skin, and hair are all several shades lighter than Elder's.

"Hi," she says, putting her hand up shyly. Her slender arm looks fragile.

"Hi, I'm Aros," I say, smiling and extending my hand.

"Oh, I...uh...I know who you are," she says. I keep my arm out. She notices it and shakes it awkwardly. "S—sorry, I didn't see you, um—" She coughs into her hand. She's probably still in her late teens by how young she looks. But Voltar's done her dirty. While Elder has his new scar, this girl looks like she's taken several beatings. Her face is bruised, her arm is splotchy with contusions, and her eyes don't seem to open fully.

"I didn't get your name," I tell her politely, retracting my hand from the overly long greeting.

She giggles at the ground. "Sorry. I—I'm V—Veronica."

"I'm Sefryn," Sefryn tells her, putting herself between me and Veronica. She takes Veronica's hand warmly into hers, and Sefryn keeps eye contact with her.

"Come, we were just about to eat," Elder says stately, beckoning toward their fire. I nod, and we follow him.

"Your faces," he says, waving his hand over. I feel a tightening of my skin, a warmth, like I'm oozing blood, and then a wave of freshness overcomes me.

I look at Sefryn; the cuts she sustained on her face are completely gone.

I look back at Elder. He shrugs. "Compliments of being a Rogvey."

Yeah, but why doesn't he help Veronica or himself?

Elder knows what I'm thinking and answers, "I like to keep this as a reminder." He points to his scar. "Chase ambushed us one night, just after we narrowly escaped some terrifying monsters." Elder swallows. We reach his fire. Veronica sits down, looking at the ground. "He killed them all. Only Veronica and I escaped, but not without harm." He uses his hand to lightly indicate the scar across his face again.

"I keep mine too," Veronica says, not stuttering, but I can see her body shake. "When I see Chase again, I will kill him with my own two hands. But when we're out of here, I think I might want to do away with them."

Elder and I exchange glances. He indicates to take a seat. I do, along with Sefryn. The grass beneath us is soft. The fire is warm, and the early night feels peaceful. Elder and Veronica must have been on this side of Voltar for a while—they've even managed to find and cook meat.

Eating feels like the most satisfying thing I've done. Sefryn did great at keeping us fed, but being so used to an omnivore diet, lacking the carnivore part hasn't been easy.

"I don't mean to touch upon what could be a delicate subject," Elder starts, the tone in his voice sounding like it belongs to a much older person. "But what of the others?"

I let out a sigh. "One of us didn't make it," I say. "Incubi attacked us in the middle of the night, shortly after we found the Eternal Flame."

Elder looks down. "I am very sorry to hear that."

I let the moment sit in silence.

"Of course, there's Arthur, who just ran away."

"Ran away?" Elder asks.

"Yeah," Sefryn interjects. "When we were attacked by the incubi, he ran away. Haven't seen him since."

Elder glances at me. "It doesn't matter, though," I say. "After he attacked one of our own, I was never going to let him go on with us."

"That doesn't surprise me," Elder says. "Despite everything I've said about not killing each other, he's probably better off dead."

"With any luck, the incubi tore him to shreds." Sefryn stares into the fire as she speaks. She kept her composure the whole time she was with me, remained strong while I could barely stay conscious. I don't yet know how strong her feelings for me are. I can see us spending the rest of our lives together, facing whatever dangers threaten the world as Ash Lords. Kreavlos always said it, and now I know he was right. I don't belong on Earth. I belong in Arteyva.

I just need to make sure that the rest of us survive this.

"We never saw any incubi," Elder says. "But Chase was ruthless."

"It was barely days ago," Veronica states. "And he murdered my fiancé, Armantha."

"He'll get what's coming to him," I say.

Elder nods. "I wanted to kill him. But I wanted to be better than that. For my son."

"Peter, yeah?"

"Yes."

"To be honest, I can barely believe he is your son," I tell him. "I thought he was in his early twenties. You barely look even thirty."

He lets out a laugh.

"My son was born when I was fifteen. I'm thirty-four now. His mother, Isabella, died many years back," Elder says, his voice even. "She was the love of my life, and I hers. We took things a tad fast. But that's the way of life in Quirlen."

Quirlen is a small country made up of islands. The land is technically ruled by the Gorgrein kingdom, but they pay little attention to it. As such, most of the people in Quirlen are closed off from the rest of the world.

"I haven't heard much about Quirlen," Sefryn says.

"Honestly, I didn't know there was a worse place in the world until I came here," Elder laughs. "My son and I escaped the islands when he was five, a year after Isabella died. We then fended for ourselves before moving east to Soulstice, where we hoped to live a better life."

"How did Isabella die?"

I shoot Sefryn a look. I want to know, but I don't have the nerve to ask so directly.

"The Gorgreins killed her when there were rumors that she was a messenger for one of the Saints."

"What are the Saints?" I ask.

Elder stokes the fire. "They're just stories about immortal creatures that watch over our world. I didn't wholly believe they were real until I saw the Azure Fox." He pauses for a moment. "But even still, I'm not too sure. The Saint that watches over our islands is said to be a sea creature, a dolphin with three tails. The Oceanic Knight, Sidoborre."

I shake my head slightly, frowning at my lack of knowledge. I've never heard of Sidoborre, but after meeting Palvadore, alongside Kreavlos and Grisla, I know the Oceanic Knight must be real too.

"We call the creatures Saints, and every now and then, one of our people is chosen to be a messenger between the immortal and mortal worlds."

"And Gorgreins are terrified of the immortal and supernatural powers," I say, remembering how they fear Voltar and the power it supposedly gives Edlyn.

Elder nods once. "Right. When those rumors spread across the seas, they came for her."

"So how did you escape?" Sefryn asks. "How did you leave the islands?"

"It is rare that anyone born in Quirlen has Magis. When I was young and showed that I had power, my parents taught me to hide it. But I always did what I could to defend my people whenever the Gorgreins came. I wasn't strong enough to save Isabella." Elder looks up at the sky. The evening is upon us. I can see hints of the first stars glowing in the sky. "She pleaded with me not to expose myself. I listened to her. But it cost her her life. After that, I knew I had to do more. I made a boat in the middle of the night and set course for Ibari."

He pauses for a moment, catching his breath.

"The trip almost killed us, but after fourteen days of sailing, we made it. Adjusting to life where we could live openly was difficult at first, and I was never able to trust anyone, so for years we kept to ourselves. But we were safe. For a little while. Gorgreins started making landfall. Their attacks were few but well-powered. I helped defend our coastal town and became highly respected by everyone. I worked with our leadership to safeguard our people from outside threats.

"Peter wanted more from life. He kept asking me to let us leave that place and move north to Edlyn, where the people with Magis lived and prospered, and the arts of Rogvey were respected. After Edlyn made a deal and said they'd protect Ibari, I knew it was time to move for my son and let him start living the life he had always dreamed of."

"He did seem very happy," I say. "I only met him that one time, but it was clear that he loved what he was doing."

Elder smiles. "I know. I've never seen him happier. In fact, he was so happy that he didn't complain when I decided to enter the Trials. He just made me promise that I'd make it back."

We let the dusk go quiet between us, hearing only the sound of the fire, the calls of the birds, and our calm breaths as we take our chance to feel safe. I feel much stronger than I did even this morning. But I still feel the fatigue of walking all day.

"Did you guys see anything in the Eternal Flame?" Sefryn asks.

They don't answer immediately.

"We never found the Eternal Flame," Veronica says quietly.

"What do you mean? Then how did you get here?"

Elder answers, "We walked through the tunnel at the peak of Voltar. But when we came out the other side, it looked like something horrible had happened. Everything was in ruins. I'm surprised that the tunnel wasn't blocked off."

"It was that night when Chase emerged from the tunnels," Veronica says.

That was just a few days ago. It is likely that we were the only group that dealt with the incubi. The others hadn't yet made it to this part of the realm, which was a good thing, at least in avoiding the incubi.

"In the middle of our escape, after Chase killed the others, it felt like we traveled into a different world. Chase couldn't follow us through, so far as I can tell. Whatever it was that brought us here, I am grateful for it."

"Those storm clouds always seemed odd," Veronica says. I get the idea she's trying to change the subject.

"That's where the Ashen Pit is," I say. "When we got to the Eternal Flame, we had visions, clues, that showed us where we were supposed to head."

Elder shuffles slightly. "Out of curiosity, I would have eventually moved toward the storms. But I didn't think the Ashen Pit would lie there."

"Do you think it's possible that nobody else got clues from the Eternal Flame?" Sefryn asks. "What if we are the only ones who know where to go?"

"Camila and Abigail know too," I remind her. "But I get it. I don't think anyone else will know where to go."

"Except for me and my new friends."

I stand quickly and turn slightly. Arthur walks toward us. Chase walks by him, while his bald companion, the one who wasn't killed by Elder, walks behind them, pulling something. I don't know where the bald man got it from, but he has a sword strapped to his back. When they are close enough, I realize that they have Camila and Abigail trapped, wrapped in some kind of rope. Their arms and legs are tied together while their mouths are bound and gagged. I don't know how long they've been dragged, but they must have just come through the barrier between the portions of the realm; the snow from the other place leaves a light trail behind as they move closer.

Elder and Veronica stand quickly. I can feel her rage, but I notice Elder holds her back. Sefryn follows me as I walk toward Arthur.

"Let. Them. Go." If it weren't for the man dragging Camila and Abigail, looking ready to hurt them if anything happened, I would already have buried him.

Arthur nods to himself as he slowly looks around, ignoring me. "Where's Clarissa?" Arthur sneers. "I knew you couldn't save everyone."

I clench my jaw but say nothing. I may not have been fast enough to save Clarissa, but at least I tried—something he knows he didn't do. He just ran. But exposing his cowardice could never be enough at this point.

"The truth is," Arthur speaks louder, slowing his steps, "you were never able to save anyone. You know it in your heart. You know it to be true."

Sefryn throws out her hand. Arthur puts up a finger. Behind him, I see a dark-skinned woman appear from seemingly nowhere. She has a spear made entirely of ice in her hand, the tip of it barely an inch from Camila's nose.

Sefryn freezes. I take a step forward. Arthur tsks, wagging his finger. The girl moves her spear closer to Camila's eye.

"See, if you step out of line, they're both dead," Arthur threatens.

"Then what do you want?"

"A rematch," he answers. "Just you and me. No one is to come between us."

I sneer. "When Abigail called down the lightning, she saved your life. I was ready to kill you then. I'm ready to kill you now."

"Good!" he shouts. "But if anyone interferes, then Gailae will kill them both."

I turn back to Sefryn. She nods. I smile to myself. Arthur is going to make it all too easy. I don't look Elder in the eye but pat his shoulder as I pass him.

"Don't go far," Arthur calls out. "I want to duel here so everyone can see up close when I kill you."

I turn back to face him. I steal a glance at Abigail and Camila. They are turned on their stomachs and are now looking forward, right at me. There's just a hint of fear in Abigail's eyes, muddled with pain. Camila stares at me, her eyes fixed with determination. She knows I'm getting her out of there. I'm not failing anyone again.

"When do we begin?"

# Chapter 17

# Fist over Fire

**Aros Caelum Hayes**

I am answered with a ball of fire that heads toward me, but Arthur's aim falters, and I barely have to step aside to avoid it. Elder takes Veronica and pulls her back. Sefryn moves out of the line of fire, watching intently and keeping an eye on Gailae to make sure she doesn't harm Abigail or Camila. I let him keep trying without retaliating, his jets of fire never coming close to me. Luckily, they fly up into the air and die out, rather than going off course and hurting someone.

Arthur begins to alternate between pulses of energy and bursts of flame. I maintain the distance between us and still refuse to attack, using my power only to deflect or smother his strikes. There's no way for me to be certain Camila and Abigail will be safe once I put Arthur down—Gailae's ice spear is too close to Camila's eye. I notice Sefryn slowly shifting her gaze. She's trying to find a way to reach our friends. I just have to keep Arthur occupied.

I run toward him, swiping away his attacks. He still doesn't get that I am much stronger than he is. When I get close, a thick wall of fire rises in front of me. I hear Sefryn shout something, but I can't make out what she says. I step back, raising my hands to block the flames. They appear so suddenly that my arms are burned before I can smother the fire.

Behind the wall, both Arthur and Chase stand, facing me with wild and idiotic grins. I can tell the fire was made by both of them. It's no surprise that Chase is much stronger than Arthur.

"Now both of you want to fight me?" I ask. The wall of fire dies out.

"Yup, but make sure your grunts stay put," Chase says. "We just want to kill you. The others will die on their own."

I look into Arthur's eyes. He cocks a smile and raises his eyebrows. "My game, my rules."

*Fine.*

I respond by palming Arthur in the face, blasting his head with fire. Chase is quick and grabs my hand before my flames can give Arthur more than a first-degree burn. He twists my wrist, and I respond by twisting his. He's strong. I may be bigger, but Chase is lean, his arms powerful, and his mind full of vengeful determination.

Arthur punches out a spark of energy. I duck, giving Chase the advantage to twist my whole arm. I punch at him, forgetting to send any sort of power. I hit him in the leg, but it does little damage, if any at all.

I yell, radiating a bright beam of energy from my palms. It hits Chase in the head, pushing it back and giving me a moment to break free.

Kicking out toward Arthur, I send a quick wave of energy that knocks him down. Chase shouts, his raging fire blasting out everywhere. I contain what comes toward me, but the flames spew in all directions. I can't see what's beyond them. Blindly, I shoot out pulses of energy. I hit Chase, and his fires die down quickly.

Chase gets up, with Arthur standing in front of him like he's protecting him. Before I can whip out a rope of fire, a tornado of flames erupts from behind Arthur, engulfing him. The tornado moves toward me, embers spitting out and sparking new fires in the land around us.

"Don't you dare fucking move!" Arthur shouts, his voice cracking with childish anger. Through the breaks in the flames, I can see him point to Veronica, who is shying away from the fires around her. He's not controlling the tornado.

I've never seen a tornado of fire before. It feels hot—hot enough to make sweat fall from my forehead. I try to expand the fire, moving it out of Chase's control, but I don't accomplish much. I take a deep breath and let it out, pushing my hands forward and creating a wave of energy to rush through the twisting flames. It knocks both Arthur and Chase down, but the fires take time to die, their flames wild and spreading fast. Streams of fire fly at Gailae, burning her hair.

Gailae screams, not for her hair, but for her ice, now melted enough that it no longer looks like a spear. She forms what's left of it into a knife, her eyes red and her face flushed with anger.

"I'll kill them!" she shouts.

Before she can raise her hand to stab Camila, I blast more fire at her. Then I charge, but Arthur and Chase stand up and tackle me from behind. I hit the ground hard, the impact of both men knocking the wind out of me. It takes me a moment to catch my breath and become aware of the random punches to my body.

I twitch my back, and a surge of energy is released from it. Chase and Arthur are tossed backward yet again. I jump to my feet and sprint toward Gailae. She throws her jagged piece of ice at me, using her manipulation to quicken its trajectory. I have less than a split second to avoid it, and it pierces deep into my shoulder blade. I grunt as the pain shoots through my body, but my momentum is barely slowed. When I'm close, I punch out a fist of energy, knocking Gailae on the side of her head.

As I pass Camila and Abigail, I notice that they are partially trapped inside ice, which keeps their hands and feet from moving.

Gailae pulls some of the ice from their bodies to defend herself. Using thin flames that cover my hand, I melt her weapon and grab her head, my palms on her face. Then I let the fire rage, burning hotter. Her screams are louder than the fires, louder than everything else around us. I keep the fire contained to her head. In her pain, it's easy to bring Gailae to the ground.

Something hits me and knocks me over. I can't tell what it was, but I look over to see Chase charging at me, fire spinning from his hands. I move my arm out in a wave, a blade of energy swiping at him. Chase tries to avoid it, but it is too big for him to jump over, and he trips, falling on his face.

I turn my attention back to Gailae. Her face is swollen and red, and her eyes are mostly closed. She feebly raises her arm, as if trying to grab me. I flick it with the back of my hand and cover her face again with my palms, suffocating her with my flames. I can feel her legs flailing behind me, but those soon stop moving. I remove my hands, letting the fire from them sizzle out. Gailae's face is charred, darker than deep charcoal; the irregular texture of her face looks like it has always been made of coal. What's left of her hair is no longer attached to her head, and other than the small mound that used to be her nose, there isn't a distinct feature left on her face.

I let out heavy, quick breaths, looking down at what I've done.

Even though I barely knew her, I know she deserved it—even if it does make me a monster.

From the farthest edges of my peripherals, I notice a blast of fire heading my way. I raise my hand, creating a thin shield of energy. It's strong enough to protect me from the fire, but not strong enough to keep me safe from being kicked in the face as Chase blasts through my shield with the force of his body.

I fall backward, flipping over, and my face lands on the ground. I can feel Chase on me, his fists, one after the other, bashing the back of my head, but the only pain I feel is in my face. I know nothing is broken, but the piercing pain is still enough to make my head spin and drown my vision. I then notice the rain falling, the water becoming heavier and heavier.

Doing my best, I try to release a body pulse of energy. I do, but it is nowhere near as strong as what I've done before. Chase is lifted off me briefly but falls back on me and doubles down on his assault.

Chase is shouting words that I can't understand. The sound of the rain grows louder. Finding physical strength, I lift my body up with my arms and try to buck Chase off me. It doesn't work. Chase lands a well-aimed punch to my head, and my face slams back down. My head gets hot. I use one arm to reach behind me, knocking away one of Chase's fists. Using his moment of surprise, I throw him off my back, pulsing out energy for good measure.

I stand up. I can taste blood on my lips, spilling into my mouth. Chase gets to his feet quickly. I stare him down, catching my breath for a second. Fires rage in all directions, none seemingly connected to another.

Chase throws more fire at me. I block it, taking care to snuff it out so that it doesn't fuel the others. There isn't much distance between us, but we aren't close enough for physical contact. Chase understands this, and it seems he'd rather fight with fists than fire. He tries to close the distance, but with each step he takes, I either take one back or retaliate with a wave of energy that forces him to take several steps back.

With the pain subsiding and my strength returning, I blast out a wall of energy that Chase must counter with fire. Enraged, he lashes out, letting flames spew from his hands, covering his arms, and igniting from his back. A heat wave detonates from his body, fire flying out in all directions. The light from it blinds me momentarily.

I fly backward as Chase tackles me to the ground. The fire dissipates from his body. His eyebrows are narrowed, there's red in his wide eyes, and he yells in my face, so close that I can see the saliva flying out of his mouth. There's an emotion of pain behind his eyes. For the seconds that Chase stops yelling, when he goes still to lock his eyes onto mine, the pain so plain and clear, I wonder if he had feelings for Gailae, if he truly cared for her, and whether the Trials weren't just about winning.

But I'm not about to find out. I knock his head back with mine. I ignore the recoil of pain and place my hand around his throat. My arm vibrates as I conjure a slice of light and use it to cut through his neck. It isn't deep enough to take his head off, but there are shallow cuts on his neck that show droplets of blood, along with a burn that looks like a bruise.

Chase gets off me, standing to his feet, but stumbles back and collapses. I punch him in the face, something I've wanted to do since I saw him almost two weeks ago. With my hand on his chest, I shove him back to the ground. Chase opens his mouth, spitting a jet of fire from it. I flip my head back to avoid it. Chase punches me in the stomach. With the breath knocked out of me yet again, drool slipping from my mouth, I elbow Chase in the face. I go for another blow, but Chase grabs my arm and pushes it back. I grab his free arm and pin it to the ground while I struggle to grip his other, but my remaining arm still struggles against his hold.

We wrestle on the ground, exchanging grips on each other quickly, always trying to get the upper hand. I wrap my legs around Chase's, trying to strengthen my hold on him. He fights it off. I'm well-built, not like Elder, but Chase is still nearly my size, and his physical strength seems to match mine. At this point, I feel the urge to prove that I am stronger than him without using my powers.

I clench my jaw and try to shove Chase into the ground. I get a grip on both his arms and attempt to press them against his neck to cut off his airflow. I lose concentration on my legs, which allows Chase to free himself and knee me in the balls. I topple forward in pain; my entire body tenses as I can barely let out a grunt.

A wave of some sort hits us, sending us both into the air, flying in the same direction. We hit the ground and roll. I can't focus on anything. Chase manages to stop his trajectory and get to his feet. I don't stop until I hit a tree. With tears in my eyes blurring my vision, I look over to see what hit us. Luckily, Chase is curious too and doesn't resume his barrage of fire.

Arthur is fighting the others, spewing flames everywhere, not caring what he hits. He sends out pulses of energy, which further ignite and spread the flames. He's taken on a fighting style similar to how Chase fought when we met, but now Chase has channeled his rage into more focused and purposeful attacks. Even with the torrent of rain Abigail called down, it isn't enough to put out all the fires.

Chase turns back to look at me, but there is something different in his eyes.

"He's out of control," Chase says, his voice loud and shaky. To my surprise, Chase launches a jet of fire toward Arthur, who has been too busy in his frenzy to notice. The force of the flaming jet knocks Arthur to the ground. All the fires around quickly die out in the rain.

Chase turns his head back to me, stares right into my eyes, and points at me, the intensity of his control keeping his arm still.

"I'm still going to fucking kill you, demon spawn," he spits. Chase runs after Arthur, who is now deflecting attacks from Abigail and Camila. I don't see Elder or Veronica.

I run after Chase. When I get close to the others, I notice Arthur wielding a sword. I look around. Chase's bald friend is nowhere to be seen. Camila catches my eye. Now free, she snaps her fingers, light pulsing out, blinding Arthur. I hadn't realized how dark it had gotten.

When Chase gets close to Arthur, Arthur slashes at him and then sends out a pulse of energy, knocking Chase out of the way. Arthur turns his arm to face me and spouts fire from it, which I counter by grabbing it, my powers colliding with the fire and creating a wall that shoots upward. Chase joins us again. I quickly glance at the others behind me.

Like I did by the lake, I pull up a ring of fire around the three of us, keeping the battle between us. Chase is still after Arthur and sends blades of blue-hot fire at him. Arthur swipes them away with his energy.

"What are you doing?" Arthur shouts as he pushes the fire coming his way into my wall of fire. "Aros is the one you hate! Kill him! He killed your brother!"

I should have joined Chase in attacking Arthur. I was so caught off guard by what was happening, and a part of me was hoping one of them would prevail, making my work easier.

Chase nods to Arthur but says, "Aros is my kill. I don't want him distracted trying to save his friends from you."

Arthur and Chase immediately resume their barrage, though only at me this time. I move my hands quickly, deflecting attack after attack. I try to use the water from the rain that falls, but it isn't enough to put out my ring of fire, and so it isn't enough to do anything worthwhile to Arthur or Chase.

Arthur swings his sword but almost slashes Chase. Chase shoots him a look right before shooting a jet of fire at me, which I dodge easily. Arthur retracts the sword but keeps it in one hand. With only his other hand free, Arthur isn't much of a threat, and he lets Chase take the lead in the fight.

Using both palms, I blast out energy that knocks Chase right into Arthur; they both topple onto the ground. Arthur shoves Chase off him, shouting something that I don't care to understand.

"Aros!"

The voice is from Sefryn. There isn't any fear in it, no dire need for me; she just wants my attention.

She calls out my name again. I pace my breathing, paying close attention to Chase and Arthur, who are just now gathering themselves.

I spread out both arms and push down, extinguishing my fire around us. Sefryn steps forward, holding her hand out, telling me to stay where I am.

Veronica makes her way toward Chase, each step she takes full of direction and intent. I didn't get to see where she or Elder came from, but I suppose Elder was trying to keep her out of harm's way. She puts both of her hands out in front of her. Her body shakes, but then she becomes still. Her eyes are narrowed as she twists her hands, her wrists looking unnatural as she does so.

I look over to Chase and Arthur, who are both standing rigidly, taking small steps closer to each other, with Arthur in the back. They form a two-person line and look like they are unable to move. Veronica walks closer, blood running from her nose, but a sliver of a smile plays on her lips—the kind born from the thrill of revenge.

She gets close to Chase, just under arm's length, and keeps moving closer.

"Fuck. You. You. Bastard."

The coldness of her voice is in stark contrast to her timid demeanor. Her eyes are hard, but the expression looks foreign on her face—like it's never known such darkness. There's a slight falter in her eyes, and I realize it must be surprise. She didn't know that she had this in her.

I move forward, ready to step in if the need arises. Veronica throws her hand toward me, and my body freezes. The sensation is unlike any other. My blood runs faster. My mind tells me to move forward, but my foot takes a step back. I can't even move my eyes to look at her, wondering how she can do this.

Then I realize—she can't. By exerting control over me and forcing me away, she accidentally releases Arthur. In a quick motion, Arthur drives the sword through Chase, slamming the hilt with a burst of energy to force it in. Having gone all the way into and through Chase, the sword digs into Veronica's chest.

Veronica lets out a gasp. The sword doesn't run all the way through her—it isn't long enough. But it makes her lose her hold, and Chase is able to move on his own, but the life in him quickly dissipates. He tries to turn his head back but doesn't make it before it drops forward, hanging there of its own accord.

"You've served your use," Arthur breathes into Chase's ear.

Veronica doesn't look good. Tears are in her eyes, and she chokes on blood until she can cough it up. I blast Arthur with a pulse. It knocks him back, but then a gust fires through, lifting Arthur into the air. Arthur lands on the ground with an audible thud, but it isn't over. In the moonlight, I can see his silhouette fly off. Abigail charges past me, moving her arms upward and in a circle, conjuring the winds of a tornado around Arthur until we can't see him anymore.

Elder rushes forward and holds Veronica. She looks at him, sadness in her eyes.

"I'm sorry," Elder tells her. He still holds her, even though she stands on her own, a couple of feet away from where Chase now lies dead on the ground, the sword sticking out of his back.

"Don't save me," I hear Veronica whisper. Elder's eyes widen as he looks at her again.

Clenching her jaw, Veronica raises a hand and curls her fingers. Elder steps away, taking his hands off her. He doesn't mean to, but she makes him.

"I want to see her again." Her raspy voice sends haunting chills down my spine, and all I can do is watch as Veronica forces Elder to freeze in his tracks as she stumbles to Chase. She pulls the sword from his body—and drives it through her own heart.

Even though Elder can now move freely again, he stands frozen in shock. After a moment, he collapses to his knees, hanging his head over Veronica, his eyes lost and full of pain. I know the look in his eyes and the thoughts running through his head. Just like I had when I knelt over Clarissa's body just days ago, he's wondering where he had messed up so badly.

# CHAPTER 18

## STORM CHASING

**Aros Caelum Hayes**

The rain has long since subsided. The moon keeps the night alive while the sun threatens to never shine again. We give Elder his time to grieve, even if he doesn't let a single tear flow. I get it. All of us do. But Camila and Abigail don't know the worst of it. They know that Clarissa didn't make it, but they don't know the horror I saw, the horror of what she suffered. Not even Sefryn knows it all, but she understands what the incubi are—a corporeal and animated nightmare. They don't. And I hope that I can keep it that way forever. What they've seen is already more than anyone should.

When it becomes clear that Elder needs more time, more space, the rest of us move away, but we stay close enough for Elder to see us. With nothing better to do, I get a fire going. My body quickly aches more and more as time passes. We don't have any food. Even though I'm hungry, I know Sefryn wants to rest, so I don't say anything about it.

"So, is it true?" Abigail asks, her voice low, already knowing the answer.

I catch her eye, and seeing the pain in her eyes, I know I can't let my own show.

"Yeah," I choke out. "I'm sorry. I couldn't—I didn't get to her in time."

Abigail moves closer to me. "I don't blame you." Her voice is strong, but when I look at her, I can see the tears she's holding back. "I know you did everything you could. And more."

I nod, looking away, unable to handle her emotions at the moment. I need her to stay strong, because right now I want to burn anything and everything that's caused me pain. I'm fighting the urge to find Arthur's body, probably blown off a cliff somewhere, and reduce it to ash, and then take a piss all over it for good measure. Chase lies somewhere dead on the ground nearby. I could do it to his body. But I remain stiff. Mutilating the dead is irrational. And I know I'm sick in the head for even having these thoughts.

"Camila?"

Sefryn's voice surprises me, pulling me from my disgraceful ideas. I look up at her, and then to Camila.

"What happened to you two? How did you escape the monsters?"

Relief fills me that Sefryn remains vague about what the monsters are. I half-listen as Camila tells the story that I've already seen. She tells the story well, but nothing can beat the detail of seeing them in action, save for living in those exact moments.

But then Camila talks about the next morning. I listen but still stare into the flames of my fire. While Camila talks, I can't help but think how done I am with this place. Aside from the monsters, it's been day to night, one after the other, of eating mostly fruit and spending endless time in front of campfires to keep us warm. I don't know if I'll ever enjoy being outside like I used to.

"We were sleeping when they came. Arthur spat fire from his mouth, surrounding us. It wasn't much fire, but waking up to it surprised us. Then we were being strangled by that large guy, and before I passed out, I saw Chase walking toward us."

"It was terrifying," Abigail adds. "Knowing that we'd just been caught by Arthur and Chase just a couple of days after fighting off those monsters."

Camila shakes her head. "I should have killed Arthur right after he attacked me."

I agree. But I should have killed him earlier. I don't say anything. That Arthur's fear was akin to the smell of blood to a starving vampire for the incubi is just one more thing I feel like I can't tell them. Camila and Abigail are amazing, some of the best people I know, and they would blame themselves if they knew that getting rid of Arthur earlier could have prevented everything.

"We spent days eating nothing, drinking from the splashed water on our faces just once a day, and listening to Arthur talk big with Chase, plotting on how to use us to kill you."

I look up at Camila as if she just said my name. She looks right at me. Of course they wanted to kill me. We've all known that. I guess Arthur figured he couldn't do it alone, and Chase knew it too. It sickens me that the only time they could get the best of any of us, including Elder, has been by ambush.

Pathetic.

Weak.

Cowards.

If I ever meet Arthur's older brother, I'll be sure to tell him all about Arthur.

"Clarissa was my best friend," Abigail says. "I'm going to miss her so much. All those years of being by each other's side, of always having one another's back, have been ripped away like they never mattered."

I can hear the pain in her voice.

"But that kind of friendship always matters," I tell her. "Just because she is no longer with us, with you, doesn't mean you never had that connection. That friendship will always be a part of you, and it will always be a part of her, wherever she is now."

Abigail gives me a shaky, watery smile. She leans over and gives me a hug, burying her face into my chest. I hold her while she sobs. I can feel her forcing her shoulders to stay still each time they shake. As I hold her, I catch Sefryn's eye. She looks worried, but not for Abigail. For me. I quickly look away, knowing that if I keep looking at her, I'll break down too.

Abigail doesn't cry for long, and she soon calms down enough to lift her head back up. But I know the tears won't be her last.

I look up at the sky. It's still dark out. Seeing the soot on the others' faces, I realize just how close we were to the fires and how much light they provided while I fought off Chase and the others.

"I think I'm going to find something for all of us to eat," Sefryn says, getting up and leaving quickly without waiting for a response. I'm grateful that she's doing it—I know it's for Camila and Abigail, who haven't eaten in days.

The three of us wait there silently, each lost in whatever thoughts come our way. I hope, for their sakes, that their minds don't go as dark as mine does. I have to constantly look out across the quiet land to gather my surroundings. My heart aches for Abigail and her loss, and it makes it worse that I can barely imagine what it must be like to have someone like that—to have a friend with whom you're so close that losing them is like losing a part of yourself. On Earth, I never had that, and I knew it. Back in school... well, I remember how much I yearned for someone to like me. All those times I looked out an open window, watching the other kids play with each other down in the courtyard.

*"Careful, Aros is watching."*

*I heard the other kids from down below. They spoke just loud enough for me to hear. Then I saw him glance up at me, a nasty smile on his face. He was ten, like I was, and the rumors had already started to spread everywhere. I thought I had friends—until I learned I never really did.*

*And then there were all those times in class when no one wanted to sit near me. It got so bad after Professor Liams left that the teachers moved a desk into the corner, away from everyone. I knew some of them were terrified of me. I could see it in their eyes every time I got too close.*

*And all those times I'd wake up screaming because the other kids wanted to scare me in the night. For what reason, I likely won't ever know. There were letters slipped under my door, threatening to kill me in various ways. Some of the kids had darker minds than I do even now.*

*Any hope I had of having friends faded away. I had no one, no family—it was something I knew but couldn't understand. It was as if the feeling of total loneliness made no sense to me, had no meaning, because why would there be such a sad word for something that was so normal? There was no silence in being alone since that was just the way of life. The idea of loving someone, the idea of having solid connections with anyone, was so esoteric that I never believed anyone could truly achieve it.*

*Now I know better.*


As those memories pass through the layers of my mind, I begin to understand the feeling of companionship, what a true friend is. I look over at Abigail and Camila. They are the best people I have ever known. Clarissa too. Sefryn feels like she's more than that. I want her to return, hopefully with a bounty of food. After we eat, I need to get us out of these Trials. Life will be easier to understand then. Right now, it just feels like a mess.

Answering my prayer, Sefryn returns. She's found yet more apples—but I think there is something different about the apples here. Eating them makes me feel full and energized. There are more than enough for us and for Elder, whenever he's ready to join. I look over toward him. He hasn't moved, but I can see his back rise and fall as he breathes.

We sit closer together in a circle while we eat. Abigail sits at one end, with Sefryn on my other side, and Camila at the other end, next to

Sefryn. It's hard to talk about much. We've already said what was on our minds. Now, it's just the feeling that this is our future; the rest of our lives spent in the deepest, most twisted parts of Voltar. Only tragedy and heartbreak await us.

Just as it was when night fell, it takes me longer than it should to realize the day has begun. The brilliant stars of the night sky have faded, their light not as strong as the star that sits closest. None of us have moved, but Camila and Abigail sleep, still sitting, leaning forward and close to toppling over, but they never do.

I hear footsteps approach. I look up and see Elder standing just beyond the dying fire. His face is solemn, and his eyes are unmoving. He parts his lips before asking, "Help me... with... her, will you?"

I nod at him. I stand and walk with him toward where Veronica lies. When we get closer, I notice how fragile she seems, just how much smaller she is now than she was yesterday when she stood frail and yet full of life as she declared her revenge.

"She never would have wanted to be buried," Elder says. His voice is steady, but it's also deep and hoarse, even though he never once screamed, cried out, or broke down. His throat sounds shredded, his vocal cords strung together by the smallest string, ready to snap with the faintest pluck. "So, I ask you this respectfully. Turn her to ash so that I may take her back home and lay her where she first met Armantha."

I place my hand on his shoulder and give it a light squeeze, then gently push him back. He goes willingly, giving me space. It pains me to do this. I never had the chance to do anything proper for Clarissa. Her family won't ever see her again, and she will become a part of the land of Voltar. But even though something inside me writhes with a sickening beat, I do it. The fire leaves my hand in a slow stream, carefully bound together like the strands in a rope, until they reach her. When the flames touch her hair, I spread them around her body, lining it until I ignite the rest of her. I keep watch, not wanting to burn her too much, but it takes a while for a grown body to be reduced to ash when I keep the heat of the fire mild.

Elder stands there, watching silently the entire time, just a step behind me. I take a deep breath and move my hands over the fire, heating it up. When I'm satisfied, I take a step back to join Elder, and we watch. I can feel the others looking at me, but I force myself not to look away.

We must stand there for a couple of hours. Elder's patience and silence tell me that he's lost more than just his wife. I know I could have done it faster, but the idea of doing it quickly feels unholy. The heat of the fire makes us sweat; the warmth of it feels like it burns my face, but from behind, I can feel the cool breeze that accompanies the late-autumn weather of the land.

Dusk begins to set when it's done. Elder steps forward and carves deep into the remaining bones, splintering them over and over until they crumble to dust. He then scoops her ashes into a pouch he made from his shirt. He can't get them all, but he does his best. He wears the same clothes as when I met him, which look like what he would have entered the Trials in. But having removed his shirt to hold Veronica's ashes, he wears only his jacket now and stuffs the wrapped ashes into a pocket.

We return to the others, where Abigail stands and gives him a hug. He returns it, and then the others follow suit. We remain silent as Elder sits like we did last night and begins to eat. I can't help but think about the ashes that must remain on his hands still, but I say nothing.

After another hour, I speak up.

"We should get moving," I tell them. I try to sound as sensitive as I can, but staying here too long will kill us all, and I can't let that happen. "We aren't far from the Ashen Pit. It's time to finish what we came here for."

No one objects, but at first, no one says anything. Sefryn stands first, and then Camila and Elder follow suit.

With a deep breath, Abigail stands. "For Clarissa."

Elder nods. "And for Veronica, and all the others who fell to this cursed land."

I nod awkwardly. They wait for me to move, so I start walking toward the stormy clouds in the distance. The storms and clouds keep changing, like they're running from us.

We pass by a set of two large animal skeletons, though none as big as the Ivory Skeleton. We can't afford to stop and investigate. Still, I can't help but wonder if there is a way I can learn the true story of Voltar, beyond the questionable tales found in books. I want to know its beginnings and how it came to shape the rest of the world. The more we go, the stronger I feel, as if I am nearing the birthplace of the source of my power. I want to know how it shaped me into what I am.

We come across a river that we must pass over. Taking our first break since we started, we drink as much as we can. Sefryn wanders off to forage for food to save for later. I drink so much that I have to leave the others for a bit to relieve myself. After taking longer than I wanted, we wrap up and get going again.

Long after the sun goes down, we find a place to rest. There's a three-foot-high stone artifact that looks like it could have been a statue, but chunks of it are missing, and it is impossible to tell what it once was.

We eat the berries that Sefryn gathered around the fire I set for us. We don't talk much, but I can feel the thousands of words that intertwine the silence.

Even though we walked for hours, I can't tell if we got any closer to the storms. Trying not to be disheartened, I think about how close we probably are. But there is a thought that nags at the back of my head. Maybe Voltar isn't ready to give us our last test. That would mean no matter how far we go, we'll never get closer to the end, not until Voltar wants us to. I can't believe it wasn't that long ago when I thought the Ashen Pit wasn't a living thing. But like Voltar, I now understand there's more to it.

But I don't know how to explain that thought to the others, and saying that we should rest or wait longer will make them ask questions I don't know how to answer. I have nothing to hide, but my connection with the Aeturnous Kitisma still feels personal and private. I don't want to share that with anyone just yet.

When it is time to sleep, I set up a bubble around us like the barrier walls I've made in caves. I know we all need our rest, so taking watches doesn't seem like a good idea. The fire keeps me warm, along with my jacket that Elder mended and improved while we walked, but something inside me feels chilly. I want Sefryn to come over so we can hold each other, embracing the warmth of our connection, but she stays on the other side of the fire. After everyone else does, I lie down. I look up at the dark, cloudy sky until I drift off to sleep.

We start our morning eating whatever is left from Sefryn's foraging. Our first hours of walking are in silence. We've all lost weight due to the lack of food and constant movement. It feels like my muscles have begun to evaporate, thinning away and turning me back into the small and skinny boy that was left at the mercy of those five kids.

My thoughts grow darker yet again with each step, and it gets difficult to keep away the memories of the recent days and weeks. I can't imagine how many bodies litter Voltar, left for creatures looking for an easy meal. With the Trials still in progress, I can't help but think that there will be more who fall to the land.

I look over at Elder. His son waits for him back in Edlyn. Somehow, I have to make sure he gets back. More so than I, since I don't have anyone waiting for me. Though the thought of Olivia flits through my mind, she feels like another life—something I have left far behind.

"I don't know what you're thinking, but I'm fine," Elder tells me, eyeing me briefly.

"I'm just thinking that your son is waiting for you," I say. "I want to make sure you make it to him."

Elder scoffs. "How can I deserve to survive this cursed land when everyone else who followed me through here perished? I failed to save them, to protect them, so if Voltar takes me, then my son is probably better off."

*That doesn't sound like someone who is fine.*

"You're a great father. I can tell," I say to him after a minute of hard contemplation about what to say. "You did everything you could to give him a great life, and I know he would want you to see him do great things with it."

Elder doesn't say anything.

"So don't say that you aren't worthy or deserving." I can feel the others listening intently. "Voltar preys on the minds of those who enter it, drawing out their fears. The Trials are designed to kill, and Voltar is a magic—Magis—beyond all our understanding. It isn't your fault," I tell him, trying to believe the words myself. Clarissa's death is on my conscience, eating at me constantly. I couldn't imagine losing everyone else too.

"Veronica loved you," Sefryn says, walking up to us. "I could tell. And I'm sure the others did too. Chase was just another monster of this land. His actions aren't on you."

Knowing we won't stop, Elder nods. I know he doesn't agree with us, but I hope that there is a small part of him that has shifted in mindset. After a little while, though, Elder tends to the injuries that Camila and Abigail suffered.

They thank him, to which Elder responds with a small smile. Then he continues on toward the dark clouds, which still seem no closer.

"Do you think we should rest a bit?" I say, loud enough for everyone to hear me.

"I want to, Aros," Abigail says. "But what I want even more is to get out of here."

I sigh. How do I tell them that we're wasting our time? I don't even know how I know it, but I know that we're getting nowhere.

The land looks the same—green grass, trees, and the mountain up to the peak of Voltar to our right.

"I think Aros is right," Elder says, surprising me. "I don't think we're getting anywhere right now."

The others look at him in confusion. Abigail opens her mouth to ask something but doesn't. Camila nods, knowing what he and I are thinking.

"It would make sense," Camila says. "Voltar has constantly been shifting; you can feel it in the air. How else do you explain climbing to the peak of Voltar, passing through it, and now we're here, somewhere where we can see the top of the mountain again?"

I'm sure Abigail has some argument, but she doesn't care to state it.

"When Voltar is ready, we'll know," Camila says. "I'm not saying we should just wait, but I am saying that it wouldn't hurt to take some breaks to make sure we are fully prepared for our final trial."

Sefryn sits down on the ground. She looks up at Abigail, who then sits next to her.

It feels a bit odd sitting on the ground and just resting. It feels like we're wasting time, like we're procrastinating. But even if someone else makes it to the Ashen Pit first, this isn't a race. That is something that is so clear now. This is about survival and overcoming the impossible. This is about who is brave enough and strong enough to be worthy of burning their souls into the Ashen Pit—worthy of the power it will bring them.

Since the sun is at its hottest for the day, I don't start a fire. The rays of the sun are warm against my skin, yet the climate of Voltar remains chilly and biting.

After some small talk, I ask Sefryn about Praellen.

"It's like here, Arteyva, I mean. Not Voltar. But it's much smaller," she says. "Everyone there has some kind of Magis, though the Fae are the strongest. But centaurs are strong too."

"Is the whole realm ruled by the Faerie Queen?" Abigail asks.

Sefryn chuckles in amusement, the sound light and airy. "Yes, but she is referred to as the Fae Empress."

A hint of red flushes Abigail's cheeks. "Oh, right. I knew that."

Sefryn lets the moment pause briefly.

"Praellen is more beautiful than you can imagine," she continues. "Between the seas, the mushroom forests, and the stunning deserts... It's just so magical. I never appreciated it enough until I came here."

Abigail frowns. "I think Arteyva is pretty beautiful."

"It is! I didn't mean to say it wasn't," Sefryn answers quickly. "So many places here are just stunning, even Voltar. But I've seen cities that weren't so pretty. Everywhere in Praellen is beautiful." Sefryn scrunches her eyes, deep in thought. "Maybe it's because Praellen is much smaller."

Abigail doesn't say anything, but she doesn't look offended. She nods, her eyes half here, half elsewhere.

"But Praellen has much more terrifying monsters," Sefryn says, her tone darker. She looks at Abigail, who seems to have possibly not heard her, and doesn't say anything more about it.

"Maybe one day you can show us," Camila says. "I mean, maybe it'll inspire me to redecorate our castle or build my own."

I look over at Camila. I know she doesn't care to inherit the throne her mother sits on. But maybe she wants her own.

"Yeah, I think I'll be able to take all of you there once we're out of here," Sefryn says, her eyes lighting up, the angles of her face glowing brilliantly. In this moment, I know that I will always strive to make her happy because I will never grow tired of seeing her smile. "The Fae Empress can't say no to anyone who's survived the Ash Trials."

Abigail shuffles her feet, moving the dirt beneath her heels and digging into the ground. She doesn't say anything. She looks out toward the sun, still not setting, and lets out a long breath.

We don't say anything for a little while. Elder remains silent, just looking out where there would be a horizon, but we can't see it from where we sit. Camila and Sefryn start talking. At first, they discuss mundane things like places to eat and visit, and then they move on to past relationships. I can't help but feel a pang of jealousy when Sefryn talks about hers. But that was two years ago, and she tells Camila that she's been single since, though she hints that she's met someone. Camila catches my eye, a glint in hers like she knows that person is me. I smile to myself. Sitting here with my best friend and my almost-girlfriend getting along better than I could've hoped—it's more than I ever knew I could ask for.

Their conversation deepens. They talk about their plans for when they return home, about the values Camila believes in and lives by. Abigail, certain of at least one thing, says she's going back to Arteyva to build a life of her own. The Trials showed her that she doesn't want to be an Ash Lord. But when she speaks, I can't help but think she's the kind of person who will always come to the rescue of someone in need.

Elder gets up suddenly. He looks out toward the sky. The clouds still flash as lightning courses through them, but they seem no closer. They move into each other at a quicker pace than I've seen before.

"I can feel them about to come," Abigail says. "They're going to head straight for us."

"What does that mean?" Camila asks. "Are the Trials about to end? Are we going to face the last volunteers?"

Elder shrugs, his face solemn.

"I hope not," I say, thinking of something quickly to give her reassurance. "I think the Ashen Pit will want several volunteers who make it through. That way, if something were to happen to an Ash Lord, it has backups."

It makes sense to me, and the others don't argue.

Then there's a brighter flash, a bolt moving horizontally through all the clouds, and then the sky goes dark. It feels as if a late dusk has fallen upon the land. I notice the clouds moving toward us slowly. I step forward. The clouds will never come all the way here; we still have to go to them. The only difference is that now we can reach them, and thus reach the final part of our Trials. To our side, the peak of Voltar still stands taller than everything else, but somehow, I feel like we are much farther from it than we were just a minute ago. The world around us has shifted, and it's still moving, like we're traveling through space into a different dimension.

Lightning continues its barrage in the clouds, striking down and destroying anything it hits. A haze of purple fills the sky in the distance, the swirling clouds lighting up with deep, brilliant colors.

"Are you guys ready for this?" I ask. I stare ahead and let out a breath. I'm ready to end this. I look around to see everyone nodding. Even Elder has that gleam in his eye, showing his determination to complete the Trials. There's a pride that swells inside me. Elder is going to see his son again. I know it. I'm not going to let anything get in the way of that.

With one last look at everyone, I lead the way toward the storm. The others walk alongside me, ready to face whatever comes next. I can't help but hope this final test will be a walk in the park compared to everything else we've faced.

Hope. It's just a hope.

We near the clouds much faster than we should, according to the laws of physics. It's barely half an hour before we stand at the foot of the storm, the inferno of rain just a step forward. For now, we're safe, but that's all going to change the second we pass through the invisible barrier that protects us from what lies inside.

A million thoughts rush through my head, but one stands at the forefront: the conflicting idea that this is going to be much worse than anything we've encountered so far, despite what I wished for. And if it comes to it, I'm not going to let anybody die, even if it means I don't make it myself.

This is the final test—the one that pushes us beyond our wildest beliefs about our limits. And with that silent, mutual understanding that the five of us share, we move one foot forward.

# Chapter 19

## Across the Bridges

**Aros Caelum Hayes**

We're instantly swallowed by darkness. Hard rain pelts our faces. Flashes of light slash across the distance as lightning strikes down, illuminating the area so briefly I can't make out where we are. The whooshing of the wind grazes my ears; my skin prickles as I sense a lot of movement around me, but it's impossible to see anything. Despite Camila being right by my side and Sefryn just behind me, I can only see them when the lightning strikes.

A faint glow of blue builds up until it shines bright enough to cut through the storm. The Azure Fox stands in front of us, her eyes unmoving as she holds her gaze. She puts one paw forward. A rush of air blasts through immediately, dissipating the weather until we can see clearly.

Up ahead, there is a large suspension bridge with four people passing over. Even from here, I can tell that they are all tense. The bridge sways in the wind but seems stable otherwise.

From the depths of the canyon, a large beast flies through, tearing into the wooden bridge and ripping it apart. The volunteers scream, flying into the air. The beast dives, opens its mouth, and swallows them all before disappearing.

Abigail squeezes my hand in surprise.

The Azure Fox looks back briefly before returning her attention to us.

"This is your final test," Grisla says. "The task is simple enough. Make it across the bridge." She pauses, giving us a second to think it over. The bridge remains broken, the two sides of it hanging down the cliff. "But know this," she continues. "If even one of you is to die, then all of you shall fail."

A clap of lightning follows, causing the Azure Fox to vanish and restoring the storm that had been raging around us. We stand there breathless, the terror of what could happen freezing our blood.

To make matters worse, a horrible snarling sound comes from within the darkness, loud enough to hear over the screaming winds and thunder. The stakes are now much higher. None of us here would ever leave another behind—we know that our lives are tied together. For those like me, which may only be Camila and Sefryn, allowing any of us to die means we won't be an Ash Lord. It makes sense. If we can't protect those around us, then we don't deserve it.

That means that I've already failed.

"I think it's time for you to shine, Camila." My bad joke barely receives a snort of amusement. Camila brushes past me. Immediately she creates a ring of light over our heads, just below the clouds. What I see looks unreal, a magical assortment of swirling and pulsing colors of clouds, both fluffy and thin, coupled with terrifying blazes of lightning. Beyond the surrealness of it all is the heart-pounding shriek of wyverns circling the land. They're waiting. Amber eyes shine in the distance, close to the ground. I look over at Camila, and we come to the same conclusion: providing some light isn't going to be enough. Camila needs to make it so bright that it looks like the sun is shining again.

I'm already soaked, not even a minute inside the vortex. Water spills from my too-long and unkempt hair, running past my eyes, down my nose, into my mouth, and over my lips. With each exhale, water spits from my face.

Abigail throws her hands up. I swear I can see her eyes flash as she tries to control the storm.

"It's no good," she cries out, her arms shaking as she tries harder and harder. "I can't stop it. This isn't real weather."

I shake my head. "You're right," I tell her. "The only way to stop this is to be the essence of Magis itself. It's just another part of the test."

"Then what do we do?" Elder asks.

In the moment it takes me to come up with a sufficient answer, Camila turns her head back briefly and says, "I got this."

Camila faces the clouds, looking up into the arena. She stands straight, her back to us. I can see her shoulders rise with each deep breath. I can almost feel her concentration.

The constant rain strikes my face and head so hard that it feels like hail. Camila snaps her fingers, the sound of it so intense it drowns out everything else. The ring hovering over our heads seems to fade, but the light disperses, strengthening and becoming dense, nearly reaching a level so bright that it would blind us if we were level with it.

All the darkness leaves and is replaced with light sourced from above, beaming down from the sun without a cloud in the sky. This must be part of it. The Trials are forcing us to overcome obstacles by other means. The Ashen Pit didn't want to see what Abigail could do—it already knows that. It wanted to see what Camila could accomplish.

The wyverns still circle out in the distance, but at least there are no beasts to accompany the eyes I could see earlier. Our entire world has changed yet again. Behind us is only a vast expanse spanning into the distance, sparse patches of grass dotting the otherwise barren landscape. I have a hunch that it leads absolutely nowhere.

I can see what lies across the canyon. There is a lone plateau just across, with a smaller bridge leading to a taller piece of land. It looks like an island, but where there should be water surrounding it is a never-ending plunge into the unknown below.

"You did it, Camila!" Abigail says, hugging her excitedly.

There's no time to celebrate. Four of the seven wyverns fire toward us, diving steeply. They all dodge my first three slices of energy. My fourth shot hits one. Abigail rains hail on another. Elder steps back, ready for whatever comes. Sefryn pulls up a root from beneath the ground, ready for when one of the wyverns gets close.

Sweat beads on Camila's face. She looks worn but determined. Two of the wyverns swoop down. Elder leaps out of the way. I ignite a fire in my hands, using it to fend off a claw that reaches for me. The beast shies away from the fire, flying up into the air again.

"Sefryn, I need wood," Elder says. Sefryn nods in response and looks at me. It's going to take her some time to pull wood up from the ground since she needs to get a tree to rise. Camila is still tired, but she looks ready to defend anything that comes her way. For now, it's going to be Abigail and me that take on the flying fiends.

Abigail brings forth clouds and generates a current of electricity that runs through them, ready to strike at anything she commands. With two of the wyverns down, the other three join in, giving us five to fight.

The wyverns, now ready to attack, dive down one after the other. This time, I shoot out powerful bursts of targeted energy, ready to tear through anything they touch. My pulses are small but quick, and I take down two wyverns in three attacks. Only one goes down permanently, the other roaring in pain. Its attacks become frantic. It gets close to me, and I stumble back, dropping to the ground to avoid it. Abigail deals with the other three wyverns, nipping them with discharges of electricity. None are strong enough to bring any down, but they're effective enough to make them wary of it.

I glance at Sefryn, and I see her pulling a thick root from beneath the grass, smaller offshoots crowning from the ground. Her eyes are narrowed with rage as she wrestles the tree up from the earth. Elder stands by her like a sentry on the lookout for attacks.

In my distraction, a wyvern grabs me in its claw, its talons piercing my skin. I cry out in pain and become breathless, the pit in my stomach plummeting as I am lifted into the air. Before I can think of how to get out of its grip, the wyvern tosses me toward one of its friends. I blast fire from my palms, scaring the beast away. No amount of fire or energy slows my descent as I free-fall toward the ground.

Everything feels silent and still, as if nothing exists, as if nothing is real. It feels like I'm falling, yet at the same time, I am suspended in space and time, completely unmoving. I can see deeper into the canyon below. Trees jut out from the sides of the cliffs.

A scream reaches me from below. Sefryn jerks her body, tossing her arm out to catch me. In place of her arm shoots a large root. I can see it wither and soften as it jets at me. It wraps itself around my torso, its impact like a kick to the ribs as it knocks the wind out of me. The controlled plummet makes my head spin. When I get to the ground, the root releases me, and I fall, tossing and rolling across the grass. Pain radiates through my body, and a piercing, stinging ring shoots from one ear canal, barrels through my head, and out the other side.

Out of my hazy vision, I see Elder carve a sword from a branch. Pulling up some smaller rocks from underneath the pile of dirt that Sefryn dug up, he imbues the sword with them, creating a menacing blade. And in that moment, poorly timed by a wyvern, he ducks, swings the sword, and cleanly cuts the wyvern's head off.

The head rolls toward me, stopping as it hits my chest. It's as big as my torso, its eyes an ugly yellow. And then the realization that we're still fighting for our lives snaps my attention back to the world around me, subduing all pain.

I jump to my feet. Creating an arching dome of energy that I fire upwards, knocking the remaining beasts off their flight path, I shout to the others, "We have to figure out how to cross the canyon!"

The words sound so simple, yet the task feels so dangerous and impossible. But I know that we need to get across. In the chaos of everything, I can see seven wyverns ready to strike at us again. No matter how many we take down, more will replace them. This isn't about fighting them.

It's about making it to the Ashen Pit despite all odds.

As if meaning to prove me right, there's a shift in the land, similar to what it felt like when the storm clouds moved close enough to us that we could reach them. Shooting from the ground, brick walls divide all of us, closing each of us off faster than the blink of an eye.

All other sound is gone except for my breathing. There is barely enough room in any direction for me to take three steps. I know it is useless to call out for the others. No, this portion of the final trial is to be done alone.

The brick walls push back and fade out of existence. I'm no longer by the edge of the cliff. The moon is out, giving me enough light to see what's around me, but not what lies beyond the thick of the trees.

A terrible scream rips through the air, loud enough to make me cover my ears. The sound becomes deafening, and the ground begins to shake. As it dies out, I recognize where it's from.

It's her. Clarissa. Her voice is crying out in my head.

The amber eyes return. I barely have a second to look at them before the creatures leap from the trees to attack me.

I fall to the ground to avoid their claws. I turn over onto my stomach and scramble to get up. After getting a close look, I realize that these creatures are a demonic form of the incubi that killed Clarissa. There is no way in hell that anyone could have thought it possible for the incubi to look even worse. But here they are, three humanoid creatures covered in slimy, scaly, and pockmarked skin.

Something tackles me to the ground. I feel claws slowly dig into the back of my neck.

Make that *four* creatures.

Between the memory of what these monsters did to Clarissa, the pressure of the Trials, and the pain coursing through my veins, I'm pissed.

Without much thought, I blast energy from my body, sending the incubus flying back. I spin around, weaving a rope of fire that flashes out, protecting me in a ring. Stopping when I face the incubus that attacked me, I let a fire burn in my hand until I change its energy to light and then fire a beam at the beast. The world lights up brilliantly for a moment. The incubus falls to the ground dead, a gaping hole right in its abdomen.

The other three incubi try jumping through my ring of fire, but I pull up a shield of energy to block them. After I hear them hit the ground, everything becomes silent once more. I can't even hear my fire.

Lowering it down cautiously, I let the smoke fully dissipate before scanning my surroundings. The land is all the same, but there isn't even a hint that there were just four incubi here.

A shimmering light materializes on the ground near the edge of the trees. Curious, I walk closer to it. When I see what it is, I really wish I hadn't.

Clarissa lies on the ground. Not only does she look unharmed, but she wears the jacket I left for her. The only thing is, her lifeless eyes stare at me—and even though she's clearly dead, they somehow manage to convey disappointment and anger.

I take several steps back, wanting to look away, but I can't. I don't know what this is supposed to be, but I don't like it. I don't know what I should do.

Before I get the chance to decide, Clarissa rises, levitating a few feet off the ground. She becomes upright, and her arms move out to the sides. Those eyes stare me down, but still, she's clearly not alive.

Gashes and tears form on her, mimicking how she looked after that night ended. My jacket falls apart and lands on the floor. Piece by piece, as if she's living it all over again, her body becomes more bare, more abused.

Transfixed, I am unsure of where to go, what to do. What to say, if that's what I'm supposed to do. I fight the memories of that night from dragging my mind down the deep end. Doing so nearly makes my head explode with both physical and emotional pain.

I can feel the same rage I felt that night boiling inside me. What does all of this mean? Why did the Trials have to be so inhumane, so deadly? Is there any purpose to it, or is it just another fucked-up thing in this world?

The feeling of guilt that I'm responsible washes over me. But I know it's not how I truly feel. I have to keep telling myself that.

Still, even though I know it's asinine, it feels all too truthful.

Arthur isn't the reason Clarissa is dead. I am. I let him live. I wasn't fast enough that night.

I wasn't strong enough. Therefore, it's my fault.

There is a quick snap in the air. I throw my arm back, palming my hand to let out a wall of energy. The incubus that snuck up on me hits it. I turn my head to look at it, tears stinging in my eyes. Using the energy from my hands, I close the flowy streams of blue around the monster and push it to the ground, holding it trapped.

Whipping out my other hand, I send two more streams out toward the trees. The energy acts like ropes and wraps around the necks of the other incubi. I drag them along the ground, having trapped them like I did the first.

Letting the hatred fuel me, I allow flames to spew from my hands, letting off on the energy trapped just enough to engulf what's inside in flames. I can hear their screams, a high-pitched squealing of anguish, and I can't help but relish in them.

As they burn, I imagine Arthur with them. Whatever happened to him was nothing remotely close to what he deserved. I may have failed Clarissa, but I won't be making the same mistake.

There's yet another clap of thunder, and I am returned to the cliffside, the broken bridge in front of me, and the light of day beaming down. There is a fire lit in both my fists, likely from the rage I felt when I burned the incubi to dust. Unfortunately, once they were dead, the Trials took me out of there, so I was never able to get the satisfaction of seeing the ashen bodies of the monsters.

I turn around, leaving my back to face the cliffs, and see the others locked in their own battles. Sefryn is clashing with Claudius DeGhore, the Supreme Ash. I step forward to help, but an invisible barrier prevents me from getting to her.

It's not real. It can't be. The incubi I fought, while very real to me, were nothing more than the imagination of the Ashen Pit. Whatever Sefryn fights, it isn't actually the Supreme Ash.

Elder clashes against three people I don't recognize. He takes it better than I did. Whatever has haunted his past, he's had time to recover and is easily able to take everyone down. After he does, Elder looks around, realizing he's where I am now.

"That was impressive," I say to him as he walks up to me. Elder scans his surroundings, understanding coming to him quickly.

"The last part was easy," he tells me. "Before they showed up, I had to fight my dead wife." Elder eyes me with a look that tells me I don't even want to try to imagine what that must have been like, but he also seems content with never speaking of it again.

Camila is surrounded by her family. She dodges their attacks but seems hesitant to fight back. But once her twin sisters spew acid from their mouths, she deflects it with a light barrier and then subsequently burns their eyes out.

When I see Abigail get knocked down, my muscles tense. I want to jump in, make sure that she makes it through. I can't have her die. Not now.

Even though I silence the thought in my head, I know it was already there. My fear was selfish. For a moment, I worried more about becoming an Ash Lord than anything else. I know that I care about her; I know that I want her to survive. So why do I feel so guilty now?

Sefryn fights Claudius by pulling roots up from the ground, but he seems to evade everything she throws at him with ease. Then Sefryn does something that surprises me. Using the roots and grass that she pulled from the ground, she caves the ground in by pushing down and then spreading her arms out. Claudius sinks to his ankles. Sefryn weaves her arms, thick vines wrapping around Claudius. Separate vines grab his hands, and Sefryn drags him to the ground. Everything disappears. Looking around as Elder and I did, Sefryn realizes that she's done and joins us.

Before Sefryn gets a word in, Camila blasts out a wave of light, similar to when I release energy from my whole body, and wipes out her family.

Once her personal trial is over, Camila breathes heavily, looking down at the ground. Something in her eyes tells me she's realized that what she fought wasn't real. She turns. When she sees us, Camila nods, but then looks out to Abigail.

Abigail is on the ground, looking up at a large man that walks toward her threateningly. She crawls back as quickly as she can. There are cuts and bruises on her face. Seeing them makes me wonder if Abigail and Clarissa had similar trauma from earlier. I know Clarissa had been beaten by her father. Even if for far different reasons than what I went through with my parents, it must have broken her. After losing her mother, Clarissa put all her trust into her father, only to have that be taken away. Looking at Abigail now, I wonder just which demon from her past is haunting her now.

Raising his hand, the man approaching Abigail narrows his eyes before swinging down. An axe materializes in his grip. I can't see Abigail's eyes, but something quickly changes. Turning over, Abigail dodges the blow. She rolls over onto her back again, facing the sky. Abigail reaches up with one hand. As quick as lightning strikes down, her world disappears in a flash.

Sefryn rushes over to her. It takes her a minute to get Abigail to stand. With wide eyes, I know Abigail is still terrified by what she just fought. Even though there is a moment of calm around us, I know better than to ask her about it.

Hell, if the memory of it is too painful for her, I might not want to remind her about it at all.

Sefryn brings Abigail over. I nod to the others, Abigail last. It takes her a second, but she steels her face and returns the nod.

We stare out across the canyon for a minute. There is no sign of danger, just the question of how to get to the other side. The answer is simple, though. Elder is with us, and he has the power to build a bridge.

But I know in my gut that this won't be as simple as just building a bridge and walking across it.

"Sefryn," Elder says, looking over at her. "I'm going to need your help. While I build us a bridge, I am going to need enough material."

"I'll get you what I can," Sefryn says without hesitation.

"Aros, watch our backs," Elder says. "This won't be without trouble. You two, please help him."

Camila stares back at him, ready to go. Abigail nods slowly, her wide eyes flitting in all directions, unable to settle.

After exchanging a quick glance with Camila, the two of us know that it will mostly be up to us to ensure that nothing attacks Elder or Sefryn.

It's messed up that the Trials are forcing us to figure out this final part after terrorizing us individually with some previous pain we've endured. Even though most of us have recovered, I know none of us are wholly unrattled. We're just doing our best to not think about it.

Elder pushes his arms out and then retracts. Part of the collapsed bridge rises into sight. Elder straightens it. The planks are wide enough for only one person to pass. Luckily, the wooden planks are still held together by rope, but there is nothing on either side, meaning a strong enough wind could knock us over.

Sefryn wrangles a tree from below, providing Elder with more wood. Elder peels off chunks of the tree, shaping them into planks. The bridge is made of light wood, so it's easy to see where Elder adds on the new section. After breaking off the unusable planks at the end of this half of the bridge, Elder attaches the new wood, roping it together with the rest. He adds on new planks.

So far, too easy.

Elder throws out his arm and pulls the far half of the bridge closer, carefully connecting the two. Once done, Elder releases it. There is some slack, causing the bridge to sink a bit. Doesn't matter. Now we have a way to cross.

So quick it must have materialized from thin air, a large beast flies upward, tearing through the middle of the bridge, breaking what Elder just made.

Camila acts fast and shoots out a beam of light toward it. It cuts through one of its wings, leaving a hole large enough that the monster can't fly. As it plummets into the depths, I recognize its features as a wyvern.

It falls so far down that we can't see where it lands or hear its thud.

"Is that going to happen every time?" Camila asks. We all know what the likely answer is. What we need to know is how to handle it. The wyverns appear quicker than we can react. Even if I put out a shield underneath the center of the bridge, the wyvern could just as easily attack another part, and I don't think I can make a shield that wide to protect the entire thing.

I voice this to the others.

"Maybe I can make a barrier of light underneath Aros's energy shield," Camila suggests. "It still wouldn't be powerful enough."

"But it would be stronger," Sefryn says. She looks over at Elder. "Have any other ideas?"

Flexing his jaw, Elder nods. "Yes. We're going to try again. Sefryn, hold the bridge together as best as you can. I am going to reinforce it."

"How?" Abigail asks.

"With the cliff itself," Elder answers. He extends his arms again, pulling up the two halves of the bridge. Sefryn helps, and they are able to connect the bridge much quicker this time. The tree Elder used to grab wood from is nearly gone.

I push out energy, directing it under the bridge and solidifying it. Camila follows with her power. She channels the light downward. There must be an excessive wave of heat radiating from the barrier of light, but I think my shield protects us from it.

Elder pushes out the rock of the cliff to the right and left of the bridge, bolstering it underneath. He does the same for the far side, but it takes him longer to do so. When he's done, the bridge looks more stable. The center part is still completely suspended over the canyon, but crossing it no longer seems as dangerous.

All seems safe, but we still wait a few moments before deciding to cross.

"I'll go first," I say, though I don't feel nearly as brave as I sound.

"I'll go next," Sefryn says.

"No," Elder says. "I'll go behind Aros. Then Abigail, then you, Sefryn. Aros and Camila are protecting our path across, so they should be at either end. You and I have to ensure the bridge remains intact, so we will similarly be positioned at the ends."

"And me?" Abigail asks.

Elder looks over at her. "You can control storms, right? Being in the middle allows you to easily reach both ends with a bolt of lightning. You are the last line of defense."

He says it strongly enough for Abigail to understand that she is important, that she does matter, but without overwhelming her with the pressure of all our lives being in her hands.

I shoot a look at Elder, which he returns without blinking. Whether he or Sefryn went after me, per his logic, wouldn't make a difference. That is, unless he thought that Sefryn would be unable to decide if saving my life was worth losing the others. Elder means for us all to make it, but he knows that, given how treacherous the Trials have been, it is just as likely that we won't all survive this.

The first steps I take are shaky. I can't help it. The planks must be no more than three feet wide. Plenty of room for me, if we weren't so high up that I swear there are clouds forming beneath me. With each step I take, it's like my mind throws itself into the worst parts it can. The voices from my past telling me that I was a demon, that I was possessed. Unworthy. So despicable that my own parents adopted another child so that they could be proud of someone.

Maybe I should have died that night. When those kids attacked me, that sword should have run straight through me. It would have killed me in an instant, but then everyone else would be happier. They'd be better off.

"Aros!"

Stupidly, I close my eyes and shake my head. Of all times, I can't believe that I remember this now, the memory worse than ever. The memory of the night Clarissa died. Her voice calling out *my* name. She believed that I could save her. She was wrong.

"Aros!"

I fall to my knees and cover my ears. I hear my name again. Forcing myself to open my eyes, my heart stops. The air in my chest constricts.

Right between the planks, I stare down into the abyss. Through the wispy clouds, I can see what looks to be a grassy landscape. I know, though, that there is at least a dead wyvern below, and four volunteers.

"Aros!"

It hadn't been Clarissa. It was Elder. I don't need to look back to know he's behind me. My eyes remain fixed, staring down below.

Something forms within the clouds, dark, large. It flies straight up. Another wyvern. Then I realize I had released my energy wall. With that, Camila lowered her shield. Without the time to think, I palm out a blast of energy. It's strong enough to knock the wyvern off course, but in doing so, it breaks the planks of the bridge.

I can't tell what happens first. My hands scramble to find something to hold on to while I fall. I grab onto something, my fingers closed over the edge. I swing with the far half of the bridge. I brace myself for impact against the cliff, but my momentum decreases.

Time blurs as everything slows to a stop. Then I'm hanging there, my grip on the plank the only thing keeping me alive at the moment. Because of the supports Elder made, there isn't a cliff face right in front of me, just open air. All the thoughts that tore me away from the present, from my focus on crossing the bridge, are gone.

Anger floods within me. Voltar has finally taken its toll on me. And then I realize that the other half of the bridge must have collapsed too.

Fuck, I hope the others didn't fall.

If they did, I might just let go from the guilt of it.

I force myself to look back. The sunlight makes it hard to see. The side of the bridge closer to the others dangles down as it had before. I can make out three figures on the cliff behind me, safe, right where they should be. They hadn't crossed over as far as I did.

But that would mean someone isn't here. That someone would be Elder.

It can't be. Elder is smarter than that. He knew something was up when I was crossing the bridge. He didn't let the others go because of it.

I look back again. Sure enough, Camila, Sefryn, and Abigail stand there. They're about a quarter of the way across, since the rock beams

Elder made stabilized enough of the bridge that even though they did start crossing, my deadly mistake didn't cost them their lives.

Someone else walks into view. His dark features make it easy to recognize him. Elder is safe. Moving his arms down in a half-circle, Elder pulls out more rock from the cliff, moving it beyond where they stand.

I look forward again, then up. The sunlight is bright, but I can still see the top of the cliff. Carefully, I reach up and grab the next plank like it were a rung of a ladder. The wood is strong enough to hold me. I keep going, thanking whatever gods I can that the day isn't overly windy or rainy.

I feel the updraft before seeing it. A wyvern rushes up, this time headed for me. A shout escapes my mouth as I let one hand go and blast light toward it. The wyvern dodges and soars higher before diving back down at me.

Again, I try to blast it with a beam of light, but the wyvern is too nimble in the air. Frustrated, I change my attack to fire. It doesn't make a difference.

The wyvern dives below. Clouds move over where it went, blocking my view of the ground entirely. Then I feel the wood move, rising. I end up lying on my stomach, my fists still clenched around the plank. The bridge jolts as it is reattached. Elder helps me pick myself off the floor.

"We have to go now," Camila urges.

I quickly thank Elder and get going. Moving my hands wildly, I reform the energy barrier I had earlier. Camila forms her shield of light.

Even though it's terrifying, my steps are much quicker. We are over halfway across now. I keep myself focused on reaching the end but pay attention to what's below me.

Three wyverns fly toward us from the side, completely avoiding my energy and Camila's light barriers. Another one tries to break through from below. The bridge shakes a bit.

I don't think Abigail can strike down all three wyverns in time. She summons lightning and gets the one to our left. The cracking sound is over as soon as it came, but I can't hear anything except for ringing for seconds after. There are still two on the right headed straight for us.

We have a mere moment before they tear through the bridge, sending us plummeting to the depths below.

The air moves so quickly that I can see it. Wind blasts heavily like a hurricane toward the two wyverns. They can't fly through it and are pushed back.

The wyverns dive down, trying to get around the blast of wind. The wyvern beneath my energy wall cuts around it.

Abigail throws out her other hand, making the same force of wind on the other side.

"Go!" she shouts at us. She tilts her head toward Sefryn and Camila, telling them to go around her.

It feels like we're in the eye of a storm; the sunlight remains, and the still air feels safe. Beyond that, there are gusts of wind and rain flying around, their forces strong enough to keep all the wyverns away.

Elder points forward. We go at an even faster pace. It feels like it takes too long, but I finally reach the end. I turn back. Elder is quick to join me, followed shortly by Sefryn and Camila.

Abigail walks backward, her steps slow and careful. She continues to move her arms around, keeping up the windstorm she created.

A roar rumbles from deep within the canyon. It couldn't be.

"Was that a dragon?" Camila asks.

Abigail must have heard it too, but she remains calm as she makes her way. I throw up a wall of energy to the sides of the bridge to help her keep her balance.

I feel helpless waiting here while Abigail fends off the monsters, but I know there isn't much else I can do.

We're lucky that whatever made the noise never shows up. When Abigail feels the soft grass of the land, rather than the hard wood of the bridge, she spins around and runs toward us. Elder catches her in his arms as she collapses.

I can hear her breathing. What she did was incredible, but it must have taken a lot out of her.

Without her power to keep up the storms, all the wind and rain die out. The bridge is fully intact. But nothing flies out of the depths of the canyon. We did it.

We all made it.

# Chapter 20

# The Ashen Pit

**Aros Caelum Hayes**

All that's left is to cross the second bridge, which, while much shorter, is also incredibly steep. Like the last, though, it isn't very wide and has no supports to help us keep our balance. Quite understandably, none of us are eager to hop on it.

A look at Abigail tells me that, more than anything, she's drained. There is no more fear in her eyes, no uncertainty. It's like something has dawned on her. Like the rest of us have known for ourselves, she's realized that she didn't survive the Trials because of sheer luck. She survived because she was strong enough to.

On top of the mesa the short bridge leads to, an oblong stone stands in the middle, reminding me of a monument of sorts. I know the Ashen Pit is inside. That gives me the confidence that the apparent ease and seeming peacefulness of the second bridge is not a trick or trap.

I start walking toward it.

"Aros, be careful," Camila says.

"It's fine," I call back, but keep moving forward, alert for danger. "It's over. We're done." I step onto the bridge and climb.

I hear the others follow shortly after. It takes over a minute to get across. The flat land is easy to navigate. Other than the sparse grass and tall structure, there is nothing else up here. We have to walk around the stone before finding its entrance. I can't see inside, but I know there are steps that go down.

Excitement swells within me while a selfish greed fuels my steps. It's like I know if I get there first, then I am bound to be chosen as an Ash Lord. It's stupid and somewhat egotistical, though, the other thought that I have. And that is that it doesn't matter. I was already chosen as an Ash Lord before the Trials even started.

Darkness swallows me instantly once I'm just a few steps down. There is no railing to guide us, just the walls on either side. I walk carefully—imagining making it all the way to the end of the Trials just to misstep and fall down these stairs to my death.

The stairs even out. I imagine walking into a large chamber, but everything is still so dark. Then I remember that I could have lit up the stairs with Magis.

I turn back to see that Camila had done that very thing. They were farther behind me, and her light made no difference to my visibility. Even now, I only know it's Camila because she's the only one who can do it, but all I see is a small orb floating in the air, slowly getting closer.

When they get to me, Camila says in a whisper, "I couldn't make my light any stronger." As if to prove her point, the light orb goes out.

I suppose that the chamber is meant to be dark since it seems to have limited Camila's power.

Blue fire lights the sconces along the walls of the chamber. The room is circular. There is enough light to see clearly, but the room is still quite dark. Up ahead, there are two stairs that lead into what I imagine to be the pit. The stairs are made of rough stone. The pit is filled with varying colors of sand.

It might be ash, though—the ash of all the previous Ash Lords.

Then, in the middle of it, the Ashen Pit burns brilliantly in an orange flame. Before we get too close to it, the Azure Fox walks out from behind the shadows. Her ice-blue aura emanates brighter than usual, casting a frosty haze throughout the chamber. Compared to outside, it is warm in the chamber, and, thankfully, the Azure Fox's presence doesn't make it cold. Her eyes graze over us, pausing for a moment to lock onto mine.

"Congratulations, volunteers," she says, her voice steady and filling me with a sense of calm I shouldn't have, given the circumstances we just went through. "Your courage, power, and the nature of your soul have been proven. The Ashen Pit has seen into your core."

Silence follows.

"I will return you to Edlyn shortly. When the Trials are complete, the Ashen Pit will decide who to call upon to burn their soul into its fire."

"I thought that the Supreme Ash was going to pick the new Ash Lords?" Sefryn asks, her voice slightly louder than usual.

The Azure Fox, Grisla, bows her head in a nod.

"Originally, and since ancient times, the Ashen Pit has chosen a Supreme Ash, but the Supreme Ash chooses the other four Ash Lords based on their overcoming great obstacles. In the centuries after Arteyva's dawn, there was no need for the Ash Trials. But the need for a true test of one's conviction, strength, and heart necessitated something greater, and the Ash Trials were created to provide that. With varying degrees of intensity and danger, the Ash Trials have served as the bar for those who were worthy enough."

"But this time, things are different?" Camila asks. Her posture is perfect, her eyes unmoving. Like I do, I can see that Camila already knows the answer and understands that there is something deeper to these Trials.

"Yes. It has been one hundred and fifty years since the last Ash Trials took place. The Ash Lords that were chosen then did not live as long as they should have." The Azure Fox falls silent for a moment. "The Magis embedded in the very nature of this world is shifting. The Ashen Pit is taking steps to ensure that this world is saved. As such, it, and it alone, is choosing each Ash Lord itself."

Grisla sighs.

"I have seen kingdoms rise and fall, extraordinary people perish at the hands of unruly and envious men, but I have never known the Ashen Pit to be so concerned for the realms that it interferes with worldly affairs. Becoming an Ash Lord is a serious matter, and this time the stakes are higher than ever before. If the Ashen Pit calls upon you, do not answer unless you are willing—not only to lay down your life but to lay down your eternity, because if you are killed as an Ash Lord, then the ashes of your soul will never leave the pit.

"Your soul is eternal, but by burning it to ash, it becomes mortal. In exchange, you'll have power beyond your wildest dreams, not unlike what you experienced during the last test. That said, I must warn you, unless you are an Ash Lord, be wary of the intensity of your powers back in Arteyva because you may not be as strong as you felt you just were."

"So, it was a test then?" I ask, remembering how my mind was so overpowered that I almost got everyone killed. I step forward, close to the first stair into the pit. I hear someone suck in a breath, and I can feel the rest tense. Not knowing that Grisla and I have spoken a few times and that I've been in contact with one of her kind for a decade, they must think I am either very brave or just very stupid. "The bridges, I mean. It was all meant to bring out the strongest of us, to see the limits of our power."

"Yes and no," Grisla replies. "The last trial served as a means to give you a taste of what you can accomplish by pushing you beyond your limits. For all intents and purposes, the last trial is for the benefit of the Ashen Pit. It wants to get a glimpse of what you can achieve were it to lend you its power."

"Lend us its power?" Sefryn asks. She steps forward like I did. Sefryn, apprehensive, finds my hand to hold. I can tell she's worried she might offend the Azure Fox, but Grisla doesn't even blink.

"Yes, you heard correctly. The Ashen Pit lends its power to the Ash Lords, making them far more powerful than the others in the world. But nevertheless, the power is borrowed."

"How do you return it?" Abigail asks.

The Azure Fox takes a few steps closer to us, down the stairs, into the Ashen Pit. The orange flames clash against the light of her blue aura. She looks directly at Abigail. "You die."

Abigail shudders. Grisla begins to circle the pit but keeps her distance. As she paces, I can't help but wonder what's coming to Arteyva. Whatever it is, it must be big enough that everyone needs to be a part of it. I know of the looming war between Soulstice and Gorgrein, something that soon will spread to Edlyn. But I haven't seen the signs of it. All I hear are rumors. Since there are Fae from Praellen in the Trials, they too must be in the same danger. But what is it exactly? Is there something coming for all of us? Or is it already here?

"Something else you should know. The Ashen Pit deems it the highest treason to kill an Ash Lord, especially if you are a Lord yourself. So, if anyone you don't... particularly like is chosen alongside you, do not get any ideas." The Azure Fox stares at all of us this time. I don't know why. The only people I wouldn't care to be an Ash Lord with are dead.

The flames in the Ashen Pit flicker brightly for a moment, their intensity strengthening. Grisla looks back at it.

"It appears that the next wave of volunteers has made it to the bridges. This means we may soon be out of time, so let me get to it." The Azure Fox walks back to the pit and sits in front of it. The flames are so close to her, and her cold, fiery aura seems to blend with the blaze. "When it is time, and if you are chosen, the Dark Wind—an essence of the Ashen Pit—will bring you back here, and you may burn your soul into the pit. Your ashes will lie amongst the others. This makes it impossible to remove the ashes of just one person, for if it were to happen, that person would cease to be an Ash Lord. Not only that, but with their soul unreturned, they would live as a soulless entity, alive only in body. No sense of person, no emotion, no thought, no will."

The Azure Fox speaks in a whisper. "The worst part? That body cannot be killed, leaving the person to rot, barely alive, but never quite reaching death."

No one says anything. The flames behind Grisla burn brighter, the fire growing taller.

The Dark Wind is an essence of the Ashen Pit? Then it's been watching me all along. How long has the Ashen Pit been waiting to start the Trials? Did it want to ensure I was strong enough to make it? Or was there something else—maybe someone else? I want to blurt out question after question. The Dark Wind, or the Ashen Pit, took me to Kreavlos, took me to Earth, and left me there for all those years. What happened in that time? The question of *why now* burns in my mind again.

"Once again, congratulations on completing the Ash Trials. Only one other has successfully made it this far, while most of the volunteers have long since perished." She pauses. "Enjoy your time back in Edlyn. While you won't wait long, there will be a wait. Few volunteers are left, and even fewer will make it."

The Azure Fox bows her head.

"When you are ready, place your hand on my head as you did before, and I will see that you make it back to Edlyn."

I let the others go first. Abigail is more than excited to get out of here. Elder follows her, then Camila. Sefryn looks back at me with a smile before disappearing. I walk up to Grisla. She eyes me knowingly. I put my hand gently on her head. As the world fades away, I notice the burning flames falter and immediately die out. The volunteers must have just made it to the Pit. The fire was unlit for us until we entered the chamber.

My gut tells me otherwise, though. We're not about to be followed by the next volunteers who successfully made it out of Voltar. No. They all just died. And the time I must wait until the Dark Wind calls me to the

Ashen Pit just got that much shorter. I let my heart feel for them for just a brief moment. But their death means my success, for better or worse, and that is a fact I cannot ignore.

# CHAPTER 21

# TENSIONS IN THE CASTLE

**Aros Caelum Hayes**

Edlyn Castle feels familiar, as if I am back home. It's light outside, but it is not long after breakfast, and plenty of people are moving about. The Azure Fox returned us to the atrium, right in front of the wall that Peter carved all our names into. But it's different now. Most of the names have been crossed out, just lightly, so that you can still read them. I feel nothing when I see *Joshua Haden Cowers* crossed out. Cowers is my so-called brother's original last name. He used "Hayes" when he got older. I wish I could burn my name away, start fresh, anew, and with no relation to my parents. But soon enough, they won't be relevant, and no one will remember them.

Abigail lets out a gasp as a slash carves through another name, seemingly all on its own. I wonder how many friends and family members have waited in front of this wall, terror drilled into their bones, praying their loved one's name won't get slashed out. That first morning of the Trials must have been mayhem here, with so many names being crossed out seconds after each other. I hear the scratching of another name being slashed. Once the Trials are over, we will be able to see everyone who made it. I wonder if our names will remain on the wall forever.

Still scanning the wall, my heart drops when I see *Clarissa Stills Snowenfeld* crossed out. Abigail sees it too. She puts her hand on the name, takes in a quick breath as her fingers dig into the groove of the slash, and quickly retracts her hand.

"How the fuck?"

I look over to Camila, who points at the wall where *Arthur Drew Theodore* remains untouched. How did he survive? I quickly look for Chase's name and find it crossed out. I knew that. I saw Chase die. But I never saw Arthur die. I always just assumed it. Even if I were to kill him the next time he shows his ugly face, it wouldn't matter as much. This wall will always remind people that Arthur survived the Trials, and people like Clarissa didn't. The world isn't fair. It never has been.

Hopefully, his name is the next to be crossed out. If there is any sense of true justice, that would be it.

Abigail leaves without a word. I know her heart is heavy. Part of me wonders just how close she and Clarissa were.

Elder mentions something about finding his son, but I barely hear his words. When he leaves, I am alone with Sefryn and Camila. I take some time to search the wall, wanting to find out who is still in the Trials. One of those names is the person who got through them before we did. I wish there was some way I could tell, but I will have to wait until it's all over. With hundreds of names on the wall, it takes me longer than I anticipated to find other names that aren't crossed out. But just as I'm ready to give up, I see one.

*Ziara Belle Sandfawn*

And then just quickly after, even though the two names are not close to each other, I see one other.

*Matthew Brickal*

I continue to look over the wall for other names, but staring at it for too long makes my vision go blurry. I hear strained voices from behind me, and I turn my head back to look. My sight immediately returns to normal, but a faint headache takes place.

"A ship was reported lingering off the Ibari coastline. Actions must be taken," comes the voice of a man.

"There is no proof that it was a Gorgrein ship. I want my resources here," replies a woman.

"Soulstice will agree to the merge. They have already said as much."

"It's a little too late for that. I want Edlyn protected."

Queen Mattias walks in, accompanied by Claudius. It's clear Claudius is suggesting some of the King's army be sent down to Ibari.

"Camila," the Queen says, her eyes wide with surprise. "You're home." Camila's mother walks up and embraces her in an overly long hug. It's slow, careful, tender, and immensely awkward. I get the idea it's more of a public stunt rather than love. I feel bad for her. At least my parents were always extremely clear about what they thought of me.

"I am, mother," Camila replies, retracting from the hug.

Queen Mattias smiles down at her daughter. She's about a head taller, which is still shorter than her husband. "I always knew you would make it."

Camila replies with a smile. She's holding back. I know what she's thinking. They sent Camila as an offering, hardly caring if she made it or not. They have three other daughters. They don't need her to keep the kingdom under their family's rule.

"Congratulations, all of you," Claudius says, walking up to us and shaking our hands. He shakes mine last, but as he does so, there's a glint in his eyes. "The Trials are no easy feat. But there's no need for me to tell you. Each one of you has seen that."

Something in his smile, the gleam in his eyes, and his relaxed, proper stature makes me feel uneasy, but a sense of admiration for him can't be helped. I'm sure I will get to know him more. He is the Supreme Ash, after all. And there is no way I'm not going to be an Ash Lord.

"Ordinarily the Supreme Ash would be charged with choosing the Ash Lords. But this time things are different." He moves slightly, shifting his stance, but he doesn't break his eye contact. "I have not seen anything that occurred in the Trials, so I wouldn't know who would be best to choose. But I do know this," he says, strengthening his voice. "The sole fact that you made it here means you've proven your worth. So, however things turn out, just know that."

"Come, Claudius," the Queen says. "We still have much to discuss."

I hear footsteps, their sound loud and echoing.

"I don't know what there is to discuss." The King emerges from the hall. His eyes are narrowed and focused on Claudius. "We will not be sending our army to Ibara, or any other place in Soulstice. There are still rumors that the king and queen of Soulstice are intending to invade Edlyn, and I will not let them have an easy go at it."

King Mattias widens his eyes when he notices us.

"These are not matters to be spoken of in front of the *commonfolk*."

"We're not commonfolk, my liege," Camila says clearly, her words carefully chosen. "I am royalty, and the rest of us here have just made it through the Ash Trials. We're anything but *commonfolk*. My companions will be given no less than the treatment our knights do."

The King stares down at his daughter. "But they are not involved in political matters of our kingdom, no matter who they might be. And neither are you. Treat them as you will. You will host them on behalf of Edlyn." King Mattias turns to face Sefryn, his mouth opening slightly, but he says nothing. Then he looks at the rest of us. "My sincerest congratulations to you all for completing the Ash Trials. I hope that the rest of your stay in Edlyn is a pleasant one. You are welcome here as long as you wish."

Without another word or look, he leads the Queen and Claudius out of the atrium. Once they leave, Camila turns to the rest of us, her eyes telling all—how sorry she is for their attitude and how, with each interaction she has with her parents, she understands more and more the rift between her family and herself.

"What now?" Sefryn asks.

"Whatever we want," Camila answers. Her arms are still crossed as she looks up at Sefryn.

"I guess that depends on what time it is," Sefryn says.

"Time won't be the same here as where we just were," I say. "This is probably going to feel like the worst jet lag ever."

Camila and Sefryn stare at me. I sigh. That was stupid of me to say, of course they don't know what jet lag is.

"The time—it doesn't matter. We need to get used to the fact that we're back." I shake my head. I need to keep spending time in Arteyva, not Voltar, and especially not Earth.

Not knowing anything better to do, Camila walks us around the castle and grounds. At first, I am surprised at the number of travelers that are still here, even if the ones they came with will never return.

Then understanding comes to me. The Trials. While not a spectating event, everyone is curious to see the outcome. Soon the world will have its Ash Lords. They're watching a thing of legend.

We stop walking near the river that divides Edlyn and Voltar and stare at its calm waters. I didn't realize I'd led them here. With everything that happened, the land of Voltar looks and feels normal. It too feels like my home.

I put my arms around them, Sefryn to my left and Camila on my right. I am still trying to understand my feelings for Sefryn. But I know that whatever I feel, it will build into something greater than anything I've experienced. Camila, well, she's something different entirely. I love her like she's the family I never had.

My ear twitches at a slight change in the air, a soft rustle of the leaves and twigs on the ground. A benign presence, I hear Abigail's voice.

"For some reason, I thought I would find you guys here."

I turn back to look at her, retracting my arms from Sefryn and Camila. Abigail has removed the blue from her hair, leaving it fully blonde, striking in shine, while her eyes remain misty. I walk up and embrace her in a hug. It will take a few days for us all to come to grips with everything that's happened.

"I couldn't help but be drawn here myself," she says into my chest. For all of us, it's probably the closest we'll get to Voltar ever again. Though a terrible place, we share a bond unlike any other. She lets go and looks up at me. "I just miss her so much."

Flashes of that night fly through my mind. Violent. Disgusting. I stare into Abigail's eyes, refusing to show any emotion. Just because I can't forget the horrors of it doesn't mean that Abigail ever has to know them. Supposedly being torn apart into pieces is a much better death compared to what really went down.

"I know," I say softly. "Me too. She was strong, brave, and one of my best friends." I force a smile. "I mean that. And I could never forget her."

"I can make sure that Edlyn honors her memory," Camila says.

Abigail smiles. "I would like that."

Camila smiles softly, but I can see the sadness in her eyes.

"And I know she is always with us. Always with you," Sefryn says.

Our moment is interrupted by footsteps. I tense, but I know that whatever it is isn't likely to be danger.

Luckily, it's only Elder, alongside his son, Peter, who carries a small figure made of stone. It resembles Veronica with eerie precision.

"I'm sorry, I didn't mean to interrupt," Elder says. He gently takes the stone statue from his son. "I just wanted to leave this here in her memory." He places the figurine on the ground, shifting dirt and pebbles from the river to hold it in place.

Elder stands up again and looks at us. He nods to his son, and they walk over to a tree. Peter breaks off a branch with his powers and shaves off parts of it until it is shaped like a body. Elder then works on it, carving out finer details until it looks like Clarissa. It isn't as clear as the stone statue they brought, but I think it's good enough.

Abigail does too. She grabs it and thanks Elder and Peter.

"Sorry I couldn't do more," Elder says. "I remember her. But I didn't know her like I did Veronica. So the details aren't there."

"It's perfect," Abigail says. She rests it next to the other stone figure. Peter gets to work, moving dirt and stones to lock it in place. I notice the change in Peter. In the time his father was away, Peter has grown, maybe not taller, but his body is noticeably stronger, his arms closer to the size of his father's than they had been. Peter then molds stones together to make a flat plaque and carves Veronica's and Clarissa's names into it before locking it down too.

"There," he says, his voice deep and kind. "Now they will always be remembered."

Abigail responds by giving Peter a hug. Taken aback at first, Peter eases into the hug, smiling to himself.

Minutes pass as we stand there in silence. When we're done, we head back to the castle, our words between each other still few.

"When do you think would be a good time to head toward the village?" I ask Camila as we step over the threshold to the castle's main entrance.

"We could go now," she says. "But to make the most of it, I think we should wait a day or so and then go in the evening."

"Why the evening?" Sefryn asks. Abigail moves her head slightly so she can hear better.

The smirk across Camila's face is priceless, and I can't help but smile too.

"We're going to have fun."

"Who is going to have fun?"

The two voices in sync make the hairs on my neck stand up. Before I can avoid it, I feel hands clamp around both my biceps.

"I don't think we were properly introduced," one of Camila's sisters says. "I'm Floria."

"And I'm Creslia."

"And he's—" Sefryn starts but is interrupted.

"Aros. We know." Again, the twins speak in unison.

"*Taken.*" Sefryn glares at them. The twins don't appreciate it, but they hold their tongues.

Something inside me feels so good right now, so validated. But I can't help thinking that Sefryn's word isn't true. Not yet. She hasn't taken me yet—something I now have an immense urge to remedy.

I walk out of their grasp and turn to face them.

"We've now been properly introduced," I say. "I'll be leaving now." I reach my hand out for Sefryn to take. She does, and I walk away with her. I hear Camila laugh as she follows us, Abigail just behind her.

"Congratulations on not dying, sis!"

Camila ignores her sisters. I don't blame her. Sefryn kisses me on the cheek before letting go of my hand. Camila gives me a look that tells me she already knew. I do my best to suppress a smile.

"What fun are we going to have, Camila?" Sefryn asks.

"There's a pub in the village. It's busy most nights, but they're hosting a 'Trials' themed night soon."

"How do you know this?" I ask since she's been with us the entire time since we've been back.

"They were talking about it before the Trials started. But the date is set to be when the Trials are over. I suspect it will be a day or two."

"Maybe sooner," I mumble.

"I just hope it isn't the type of thing that shows just how little they know what the Trials are," Abigail says. There's that tone of voice I know from when I first met her, but it doesn't annoy me; if anything, it makes me happy. I think the night out will be good for us; the quick change in tone from somber to planning a night out suits us.

Camila leads us to the Grand Room where we've eaten before. The room is almost empty, with just a few servants moving around, cleaning rarely used tables. But there is something different. The long tables are polished, thick legs of petrified wood are used to support the wood and black quartzite tops. Smaller chandeliers hang from the ceiling with a sleek, Earth-like clean appearance, in contrast to the old-castle style. The small fires that burn inside are so steady they look almost like lightbulbs.

We sit at one of the tables near the swinging doors that lead to the floor below. I wonder what the King and Queen intend to use this room for now that there are so few of us left.

As I sit there, it dawns on me that we've been awake for more than a day, but I am not tired. I also don't feel any of the injuries I sustained while we traversed across the bridges to reach the Pit. I can only imagine that the Azure Fox, or the Pit itself, healed us as we were returned to Edlyn.

With just a slight raise of her arm, Camila calls over a servant. He's shorter than Camila but has the same dark hair color she does.

"Bring us the royal lunch."

The servant raises an eyebrow.

"My companions are to be treated like royalty," Camila says. "Bring us the royal lunch."

The servant nods and walks away.

"I would bring you upstairs to where my family usually eats," Camila tells us, "but they likely would be there, and it is best to avoid them."

Abigail looks curiously at Camila but doesn't say anything. The two sit across from Sefryn and me. The teeny moment of silence is interrupted by Camila's oldest sibling.

"That's not a very nice thing to say," the older sister says. "We are your family, after all." She sits down next to Camila. She looks at me briefly, and then she smiles politely when looking at Sefryn and Abigail. "Hello, I'm Mavia."

I stare at her, remembering vividly how she refused to tell me her name when we met before the Trials started. Mavia shoots me a quick smirk.

"I'm sure you've been given more congratulations than you care for," she tells us. "But I wanted to give mine anyway. Truly, I am honored to be in your presence."

Camila scoffs.

Mavia looks at her sister. She urges Camila to scoot over so she can sit properly and not half off the bench. Rolling her eyes, Camila makes space for her sister.

"I mean it," Mavia says pointedly, staring at her younger sister. "You guys were brave enough to do something that not many would."

"There were hundreds of volunteers," Sefryn says. "But most didn't return."

"I am sorry for those who didn't make it," Mavia says. "But that is the point I am trying to make. There were only hundreds of volunteers out of millions of people. There are parents, daughters, friends, husbands, who came here with someone and left alone. No one knew the Trials would be that dangerous."

Again, Camila scoffs. "We did. Our family knew how dangerous they would be."

Mavia nods. "And they still forced you to offer yourself up," she replies. "Messed up, but I envy you, Camila."

"Why? Mom and Dad didn't throw you to your death like they did to me." It surprises me that Camila speaks of her parents as her parents, and not by their titles.

Mavia shakes her head. "You may see it that way. And maybe you're right. But I see it as they didn't think I was strong enough to make it back."

"No, you're just their prized princess."

"And if I weren't alive, they'd find a way to make sure you sat on the throne."

Camila stares at her sister.

"You think our parents would ever allow our twin sisters to rule over Edlyn?" Mavia lets out a laugh. "They'd fuck their way to Edlyn's demise."

A chuckle escapes Camila's mouth. "Still, they couldn't risk your life."

Mavia shrugs. "Maybe. But I know that they figured your chances of survival were good. Especially after you became friends with *him*."

The word carries a touch of resentment.

"Do you have a problem with me?" I ask, even though I don't care what her answer is.

"One of those boys you killed ten years ago—I was seeing him."

"Of course you were," I say, not understanding why my temper is rising. "They were assholes and deserved what they got." I look into Mavia's eye. "If you're still mad about it *ten years later*, then you have bad taste in guys. Which means you're no better than your twin sisters."

Mavia's lips curve downward and her eyes narrow. "You're the asshole. My mother and father will see you for who you really are, and when they do, they will treat you appropriately."

I lean forward. "No, see, your parents feared me before the Trials. When I become an Ash Lord, they'll do anything I ask. They can't afford not to have me on their side, and they know it even now."

Mavia glares at me. She knows I'm right. I don't need the King and Queen to be loyal to me, and I don't care about their issues with the other countries. Whatever Camila needs me to do, though, I'll be there.

"Fuck you."

"I'll be seeing you around," I tell her. I smile viciously, the glare in my eyes making it clear that she should leave. With a final scowl, she gets up and walks away.

I look over at Camila. I see Abigail with her mouth open, obviously with much to say, but her shock keeps her silent.

"She hates you," Camila says. "But that was awesome. Harsh, though, and I should condemn you for speaking to my sister like that."

She laughs. "But awesome."

I'm saved from the need to respond when two servants come to deliver lunch. Gold-rimmed stone plates are placed in front of us, accompanied by platters of no less than seven different kinds of meat, cheeses, and fruits. The four of us look at each other, and then we eat everything but the fruit. I had forgotten how good real, properly cooked meals are. We eat so fast that the servants apologize profusely for not providing enough food, promising that they will remedy it immediately. Camila thanks them and tells them that we've eaten enough. While true, I still wish I could eat more.

Reading my thoughts, Camila tells me, "Every meal we eat will be like this. It isn't like we're about to go into the Trials again."

She has a point, and I allow myself to feel full.

Abigail burps, which causes her cheeks to flush with embarrassment. We laugh, and to help ease Abigail, Sefryn burps too. Camila follows, and in the end, I am the only one who doesn't burp. When I try to, I just hiccup instead and then deal with the fit of laughter from the girls that follows. But when they laugh at me, they regret it almost immediately, since they hiccup too.

I revel in the moment, feeling as if we might just have a normal life. But I know better. If we're going to be Ash Lords, the Trials won't be the last horror we'll live through. We will be way stronger, though. After everything, I'm enjoying not feeling like something is going to kill me at any moment.

Lunch is followed by a long walk around the castle. We pass by the fields where many of the volunteers trained before the Trials. There's a lake on one side of the castle, and when we reach the other entrance, I can see into the valley below. Structures are built along the hills and cliffsides, leading to the village nestled at its base. The land continues its slight descent toward sea level, though the ocean can't be seen from here. Since Edlyn Castle stands by itself, the village has a much homier feel. I can't help but wonder how lonely the corridors and chambers can get. I know that the servants don't stay in the castle—not the low-order ones, at least.

We move on from the view and walk the grounds some more. Camila offers to assign us sleeping quarters, but I tell her to show us after dinner. I want to get used to being back for a bit before I head to bed, knowing that once I see one, I will want to fall asleep immediately.

The afternoon goes by quicker than I anticipated, despite doing little. As twilight falls, we return to the Grand Room for dinner. This time, when Camila orders the servants to feed us, they do it without question or hesitation. As we eat, I notice someone walk in. She has light brown hair and matching eyes that contain such a presence that I can't help but look into them as she catches mine for a moment. She looks away quickly, seemingly realizing that she was caught staring. She reminds me of someone. I shrug to myself and keep eating.

Elder and Peter join us. Peter is given the same treatment upon Elder's demand, and Camila nods to the servants to approve it. She then walks away for a moment, coming back minutes later.

I'm too tired to ask where she went.

Our dinner is graced by the presence of the King. He smiles as he stops by our table. "I hope dinner is to your liking," he says but doesn't let us respond. He turns to Camila and calls over a servant. "The winners of the Ash Trials will stay in Tower Four," King Mattias says. I don't know where Tower Four is, but that's probably the point—calling it the "northeast" tower would be too obvious. "Ensure their stay is as every bit comfortable as you make mine."

The servant nods and hurries away. The King nods to his daughter and leaves without another word.

"I should tell you that the royal family sleeps in the towers," Camila says. I look at her, confused, as I know she went to a different room to sleep before we left for Voltar. "I had to keep that a secret," she tells me.

"Rules I have to follow. I'm sorry for lying."

I nod. I understand and don't care. Sefryn smiles and continues eating. When we're done, Camila leads us into the atrium and up a staircase. We walk toward the west end of the castle where a servant is waiting by a wooden door.

"All the rooms are ready, Your Highness." The servant bows.

"Thank you," Camila says politely. We go through the large doors, walk down the hall for a while until we reach the other side of the castle, near the library, and then up a spiral staircase.

"These doors lead to the other floors," Camila points out. "And near the top, there are chambers—three on each floor. They're big. But if you ever wanted a bath in a tub so large it could be called a lake, just take these stairs all the way to the bottom."

Camila takes us to the top floor.

"Choose your rooms. Someone has to sleep on the floor below, though."

"Peter and I will," Elder offers.

Camila nods and then gestures to the three doors that are just ahead of us. With how much space there is, there could be another three doors, and still, each unit would be larger than some apartments in the crowded cities on Earth.

I walk over to the one on the left. "Good night. And thanks," I say, looking at Camila. She smiles and nods, her graceful presence taking over as she represents her family. Sefryn takes the middle, and Abigail goes to the right.

I don't see a bed when I walk in. The chamber is huge. The entry is a living room, with no other word to use to describe it. There is a large couch that faces the window, which is nearly as tall as the room, and overlooks the village of Aeilvow, though the towers on the side of the Grand Room are closer to it. With the onset of night, the village shines brightly like scattered stars.

Through an open doorway, a short hall leads to two separate spaces: on one side, a bedroom; on the other, a narrow, curved room with a table, shelves lined with books, and a cozy nook for reading.

The bedroom mirrors the living room, with a massive window and nearly as much space. The bed rests within a large frame—regal and inviting. I open the curtains at the window so I can look out at the night.

Connected to the bedroom is a bathroom with a wide, sunken tub carved five feet into the floor. I step down into it and take a shower, the water falling right down from the ceiling like rain. I turn it hot since I haven't had access to plumbing for a while. I stand there, the water running down my face. I chuckle at the immense selection of soaps. I choose one at random: redwood and shea butter.

Running my fingers through my hair, I'm surprised how long it's gotten. The grime matted it down so much, I hadn't noticed. I don't know how anyone tolerated the stench we must've carried when we returned.

I finish my shower, now feeling more awake. And now I realize my mistake. Sefryn. The Trials are over. She's as much admitted her feelings to me, just as much as I've made them known to her.

Looking into the mirror, I immediately grab a Rogvey-designed razor. I trim the wild facial hair, leaving a short stubble behind. I've never grown it out before, but something about it feels right. The result isn't perfect, but maybe tomorrow I'll find someone to shape it properly.

Letting out a long breath, I prepare myself to see Sefryn. I've been an idiot. A total, complete idiot.

I open the door to my chambers, ready to storm to Sefryn's. But she's here already, hand raised and fist curled, ready to knock.

"I've been an idiot," she says to me. She lowers her arm and puts both her hands on my chest, pushing just slightly, but she closes the distance between us. Sefryn kisses me with more force than I thought she would, like she wants me just as much as I want her. I pull her close to me and into my room, shutting the door with a flick of energy. There's a hint of vanilla in how she tastes, and like an insatiable sweet tooth, I go for more.

We find ourselves gasping for breath, her mouth still so close to mine that we share the same air. I lean in and go for her neck, the scent of pine enters my nose, and I can no longer associate it with anything else but her. And with all the time I've spent feeling everything that I have for her, my body feels ready to release, like it's never experienced anything like this. I hold back. No way. No way am I going to let that happen now.

But it gets harder with each graze of her skin against mine, the short nibbles on my ear, on my neck, ready to go lower. She doesn't need to. All my blood has already rushed there.

She looks up at me and takes off her thin silk gown. There's nothing beneath it, and I take in the sight of her. I lean down, ready to get on my knees when she speaks.

"No," she breathes out. "I'm ready for you now."

I'm ready too, and I want nothing more than to satisfy my urge, but I keep myself in check. I use my tongue and trace upward. I get to just above her waist and look up. She shudders a breath.

"Please."

I want her to say it again, but I don't tease anymore. I stand to my full height and kiss her again. I place my hands beneath her thighs and lift her up. She wraps her arms around my neck. I ease her closer, sliding into her slowly. I walk over toward the window, her back almost against it, the village lights glinting behind her. Starting slow, she moves her body closer to take in more, to take it in faster.

I concentrate on her, on making sure this moment lasts as long as she needs it to. Sefryn's eyes shine with pleasure as she tilts her head up, and I can't fucking believe I'm this lucky. I gently kiss her exposed neck and leave my lips there. I circle my tongue against her skin lightly before increasing the pressure. She lets out a small cry and puts one of her hands in my hair, pulling slightly. My mouth opens, the feel of her touch coursing through my body. Gritting my teeth, I keep at it, lost in the way our bodies perfectly match as if they were meant to be together.

My legs burn and my arms feel heavy, but I don't stop. Bending my knees slightly, I take the reins. She lets out another cry and kisses my neck, and I fail to suppress a low moan. She's giving me everything, and then more. I've never been with a girl this intimate, and I know that this is more than just sex. All the pent-up feelings for her create this energy that I use with each movement I make, from the thrusts to the kisses to the slight shift of my hands.

I look into her eyes and use one hand to push her back, bending over slightly so that she can lean away. I support her with my other hand on her back. I suck in a breath as I look over her body, her stomach taut, her breasts irresistible, and her lips so inviting that I'm ready to pull them back up to mine. Sefryn holds my hand in hers. At her first scream, I can't hold it in any longer. For a short moment, it feels as if we're in sync, each pulse from my body yielding those loud gasps from her that caused me to lose control in the first place.

When we're done, I lift her back to me. Still inside, I walk over to the couch and lie her down, kissing her again before pulling out. She looks up at me, and I'm ready to go again. No words need to be spoken, and I let myself lie there, the full weight of my body on top of her, her arms around my torso while we enjoy the feel of each other until my body is ready to start once more. Her nails dig into my back, making me go harder, and even though my body feels exhausted, I know my efforts are worth it.

# CHAPTER 22

## FINALISTS

**Aros Caelum Hayes**

We made it to the bed. Eventually. Even later, we finally made it to sleep.

Even though it's no more than five hours when I wake, it feels like the best sleep I've had in a long time. Sefryn hugged me the entire night, and I wake up smiling. She wakes up with me, and we let ourselves enjoy this moment, embracing each other as we allow ourselves to feel happy and safe for the first time in a while.

The bedroom door opens. I sit up slightly, the thick comforter covering my private areas, my chest exposed. Camila walks in. She catches my eye. Damn, she really does feel like my sister. Sefryn sits up, too, holding the blanket up to her collarbones.

"Knowing what was going to happen, I wouldn't have come in, but since we need you, I figured it was better me than someone else," she says, staying at the doorway. She looks a little awkward. "I should let you know that Arthur made it back earlier this morning. It is likely the Trials are about to end."

I sit there, cursing to myself. The Trials ending is good news. Arthur isn't.

"I'll be with the others at breakfast. See you soon."

Camila walks away, and Sefryn and I look at each other. I could repeat last night for the rest of eternity. But Sefryn and I both know that we need to face everything that is about to follow. I give her a light kiss, and we take a quick shower. She takes one of the shirts from the wardrobe in my bedroom. Meant to fit me, it is big on her. As we walk down into the atrium, Sefryn grabs my hand softly.

"I need to go take something," she says. "I'll be in there soon." I look at her, wondering what she means. Does she feel sick? She senses my puzzlement. "I mean I need to take something because of last night. Reserved isn't a word I could ever describe you as." She whispers her next words. "And as much as I like you, I'm not ready for kids."

I blink and open my mouth. "Shit, I'm sorry. I wasn't even thinking."

Sefryn laughs. "I know." She takes her hand away. "I'll see you soon."

She walks away, and I head into the Grand Room, my ego feeling dangerously oversized.

Breakfast seems to be a pleasant affair. Camila is already eating, along with Elder, Peter, and a girl I don't know but recognize from yesterday, with wavy, light brown hair and matching eyes. There is a small buffet of food at the table. As I sit down, she gets up to leave. Camila wishes her goodbye.

"Who is she?" I ask.

"That's Ziara," Camila answers. "She's staying over in my tower, not far from me. She was the first one to complete the Trials."

"Oh," is all I manage to say.

"She doesn't talk much about them. But after I tracked her down and offered my family's compliments, she warmed up and started talking a bit."

"Well, if she got back all alone, I can't imagine what she went through."

"Seriously. I would never have survived without you guys," Abigail says as she takes a seat next to me.

I start putting food on my plate, my appetite huge. After cleaning my plate and grabbing more to eat, Sefryn joins us. She sits on the other side, next to Camila.

Probably for the best. I'd happily pretend last night never ended and go right back at it.

"So, what now?" Elder asks.

"I think I might remain in Edlyn," Abigail says. "I suppose it's time to move ahead." She pauses, taking a deep breath to hold back her emotions. "Maybe become a knight?"

"It will be done," Camila promises. Abigail smiles at her.

"I need to keep training," Peter says. "Sculpting is my passion, but I know I need to learn how to fight."

"He's been training since the Trials started," Elder informs us. "And now that we can use the knights' facilities, it will be much easier."

"What have you been doing for your training?" I ask.

Peter shrugs. It amazes me how much muscle he has put on. He looks like a younger version of Elder. He's handsome too. "It's just been physical combat training. I was waiting for my father to return before learning the battling arts of our kind."

I can't help but wonder what Peter would have done if Elder hadn't made it.

"Yes, well, that is a lot more complicated," Elder says. I get the feeling he doesn't want Peter following in his footsteps.

"I've seen you in battle before. If we weren't friends, I'd be terrified of you," Sefryn says. It surprises me, but the shock is nothing compared to Peter's. He swallows too much food and coughs. I know he knows about what his father can do, but I don't think he's ever seen it.

"That's for a different time," Elder says, the tone in his voice urging us to change the subject.

"No, Dad. I need to learn," Peter tells him. "The Azure Fox connected me to the Trials and the breath of life of every volunteer." He shudders. "I felt every single death as their names were crossed out. I know it wasn't my fault, but after feeling so much death... I can't live a life of peace. That first morning was the worst; it felt like my insides were being ripped to shreds."

No one says anything. I can't imagine what that was like. I don't think any of us can. Elder's eyes are filled with shock and sadness.

"What if you hadn't made it back, Dad? I'd need to know how to protect myself. We escaped the Gorgreins, but if they are coming here... I can't just keep running." The look in Peter's eye is almost heartbreaking.

"I never wanted this life for you," Elder says quietly.

"I know, but you can't control the whole world. The best thing I can do is learn to control my own fate."

Elder looks out at us, as if realizing that we've been there the entire time. He turns to face his son. "After breakfast, we'll start training with your Magis." He looks pained as he says it, but Peter is right, and Elder knows it.

I keep eating. Sefryn doesn't touch the food. I suppose whatever she took as birth control subdued her hunger.

As we eat, we're approached by the King and Queen, with Claudius right behind. Camila's three sisters also accompany them.

"The Trials have ended," Queen Mattias says. "We will meet in the Atrium to congratulate all of the winners."

They walk away. None of us get up. Mavia turns her head and beckons for us to follow. We look at each other, nervous and excited, and then we follow the royal family to the atrium.

The atrium is packed with people. Claudius ushers us to the wall where all the names are scribed. He holds Peter back. We stand, ready for whatever comes next. Arthur glares at us as we catch his eye. Someone I don't recognize stands next to him. Ziara makes a point to stare directly ahead.

"It is my great honor to take part in this moment in history," the

King says, bellowing out to the crowd. Despite the vastness of the atrium, it isn't big enough to hold the crowd. Curious faces watch us through the atrium's open doors, standing beyond the castle walls. "The first Ash Trials to take place in over a century! Let us welcome with open arms and reverence the winners of the Ash Trials!"

As commanded, the people clap and cheer. In the dissonance, I can make out some less-than-pleased people, probably those who lost loved ones to the Trials.

"Announcing our winners will be the hallowed Supreme Ash, Claudius De Ghore. He will help lead our kingdom to freedom, and four of these winners will stand by him, as we, the people of Edlyn, stand by them."

Claudius steps forward. He puts his hand up, and the crowd suddenly goes silent. It's a little too sudden, and I wonder if he used his Magis.

"Ziara Belle Sandfawn, Aros Caelum Hayes, Sefryn Loste Ambers, Elder Jordas, Abigail Morre Coriffer, Camila Vera Mattias, Arthur Drew Theodore, Matthew Brickal."

The crowd claps gently, a moment of grace in their otherwise riot-like cheers.

"I guess that not many people from another continent made it through," Elder whispers into my ear.

Edlyn and Soulstice—both part of the continent Cameleair—and the Fae Realm tend to follow a three-name tradition. Other regions usually don't. It isn't all the same everywhere, but it's an easy way to tell where someone is likely from.

"I suspect the Ashen Pit will choose soon," Claudius says. He turns back to face us, rather than the crowd. "Your time in Voltar must have been tough. No doubt you've found and strengthened friendships, as there can be no stronger bond than making it through the Ash Trials together." He pauses for a moment, smiling, as if recalling his time in the

Trials. "But I know there was also strife, ill intentions, and bad blood. Be warned, the Ashen Pit will not take kindly to harming each other. Not until it has picked those it deems worthy of burning their souls into it."

Claudius De Ghore turns to the crowd again, the mere gaze in his eyes commanding everyone's attention. "Once the Ash Lords are chosen, Aeilvow will host a celebration in their name! May their lives be forever honored within these walls."

With more cheers, roars, and boos from the crowd, I feel like there is little meaning to all of this, except for Claudius to show his alliance with Edlyn. Are the Ash Lords due to follow his lead and ally themselves with whom he chooses? Or do we have more freedom than that?

*Do we.*

I'm already thinking that I'm an Ash Lord. It is just a matter of time.

"Thank you," Claudius says, dismissing the crowd. It takes a while for everyone to leave, and the eight of us winners are trapped between the wall of names and the shuffling crowd. When the crowd clears, I make my way back to the Grand Room. Someone makes a point to shove past me, running into my shoulder and pushing me aside. Arthur turns his head.

"If I were you, I'd be watching my back," he sneers at me. The other guy I didn't recognize does the same, purposefully running into me. He turns his head to smirk at me, but then he follows Arthur into the Grand Room without a word.

I no longer feel like going back to breakfast.

"Shame, it would be an easy kill," Camila says, staring at them as the two grab their places at a table. "But we won't have to wait long. Once the Ashen Pit chooses, we can dispose of him."

"Good riddance. Feed him to the fucking monsters in Voltar," Abigail says.

I hear giggling behind me. I turn to see Camila's twin sisters walking into the Grand Room. They sit by Arthur and Matthew.

"My sisters have the worst taste," Camila says with a heavy sigh. "Maybe Mavia is right; my parents would never hand the kingdom over to them."

"Hey, so where are Elder and Peter doing their training? I think it might be a good idea to get some workouts in," I say, changing the subject. Talking too much about killing Arthur just might push me to do it.

"I'll show you," Camila says.

"Hey, I'll catch up with you later," Sefryn tells us. "I think Abigail and I are going to spend some time outside, maybe by the lake."

Abigail looks over at Sefryn but doesn't say anything.

"Okay," I say with a smile. "I'll see you later." She looks at me awkwardly and begins to walk away.

"What are you guys, embarrassed? Don't be so weird about it," Camila tells us. "We've all known about you two." I let out half a chuckle. Camila turns to look at me, a glare in her eyes and her arms crossed.

"Come here," I say to Sefryn, grabbing her hand and pulling her toward me. I kiss her. She's stiff at first, then relaxes and kisses me back. When we part, I smile at her and say, "I'll see you at dinner."

Sefryn smiles, the awkwardness that overcame her just moments ago gone. Abigail laughs and puts her hand on Sefryn's shoulder. "Shall we?" Sefryn nods to Abigail, and the two of them leave.

I shoot a quick look at Camila. When I catch her eye, a smile graces her face, and she blushes slightly. "Sorry, thought I'd wingman you there."

"I don't need a wingman," I tell her.

Camila laughs. "Oh, I know. Still, you two must have waited for a while. The Trials aren't the best place for love."

"I don't know if I would call it love."

Camila shrugs. "You know what I mean."

I let out a breath through my grin. "I do."

We look at each other for a second before Camila jerks her head a bit. "Let's go." She leads me upstairs. We walk along the corridors on the third floor before heading up to the sixth, the morning sun beginning to shine through the windows. A knight passes by, bowing his head slightly at Camila. He is dressed in light chain mail and short, sturdy shoes, with lightweight, woven pants fortified so that they won't be easy to tear through. His hair is brown, and his green eyes are framed by clean brows.

"Do you know him?" I ask Camila.

She shakes her head. "Due to the threat of war coming to Edlyn, my family has been recruiting knights from all over. With a chance to turn your family into royalty, there have been a lot of new knights."

To prove her point, Camila opens a door that leads into a long and wide room that must cover the entire corridor. Full of equipment, weapons, mats, and people, this is where all the new knights must train. With swords, punching bags, and even a nook with stone statues to practice Magis, this is the exact place that Peter would want to be.

An older man walks up to me. He wears a flower-patterned robe, tied together in the middle with a sash. His feet are bare, and I get the idea that the robe is the only thing the man is wearing.

"Are you here as a new knight?" he asks, his voice muddled with a low croak but otherwise pleasantly sounding.

"No, I came here from the Trials," I tell him, extending my hand. He takes it. "I'm Aros."

"Well then, it is a pleasure to meet you," the man says. "I am Kitinger. I was the first knight under King Mattias's rule."

I nod. "It looks like your hands are pretty full here," I say. "I'll come back later."

"If you like, we have private rooms on the other side," Kitinger tells me. "But I wouldn't mind seeing your performance here." He looks around at his students. "What is it that you would like to accomplish?"

"Here? I'd like to work on physical combat," I tell him. "I think I'm well ahead in using my Magis."

Kitinger smiles at me, holding his mouth curved up. Just before I start to feel uncomfortable, he speaks again, "I'm sure. But don't let your victory in the Trials inflate your head with egotistical thoughts."

I'm not sure if he's insulting me or just giving me a warning.

"Let's see for ourselves," he says and walks away. Camila and I follow him. He wordlessly calls over one of the knights, who promptly stops his sword training and follows us. Kitinger walks across the corridor into an empty room. This one is much smaller, but still large enough for thirty people to comfortably train in. Kitinger waves his hand, and the glass over the windows dissolves.

"That's so you guys don't break anything," he tells me. The student who followed us walks to one end of the room. He is shorter than I am by a few inches, has a similar skin tone to mine, and matching eyes and hair so short that if it were to be cut, he'd be bald.

Kitinger stares at me. I'm not sure what I'm supposed to do.

"Well, go for it," he tells me. "Try to land a hit on him."

I give myself a mental shrug. I step forward, centering myself in the room. Camila pulls Kitinger back.

I punch out a burst of energy. The guy dodges it. He's quick. But I can be quicker. I send out another three bursts before swinging a thin wave of fire at him. The student jumps over the fire, dodging all my attacks. He cocks a smile at me. Several figures fly from his body, all looking exactly like him, until I am surrounded by copies of the knight.

This is something I've never seen before. But I know they can't all be corporeal, though if he has other Magis, they may be able to attack me. Not losing focus, I blast more fire at where the original was. He dodges it, and then all of the figures move back and forth so quickly that it looks like all of them are glitching out.

I steady myself. I flick out a small burst of energy about thirty degrees to my right. When it hits him, all of the copies disappear, and the knight flies back, landing on the floor just before hitting the wall. He jumps to his feet.

The room goes dark, and then trees sprout from the ground. The moon shines brightly, an ominous air about us. I can't see him anymore. But this was his mistake. The copies he made weren't real. This terrain isn't real. He can manipulate minds, and he's good. But now I know what I am up against. If he wanted to get the best of me, he should have been more subtle about his powers.

He punches me right in the face, and I almost topple over. I do when he kicks me. Pain shoots through my stomach, and all air leaves my body. While on all fours, he kicks me again, right in the middle of my face, like an uppercut. Blood spills from my nose.

Fine, this is fine.

I do nothing as he attacks me again. I can hear voices around me, but I put my arm out, calling for them to stop. Camila knows I can make it through this, and she is likely preventing Kitinger from stopping our brawl.

If this knight wants to play dirty since I bruised his confidence, so be it. I'll let him use his mind tricks.

Another three successive punches hit my body, but I feel immune to the pain. And then another three. I make sure he can't knock me down again.

That's when I feel it. Another kick comes for my torso, and I reach out to grab it. As I do, the world around me disappears, and I am in the room again. I shoot my palm out to face the knight and blast his head with a surge. I let go of his ankle so that his body can fly back. He rolls into the wall with the open window.

The knight looks up at me, and it is hard to tell if there is more anger in his eyes than there is in Arthur's. He throws his hands out. More mind tricks. But I've been ready, and I surround his body with fire that nearly touches the ceiling.

While the forested and dark land surrounds me again, nothing else happens. I hear more shouting, but I am waiting for something specific. I can't see my fires, but I can feel them. I push them in closer. I hear him scream.

I am returned to the room again. From the fire, another projection of the knight appears, but his arms are up in surrender. I lower the fires until they die out. The knight looks red, the fires having been so close that he must feel like he's had a sunburn. He's lucky I was holding back. I know this was all a test, with Kitinger wanting to prove to me that I need training.

I do. Just not from him.

"I see," Kitinger says. "It appears you have a right to your victory in the Trials."

I turn to look at Kitinger. "All of us do."

The knight walks up to me. He extends his hand. I look at him for a moment, eyeing his expression before taking it.

"Elias."

"Aros."

He lets out a small laugh. "I know. It's actually an honor to have sparred with you."

"You didn't seem so happy at first."

Elias turns to look at Kitinger. "Well, Kitinger seemed to think I'd best you," he says. "I wasn't expecting you to be that strong."

"Neither were those kids who attacked me ten years ago," I say, dropping his hand. I turn my gaze to Kitinger. "I think it's better that we don't forget that."

Kitinger doesn't say anything but gives me a slow nod.

"Hand-to-hand combat—that's what I want to train in," I tell them sternly since they clearly didn't hear me before. "But I think I've had enough for today."

I look at Camila and move my head toward the door. She walks out, with me following her.

"Aros!"

I turn to see Elias holding the door open. "Will we see you down at Snake and Mammoth tonight?"

Camila catches my eye as I silently ask her what that is.

"The pub I was talking about," she says. Then when I raise an eyebrow at her, she adds, "Ironically, it's called Snake and Mammoth. I know."

I give Elias a warm smile. "You will." He smiles back with a nod and lets the door close. Camila walks me back down to the atrium. I tell her I want to head to my quarters and rest a bit. She waves me goodbye.

I take another shower and lie down for a while. Millions of thoughts race through my mind. How long will it take for the Ashen Pit to decide? How much longer must I wait? Will all this—the suffering, Clarissa's death—be worth it? Can it be?

I'm surprised by a knock on the bedroom door. A moment later, Camila appears, along with Abigail, Sefryn, and Peter.

"Are you ready?" Camila asks.

I look out my window. The sun has nearly set. I didn't realize how dark it had gotten. Feeling extremely hungry for a moment, I get up and yawn.

"Yeah, let's do it."

# CHAPTER 23

# THE SON OF THORNE

**Aros Caelum Hayes**

The cold air outside feels pleasant against my face. I'm wearing a dark coat, more than warm enough for even the coldest parts of Voltar. I'm enjoying wearing proper clothes again. Sefryn's clothes were nice, but they don't compare to the feel of fur and the Rogvey touch.

We walk along a winding dirt path through the grass fields that lead into the valley of Aeilvow. The moment the road begins descending into the valley, the dirt path gives way to neatly laid cobblestone. As the sun finalizes its descent below the horizon, the lights of the village burn bright, welcoming us to something magical.

My arm is wrapped around Sefryn. She leans in close as we walk. Turning to see Camila, I put my arm around her too. And then I realize something: I'm happy for the first time in a long time. It feels like when I first knew everything was going to be alright after Kreavlos took me to Earth. It was so freeing. And now, I taste the same breath of fresh air, the scent of the wild, and this thing inside me grows—stronger than just a hope—and I know that all is going to be okay.

Elder didn't join us. He said he might stop by later, but I know better than that. I forget that he's older than us. Getting drunk with a bunch of twenty-somethings probably doesn't interest him. Peter, on the other hand, is full of life and wonder as he explores the new world that has been offered to him.

It takes us just over ten minutes to reach the bottom. Edlyn Castle is long out of sight. We can't see anything above the cliffs. It's like we've entered a cozy, secluded part of the world. As we walk down the main road, lined with artfully built shops and houses made of rock and wood, I begin to realize why the people of the Edlyn kingdom are happy and why they don't demand that they live up where Edlyn Castle is. They have their own fortress here. With the music seeping into the streets and the outdoor market full of lively people, life in Aeilvow feels more comfortable than it does in the castle.

"I love this place," Camila says in a loud whisper. "It's too bad I don't get much time to visit."

"What, with being a princess and all, aren't you too good to be here?"

The voice comes from the side. I look over and see someone just taller than me jogging over. He has blonde hair about an inch and a half long, pushed up. With bright hazel eyes, he almost has the same charm that Claudius De Ghore has, but loses it all with his brash attitude and pompous drawl.

"*Because* I'm a princess, I can go where I want," Camila retorts.

He laughs. "My offer still stands," he says, ignoring the rest of us. "I can show you where to have a good time. The who? Well, that's with me, your highness." He places a hand over his stomach and gives Camila a mocking bow. "Plus, I want that sweet taste of royalty, behind the curtains," he says, leaning in closer to Camila, though he still keeps some distance. "If you know what I mean."

Camila raises her eyebrows. "Smooth."

The guy huffs. "If you weren't so stuck up and forced to be a prisoner to whatever lame man your parents choose for you, I'd show you dick so good you'd think you'd never had one before."

I step forward quickly, ready to knock him down and then blast his face with fire just for good measure, but Camila grabs my forearm and holds me back.

"My parents don't dictate who I be with. I get to choose," Camila says in her low voice. She steps forward and looks up at the guy. I don't know how the dude isn't pissing his pants from the look in Camila's eyes. "And I choose not to be with you, Liam."

For the first time since he appeared, the douche named Liam glances at the rest of us. He sneers. "Your loss, Miss Never-to-be-Crowned. And even if you were, the village doesn't give a shit what your family says." Liam walks away, down the road in the same direction we're headed. For obvious reasons, we don't immediately resume toward our destination. It helps, too, that only Camila knows where we're going.

"Do you want me to get rid of him for you?" Abigail asks, her Earth-English accent sounding much stronger. "One tornado aimed at him, and he'll be gone forever. Or I could do a hailstorm, a long and sharpened piece of ice straight through his eyes. Your choice." Camila looks up at her. "I mean it!"

Camila laughs. "I think his life itself is enough punishment."

Peter shifts, his discomfort palpable.

"Alright," Camila says, breaking up the moment. "Let's keep going."

Leading us down the road, Camila stays quiet. Peter and Abigail take up the rear.

"Are all the villagers like that?" Peter asks.

"No, just some who think the royal family of Edlyn can give them more," Camila answers.

"More what?" Abigail asks.

"Protection, food, or other resources," Camila says, pausing before she elaborates. "Despite being down here, the village is well protected by our knights. The Rogvey-designed arrows can rapidly travel long distances, meaning intruders can't reach Aeilvow. But sometimes there are incidents within the village."

"But why does it seem like there is such a strong division between the castle and the village? It doesn't seem like Aeilvow is full of criminals," Abigail says.

"You're right. Aeilvow is mostly safe," Camila answers. "But the King and Queen think it is best to remind people where they are, so even though they offer protection from outsiders, the protection is still limited. Whatever happens within Aeilvow, the King and Queen do not consider it to be their concern. Even so, my parents host festivals at the castle for the commoners as a gesture of gratitude. Edlyn pays all expenses.

"My family holds a lot of pride in their kingdom. They do their best to make sure no one goes homeless or hungry. But the further one is away from the castle, the harder it is. But down in this village, the people of Aeilvow live happily." Camila sounds like, while she isn't happy with how her parents rule over their kingdom, there's a part of her that wants to defend them.

"They don't sound like bad people," Sefryn says.

"They aren't," Camila replies. "I just don't usually agree with their methods. Outsiders aren't given the same treatment. That's why there's tension between Edlyn and Soulstice. Even if Soulstice did agree to come under the leadership of Edlyn again, the King and Queen will use them as a first line of defense. Only after the war—that's when the King and Queen will step in and help them. Soulstice knows it, but the alternative is worse."

"Especially if Gorgrein is readying themselves to invade," I say.

"Yup. The Gorgreins could climb up the mountains in Voltar, which would be suicide, or they can land in Soulstice and make their way to Edlyn. They'd never reach it, though. There's too much land between the two kingdoms that our army will wipe out any threat long before they get close."

"What do you want to do about it?" Sefryn asks Camila.

"I don't know."

The grim silence that follows is uncomfortable. While I feel nothing to ally myself with Soulstice, I don't want innocent people to be killed in the line of fire.

"Let's just hope that if the war happens, we've become Ash Lords first," I say. "Then we would be able to wipe out the Gorgrein ourselves."

"I'll be there too," Abigail says. "Even when I'm not an Ash Lord, I know I'm strong enough to protect them."

We fall into a silent walk, and I allow myself to admire the village.

It's hard to imagine anything else existing near the town since, from the bottom, the cliff tops look so high. It's only because of the structures that are built alongside the cliffs, some built into them, that I can tell one side is taller than the other. The sun has fully set down here, and the town looks just as dazzling from this view as it does from a turret of Edlyn Castle. Despite the excessive display of lights, the stars keep their wondrous shine and brightness.

Up ahead, there's a crowd of people and more noise. It becomes clear where the pub is. Nestled slightly into the cliffside, two stories tall, and with a large, open sitting area in the front, the pub is obviously quite popular. Among the crowd of people is a line. Camila walks us past them and through the sitting area, where people who want a quieter spot hang out.

Before walking inside, I catch the sign above the doorframe; the letters spelling out the name of the pub are adorned with a drawing of a snake wrapped around tusks. Upon entering, I almost drop my jaw in shock. I can't see how far in it goes, but the pub is huge. The ceiling is made of wood near the entrance but is soon replaced by the rocky earth of the hill that it rests under. Live plants dangle from the ceiling, colored lights beam down in all directions, and there are at least three bars that I can see.

"Hey! It's the volunteers!" someone calls out. A man, probably just short of fifty years old, walks up, his stomach protruding slightly and his hands wide. I get the idea he was waiting for us. "Congratulations! This night is for you!" He points to a banner on the wall, which depicts the mountain of Voltar. Next to it are pillars that look like decorative pieces. On a circular stage located just off the entrance is a small fire. Abigail and I exchange raised eyebrows. "First round of shots is on the house!"

Someone grabs my arm lightly. I turn my head and see Peter. He whispers into my ear, "Hey. Uh, I don't actually know what a shot is. I've heard of it, but I—"

"I got you," I say.

"Hey, could I have one first real quick?" I ask the large man. Camila and Sefryn catch on quickly. Abigail doesn't say anything, but she's too busy looking around with a scowl on her face that I don't think she notices.

The guy laughs. "Sure, but with what money? From what I've heard, you've spent most of your life on Earth."

He's right, just like when Camila called me out the first night I arrived. I have no money here.

"With royal money, of course," Camila says. "My friends right here are covered under my tab, all sent to my family to be paid."

The man laughs. "The Queen cut you off."

A moment of anger flushes through me, making my mind feel like a solid block. Does her mother really hate her that much?

"My mother cut off my twin sisters, and for good reason," Camila answers. "But my other sister and I still have our money. So, yes, their drinks go on my tab, and you will be paid."

"Fine," the guy says. He calls for a bartender behind the bar, puts up one finger, and then all five afterwards. Six shot glasses are served to us on a wooden platter.

"So, what do we do?" Peter asks.

I look at him and crack a smile. "This." I grab one of the glasses and shoot it down. The initial bitterness gives way to a sweeter taste—exactly what I expected—but then something else hits. It feels like I just drank water.

In the time I spent reading before the Trials, I learned that some alcohols are made by the Fae. Easier to drink, less gagging for those who can't handle strong liquor—but far more dangerous, since it makes it all too easy to have another. And another.

"That seems easy," Peter says. He picks one up and tosses it back. He coughs and sputters a bit, almost choking, but gulps it down.

I laugh. "Usually, you wait for everyone else," I tell him as the rest of us grab our shots.

"But you just drank one!"

"Yeah—to show you what to do."

He nods, his eyes dropping slightly. Camila calls for another round, and it's brought over immediately. I notice a crowd gathering around us.

"Ready?" I hold out my shot. The others do the same, as well as many in the crowd.

"Yeah," Abigail says. "This is for us."

"To us," Sefryn, Camila, and I say in unison. Peter mumbles the words right after. We take the shots, and the crowd around us claps and cheers. The crowd quickly clears, having honored us enough to say they did, which is just as well.

We stand there, almost feeling out of place, while everyone around us dances and socializes as if there is no one around but themselves. I've done the same before, but on Earth. Here? I barely know anyone.

"Let's dance!" Abigail says, pulling Camila and Peter with her. I follow behind with Sefryn. We shove our way through to the crowded dance floor.

To my surprise, Camila enjoys dancing. She moves about as she pleases, she and Abigail taking turns dancing with Peter, who does his best to keep up. Dancing is not my thing, but Sefryn joins in on their fun, and I know I can't let them down. I call for another shot, and then another, until I feel that tingle of a buzz and my inhibitions fade.

I jump in, moving wildly at times and taking turns dancing with the girls, until I decide to sweep Peter off his feet and onto my back, almost regretting it instantly. The dude's heavy. But I don't drop him as I hop and dance with the others. Peter throws his arms up, enjoying the time.

When I start to feel the weight of the world push down on me, I lower Peter off my back. Whatever buzz I had is gone, no doubt thanks to the constant activity. Peter asks for another round of shots. We take them. Slowly, we dance our way off the dance floor.

"Want to go outside?" Camila asks. I look at her, nodding. She knows.

"Hey, Aros!" I hear the voice from everywhere. I look around, trying to see anybody I recognize. The trouble is, I saw so many in the castle and at Claudius' announcement that everyone seems familiar while simultaneously being total strangers. "Aros!"

When I hear my name again, I look ahead, eyes scanning the crowd of people. Then I see Elias, smiling, his white teeth standing out against his dark skin. He walks up to us. There is a girl accompanying him with tightly curled hair braided down her back that's almost the same color as her skin. With straight posture, she's almost as tall as Elias.

"Hey, man," I say, shaking his hand.

"This is Natasha," he says. Natasha shakes our hands as we introduce ourselves. "She is also one of the knights in training."

As if deemed by law, she bows when greeting Camila, who promptly tells her to stop.

"I'm at a pub having a good time with my friends. Here, we're just people," Camila tells her. "If I were to give any command to you at this moment, it would be to treat me just the same as anyone else here."

Natasha smiles warmly. There is something so perfect about it, so genuine and radiating confidence.

"It's loud in here, isn't it?" Elias says. I move closer to his ear so I don't have to shout so loudly.

"Yeah, we were going to head outside."

I start heading for the door, but Camila tugs me back.

"We're not going that way."

Leading the way, using her light to shine in people's faces to move them out of our path, Camila heads toward the dance floor. Instead of going through, she moves around it. I turn back. Sefryn looks at me. Elias shrugs. None of us knows where we're going.

Toward the other end of the pub is a doorway where the hall turns out of sight. We are stopped by two guards. Camila speaks to them, and they move aside, letting us through. A winding passage leads us to an irregular oval-shaped room. Light shines down. I look up and see the moonlight peering through a set of crossed bars blocking the opening above. We're so far down that even if someone tried to climb through, they'd fall to their death.

There are many sets of tables and chairs, and even couches along the rocky walls in the back. There are three others in the room. There's one tall guy who stands as we enter, with short, perfectly messy light brown hair and matte blue eyes a shade darker than bright. There's something striking about him. Two women stay seated, both of them petite with dark hair and fair skin.

"Camila," the guy says, his tone short but cordial.

"Silas."

The guy turns his head slightly and whispers to the two girls. "Leave."

They both look up at him, glare at Camila, but follow his direction and walk out.

Silas and Camila look at each other. Camila has to look up to meet his eyes.

"I can go, too," Silas says, starting to walk out.

"Stay," a voice comes from the passage. I turn my head back. Mavia walks in, her strides purposeful, as if she intends to get what she wants. "There's no reason why you should have to leave just because my baby sister is here."

There's a tension in the room that I don't understand.

"You being here doesn't help," Silas says, glaring at her.

"Come now," Mavia says, walking up to Silas and running her hand down his arm. "You don't represent your whole family, just like my sister and I don't represent ours."

Silas scoffs. "Yeah, the both of you do. Just like I do. There is no running away from that."

Impatience builds in me. "What is going on?"

Camila looks up at me. "Silas is one of the sons of Thorne."

The kingdom of Soulstice has been under the Thorne family for decades. King Marcus Thorne and his wife, Queen Yvette Thorne, have three children. Two sons, and one daughter. I never learned their names. Still, other than the current state of affairs between the two kingdoms, I don't understand why they don't seem to like each other.

Mavia kisses Silas on the cheek. His lips curve into a frown, his eyes narrowed in disgust. "Don't touch me," he growls at Mavia. "Neither my brother nor I are interested in you. That is something we have always agreed on."

"Mavia, have some dignity," Camila snaps. "You're acting like our twin sisters. I thought you were better than that."

Looking at me with those dagger eyes that she loves so much, Mavia says, "It's been ten years. I'm just getting over it and moving on, just like Aros told me to." She shoots a look at me and tilts her head mockingly. "Isn't Aros just *so* smart?"

Something lights in Silas's eye as he darts a look at me, but he keeps his facial expression impassive.

"What's going on?" I whisper to Camila.

Camila steps forward. "Let's just clear the air, okay? I hold no grudge toward you." Mavia looks right at Camila, appearing both surprised and offended.

"I can't believe that, considering what my brother and I did." Silas steps forward, but I think he's trying to get away from Mavia rather than confront Camila. "I can't trust that you don't want revenge."

Camila shrugs. "I don't. You did what your family forced you to."

There's a silence that follows.

This time he walks up to Camila. He lowers his head a bit, his eyes sad and caring. "Look, I am here on behalf of my family. Again." Silas sighs. "I'm here to finalize the agreement to turn Soulstice over to Edlyn."

"Good luck," Camila says. "My parents aren't known for playing nice."

"Neither are mine." Silas gives her a half-smile and walks away.

"Forgive him, girl, that man is F-I-N-E," Abigail says, her voice high-pitched and sounding British again. I think she's still drunk. "I forgive him."

"Me too, I forgive him," Peter blurts out, clearly drunk. "He's incredible."

I chuckle. I turn to Sefryn. She's smiling at me. I shrug. "He's kinda gorgeous, you gotta admit," I tell her.

"Sure, but I only have eyes for you," Sefryn tells me before kissing me.

Camila sits down on the couch Silas was on before we walked in.

"I never said I don't forgive him," Camila says, raising her voice to cut through the others. "Actually, if anything, I think I already said that I do forgive him." When we're all silent, Camila turns to her sister. "You're welcome to stay, Mavia," Camila says, "so long as you behave yourself."

"I don't take orders from you," Mavia says.

"No, but if you don't behave, my friends will treat you like shit,"

Camila answers. "It's your choice."

Mavia crosses her arms, stares at us, but then sits down at a table. We all sit close enough to talk. Camila, Sefryn, and I on the couch, and the rest at the tables just by us.

"So," I say, letting out a breath and looking at Camila, "what happened?"

"Five years ago, Silas and his brother, Xylen, sought revenge on behalf of their parents," Camila begins. "When my parents refused to concede to the threats from the Thorne family, they snuck into the castle and kidnapped me. They took me across the river and chained me to the floor in a small cave. Winter had just started, so you can imagine how cold it was." Camila then adds, "Xylen can manipulate minerals. He made the chains right in front of me from the walls of the cave."

"That's awful!" Abigail says, her eyes wide. "I take back what I said about him."

"I didn't know there was so much tension between the two kingdoms," Natasha says.

Camila shrugs. "Honestly, I don't care," she says. "Silas was hesitant, and Xylen was so silent the entire time I don't think he wanted to be there. After a few hours, the Azure Fox came to save me and brought me back to Edlyn."

"What did your parents do?" Sefryn asks.

"They saw it as an act of power," Camila says. "Because of it, Soulstice got the protection they sought—even if my parents forced them to give up their kingdom in exchange."

"Wow," Abigail says, sounding disgusted.

"My parents have their ways," Camila says. "Like I told Silas, I don't hold a grudge. I don't even hold one for Soulstice or my parents. And I understand the strife between the two kingdoms. Edlyn took Soulstice under their rule. But that didn't last. Now it looks like Soulstice wants to forfeit their sovereignty again."

Elias says, "How could you *not* hold a grudge?"

"Because holding a grudge does nothing for me," Camila says. "I just need to make sure that I'm strong enough so that I can protect myself and anyone else who could become collateral damage."

Learning about this from Camila, after all this time, makes me believe that she wanted to volunteer for the Ash Trials. Her parents would not have had to force her. "Do you trust Silas?" I ask her.

"I think he and I are a lot more alike than others think."

By the time we finish hanging out, everyone has sobered up. Elias and Natasha leave first, followed by Mavia, who makes a clear effort to wish everyone good night except me. We head out, walking back up the valley until we reach the doors into the castle. Peter and Abigail give us hugs before going upstairs to their rooms. Sefryn, Camila, and I hang back in the atrium.

"You okay?" I ask Camila. The fires in the lights flicker quietly, their flames staying constant. Camila looks over toward the wall with all our names.

"Yeah, I am," she says. "I meant what I said. I've seen enough to understand that we, as the children of royal families, cannot be judged based on our parents' decisions. I don't think Silas would ever do something like that again. Plus, it was five years ago. Between the ages of seventeen and twenty-two, one can change a lot."

"What about his brother?" I ask her.

Camila shrugs. "He might be more like his parents," she tells me. "He's the oldest, and there are rumors that he's cruel. But he'd never do something like he did to me on his own accord. Not yet, at least."

"But when Soulstice merges, won't they no longer have a royal family?" Sefryn asks. "The power would shift to yours—to Edlyn."

"Sure, but that kind of shift takes time," Camila answers. "Thorne will still have power over the land of Soulstice, except they will have to answer to Edlyn."

"I wouldn't trust them," I say quietly. "How do you know Silas isn't here to do something like he did before?"

"First, because it wouldn't work," Camila answers. "My parents won't care this time. Second, because I have to believe that Silas is better than his family. I have to give him the chance. It's exactly the chance I would want people to grant me."

"What do you mean?" Sefryn asks.

Camila starts to head toward the stairs. I can tell she's worn out. "My family has made a lot of enemies. I think it was unnecessary. But people out there hold their own grudges and hatred. I'd like them to see me as me, and not as an extension of my family."

I nod slowly. There's a lot to unpack here, and I can't help but think the truth might be buried deeper than I'll ever reach. I don't think Camila would lie to me—but there are things even she might not know. I just hope her parents don't do something so stupid it gets her killed.

Reading my thoughts, Camila says, "I can take care of myself."

I smile. "I know. Goodnight."

She waves and walks up the stairs, disappearing from view.

As Sefryn and I head toward our tower, I see Silas enter the atrium. He nods slightly as he passes.

"I'll see you in the room," I whisper to Sefryn. She smiles and heads up the stairs.

"Silas."

He stops. A second ticks by, then he turns. I walk up to him.

"If you bring any harm to Camila," I say, locking eyes with him, "I will kill you."

Silas smiles—and leans in, just close enough to make my blood rise. Damn, he even smells good.

"If I even think about hurting her," he says, "I'd count on it."

He turns and walks away.

"Goodnight," I call after him. There's not a shred of warmth in my voice.

He lifts a hand in a half-hearted wave and disappears down the hall.

What a majestic prick.

# CHAPTER 24

## CHOSEN

**Aros Caelum Hayes**

Snow arrived in Edlyn. Last night, it must have stormed in, layering the ground in white. After breakfast, I had to return to my room to dress accordingly. Stepping outside, my boots sink into the ground, the snow reaching above my ankles. We don't make it far before a horn blares across the land. I turn to Camila.

"That means there's an announcement," Camila says. Sefryn looks back at the castle. "But it isn't until lunch. It gives time for the people in Aeilvow to make it to the castle if they want to be present. It's rarely used. I suppose this must mean it's over."

Finally.

"Sounds like lunch can't get here soon enough," I mumble.

"Even if the announcement has anything to do with the Ash Lords," comes Abigail's voice from behind us, "what would it change?"

"I'll be an Ash Lord," I answer.

"Yes, but then what?"

I don't know how to answer her—because honestly, I don't know myself. There's a whole new life I have to build here. I don't know how long King Matthias will let me stay in Edlyn Castle. Camila will do everything she can to make sure I stay as long as I want, but the King could change his mind at any moment.

Still... after everything I've been through—everything I've done—I've earned this.

Becoming an Ash Lord doesn't feel like a reward.

It feels like a right.

"How about we cross that bridge when we get there?" Sefryn suggests, her eye twitching at her choice of words.

"Really, Sefryn?" Abigail says.

I chuckle silently. Compared to all else, the bridge was *almost* anticlimactic. After the fact, that is. I hated it, but it felt like the most controlled part of the Trials. Everything that happened before felt like plain bad luck.

Maybe after lunch, when I'm an Ash Lord, I'll drag Arthur back to the bridge and toss him into the ravine as a snack for the wyverns.

We spend the morning sparring with each other in the fields, but this time with our Magis. Sefryn does her best to pull roots out from the ground but looks like she struggles. She's been able to before, so I don't understand why.

"I need to be quicker with it," she answers when I ask her about it. "More subtle."

Camila weaves orbs and discs of light, tossing them into the distance and controlling their trajectory. Abigail focuses on directing her storms, whether it's causing rain over just a radius of two feet or moving the wind toward a target, and nothing else.

When it's close to lunchtime, Camila dimly flashes light over our eyes to get our attention so she can point to the castle, reminding us that we are only training to pass the time.

I look over at Sefryn. She nods.

"Can't wait," Abigail says. "Let's get this over with. Then I can forever forget about the Trials."

We say nothing more as we trudge through the snow back to the castle. Camila leads us toward the open portcullis that leads into the atrium. There are guards with tall spears on both sides. They nod their heads in a slight bow when they see her. We have to push through a lot of people to make it to the front.

We are greeted by the King and Queen of Edlyn, as well as the Supreme Ash himself. The guy named Matthew is there too, alongside his new best friend, Arthur. Elder nods with a smile as he sees us. I don't see Ziara.

"We're early," Camila says. I look around at all the people who are already here.

"How do you figure that?" Abigail asks.

"Because we were able to make it to the front."

This time, people are standing in the Grand Room too, and others are lined up at both entrances to the atrium, as well as on the staircase.

"Important announcement, I guess," I say. We all know what it is, but no one has confirmed it.

Waiting here feels exhausting. Each passing second gets worse. It's hard to tell when more people arrive, other than by the rising volume of all the voices speaking at the same time.

The royal family stands in front of the wall of volunteers. Even Camila's sisters are there. Camila has to remain with us, though, off to the side and not in the line of sight of the royal family. Today, she isn't one of them. She's one of us.

I can barely hear what is undoubtedly a bad joke from Arthur, probably something snide about me, but I block out the sound of his voice.

Then she appears. There's the faint blue haze, the shining aura around her. Grisla. It's fitting that the Azure Fox opens and closes the Ash Trials.

"Three hundred and twenty-seven," the King roars, and the crowd quickly falls silent. "That's how many volunteers participated in the Ash Trials." He goes quiet for a moment, letting it sink in just how many people were lost during their time in Voltar.

Three hundred and nineteen people died. In what, two months? And over half of that on the first day. We didn't see that many people during the Trials. I wonder if we were lucky to head in a direction that was somewhat correct—as in, it would lead to the valley. Others probably went down the mountain to avoid the monster attack, all those wyverns and the goblins jumping down. That would have made it harder for them to climb back up the mountain.

Then, of course, there were those who succumbed to the elements.

"Completion of the Trials itself is worthy of the highest honor," King Mattias goes on. "In that, know that the people who stand before you are braver than you can imagine. Braver than even I. So, to announce the winners, I present to you the Azure Fox!"

My body freezes. When does it happen? Will the Azure Fox announce those that the Ashen Pit chooses, and then we go off to burn our souls into it? Or has it already chosen, and she's to tell us who the new Ash Lords are?

Just as the worst of my thoughts start to boil, I feel a rush of wind, and everything goes dark. The howling continues. I can't see anything. I can tell there is no one else around.

When my senses return, I see it. Dug into the ground, a circular rim and dark gray rock finish, the Ashen Pit burns with an ethereal fire. This time the flames are blue, much like the minimal light that shines down on it from above. I can't see where the light comes from. Everything else around is so dark that I don't think even space itself exists beyond what I can see.

"At this point, I ask the victor if they would like to burn their soul into me," the voice comes from all around—deep, beckoning, and dangerous.

"But you, Aros... *owe* me."

The last two words are spoken in an even deeper voice, a threatening growl behind the words.

I say nothing.

"Proceed," the voice commands.

The Ashen Pit doesn't need to ask me. Now knowing that the Dark Wind is an essence of it, I understand that I do, quite indeed, owe him. If he hadn't saved me that night in Voltar, I probably would have died.

I step forward.

The flames surge—bluer, hotter, licking toward violet. The heat slams into my face, burning as if the fire is already touching my skin.

I stop, unsure of what to do.

"Go on."

I take another step forward. But, hesitant, I keep my feet planted. The waves of the fire rage at me. My face feels charred, the rest of my body screaming from the sensation, shouting at me to retreat.

"Do it. *Now.*"

The Ashen Pit doesn't wait.

Something grabs hold of me—not physically, but from within—and drags me forward.

I'm forced to take a step. Then another.

Forward again.

Four more and I descend into the pit. My skin catches fire, the heat and smoke producing tears in my eyes. I can't breathe. All I can see is the flickering rage of the flames, a deep blue, white, and then they fade, harder and harder to see until I see nothing. I can feel it still, the fire. But instead of burning, it feels like it peels off not my skin, but my very soul, layer by layer.

My skin prickles. But I know I'm okay. My clothes don't burn. Even under the layer of winter clothing, I no longer feel warm. I breathe in normally, and this time my lungs catch air, light and pure.

But then a sense of dread washes over me, drenching me in its cold embrace. I shiver and simultaneously sweat—the sensation making me feel worse. The fire cracks louder, like fireworks exploding in my ears.

What was left of the light above disappears, and the ultraviolet light from the fire burns hotter once more. The blazing heat rushes through me. I'm about to scream out when everything fades, and I am left in an empty darkness once more.

Another howl of wind, and I am transported elsewhere. I think. There is still darkness all around, but I don't think I am standing inside the Ashen Pit.

It builds up too quickly for me to control.

Unable to stop it, I let out a surge of energy from my entire body. The force of it is so strong it feels like my spine cracks from the pressure. The energy whips through the empty space—and a thunderous, echoing crack follows.

After releasing that much power, I'd be breathless.

But I feel fine.

I feel stronger.

I squint as the light of the atrium returns. I face the crowd. Looking behind me, I see the wall of names, the entire thing essentially a cacophony of slashes. The royal family stands where I stood just before the Dark Wind took me.

Next to me are Sefryn, Camila, and Elder. Just the four of us.

"Your Ash Lords," says Claudius, egging on everyone to cheer. I catch a scowl from Arthur before he turns and wrestles his way out of the atrium. Abigail stands with the crowd, facing us. She has the widest smile I've ever seen on her face. I can see the pride in her eyes. I can't help but smile too.

I'm not sure what comes next. This is all I cared about since I arrived in Arteyva. My plans never went further. Maybe it was because somewhere deep inside, it never seemed real. But it was. The Trials were very real. And I can't help but think that whatever we face next is going to be a hell of a lot worse.

"A celebration is in order!" the King declares, stepping up onto the low platform we stand on. "In three days, on the night of winter's dawn." The king pauses for a moment. He bows his head slightly. There is a sliver of a glint in his eye. "See you there."

The night of winter's dawn is exactly that: the start of winter. It's also a day of celebration, the closest thing to Christmas that Arteyva has to offer—meaning it isn't a celebration for us as Ash Lords. Traditions vary from kingdom to kingdom, but if Edlyn is anything like Soulstice—as I'm sure it is—then it'll be a night of dancing, gratitude, gifts, and more.

"Kill them!"

The scream slices through the atrium. It comes from a man, but the voice is high and cracks. I look out at the crowd to see where it came from. Then I'm shoved backward, but I keep my feet on the ground.

Looking up, I see a man probably about twice my age. He has a full head of graying hair and blue eyes. Saliva spits out of his mouth as he screams words I can't hear in my stun. Suddenly, he releases my coat and steps back. His eyes widen in confusion.

"There will be no room for this sort of behavior," Claudius says, booming his voice over the chaos.

The man who went after me raises both his arms.

Claudius watches him with the faintest, most twisted grin I've ever seen. His eyes gleam in the light—cold, calculating, terrifying. And somehow... mesmerizing.

With eyes still wide open, the graying-haired man walks over to the nearest stairs, kneels down, and proceeds to bang his head against the stonework of the newel post. He does it quickly, two to three times per second.

Even from where I stand, I can see blood spill down his face in lines. Each smack against the wood produces a smushing and cracking sound, and even when the man's eyes close, presumably from unconsciousness, he continues to throw his head against the pillar with more and more force until his body goes limp and collapses to the floor.

One of his arms lays against the first few steps. His eyes are open, but there is nothing behind them. His face is hard to discern since it's so covered in the blood still pouring from his forehead.

"The Ash Lords, as well as the victors of the Trials, are to be regarded with the highest respect," Claudius says, turning away from the deceased man. "I will not stand for anything less, and any further attempts to attack an Ash Lord will be dealt with as you've just witnessed."

The crowd is silent. I understand why. It isn't because of what just happened. Not directly. It's because of what Claudius just announced that he is.

I've always known he was a Maleficium, just like me. He told all of us the day we arrived in Voltar. But his power is beyond what I can even imagine mine to be. He is a Maleficium who can control people—their bodies.

By the look in the man's eyes, Claudius wasn't in his head. He just forced the body to move as he wanted it to.

With a forced nod to Claudius, the King holds out his arms and addresses the crowd. "See you in three days!"

Getting the message, the crowd shuffles out of the atrium, most people waiting until they are outside before speaking. When most everyone is gone, the royal family leaves. Except for Camila, of course. I don't see Abigail. Peter stands close to Elder.

"Come with me," Claudius says. He motions with his head to follow, his movements seemingly harmless and welcoming.

He doesn't wait for us but walks up the staircase, stepping over the man he just killed without looking down. We start to follow just as some of the servants come to clean up the mess.

Once we reach the third floor, Camila is brave enough to speak.

"Who was he, and why did you kill him?"

Claudius barely turns his head back as he walks along the corridor. "He attacked one of you," Claudius answers. "I will not stand for anything like that. I lost my fellow Ash Lords once. I will not lose them again."

We don't say anything.

"Don't worry about the way I did it. That man was the father of a Fae-Blessed who died on the first morning of the Trials. It would appear that he stayed in Edlyn the entire time to exact revenge for his daughter," Claudius says, turning around to face us. "Again, don't you worry about how I did it. Even with my power, taking over the body of someone with Magis is difficult, let alone the body of an Ash Lord."

"What do we do, exactly, as Ash Lords?" Elder asks in a disapproving tone, ignoring what Claudius said.

"You protect all life in this world," Claudius answers. "Something big is coming. We need to be prepared."

"What is coming?" Elder asks. "I've seen some of the worst that this world has to offer."

There is a small tick of Claudius's head. "No, you haven't. But you will."

Claudius leads the way again, down the corridor and then up a set of stairs. As I guessed we would, we enter the sixth floor. This time, we walk farther down the hall, turn the corner, and keep going. We get to a door that Claudius opens and walks inside.

Lined vertically are several tables, all covered with a variety of items. The first thing I see is clothing, but then the small weapons quickly catch my eye.

"You'll find a table with your name on it," Claudius says. "Your armor has been custom-fitted. It can withstand even the sharpest blades—but it isn't impenetrable, especially against the strongest Magis. It will feel no heavier than ordinary clothes."

He gestures down the room. "Beside the armor, you'll find two daggers. At the far end of the table, a sword."

Claudius stands at the far side, directly across from the hall's entrance.

"To your left is a room stocked with additional weapons, in case you favor something else. To your right, you'll find a chamber designed for training with your new powers."

He chuckles lightly, letting the weight of his words settle. Technically, we don't have *new* powers—but the strength pulsing through us now feels like something entirely reborn.

"Just be mindful," he adds. "The castle wasn't built to contain your full strength. If you want to test your limits, head north—there's a clearing by the river of Voltar."

We don't say anything.

"Train. And be prepared. When the worst comes, it will be sudden."

The door opens behind us. I turn back and see Silas walk through it. He gives me a small, upward nod and turns his eyes to Claudius.

"You wanted me here?"

"Yes," Claudius replies, walking over to Silas. "As part of the agreement your family has made with Edlyn, you will stay here and fight alongside the knights."

"I know that," Silas responds, his words short and clear.

"You will train with the Ash Lords and the other victors," Claudius tells Silas, though it feels like he's speaking to all of us. He then looks around the room, making it clear he is addressing everyone. "I'm going to take it that you all understand how to follow directions, so I will leave you be." He walks off but then pauses at the door. He turns to face us again but looks me in the eye. "I suggest you spend your first day outside, beyond the training grounds of Edlyn. The power you hold now is greater than you think it is."

Claudius leaves the room. I turn to look at Camila, who has her eyebrow raised as she returns the gaze.

This is it, then, I suppose. I'm an Ash Lord, and I've now been ordered to train for battle. I don't mind since I have nothing better to do, and now I don't need to wait for anyone to help me train.

"Wouldn't it make sense to make sure he went back to Soulstice?" Sefryn asks us, clearly referring to Silas. "That's where the war is supposed to be."

"I think that's the idea," Silas says. "Keep me away from Soulstice. For what purpose, I don't know." He sighs. "I don't think I'll ever truly understand my parents."

"See? Silas and I are not unalike," Camila whispers to me. I nod. Looking back at the table, I walk until I find the one with my name on it, which happens to be the one in the center. I take off the top layers of my clothing so I can put the armor on. The others do the same.

There is a table for Silas, Abigail, and Peter. There's even one for Ziara, but it is already empty. I don't see a table for Arthur or Matthew. But after we were chosen, I don't think they wanted to stay in Edlyn.

Following Claudius's advice, we head downstairs and make our way out into the forest. We walk for a while, not knowing where the clearing Claudius mentioned is. Just as I'm about to give up and suggest we go somewhere else, Camila's joyful shout stops me.

"There!"

Not far from the river and through a patch of grass, we spot a clear arena for training, which is just dirt with the odd stone here and there.

"Who wants to go first?" Silas calls out. He holds Peter back as the rest of us make it to the center of our training field. It's large enough to hold a small stadium. It is certainly larger than any of the training rooms the knights use on the sixth floor.

"Aros," Sefryn says. "Aros does."

She's right. I do. But I didn't want to say it. I don't even know what I'm going to do.

"That sounds about right," Silas says. "Here, Aros, let me spar with you."

I laugh. "I don't think that would be fair," I tell him.

Silas cracks the faintest smile. "You aren't the only high-order Maleficium from Soulstice." I stare at him. Is he serious? Or just delusional?

Either I am going to have a lot of respect for him, despite what he did to Camila, or I'm going to have another "Arthur" to deal with. But this time, there isn't anything stopping me from killing him.

"Of course," Silas calls out. He motions for the others to stand behind the circle, and they do so. "I know that you're stronger than me. Even more so now that you're an Ash Lord. But I would like to think I can hold my ground against you."

"Fine," I tell him. I step back to put some space between us. If we're battling as Maleficium, then we should truly show what we're capable of. "I'll give you the first shot. Go ahead. I won't even block."

I think I see Silas narrow his eyes, but it's hard to tell from this distance. He stands there, seemingly unmoving. Then, like a quick draw, Silas throws both his hands in front of him, releasing a pulse of energy that rushes at me. When it hits, I'm thrown off my feet and fly backward. I don't get the chance to land my fall, so I hit the ground, tailbone first, sliding across the dirt until I reach the grass.

He wasn't lying. He is strong.

"Believe me now?" he shouts, swinging his arms in pride.

I get up and laugh. I respond by throwing my own wave of energy at him. He catches it and sends it back. Adding more power to it, I throw it his way again, which, of course, he deflects back in my direction. What is normally a faint glow, even from my stronger attacks of pure energy, is now glowing white and blue and very much tangible.

When it gets close, I grab it and toss it across the river. It goes farther than I intended, past the water, beyond the riverbank, and into the side of the mountain. There is a blast like an explosion, and chunks of rock twice the size of a man's head fly everywhere. Silas and I conjure up shields to make sure the rocks don't hit any of us. When it's clear that the danger is gone, we face each other and attack with more bursts of energy.

Silas dodges and whips his arms out toward the river. A stream of water flies out, freezing to ice, and soars toward me. I shoot fire at it, melting the ice before it can impale me.

In retaliation, I bring forth an eruption of fire right out from the ground. The power is easy to control. While I've done it before, I feel like I am in sync with the fire, moving it effortlessly in trails around Silas until I throw them at him.

All in all, I feel more in control. Stronger bursts of energy and power are easier to conjure, and I don't feel as drained because of it.

A vortex of water surrounds Silas, but it dies out quickly. It doesn't matter. It extinguished the fires. Silas looks at me as if he is confused that I tried to kill him. What does he expect? He just sent a spear of ice toward my face.

Silas draws from behind him. The shadows from the trees lunge at me. Not understanding it, they wrap around my arms, pulling me down to the ground. I struggle with them as I try to keep my footing. I flatten my palms, releasing light from them. I have to twirl my fingers to move the light like streamers, but the shadows are too prevalent. I curl my hand into a fist before quickly exposing my palms. A flash of light bursts out, blinding all of us for a moment. When it's gone, so are the shadows.

Breathing heavily, Silas throws another bolt of energy toward me. My torso twitches, and with both my arms out to my side, I produce energy in the shape of me that circumvents his energy. As I catch his attack in my hand, sizzling it out, the energy from my body punches Silas in the face and knocks him over.

His coarse hair hangs over his forehead as he recovers from the blow. He stands up again and chuckles.

"That's a new one," he says. "Never seen it before."

Someone claps from the side. For an instant, I think it's the others, but I soon see Claudius walking alongside the King and Queen.

"There you have it," Claudius says, "there is nothing to worry about." He turns to face the King. "Us Ash Lords are more than powerful enough to defend Edlyn, should the time come. But it will be weeks before any army can reach here, that is, if they even make it through Soulstice."

The King and Queen exchange some words I can't hear.

"May I remind you," Claudius says, his tone deeper in warning, "Soulstice will be torn to shreds if they do not get the support of your army."

The King walks over. I move toward Silas. He beckons for his daughter to come, and as she does, she calls for Sefryn and Elder.

King Mattias kneels before us. "Will you stand with Edlyn?" he asks, his voice full of admiration but also a tinge of bitterness.

"We will," Camila answers.

"Thank you, daughter," the King replies. "But I need to know that this is their choice."

"When it comes to where our alliance lies," I say to the King, "we will go where Camila goes." I turn my head to the others. "Right?"

They all agree. Silas, too.

"So, yes, we do stand with Edlyn."

The King stands up, nodding and shaking all of our hands. Queen Mattias strolls up.

"Silas, you will remain here, as we discussed," she says. "Your mother demands it."

Silas nods. A faint smile appears on the Queen's lips before she turns away, brushing against her husband, signaling for him to follow her back with Claudius.

"Soulstice will have our army," the King says. Claudius smiles, and they make their way back to the castle. Other than a few approving words from Claudius, I can't hear anything else.

"I don't understand why my mother wants me here," Silas says. "They'll need my help to defend themselves."

"Maybe she trusts Edlyn's army," Camila says, though I know she doesn't believe it. Neither does Silas, but he doesn't say anything else.

Deciding that Silas and I are done, Camila steps forward with Sefryn, and they go at it. It's a little slow at first, with Camila holding back her power with light so that she doesn't hurt Sefryn, while Sefryn refrains from using too much strength for the same reason.

Then, as if they had been speaking telepathically, they charge at each other with the same vigor Silas and I had. Sefryn is able to pull up roots thicker than an ogre's thighs from the ground, while Camila blasts light at them, burning a hole right through them. Then Sefryn creates an octopus that surrounds her, all from the roots of the nearby trees. They strike at Camila, who builds up a barrier of light in front of her. As the roots pass through it, they disintegrate, leaving Camila unharmed. Smiling, the two girls nod to each other and hug their truce.

Asking to train with Peter by himself, Elder takes up his stance in the arena. The rest of us leave. I don't know what Elder is doing, but I trust him to have good reasons. I am curious as to what Elder can do now. Before, he was terrifying in how he could just tear into someone. But as an Ash Lord? There's no telling what he *can't* do.

"You're strong, Aros," Silas says to me as we make it back to the castle grounds. "I know you know that. But I just want you to know that I respect that. I respect you."

"Thanks," I tell him. "You too. You surprised me, but I can honestly say that I am glad we're on the same side."

He leaves with a smile, and I can't help but sense that underneath everything, he feels just as lonely as I used to before the Trials. Camila bears no ill will toward him. In that moment, I realize that I don't have the right to judge what he's done.

I really am glad we're on the same side. I don't know what's to come, but I have a feeling we'll need all the power we can get—even as Ash Lords.

# CHAPTER 25

---

# DAWN OF WINTER

**Aros Caelum Hayes**

The slush of frost barely misses me, the small shards of ice nicking my face. Even with the following two days of training we've done, while I've gotten much stronger, so has Silas.

We decided to use the arena Claudius directed us to so that we can practice our skills. We also decided to keep our sparring partners, at least for the rest of the week, before switching it up. Abigail joined us today, and she spars with Elder. Peter only tagged along the first day, and he now spends his time with the other knights. There's a handful of Rogvey specialists, and even one of the highly respected masters of the art came up from Soulstice to train the knights.

I throw a dagger at Silas. He catches it in his hand, his palm wrapping around the blade. I spew a stream of fire at him. He washes it away with a wave of water, which I take from his control and throw back at him.

Even though I try, it doesn't turn to ice.

Drenched but unhurt, Silas runs at me, wielding a sword. I draw mine from my back, and the blades clash against each other. I release heat from my hands, directed at the hilt of Silas's sword. He drops it in pain.

I go for the final blow.

A sliver of shadow pulls my wrist back, giving Silas enough time to disarm me. Holding my sword in his hands, Silas stabs at me with it. I grab the blade, much like Silas did, and burn through the iron. Part of the blade falls to the ground.

Silas tosses the sword aside and goes in for physical blows. He manages to knock me to the ground. I kick out and trip him. As he falls, I get back up, ready to kick him in the side.

Once we got comfortable, we stopped holding back. Sure, I've been hurt the past few days, but it's all for a good purpose.

Silas blasts energy at me, throwing my leg back. I keep my balance. In that time, Silas returns to his feet. We trade blows of energy bursts. The distance between us grows. At this rate, we'll rarely hit each other.

I sprint toward him, swiping away his attacks. Surprised, Silas doesn't change his tactics, and I tackle him to the ground. He grunts as he hits the floor. Playfully, I smack him across the face. He tsks and tosses me off him. Before I can get up, shadows tie me down. I have to release a body-form energy burst to deal with Silas, distracting him from the shadows so that I can free myself.

"Guys!" I hear someone shout. I jump to my feet and blast fire toward Silas. He catches it in a ball of energy, the swirling flames unable to escape it. He can't control it, though, and I have to subdue it before vaporizing the energy so that it doesn't explode.

"Hey!"

I look over. Camila is shouting at us. I look up at the sky. It's been hours since lunch. Breathing hard, I look around. Sefryn stands by Camila. Elder and Abigail have already left.

"We should get ready," Camila tells us.

Silas and I bump fists, and we head back with the girls. The last two days were completely spent training—well into the night, too. Without much time for talking, I've still developed a bond with Silas that won't be broken easily.

We pass through the Atrium. I'm tempted to eat—very tempted—but I don't say anything. I know the celebration will have more than enough food.

"See you later, Aros," Silas says, patting me on the shoulder and giving me a half hug. I smack his back, and he walks off. Camila says she'll see us this evening and walks away. As we get to our tower, Sefryn goes for her room. She hasn't slept in it yet.

"Where are you going?" I ask. She also hasn't used it, as far as I know. She's taken showers in my chambers and even has clothes in there.

Sefryn smiles. "You'll see." I watch her as she closes the door to her assigned room, mesmerized, wondering what she means.

As I'm taking a shower, I realize just how much I've been cut up and bruised from today alone. I reflect on the training we've done. My fighting isn't bad—I know that much. But my use of weapons could improve. I've just never needed anything like them before. There are people on Earth who could take me down if all we did was fight hand-to-hand.

I let my thoughts override my mind. There's a lot of improvement in the Magis department. Still, as an Ash Lord, I should be immeasurably strong, but Silas can keep up. He can do more than keep up. Surely there are others who can match my power. While I feel stronger, and I know I am stronger, it just feels like there is something holding me back.

Knowing that this is a special occasion, I take care to pick out appropriate attire. I can't find anything that I feel is suitable, but then I notice something out of the corner of my eye. On the bed are three sets of formal wear.

In Arteyva, the formal wear resembles what men wear on Earth, without the copy-and-paste of a tuxedo. There are more choices in color and varying degrees of flair. Aside from the overly lavish and disgustingly adorned clothes, I generally like the style in this realm. Each set has a plain shirt made of woven fanglac and diamondite, which is exactly as it sounds—just extracted diamond fragments made so that they can be worn. The shirt is an off-white, and it's hard to make it look anything special without sacrificing its protective armor-like properties. I grab one and put it on.

One of the sets is made of dark fabric. It looks great, but it's the closest thing to a tux. The next set is almost the opposite, with white, cream, and light brown. But the last set makes me feel like I truly am in Arteyva.

It has a deep burgundy vest that covers the entire undershirt. The vest has an intricate design of straight lines that shift direction, just a few shades lighter than the rest of the fabric, with navy buttons and a black collar. I put on the navy pants and notice that the inside is lined with tight leather. Not impenetrable, but better than regular clothes. Then there's a dark jacket, not unlike a black suit jacket, which I put on and leave unbuttoned to show off the vest.

The shoes are black, with high tops and thin laces that end midway, like a dress shoe I could run in should the need arise.

There is a knock on my door.

"Come in!" I call.

Camila enters. She's wearing a royal blue dress that flows behind her. The edges are pearly white, and she wears a golden bracelet on her left wrist. "I see you found the clothes I left for you," she says. "I had a feeling you'd go for that one. Most guys would just choose the black."

"I don't blame them," I say. "Most men would look sick wearing it."

"Why would they look sick if they wear the clothes?"

I look at her and suppress a laugh. "No, I mean," I let out a chuckle, "I mean that they would look really good in black."

"Oh," Camila says. "I agree."

I check myself out in the mirror.

"You ready?" Camila asks after a moment.

"I think so," I tell her.

"Let's go," she says. "Sefryn is going to meet us down there."

I follow Camila out of my assigned chamber. When we get downstairs, it's clear a lot has changed in the hour I spent upstairs.

The whole atrium has lights of pale blue fire that flicker just under the ceiling, looking almost like large snowflakes. The entrance into the atrium from the Voltar side has been shut. People come in from the entrance closer to Aeilvow, through an erected courtyard. I walk outside, taking in the transformation.

"Every year, Edlyn's finest Rogvey outdo themselves," Camila explains to me as we walk down the few steps. The ground has been laid with a stone floor. Three-foot hedges line the courtyard, and tall pine trees have been planted throughout, with glass orbs lit with burning fires strung across them. Guests gather in clusters, holding glasses of wine and other drinks that are served at round tables, each with a bartender behind them. More and more people flood in as we watch.

"Let's go back in," Camila suggests. "I think the others are in the Grand Room."

I follow Camila back inside. I turn to head into the room where we usually eat, noticing the distinct lack of tables.

"Aros," I hear Camila say.

I turn—and forget how to breathe.

Sefryn descends the wide stairs in the atrium. Her hair is pulled up and falls right down her back, shimmering in the ambient light. She wears a floor-length gown of white and silver that shimmers with tiny amber gems. The contrast is subtle but striking. The dress leaves her neck and upper chest exposed, elegant and deliberate.

As she approaches, I spot a silver necklace resting just above her collarbone. Her heels, looking like glass, match the ethereal tone of the gown—but I know they're made of the same material as mine.

"Damn," Camila mutters.

Good for her, because I forgot how to speak.

Sefryn makes it to us. She gives Camila a graceful and formal hug, but unlike when her mother does it, there is nothing awkward about it.

"Aros," Sefryn says. I look right back into her eyes. "Are you alright?"

It takes me a few seconds to respond.

"Yeah, I—uh," I say, hissing slightly in my stutter. "I—I... You look beautiful."

My face feels hot, and I try to clear my throat.

Sefryn smiles and puts her arm through mine.

Silas comes up to us. He wears a suit similar to mine, though it features a dark charcoal jacket and matching pants, with a forest-green vest and dark shoes. His smile is warm, and his eyes draw into mine.

He's a bastard for being so handsome.

"Shall we?" he asks, extending his arm for Camila to take. She looks at me with a smirk of amusement but takes his offered arm. Silas definitely comes from royalty, and he knows his manners.

We head into the Grand Room. The tables have been pushed against the walls, all carrying more food than I imagined existed. The ceiling has snowflake lights hanging from it like the atrium, but it also has orbs of fire like the courtyard does, though instead of being strung, they all seem to float near the ceiling, bobbing up and down slightly.

A mosaic of Voltar and the surrounding landscape has been placed over the floor, but there is something so immensely inviting about it when turned into art. A short stage has been erected near the wall where the doors to the kitchens are, and people play live music with violins, a guitar, and pianos.

"Hey guys," I hear Abigail say. I turn to welcome her with a warm smile and hug. She wears a dress, shorter and tighter than Camila's, with similar colors. The blue suits her blonde hair. Peter stands next to her, wearing the black set. He's intensely striking in it, his eyes gleaming with a confidence that I haven't seen in him before.

I shake Peter's hand and give him a one-armed hug. Elder joins us, wearing a matching black suit, and I greet him similarly. "Good to see you," I say, my cheek close to his.

"I'm going to get us drinks," Sefryn tells me and heads to one of the tables.

People start filling the room, some claiming the space near the center to use as a dance floor. The King and Queen make their appearance, greeting everyone cordially, only stopping to briefly speak to a few people. I don't see Claudius.

"So, the chosen Ash Lords."

Arthur's voice has that same irritating drawl that always manages to piss me off. I lock my eyes on him as he walks toward us, wearing a black suit that might've looked decent on someone else. But his increasingly pudgy face and his growing beard—that he probably spent way too much time attempting to style—ruin any shot he had at looking polished.

Man, he really isn't good at anything.

"What are you still doing here?" I ask him. The others stay silent but watch him intently.

"Two women wanted me here," he answers. "That's more than you have for yourself, am I wrong?"

"*Wanted*," comes a voice.

"That word is past tense," comes another.

Camila's sisters walk toward us. They, too, wear dresses like Camila's, and I figure it must be the style they have to wear for these occasions.

"I've seen dwarves packing more than you," Floria says, jabbing her words with a disgusted look at Arthur.

"But who do we have here?" Creslia says, walking up to Silas and running her fingers along his shoulder.

"Someone who is not interested," Silas answers flatly, grabbing Creslia's hand and throwing it off him.

She huffs. Looking at her twin, the two walk away.

Arthur turns around and throws a wave of energy at the twins that sends them face-first onto the ground.

"You've seen nothing," Arthur seethes. "If you were prettier, then maybe I'd have more to show you." He storms toward them. The two sisters look back, confused. They just start to get up.

"Hey!" Camila shouts, running at Arthur. Arthur ignores her. "Hey!" Camila says again, catching Arthur's wrist and turning him around. "You don't attack my sisters."

"Fine, I'll settle for you," Arthur says. "We have unfinished business, or did you forget?"

Camila answers by throwing a thin wave of light across Arthur. It's as bright as it burns, and soon Arthur's torso is fully exposed, his soft belly spilling out, pale and unprotected. It appears he didn't have an undershirt made to serve as armor.

Everyone in the room notices, including the King and Queen. Everything goes silent—even the musicians stop playing. It looks like King Mattias is about to say something, but I hold out my arm, telling him to stop.

Arthur throws fire at Camila. She wraps it in her light, diminishing the flames, and then shoots two arrow-like beams at him. The light hits Arthur in the eyes. He screams, moving his hands up to his face.

Camila walks right up to him. Even though he's taller, she reaches up for his neck and pushes him to the ground. He doesn't fight back, his eyes pooling with tears of pain. I hear him whimper.

The twin sisters stand up, back away, and watch, a vague look of appreciation in their eyes. I walk up, getting closer to Camila, but she doesn't need my help, so I don't do anything.

"I am officially banning you from Edlyn," Camila says, her words dark and final. She calls over two knights dressed in guard armor. Camila leans in closer to Arthur, who still has his hands over his eyes. Sniffling is the only sound he can make. "I should throw you back into Voltar and call for the incubi. Which is. Exactly. What. I. Will. Do. If I ever see you again."

Camila knows about the incubi. Everyone else is too far to hear. I'll have to ask her later about it.

The guards lift Arthur to his feet, pulling his arms away from his face. His eyes are swollen. I can't tell if they're open or closed.

Briefly, the knights glance at the King, who nods his approval. The knights take Arthur away. The King clasps his hands together and indicates to the musicians, who at once continue playing. Everyone else follows the direction and gets back to what they had been doing as if nothing had happened.

The King and Queen resume their business without so much as another look toward Camila. The twin sisters have already disappeared.

"Let's get some air," Sefryn says, holding two drinks. She gives one to me and the other to Camila. I'm sure it was meant for herself, but Sefryn goes back and quickly grabs another.

"You're such a badass," Abigail tells Camila as we walk out of the Grand Room. Camila doesn't say anything, but her face is bright.

Peter finds us a large table outside near the hedge, with chairs and two garden benches around it. Sefryn and I take a bench, while Silas and Camila take the other.

"One second," Abigail says, giving Peter a light kiss on the cheek before walking away. Peter looks shocked for a moment but smiles to himself. I wonder if she's already drunk.

"Aros!"

I look up and see Elias approaching, Natasha at his side. Both of them wear black, dressed like they're ready for battle. Natasha moves with her back straight, eyes locked ahead, a faint smirk tugging at her lips—a quiet, commanding confidence that's hard to look away from.

I offer them a seat. Abigail returns with a plate of drinks as Elias and Natasha sit.

"It's a good thing I brought extra." Abigail sets the plate down, with more cups than we need filled with the same chocolate drink I still haven't touched. A jug sits in the middle of the table, filled with it. Camila and I lock eyes, then down the drink Sefryn gave us. It's sweet, like chocolate syrup laced with vanilla—definitely spiked with something stronger.

Abigail takes the seat next to Peter and lifts a cup. "Congratulations to the best people I know," she says, smiling. "And the newest Ash Lords."

The others raise their cups with hers, even Elder. I hastily refill Camila's and mine.

"Aros, Camila, Sefryn, and Elder."

The others echo our names, and we drink. Abigail pours drinks for those who want more. Despite the chill that the onsetting winter weather brings, I feel warm inside, thanks to both the drinks we have and the fiery lights above us. Many people walk about, heading in or out of Edlyn Castle.

"How's the training been?" I ask Elias and Natasha.

"Good!" Elias answers. "They're actually sending us to Soulstice tomorrow."

"Any reason, or are they just getting ready?" Sefryn asks.

Natasha shrugs. "I think with everything that's about to go down, they just want to make sure that Soulstice is prepared for an invasion, should it come."

"But there are more Gorgrein ships appearing near the coastline of Ibari," Elias adds. "So, it is likely they are preparing."

"With the merging of the kingdoms, I think that the Gorgreins believe that Soulstice will be vulnerable." Natasha takes a sip of her drink.

I laugh.

"What is it?" Elias asks.

"If you're there, then they don't stand a chance," I say to Elias. "What you can do is terrifying."

Elias leans back into his chair. "You were able to make it through."

"After the Trials, it wasn't a problem for me. But the Gorgrein army?

They have no idea what they're about to get into."

A laugh erupts from Elias's mouth. "You should see Natasha in action."

I look over at Natasha. She grins mischievously.

"Don't leave us hanging, tell us!" Abigail says.

Natasha decides to show us instead. She touches one of our empty cups. It disappears and reappears at the other end of the table.

"I can only really do it with small stuff," Natasha adds.

I nod. If she's smart—and even if she isn't, Edlyn's commanders are—she'll know exactly how to take advantage of her abilities.

As if reading my mind, Natasha raises her leg and puts her foot on her chair, revealing no less than eight blades strapped to it. All she has to do is touch one of those and make it appear in someone's neck, and they'd be dead instantly.

Peter whistles. He understands. The creativity of one's abilities plays a huge part in how strong one can be.

"Remind me to never get on your bad side," Elder says. We all laugh.

It hits me that I feel like I belong here. Earth was never that to me—just a lone sanctuary that supposedly kept me safe but never truly let me live. And now, with the Trials done, I feel like I can make connections with the others without constantly fearing for my life or theirs.

We drink more, with Abigail going back another three times to refill the plate. Peter gets us an array of finger foods to chow down on. I had forgotten how hungry I was. Silas looks over at Natasha, a glint in his eye, and I know what he's thinking.

The night goes on. Elias and Natasha go off to bed, stating that they have to leave early tomorrow to head for Ibari, which is easily a five-day trip. After some contemplation, Silas excuses himself and chases after them.

"I should make an appearance with my family," Camila says, sighing as she gets up. "Perks of being a princess. I'll see you guys tomorrow."

I wave goodbye to Camila, and she walks off, her posture straight, just like she does when she means that she's on royal business. Elder, Peter, and Abigail soon leave too, and then it's just Sefryn and me. She curls up against me, and I listen to the soft sound of her breathing.

"We should go," Sefryn says. I follow her.

The other doors in the atrium have been opened again, but they aren't wide like they usually are. Several people mill about just on the other side. There are no decorations out here, but I suppose the number of people that came made it necessary to open the doors, just to increase the available space.

"Where are we going?" I ask Sefryn as we jog past the people hanging out. I thought we were going back to my sleeping chambers. She doesn't say anything but pulls me closer toward the trees. We walk for a bit, heading toward where we usually train.

I shoot out two orbs of light to make it easier to see in the dark. Being so far from the castle and even farther from Aeilvow, it's pretty much pitch black out here. Through the thick of the trees, the light of the moon struggles to make it down to the ground.

Then we reach our arena. Light reflects off the waters in the river. Despite everything else around us, the place feels safe.

Sefryn tugs my hand, and I get closer to her. She looks up at me. The gray of her eyes draws me in, and I soon find myself kissing her, reveling in her calming scent, the taste of that chocolate drink faint but so much better now coming from her.

She pushes back my coat. I help her take it off while keeping my mouth locked onto hers. She starts unbuttoning my vest.

"It's cold out," I whisper, keeping my lips close.

She smiles. "You can fix that."

I draw my head back a bit. I stretch out my fingers, and a ring of fire surrounds us, far enough away to not burn, but the flames hot enough to keep us warm. Sefryn grabs my hands and leads them to her back, where

I find hidden laces that keep her dress closed around her. I pull them, one by one, loosening the fabric tight around her body. She lets out a breath as she pushes the dress down, stepping out of it. Like me, she wears an armored shirt underneath. She pulls it off over her head. I pull mine off too.

I kiss her chest, then slide down as I go, until I'm on my knees. Suddenly, I want all of her bare. I go down further, running my hands along her thighs, and then I press my mouth against her, teasing her with my tongue. Even through the sound of the raging flames, I can hear her gasp.

Sefryn grabs my hair and pushes me in more. I keep moving my mouth, my lips pressing against her, my tongue not knowing which liquid is mine or hers—except when I get that rush of her taste that makes me want to devour her.

I remain on my knees, my lungs gasping for air, but I'm begging for more of her. I keep going. If only these moments could last forever. I struggle with myself, wanting to keep a tender touch while also going deeper, going harder, and showing her just how much I want her.

I press my mouth against hers more firmly, pulling her closer, paying careful attention to what makes her moan. To what makes her want more. I slide in a finger—another gasp. Then two, moving my fingers as if telling someone to come toward me, inviting her to climax. I keep going, feeling her pleasure with every movement and touch. I move my mouth up, my tongue gliding over, up one side and the other, until I reach the top, my lips and tongue applying pressure as my fingers continue to work inside her.

Sefryn grabs my hair and pulls me toward her, as if I can't possibly be close enough. I revel in her pleasure. She gets louder, her body shaking. And then it's like the fires don't exist, and all I can hear is her crying out to the sky as she collapses against me, barely able to stand.

Breathing heavily into my hair, she reaches for my face. I move away and look up at her, still on my knees. She bends down to my level, kisses me, and pulls me up. She releases me, her warm breath tickling my lips. I grin and tilt her head up, staring into her eyes for a moment, the flames dancing in their reflection before kissing her again. I draw the fire closer to us. I kiss her neck as she holds the back of my head, her fingers brushing through my hair.

Sefryn lets go, her hands sliding down to my pants. She undoes me, exposing everything. Then it's her sliding down, faintly brushing her tongue against me for a split second. She stands up to her full height. I step out of the last of my clothing. She puts her hands on my shoulders and looks at me, deviousness in her eyes.

Something catches my wrists and pulls me backward and down. I land on the soft ground. I touch it with my hands. Grass, pulled up by Sefryn. She sits on my pelvis and leans forward, opening my mouth with hers. She lets go and traces her tongue in a line down my torso. She doesn't even get all the way before I'm ready to be inside her. But Sefryn has other plans. Her tender roots pull me down again, my back now flat against the grass.

She takes me in her mouth, teasing me with her tongue. She releases, her tongue grazing me. Her hot breath fans across the rest of my private areas, sensitive to even the slightest rough touch. I shudder. She nips me gently with her lips, sucking a bit before tickling me with her tongue.

I can barely contain myself. Hearing me let out a deep moan, Sefryn takes me in her mouth again, deeper this time. I lift my head slightly to see the top of hers. She senses me and looks up, but she doesn't stop. My arms are still tied to the ground, and I feel more vines wrap around my ankles.

"Sefryn," I call out, but she doesn't stop, and it isn't long until I fill her mouth.

She takes it all in, and in those moments, I feel so sensitive—so vulnerable.

When I'm done, I can feel her swallow, and she then slowly lets me out.

Taking a quick pause for a breath, Sefryn looks into my eyes before crawling over me, reaching my neck and face. She kisses my neck once and then again on the other side. She lays against me, her cheek pressed against my chest. It doesn't take long before I want her more—if it's even possible—and I move my arm to run my fingers through her hair, but her roots tighten around me. I feel a quick slash.

I let out a gasp. Sefryn looks at me, her eyes wide. I turn to see blood running down my forearm. It doesn't hurt now, only when the initial cut happened.

"I'm so sorry!" she cries out. "I must have been..."

I laugh. "It's okay," I tell her. She lets the vines go, and I grab her face. Staring into her eyes, I smile, and then I kiss her.

She lies on top of me for a while, and I hold her close, her heart beating softly against my chest.

"I didn't expect this to end so quickly," I say, laughing lightly.

"Neither did I," Sefryn says. "But after you went down on me, I couldn't help myself."

"Hah, I've been waiting for days to do that," I say.

Sefryn looks at me, our noses touching slightly. "You could have any of the other nights," she responds.

"I know, but I wanted it to be memorable."

She laughs. "Trust me, no matter when you did it, if it was like that, it would have been."

And there she goes, inflating my head again.

We lie there in silence. Sefryn rolls off and onto her back. I grab our clothes to cover our lower halves, using them as makeshift blankets.

"It's so beautiful out here," Sefryn says. The fires still rage beyond us, a safe distance away. There's a beauty in it, too. "There's so much that reminds me of Voltar, but everything is so different now. We're safe.

We're home."

Sefryn then says something that makes me melt inside.

"And we have each other."

"We have each other," I echo back softly.

# CHAPTER 26

# INCRIMINATING GRASS

**Aros Caelum Hayes**

"We will be sending more soldiers."

My stomach growls. We sit at a long table, but there is no food—just the entire royal family, Claudius as the Supreme Ash, and the rest of us Ash Lords. None of us have spoken except for Queen Mattias and Claudius. Even the King has been silent.

"They need all you can spare, and more," Claudius urges. "My sources tell me that there are more ships on the horizon, meaning war is imminent."

I stifle a yawn. I didn't get much sleep last night. There was something just so comforting and relaxing about lying in that patch of grass with Sefryn.

"I don't think we should send our entire army to Soulstice," Camila speaks up, surprising even the King. But now that she's an Ash Lord, he has to respect her the same way he respects Claudius. His demonstration the day I became an Ash Lord demanded nothing less. "I want to protect them, I do, but we can't be left defenseless either."

"We won't be," the King replies. "We have you."

Is that pride I hear in his voice? I steal a glance at Camila, who sits next to me. She must be wondering the same.

"I think Soulstice should have Ash Lords as well," says Camila. "Make sure that they have the same fighting chance as we do."

Claudius thinks this over. The King and Queen both look at him. In their eyes, I think they'd rather be listening to Camila, whatever they thought of her before. But they can't ignore the Supreme Ash—not when things in their kingdom seem so delicate.

My stomach rumbles again. Man, I wish I had gotten up early enough to get breakfast. I thought I did, not having any set schedule. But before I even made it to the ground floor, the King approached me and told me to follow him. I don't care much for the politics going on, but as I promised the other day, whatever Camila needs, whatever she wants, I'll be there for her.

"I can't let you guys be separated just yet," Claudius answers, his tone understanding but firm. "I will not be losing any Ash Lords again, especially not so soon after you have been chosen."

"But then what is the point of being an Ash Lord, of all this power, if we cannot use it to defend those who need us?" Elder asks, almost accusatively.

"The time isn't right," Claudius answers, his voice sharp. "Soulstice is not being left defenseless. There are more than enough highly skilled and powerful Magis there. The Kingdom of Gorgrein stands no chance."

"Then I think my parents would agree that Soulstice does not need any more of our army," Camila snaps.

"Agreed," the King says. "We will send the last units as discussed, and the rest of our soldiers will stay in Edlyn."

Claudius nods gracefully. If there is any displeasure or aggravation on his end, Claudius hides it well.

"You may leave," the King says. The four of us Ash Lords get up, as well as Camila's three sisters, all of whom said nothing the whole time, barely paying attention. Though Mavia listened intently after Camila spoke.

Maybe Mavia isn't so bad. She just needs to get over what happened ten years ago. It's not like I did it on purpose. Not that I wouldn't do it again.

Knowing how hungry I am, Camila takes us down to the kitchens and orders a couple of servants to get us food immediately. Elder goes off to continue training with his son where the other knights train. I was hoping to get in a last goodbye to Elias and Natasha, but Camila tells me that they left first thing this morning.

Abigail strolls in as we eat. It's probably about an hour until lunch. I'm amazed at how normal the Grand Room looks, since last night it was decked out so impressively I thought it would take weeks to revert.

"Hey, I was wondering where you guys were," she says, sitting down across from me and taking one of the pastries off my plate.

"Sorry, had a late start to the day," I reply.

"Well, I hope you feel energized after eating," Abigail says. "I'd like to train today!"

"Sounds like a phenomenal plan!" Despite facing the entrance to the Grand Room, I didn't even see Silas walk in. He sits down, too, right next to Abigail, though he doesn't steal any food off my plate.

"If we eat now, then we can train through lunch and until dinner," Silas says.

I chuckle. "If anything, I think I might have an early day today."

"Late day and early start, huh?" Silas says. "Sounds like you had quite the night."

"Wanna tell me about yours?" I jab back. I know there's no way in hell that Natasha would have turned him down.

Silas answers with a smile.

"I think I'm going to head home to Carroldore tomorrow to say bye to my family," Abigail tells us.

"Why tell them goodbye?" Sefryn asks.

"Were they not here for the Trials?" I ask.

"They were, but Carroldore is almost halfway to Soulstice and on the east side, so they didn't wait around. They had someone check on the wall daily so that they could know if, you know, I didn't make it."

Makes sense to me. Either way, the anticipation would be the same.

"Are you leaving Carroldore?" Sefryn asks.

"Yup!" Abigail's face lights up with excitement. She looks over to Camila, who smiles and nods. "I'm going to move up here to Aeilvow. There's something about that town that I just fell in love with almost immediately. Plus, I'm going to train myself up and become a knight."

"That's amazing!" I tell her.

It sounds like Camila worked her way to her father and got him to agree that Abigail should be slotted to become a knight. I'm not sure how it all works, how they're chosen, or if they have to already have royal ties, but I'm happy it worked out.

Plus, I totally understand her wanting to move to Aeilvow. I'd move too if I didn't have a place here in Edlyn Castle. I've never been told if my chambers are permanent, but it's easily assumed considering what I am now. It's also nice to hear Abigail sound happy and make plans, since I'm sure that weeks ago, she wanted to be as far away from Voltar as possible.

"I think that's such a great idea!" Sefryn says.

More food is brought out, and the others eat, taking in their early lunch. I try to force more food down, knowing I'll be outvoted when I ask to head back for lunch.

"We ready?" Silas asks.

"Sefryn, there you are."

The sound of Claudius's voice annoys me for some reason. He walks up to us, his alluring charm impossible to ignore.

"I need you to come with me," he tells her. "There is a technique I want you to master, considering what your powers are. Now that you have the power of the Ashen Pit, this shouldn't take long."

"What power?" Sefryn asks. I'm glad she did because I'm curious too.

"You'll see," Claudius says. "But until you can accomplish it, I'd rather keep it between us. That way, no one is disappointed if, for whatever reason in Kreavlos's name, you don't manage to."

Sefryn looks at us. None of us know what to say. It isn't like we can tell the Supreme Ash no. I put my arm around her in a small hug and kiss her on the cheek.

"I'll see you later, then," I tell her. She kisses me back and leaves with Claudius.

"Wonder what that's all about," Silas says.

"Yeah, we all do, Silas," Camila retorts. I chuckle. So does Silas.

We head out of the Grand Room and to our training grounds. Everything seems so different during the day, but the scent of the trees remains the same.

"Look at that!" Silas says, pointing straight ahead. "What is it?" He runs over to the arena. The three of us chase him. And then it all becomes clear what he means.

Right in the middle, and immensely out of place, is a large patch of grass surrounded by an oval of burn marks. It looks like some sort of dark ritual took place.

My face goes hot.

"What happened?" Abigail asks, looking around.

It takes all of three seconds for Camila and Silas to turn to me. Both of them wear smirks that make me want to punch them.

"This why you're tired today?" Silas teases.

Abigail stares at me, and then her jaw drops in understanding.

"Right, so... right here," Abigail says, walking right up to the grass and pointing down. She's careful not to step on it. Not that there's anything gross there. But I get the idea.

"Yeah," I say. "Don't worry, I'll burn it," I tell them. I hope my face isn't red, because it feels like it is.

"Wait," Silas says, his hand against my chest to stop me from moving forward. "You sure you want to destroy this memory?" Camila laughs.

"I'll make more," I tell him. "I promise." I snap my fingers, and a fire starts at the edge of the grass. I make it burn quicker, and it takes just over a minute to burn the grass away.

Abigail looks to the sky. "I'll handle the rest. Mind you, you're gonna get a bit wet." Abigail makes it rain and picks up gusts while she's at it. She, too, has gotten stronger. The rain covers the whole field while she directs the wind to blow around the dirt, hiding the evidence.

"Loverboy, I'll take you on first," Camila says when the sun comes out again.

"Should I stick to using only light?" I ask her.

"Why make it fair?" she retorts. "Few people have my ability. It's best I train for anything that might come my way."

"Agreed," I say, then chuck a ball of fire at her. Camila falls back to avoid it, then jumps to her feet with surprising agility. The others quickly back away, not wanting to get caught in the crossfire.

I've seen Camila train with Sefryn, but something tells me that she hasn't gone all out. Sefryn hasn't either, despite looking like they have. That seems to be something only Silas and I have done.

Camila zaps out a bolt of light. It moves erratically and impossibly fast, hitting me in the chest and knocking me back before I have a chance to defend myself.

As I get up, I see Camila running toward me. She flashes a ball of light, chucking it at me. I swipe it away, taking control from her. I stand on my feet, and Camila skids to a stop. She twitches an eyebrow, egging me on to make the next move.

I push out a jolt of energy, following it with a me-shaped attack. Camila smiles. She was waiting for it. As the energy rushes toward her, Camila shoots light into it, dissolving my energy and sending it right back, my energy now Camila's light but still in the shape of my body.

It burns bright as it nears, and I hold out my hands to dissolve it.

Camila never meant for it to hit me. She knew it wouldn't. But she used the distraction and my inability to see anything beyond it as a cover to charge at me. She lunges into the air. I catch her outstretched arm and toss her behind me. Something trips me, and I fall. Taking a quick look, I see a rope of light near the ground. She is absolutely stronger than she was before.

Falling onto the ground, Camila leaps on me. I toss her over and pin her to the ground with my body. She laughs in my face, and I understand why. There's a knife right at my neck, sizzling and burning bright. She barely touches my skin with it, but I can feel the burn. I get up quickly, looking at her, confused. Not because she hurt me, but because of what she did.

Camila stands up, brushing her pants off.

"Thanks for that," Camila says. "I had to see if this would work, and you were the best person to test it."

She's cocky—but after what she did, she deserves it.

When Silas and Abigail train, I can tell Silas holds back. Despite not being an Ash Lord, Abigail's power has grown. She's been able to control and direct the weather, striking down bolts of lightning, making it rain over just one person, or summoning clouds over Silas's eyes so that he can't see. At one point, she even covers him in snow clouds, and Silas comes out of them shivering.

When we reach midafternoon, I tell the others I want to call it a day. Now, fully understanding why I'm so tired, they agree, and we head back. I nap for a bit but go down to dinner after Sefryn comes to get me.

Because Elder and Peter are here, no one teases me or Sefryn, which I appreciate greatly. Still exhausted, I head back to my chambers with Sefryn behind me. We take a bath and do little for the next few hours. Come bedtime, I'm ready for sleep.

"They found out, you know," I tell Sefryn as we lie together.

"Who found out what?"

I chuckle. Looking back at it now, it's quite funny.

"What we did last night," I say. "When we went to train, the grass was still there, as well as the burn marks around it."

Sefryn lets out a laugh that makes me love her even more.

"My grass sold me out."

That warrants a laugh from me. We lay there in silence. I'm tired, but my eyes don't seem ready to close for the night.

"Hey, did you ever see things in your dreams?" Sefryn asks. "I mean, while we were in the Trials."

"Why? Did you?" I ask.

She nods. "Yeah. But I mean beyond the Eternal Flame. Like when we were camping out after the incubi attack."

"Like when you watched over me while I recovered?" It's not really a question. I know exactly when she means.

"Yup," she says. "One night, while I slept, I could hear a voice. It reminded me of the Azure Fox, but it belonged to a man. He told me to stay put, to not leave that spot until it was safe."

I turn to look at her.

"The Azure Fox isn't the only one," I say. "They are called the Aeturnous Kitisma. I still don't fully understand them, but they watch over Arteyva."

"How many are there?"

I shrug and wrap my arms around her. "I don't know," I answer. I know I shouldn't tell her. Not until they reveal themselves to her. They aren't my secret to tell, but I want to so badly.

"Well, whoever they are, I am thankful for them," Sefryn replies. I'm relieved she doesn't ask more.

"So, what did Claudius want to train you on?" I ask.

"Oh, that," she says, sounding a bit annoyed. "He wanted to see if I could pull a tree right out from the ground. And I mean a fully grown tree."

"That sounds—"

"Impossible, I know," Sefryn says. "But I was able to pull up a whole stump," she adds. "I didn't understand why the first thing that came out wasn't the canopy, but then Claudius explained it to me. He said I must possess the power to grow plants from almost nothing. So no, I won't pull trees from the ground. But maybe soon. For now, it seems like I can grow them, or at least materialize them as if they were fully grown. It's kinda hard to explain."

"Honestly, that sounds way more powerful," I reply. "Even if I don't totally get it."

Sefryn puts her hand on mine. "I know," she whispers. She turns around to face me and touches my face gently. I smile, thankful to have her here, our bodies fitting perfectly as we hold each other—I couldn't imagine anyone else beside me.

# CHAPTER 27

# DARK IN THE DAY

**Aros Caelum Hayes**

I wake much earlier than I thought I would. Sefryn sleeps peacefully next to me. After my attempts to get more rest fail, I get out of bed carefully so as not to wake her and head downstairs. The earliest moments of dawn feel desolate and dark, but a sense of calm washes over me. Maybe it's just the stillness of the morning.

My heart beats faster for a moment, remembering just how deadly the still atmosphere became. But this isn't the Trials, and so I allow myself to enjoy the calm.

Awake and hungry, I head to the Grand Room.

I spot Camila sitting at our usual table. She looks at me as I walk closer, probably wondering why I'm up so early. I sit in front of her, my back to the entrance, which is unusual for me.

"Food?" Camila asks as a large platter is brought to her. There's a set of plates too.

"Yeah, thanks."

We eat silently for a bit. When she can tell I'm fuller, she then asks me why I'm up so early.

"I couldn't sleep anymore," I answer her. "I tried to, but I was just awake."

"Me too," Camila says.

"Why?"

Camila shrugs as she pops some bacon balls into her mouth. "Just this feeling, I suppose. I keep worrying about Ibari." She pauses. "I think my family should focus on evacuating the citizens there and prepare for an attack. Ibari can be used as a sacrificial war zone, but the people don't have to be."

"You should just tell them," I say.

"Oh, I did. After you went up to your room, I found my parents and told them everything."

I look at her curiously. "What do you mean?"

Camila sighs. "I told them off for always treating me like I was worthless. I screamed at them for sending me into the Trials. I only told them some of the things we saw. They tried to apologize." Camila scoffs. "I think they might fear me now. They probably never thought I'd make it, despite what words they may have said.

"I told them their apologies wouldn't cut it. I demanded that they start taking me seriously. Claudius may be the Supreme Ash, but none of us know him. We know each other. You, me, Sefryn, Elder, Abigail—I trust all of you far more than I trust Claudius."

"I don't blame you," I tell her. "Part of me agrees with you."

"And the other part?"

I sigh through my nose. "He's...strong," I say. "What he did to that guy after we were chosen? I know he says it's harder to do to someone who has Magis. That part I'm sure is true. But no matter what he says, I think if he really wanted to—if he got enough power—he could do it to any one of us. So, I wouldn't say I trust him, but I want him on my side."

Camila nods grimly. "We're going to have to learn how to protect ourselves against that kind of attack. Especially if the stories about the blood witches are true."

We sit in silence, picking at our food, probably both hoping it never comes to that. I look over to my left. The arched windows are always frosted, blocking most of the early morning light. It almost feels like there are no windows at all, and it reminds me all too much of a prison, even if it is beautiful.

A few more people wander in, but none of them are here for food. Based on their brown and tan robes, they are servants of the castle. Some begin to wipe down the tables while others head into the kitchens.

"How long do you think we need to stay here?" I ask.

"That's something I need to bring up to my parents," Camila answers. "But it's safe to say that neither they nor Claudius want us leaving until after Gorgrein invades."

"What if they never do?"

"That's what I'm concerned about," she tells me. "What if Gorgrein never comes for Soulstice? What if they never planned to?"

"Well, someone seems to think so," I say. "I've heard about this since the first night I arrived."

"It's unlikely that they aren't going to," Camila says. "They have a reputation, though they lack the triumphs to truly instill fear."

"I don't want to stay here forever," I tell her.

Camila raises her eyebrows quickly and drops them. "Neither do I. But where would you want to go?"

"There's that mountain range toward the east, slightly north of Soulstice," I answer. "I always wanted to go there when I was a kid."

"I know where you're talking about," Camila says. "I've never been, but it would be nice to—"

The piercing sound of shattering glass tears through the room, accompanied by a screech that reverberates off the walls and shatters the other windows. Camila and I lay our heads against the table, covering ourselves, as a giant shadow passes over us, plunging us into momentary darkness. Screams erupt throughout the Grand Room and are quickly drowned by the shriek of something else.

I peek out from under my arms. A massive bird hovers over us, its wingspan covering a third of the room, giant feathers swaying at their edges. Its beak is so big it could easily pluck any of us up into the air before devouring us—or it could tear us to shreds first with the razor-sharp talons extending out from its muscled legs.

The approaching morning sunlight pours through the open windows, and we are plunged in and out of darkness with each flap of the bird's wings. The large avian shrieks again and lowers itself. I bend down, putting up a shield of energy around Camila and myself.

The servants who didn't move don't make it. The bird goes on a quick and brief rampage, flinging people into the air to either swallow them or chuck them at the stone walls, resulting in sickening thuds before they drop to the floor.

It's at this very moment I realize I am not wearing the armor shirts that could very well save my life.

I grab Camila's hand, pointing to the windows. We make a run for it. Without looking back, I shoot out walls of energy to protect us in case the bird creature comes after us. It doesn't, and we are able to hop over the windowsill and out of the castle.

I look back into the Grand Room. The creature lashes out, knocking into the walls, destroying everything it crashes into.

Another shrieking caw comes from behind. Flying over the trees, another bird-beast heads toward us. It detours, rising high into the air, right where the sun starts to appear. It holds its position, its wings flapping slowly, their strides large. It's hard to do anything but look. The sun shines like a beacon behind it, its feathers glowing in the sun's rays. Were one of them not terrorizing servants before ending them, I would think the creature was majestically beautiful.

Another cry. A third avian soars down, purposefully crashing into one of the towers. The rocks quickly come crashing down, and a massive chunk five times the size of me plummets toward us. We're not going to make it. I throw my hands up at it, jabbing bolts of energy in an attempt to break it apart. When it gets closer, I put up a shield. Camila blasts light from her hands. The chunk of the tower breaks through my shield. I was ready for it, and there's another shield waiting. Everything goes white, my eyes stinging and starting to tear.

Looking around, we are surrounded by the stone of the fallen tower. But we are unharmed. Camila looks at her hands. Steam flows right out of them. She burned through the entire stone, saving our lives.

There's no time for praise. The bird that crashed into the tower dives toward us. Combining our strength, we blast blinding light at it. Unable to see, it retreats, crying out into the wilds.

"Was there anybody in there?" I ask, indicating to the tower remains around us.

"Not that I know of."

I climb up the stonework before turning back and pulling Camila over it. We jump down. The bird we hit has flown off somewhere. The large one inside still rampages on, trying to get through the doors into the atrium, but it's too big. Then there's the one that just stays put, looking down at everything as if pondering where to grab its prey.

"We have to get the others," I tell her.

"I have to make sure my family stays safe," Camila says as we run toward the castle. We almost make it, but then the loudest screech yet erupts around us. Windows shatter yet again. My entire body freezes as the sound tears through my eardrums, threatening to shred them apart.

I turn back, looking up at the sky. The sun is fully out now, the light of day beaming down. But then the bird climbs into the air and, as its massive body passes across the sun, all the solar light diminishes, imbuing the land in darkness.

The enchanted castle lights flare to life at the abrupt darkness. The moon, though turning away from this part of the world, provides just enough light so that it isn't pitch-black out.

"Let's go," I say, pulling Camila with me. We run through the atrium, leaping up the steps. Up ahead, I see Sefryn and Abigail running down the stairs.

"What's happening?" Sefryn asks.

Another roaring screech, so loud that the beast itself must be inches away from me. I turn. Somehow, in my worry, I completely missed it. The first winged monster still attempts to pass through the doorway from the Grand Room into the atrium. It snaps its beak out, trying to grab onto anything.

"What is it?" Abigail asks.

"Dead," I answer, running back down the stairs to get closer. I stare up at it and, in that moment, it calms, looking at me curiously, as if wondering why something so small seems not to fear it.

I blast hot fire from my palms, quickly increasing the heat, the flames turning blue. The monster rears its head back. It struggles to retreat, but it got lodged in the doorway. My scorching flames feel hot against my skin, but I know it's nothing compared to what I'm delivering to the winged creature.

Through the blinding fire, I see something that makes my core tense and my heart stop. Coming back at me, lighter and hotter than my own flames, is fire from the monstrous bird. I quickly extinguish my flames, replacing them immediately with energy, forcing it out as strong as I can. Creating a wall, the bird's flames collide with my energy, turning my output into a barrier, which the fires then scale, unleashing high into the atrium and spreading far.

There's nothing I can do to stop the fire from spreading, not without letting my shields down, but that would mean I'd be torched to a quick death. And then who knows what will happen after that? I pulse out more energy, screaming from the force of it. The flow of the fire breaks, throwing us into a moment of stillness. The bird pauses, surprised. I quickly clasp my hands together and form a beam of light into a javelin. I launch it toward the beast's head, fueling its force with more energy—

The spear shoots right through its head with such force that the beast is blown back. Crashing into the top of the door frame, I hear its head crack. Splintered lines run through the stone, but the doorway itself remains intact. The creature slams against the floor, the thud like a pulse wave radiating out in all directions.

Slain. The monster is dead. It's larger than any wyvern I've taken down, larger than any incubi I've seen.

Camila, Sefryn, and Abigail run down the steps.

"Camila!" The booming voice comes from the King. Looking over the balustrade, his eyes widen when he sees the creature lying on the floor. "Are you hurt?"

"No, Father," Camila answers.

The King jumps down, landing surprisingly well on his feet, despite the distance of the drop. He takes a closer look at the monster, then he looks outside and gasps. "Oh my..."

He's right. Looking out the entrance toward the village, I notice Aeilvow is in trouble. There may have been two monsters that attacked the castle, but several more fly toward the valley. By the look of it, other creatures jump off their backs, all running toward the town. To make it worse, the figures of the creatures look all too much like incubi.

The King walks out and raises his hands. Light seems to form from nowhere, spreading out. It doesn't take all the darkness with it, but in its radius, the light shines bright. The King peels discs off the light source, chasing the creatures and cutting through any that they touch.

"We have to save them!" Abigail says, running toward the village before we can respond. The three of us follow, ignoring the shouts from Camila's father to stay back.

Way in front of us, Abigail looks wild as she dashes across the fields, throwing her hands into the air. She moves her arms back and forth erratically, changing the positions of her palms, stretching out her fingers, all while never slowing down.

Breaking through the shroud of darkness, I see sunlight filtering through the sky. We catch up to her. Abigail doesn't stop, not even as we reach the zone of the flying creatures. These creatures are nowhere near as large as any of the avian from before, but I don't know what they are. A slimy grayish-blue, they look like serpents with a set of wings—no claws, no talons, no feet. Just snake-like bodies and bat-shaped wings.

I'm filled with relief. From a distance, the other monsters that dropped off their backs looked like incubi, but these are just tall imps that charge down the hill. They lack any set of eyes, and I wonder how they see.

The more the sun comes out, the easier it is to gather my wits and direct my attacks, most of them hitting despite the constant movement of my targets.

We run down the slope we walked the night we went to the pub. I deflect falling debris as the monsters above crash into the ledges of the cliffside. Having brought the sun out in full, Abigail now draws lightning from the skies.

The village is in turmoil. Several of the townsfolk run for their lives, but it's hard for them to know where to go. Buildings get demolished as flying beasts crash into them while the humanoid imps tackle people to the ground, gouging out anything within claw's reach.

Keeping a close eye on the people near me, I shoot bullets of energy at any monsters I see. Camila takes from her father and holds an orb of light in front of her, sending out discs of it to sever through the torsos of the creatures.

I never noticed it before, but in the opposite direction of where the pub is, the valley widens and the village extends, with more streets winding through housing and other buildings.

Sefryn breaks off branches of the nearby trees and tosses them like spears, shaving off excess wood and shaping her weapons for lethal impact. She uses the wood from the houses that are built into the cliffs, all of them seemingly vacant.

There are imps ahead and behind us. The four of us work together, saving each other's backs while doing all we can for the people below. When we're near the bottom, I see something that both gives me hope and sends chills of panic throughout me.

Elder is caught in the middle of it all, but he's doing well for himself. He stomps on the stone path, part of the rock breaking off, and then he tosses it with surprising strength and speed. As it soars toward its target, the stone shapes into various weapons. Peter is by him. He isn't as strong or quick as his father, and that terrifies me. He's in over his head.

Judging by the look in his eyes, he knows it.

A flying creature lunges toward Peter. I toss out a web of energy. I catch the creature and pull it back. It roars into the air, struggling to break free. Twisting my hands, I spin my energy around and break the monster's neck, causing it to quickly fall to the ground.

We make it into the village proper. I can see Snake and Mammoth in the distance. It felt much farther away that night than it does now.

"Toss me some energy!" Elder shouts at me as he sees us approach.

Not knowing what he means, I do it anyway. Elder catches my ball of radiating blue and throws it into the air. It turns into something that looks like an electric current, though it keeps its original color. Elder zips my energy through the air, crashing through beast after beast, bringing each down as soon as it makes contact.

I hear something behind me, the noise making the hair on the back of my neck rise. I spin around and see up close a small imp leaping toward me. The creature chucks two small daggers, both hitting me in the right shoulder.

Wincing from the pain, the damage minor, I reach out, grab its small arm, and swing down. As I let it go, I release a pulse of energy at it. The imp hits the ground with enough force that it cracks the stone path.

Then I hear another one of those terrifying shrieks. It reverberates through the village, the sound waves acting like wind as they rush through. Then the temperature drops, first cool and then quickly turning cold. Snow begins to fall before I see anything else.

Humans and creatures alike stop to look around, curious as to what made the noise.

I don't let the sound distract me any longer. Though cheap shots, I blast out at any creatures I see, putting most down in one hit. The commotion continues. Gradually, the snowfall increases. Abigail does her best to deter the snow between her flurry of attacks, but she can't quite seem to stop it.

More of the winged serpents drop imps upon us, making it hard to ensure anyone I save remains safe.

Sefryn does a great job of pulling up trunks and roots from the ground. Even though she destroys the stone pavement, it's worth it when her attacks become lethal to anything she goes after. Elder and Peter use the broken stones and the wood from the trees to forge weapons. Elder, moving objects like it's some form of art, constantly strikes down the monsters. We'd easily beat them and have it all over with, but they don't seem to stop coming. Peter, having trained in the use of weapons, fights off the monsters he sees, moving from one to the next, quickly forging another weapon anytime one of his breaks or he is disarmed.

Camila pushes out rings of light above us, covering a wide area. At their brightest point, the rings burn through anything they touch, but otherwise most of the dropping monsters receive a minor burn at worst.

Another shriek cuts through the sky, making my eardrums rattle. The wind picks up, the falling snow increasing, the flakes sticking to my face and not melting as fast as I would like them to.

I hear the flapping of wings, rhythmic, in sync, and massive. Looking up, all I can see is the gray and white rush of the snow. Then there's the shadow, its shape indiscernible at first. But then it descends beneath the cover of haze. As large as the other three, this monstrous bird has white, frosty feathers and ice-cold blue eyes.

"Stoichea," Elder says, looking up at the bird.

This monster is closer to us than any of the others. It feels like any movement I make, no matter how slight, will only serve to make me its next meal. With that thought in mind, I stay as still as possible.

"What?" Sefryn dares to whisper.

"Stoichea," Elder says. "They are four elemental creatures from myths of my culture."

I can't believe the bird stays put, not seeming to care if we speak to each other.

"This one is the god of water."

*God?*

Apparently getting bored, the supposed god lowers its head and opens its beak. It lets out a rumbling sound as a fog of frost is spewed from its mouth. I jump in front of the others and throw my arms in front of me in a defensive position, erupting flames from my hands, the fire so dense it looks like a glowing wall.

After what feels like a full minute, the bird stops, and I let down my fire. Nothing seems different until I turn back.

Everything as far as I can see has been frozen over—human, imp, or flying snake; they're all frozen dead in place as they were when the ice took over.

Frozen roads make it impossible not to slip. The chill of the air pierces my bones, making my whole body feel like I'm frozen just like the unfortunate people who actually are. Since it killed most everything in sight, the Stoichea resumes its position above us, looking down but not attacking.

"How do we beat it?" Sefryn asks.

None of us can answer. But there must be a way. Camila drove off one of them. I killed another. The only difference now is that it feels like the beast has us pinned down.

And the only reason it hasn't killed us yet is because it hasn't decided to.

"If I can get up there, do you think I can burn it down?" I ask.

"No, it would just drown your fire. You'd probably die before you even touched it," Elder snaps.

I take a deep breath, still scared shitless that the creature will see me move and decide to kill me immediately. "As Ash Lords, there's something we can do about it."

"Comforting for you," Abigail says through chattering teeth. "Right now, I'm kinda wishing I became an Ash Lord."

"Abigail, you brought back the sun. You're fine," Camila says.

"Yeah, but I can't do that now! I've been trying!"

An idea comes to me. "What if it's distracted?"

The others quickly look at me, their expressions both telling me I'm insane and begging me not to.

Too bad. At worst, I die, but maybe they live.

I push out my arms and blast fire at it. I can't see how far up the flames go, but I soon feel the push back as the monster counters my attack with its own. I don't hear any screams of protest, so the others must be fine.

Knowing that its ice attack isn't doing anything, the Stoichea shifts gears, turning its frosty breath into a cannon of water. As Elder predicted, my fires start to go out, but steam rises from our clashing elements, my fire hot enough to evaporate some of the water before it hits me.

Roaring into the air, the Stoichea ascends, dodging my fire blast. I back down from my attack, ready for whatever it does next. I take a quick look at the others. They're looking at me with that same look that tells me they think I'm insane.

Another cloud of ice shoots toward us. I counter it again with fire.

As if the bird wanted this, it changes its ice to water again—this time much quicker. I don't even try to fight it with my flames. Concentrating as hard as I can, I push back the water to the best of my ability. The power of the Ashen Pit that resides in me has made me much stronger, and the water erupting from the beast's mouth is rebounded with much more force, knocking the Stoichea out of the sky.

It quickly recovers, regaining its position.

"Camila!" I shout.

She and I burn as much light as we can toward the creature, aiming for its eyes. It worked before. Maybe they just don't like light.

The Stoichea recoils, screaming as it flies back and over the crest of the valley, out of sight. I want to celebrate. I want to believe we're safe now. But something doesn't feel right.

Silence can be the dirtiest trick of all.

There is no warning before it happens. If we hadn't been looking, we'd all have been caught dead in it.

A providential amount of water pours into the valley. It can't be real. There is too much to be conceivable. I throw out my hands, pushing back some of the water before it reaches us.

A sharp pain in my back makes me cry out, losing all concentration on the water. I turn around. From the air, another one of the winged snakes soars by, carrying a larger imp on it who wields a bow.

The rush of water hits us, knocking us off our feet and sweeping us away in different directions. My head goes under several times. I do my best to stay above water. I don't even attempt to breathe; I just hold my breath, hoping that this will stop soon.

My head underwater, I close my eyes as my body spins around so quickly I can't tell which direction is which. I'm lucky no debris has hit me.

Almost as quickly as it came, the water disappears—some of it running through the village, wiping out anything that's left in its path, and the rest evaporating.

I touch the part of my back where I felt the pain. There isn't anything there except blood. Looking around, I first see Camila, then Sefryn. Ignoring the pain that's everywhere, I run toward them. Camila is coughing up water but otherwise seems fine. Sefryn looks unharmed.

"Aros, you're bleeding."

"I don't care," I respond, not knowing what she's talking about.

I can't feel pain at this point. Either from the water or something else, my whole body is numb.

Peter slaps me on the back, just off and below my shoulder blade. I feel a stinging and a relaxing warmth. Without spending too much time, he heals me enough that I might be able to get through this.

There's another shrieking. The Stoichea has returned, but this time it rages in the valley. We're far from the pub now. Instead of the single street that I'm used to, there are three. Or were three. Debris is littered all around, and only because of the lack of road in some parts can I tell that there used to be structures here.

"Aros!" Elder shouts from afar. He's using wood and stone from the fallen structures as weapons and throws them toward the bird. I run toward him. Abigail runs too, one arm stretched toward the sky.

Then I see another winged beast fly at us. This one is different from the rest. I can't believe what I'm seeing because it's a freakin' hippogriff. It lands, its wingspan almost as massive as the Stoichea's.

A girl hops down. "I need you to come with me."

It takes me a moment to place her wavy light brown hair and matching eyes. Then it hits me—Ziara, the first person to complete the Trials.

I ignore the near-crippling fear in my gut as the Stoichea caws again, while Elder and Abigail fight it off.

"We're busy."

I don't mean to be short, but I can't help it.

I walk toward the others, Sefryn and Camila quick to follow. Ziara puts her hand on my chest and forcibly holds me back. Not that she is strong enough to restrain me, but the surprise of it stops me in my tracks, and I turn my head to look at her.

A bolt of lightning strikes down. Its flash lights up the world brighter than I've ever seen. I missed whatever happened, but from what I can tell, Abigail hit the Stoichea.

Unfortunately, the Stoichea doesn't go down, but I can tell it's hurt.

I start to rush over, but Ziara stops me, this time with her hippogriff. Twice my height, the beast would be terrifying if I hadn't seen much worse before.

"This is all a distraction!" Ziara shouts.

Camila and Sefryn head off toward Elder and Abigail.

"Camila!"

Camila ignores Ziara. Sefryn works to pull up a tree from the ground. This time she does it, and Sefryn is able to rise into the air. She shoots out vines and sends them to catch the Stoichea.

"Someone very powerful is behind this, and their target isn't Aeilvow—it's Edlyn."

Another shriek comes from the Stoichea. Looking over, I see it break through vines, its force so strong Sefryn almost falls out of her tree.

"Later," I say as quickly as I can and run for it. I shoot out rockets of energy. One of them gets the giant bird, but the bird recovers quickly.

Diving down, the Stoichea heads for Abigail. Abigail conjures wind to blow the monster away, but it isn't strong enough. Knowing that, Abigail starts to run for it, but something stops her. As I dart toward her, I shoot out more attacks, switching between fire and energy. Elder throws spears of wood at the creature, but the Stoichea is impossibly nimble that it dodges everything.

It happens in just a second. Rooted to the spot, Abigail is swept up in the beak of the Stoichea. Rising high into the air, I can barely see the creature. Elder shouts, throwing more weapons at it, but the beast is too high up.

I see something large fly past me. Ziara and her hippogriff. They chase the Stoichea. Catching up, they barely dodge the frost attack and quickly retreat.

There's nothing more I need to know. Even from so far away, I could see enough. Nothing fell from the sky. The Stoichea was able to open its mouth to release its ice-cold breath. Elder runs up to me. Sefryn isn't far, but her face falls when she looks at me.

Ziara returns, shaking her head.

The heat that burns inside me threatens to consume the immense rage that poured in just seconds ago. The monster devoured Abigail, and she's gone. All her plans for her future were voided by the avian's jaws.

It's no god. It's just another fucking monster.

And then everything feels like Voltar again.

Fuck this land.

Fuck this place.

The Stoichea charges toward us, descending quickly.

Releasing the volcanic wrath inside me, I shout, my right hand raised toward the sky. There is a flash of darkness as the clouds above us turn dark, and a colossal bolt of lightning strikes down, catching the monster. Light returns to the sky, and landing under a hundred feet from us, the monstrous bird hits the ground, already dead. Inside, I feel nothing. No spark of life, no power. If it weren't for the Ashen Pit, I'd be worried I burned out all my Magis.

"Aros."

I turn to look toward Sefryn. Other than the breeze and the call of my name, it's quiet. The chaos and turmoil here are over, and all that's left is the wake of destruction.

"Aros."

It wasn't Sefryn who called me. It was Ziara.

"I—I don't mean to be insensitive, but I need you back at the castle."

Camila touches my arm, as if reminding me that it's her family that's in danger.

"Go," Sefryn tells me. I stare at her. I know it's safe now, but part of me wants to kiss her, just in case it will be the last time. "I'll be fine," she promises, her smile all the reassurance I need.

"Find her," I say, looking toward Elder. I know that they probably can't. They know it too, but they both nod.

Camila and I climb onto the hippogriff. Even with it lowering its body, it isn't easy, and I have to help Camila up. The hippogriff shakes slightly, as if protesting the weight it now carries. Ziara pets it on its head, soothing it.

We lurch into the air, the jolt so sudden it feels like every organ inside me has been left behind. The rush of the wind feels bright and alive against my skin, reminding me that I'm here, and I've still got people to save. Even if it's awkward, I lean close to Ziara, my arms holding onto the feathers of the hippogriff. Camila does the same behind me.

Though far from the castle, we make good speed. The hippogriff lowers itself closer to the ground as we approach. The land is littered with fallen creatures, all of them the flying snake monsters or the tall, human-like imps. Something glows over the castle—a barrier of energy. As we rush to it, a space opens up. Once we're inside, the hippogriff lands. The impact is rough, and Camila and I fall off it.

"Are you okay?" Ziara asks, leaping off her beast and helping us up.

"Yeah, fine," Camila answers, her tone sour.

"Sorry, he isn't used to carrying more than one person."

"What is this?" I ask, pointing to the energy shield around us.

"Claudius," Ziara answers. "He's protecting the castle from the creatures. But it's so massive and has withstood so much, it's all he can do."

"Where is my family?" Camila asks.

"Inside, safe—last I knew."

*So, what are we doing here?*

As if sensing our arrival, the Azure Fox appears. She stares at us for a moment before speaking.

"There is a threat to this kingdom," she tells us. "Claudius is protecting it from the monsters outside. But something wicked is inside the castle, and I cannot find it."

"What do we do?" I ask. "How do we know what it is?"

The ground rumbles, shaking like we're near the epicenter of an earthquake.

"Follow me."

As ordered, the three of us follow the Azure Fox into the castle. Ziara's hippogriff remains outside. The atrium looks almost as we left it. The fallen Stoichea is still there, the walls are mostly damaged, and the whole place is empty.

Acting like an animal for the first time, the Azure Fox sniffs the ground, walking slowly, trying to follow a scent.

We head up the stairs, pausing for a moment at the landing as the Azure Fox decides where we're going next.

I hear running footsteps. It's Camila's three sisters. Their eyes are wide. "Camila!" Surprisingly, they all hug their sister.

"Where are mother and father?" Camila asks.

"Mother is downstairs attending to some of the knights," one of the twins says.

"That other Ash Lord girl told father to go with her, claiming he was in danger," Mavia tells us, looking at me briefly.

My heart missed a beat.

Sefryn?

She's the only Ash Lord that Mavia could be speaking of since Camila is right here. But she's down in the valley with Elder. There's no way she beat us here.

"Where?" the Azure Fox demands of Camila's oldest sister, her voice bellowing, sending chills down even my spine as I realize what might be happening.

"T—t—t—"

"Where?" I shout.

"The northwest tower," Mavia barely manages to speak. But once said, the Azure Fox bolts in that direction, with me, Camila, and Ziara following after her.

We run down corridors I've never seen before, walking on the other side of the castle, the one closer to Voltar. Most everything seems to be untouched. Whatever battle happened on these grounds, it stayed in the Grand Room, atrium, and outside.

The Azure Fox breaks through the door that leads into the tower's stairwell. She skids to a stop. There is a massive trunk running up it, right in the center, somehow positioned so that it did not destroy the stairs.

"That isn't normally there, is it?" Ziara asks.

I already know the answer. And with the thoughts that run through my head, nothing now can be real. Nothing is right. A part of me wants to smash my head into the wall or jump off the tower—do whatever it takes to wake up. Because what seems to be can't be true.

"Find Claudius," the Azure Fox tells Ziara. Reacting immediately, Ziara runs off. She probably knows where the Supreme Ash is.

Leading us up, the Azure Fox hops the stairs, her graceful steps quick. We reach the top and barge into the room. There is no door. Instead, a large branch of a tree hangs inside from the spiral staircase.

Back facing us, I can see the ash-white hair that's so unique to Sefryn. In front of her, facing us, is the King. The vines wrapped around his neck seem to render him unconscious.

Hearing us, Sefryn looks back. Her gray eyes dilate when she sees me. She turns her attention back to the King. His dark beard shines like it's drenched with something. Blood. His face quickly turns red, his eyes opening and bulging slightly.

Then Sefryn seizes, her back arching, and she rises into the air. I hear something behind me. Accompanied by Ziara, the Supreme Ash charges in, his arms thrown forward. I can see veins on his neck and arms, popping the more he struggles.

Several sets of vines and branches crash through the large window that overlooks the forest. The room looks like my chambers, just smaller.

I'm pinned against the wall with the others. Sefryn turns her head back, her eyes dark with malice. She jumps out of the open window, a tree branch carrying her safely down and out of sight.

Setting the tree on fire, I break free and run toward the window, ignoring the King. Sefryn is gone. No matter where I look, there is no indication of where she went.

"Aros."

The voice is soft, frail, imbued with both sadness and numbness. I turn around. Camila kneels in front of her father. I step closer.

The King leans against the stone wall beneath the sill of the wide windows. The vines around his neck are red, the blood of the King dripping down them. Looking closer, I see thorns jutting out of it, right into his neck.

It must have started as a slow job, like some sort of revenge, and when we surprised her with our arrival, she had no choice but to make it instant. I still can't believe what I saw. But it was Sefryn. She did it.

The King of Edlyn is dead.

# CHAPTER 28

## LONG LIVE THE QUEEN

**Aros Caelum Hayes**

Aftermath is a varied thing. People suffer from different losses. Some are worse than others. People have lost their lives. Aeilvow lost its homes. For Camila, she lost her father. For Edlyn, well, they just lost their king. We lost Abigail. The feelings start subtle, the sense of shock overwhelming them, until the truth emerges, reality evoking the raw emotions attached to it.

I want to say I lost Sefryn. But that wouldn't quite be the truth. See, if Sefryn was always going to betray us, then I never had her.

Everything was a lie. I trusted her. I was falling in love with her. Fuck, I *was* in love with her. We had each other, and those moments we spent together made everything else seem fine—like all the bad I had gone through my entire life was worth it if it led to her.

She made me feel like there wasn't anything I couldn't live through.

Little did I know, she was just the next phase of the shit-show my life has been.

So, no. I didn't lose her.

What I lost was the ability to trust myself.

Down in the dungeons, Camila and I lie against the grim-looking walls. The cells are open and used as medical wards. The Queen has the ability to heal anyone. She's strong. That gift is extremely rare for someone who is not a Rogvey. I can only heal the ordinary back on Earth, and even then, my power is limited.

Upon our arrival, the Queen patches me up instantly—no emotion behind her eyes. She makes sure Camila is okay and then returns to attending those who fled into the castle when they were hurt.

Camila blurted out what happened while her mother healed her. A moment of shock flashed across the Queen's face, but she gathered her composure and returned to doing what was most needed.

It's been about an hour. I don't know where Ziara went. The Azure Fox demanded that she speak with Claudius, so he is also gone. I know nothing about Elder or Peter. I didn't even see Peter after he healed me when we were in the valley.

Servants pass us, bringing supplies to the Queen and the other attendants who help those who were injured. I am amazed at how many people from Aeilvow made it into the castle.

So many things run through my mind. Abigail. Seeing her swept up—just like that. One instant she's there, and the next she isn't. The memory plays over and over again, all to remind me of what a failure I am. All the power that flooded me after she died... why couldn't I have done it earlier?

I have to think of other things to keep from thinking about it—even remembering all that happened in Voltar is better than thinking about how Sefryn betrayed us. Betrayed me. But it doesn't work. Every time I see Camila let out a shaky breath, every person that's brought in on some sort of old, wooden stretcher, every time the Queen passes by, I can't help but think of Sefryn and everything she's done.

And I can't stop thinking about how she helped make the hell of Voltar so much easier, how she spent a week with me, attending to me, to make sure that I would be alright. How she promised me that she would never leave.

I can't believe how stupid I was. I've known all my life that I would never know what love felt like. My parents made sure of that. Ever since I was born, I've been cursed. A solitary life is all I've ever been destined for.

I didn't even realize I had stood and begun walking away until I saw Claudius and the Azure Fox standing in front of me.

"Aros!"

I look past Claudius and see Silas with his hand up, looking for me. He's carrying something behind him, someone helping him further back. When they come close, I see Elder lying on the cloth. His eyes are closed, but looking closely, I see his chest rise and fall.

Queen Mattias rushes over and directs Silas and the other guy to put Elder down. She starts working on him, running her hands over his body, not quite touching him.

"I found him over on the hillside, a little too close to the cliffs into Aeilvow. I'm surprised he didn't fall over."

I hear Silas, but I don't know what to say.

"Sefryn must have ambushed him after you and Camila left," Claudius says. "Luckily, he's an Ash Lord, so killing him wasn't an option for her."

"Are you alright?" I manage to ask Silas.

"Yeah, I am," he responds. "I was still in the castle after the attack started. I had to help the princesses get to safety, but then there was that large bird to deal with. It produced winds so strong I don't think most storms could even match them." Silas lets out a sigh. "I don't know how the castle withstood it."

"There was another one?"

"Another one?" Silas asks, clearly confused as to what I mean.

There's too much to deal with. While I was down in Aeilvow, the castle was being targeted too. It doesn't make sense how all of this was Sefryn's doing. But she is from Praellen, so maybe there are other Fae who have been helping her. But how did they call upon those monsters?

"We fought off two of those things," Camila says.

"Three."

"I scared one away, it doesn't count," Camila says.

"It does in my book."

The Queen walks up to us, taking a break from her work as a healer. From all the things I've heard in passing conversations, there is only one other Tavtka healer in Edlyn, and he isn't anywhere near as powerful as the Queen. "Those monsters threatened every life in our kingdom. So dead or gone, that's a win, and you shouldn't think anything less of it."

Silas looks over at me. "So that was you, I mean, the giant bird in the atrium?"

"Yeah," I say. Also the one hopefully now rotting in the ruins of Aeilvow.

"Aros, Camila, come with me," Claudius interrupts. I turn back to take another look at Elder. He seems fine. Unconscious, but I know he'll be okay.

"Has anyone seen Peter?"

Silas shakes his head.

"The valley. He has to be there somewhere. Maybe beyond the village. But he's somewhere," I tell Silas. I don't want to imagine the worst. Peter isn't dead.

Understanding, Silas clasps me on the shoulder. "I'll find him." He turns to leave.

"Now," Claudius says. Camila and I follow him out of the dungeons. He leads us out of the castle. We head toward Voltar.

Passing through the trees, we finally reach the river. The Azure Fox trots ahead, takes a drink from the water, and turns around.

"The Ashen Pit has yet to contact us," Grisla says. "Sefryn... There's nothing we can do now. She is an Ash Lord. How she managed any of it may forever be unknowable. The Trials test a person's strength and character at their very core. The choice should be infallible."

We don't say anything. Even Claudius seems to listen intently.

"That is how we could tell you that Arthur would never become an Ash Lord." I feel Camila shoot a look at me, but I don't return it. I can explain it to her later.

The Azure Fox walks up to me.

"You will be returned to Earth," she tells me.

I want to ask her why. I want to argue. But truthfully, I don't care. Maybe I'm exhausted. Maybe part of me wants to go back.

"Aros, can I speak with you?" Camila asks, using that stern voice she does when she's speaking as royalty.

Without responding, I begin to walk away with her.

"Wait!" Claudius calls out. Camila doesn't stop, so neither do I. Faintly, I can hear the Azure Fox telling Claudius to let us go.

When she's sure we're out of earshot, Camila says, "I don't know why they are bringing you back to Earth. There's probably nothing we can do to change that." She sucks in a breath. "But just promise me this," she says, holding me back and making me face her. "Don't make it another ten years before you come back."

It takes all my energy to focus on her. Camila's been my true best friend. She and I developed a bond that has no limits. At the moment, it's just hard to see anything. It feels like there is this heavy fog surrounding me, pushing down on my head and clouding my vision.

"I won't let that happen," I tell her.

After a minute, Camila says, "I can't imagine what you're going through."

I shake my head. "Don't worry about me," I say. Focusing on helping her is making it easier for me to go on. "You just lost your father."

"We're both in pain, yes," Camila says. "Being raised as a princess, we're prepared for something like this to happen." Camila looks down at the ground. "It's sad. But I can't feel the pain of losing him. It's like I was raised to be numb to it."

I don't know what to say.

"In my eyes, it's nothing compared to what you have to deal with."

Blinking away tears, I look over Camila's head. The sun has been setting for some time now. The battle went on for a while.

"When you need me," I say, struggling to find my voice, "let me know." I look down at her. We lock eyes for a moment. I kiss her on the forehead and walk away.

Not thinking of where I'm headed, I walk beyond the castle and to the valley where it drops down into the village. Looking down, all I see are the fresh ruins. Right about now, since the sun has nearly dropped out of the sky, Aeilvow would be shining brightly. The twinkling lights of the city provide a magic that this world couldn't otherwise offer.

I can't stay here any longer. I head back to the castle. They've begun trying to clear out the atrium, but moving a beast that large is going to take time, especially when many of those who could move it are hurt or dead. I walk past them and head up the stairs. Before I realize it, I'm in the tower where we stayed.

Three doors. One for my room, one for Sefryn, and one for Abigail.

Swinging open my door, I walk through the main room and into my bedroom. My footsteps feel numb, just like my vision. I see it all. Sefryn and I shared this bed. We first shared each other just outside this room. This floor in the tower hosted some of the best people I knew.

Yelling, I produce energy from my hands, hold the power there, and grab everything in sight. I throw the mirror across the room, making sure the glass shatters on the floor. I shoot down each bedpost, one at a time, until the whole thing collapses. There's an armoire full of clothes. I open it and set it on fire. I shove it toward the window. Taking several steps back, I blast it, and the whole cabinet goes flying, breaking through the glass and falling to the ground somewhere six floors below.

Shouting again, I light everything on fire. The heat threatens to consume me, and there's this moment where I want it to. Everything in this room can burn to ash—me along with it.

But no, that can't happen. The Ashen Pit wouldn't allow it. It already has my soul. Calming myself with an understanding of my rage, I put the fires out, the flames shrinking until they seem to seep under the floor and out of existence.

The walls are undamaged, but everything else in here barely looks recognizable. I climb out the window. Pulling myself up on the various ledges, I make it to the top, sitting back on the slightly slanted roof. I stare at the stars. I refuse to move. I can't sleep in that room. I can't close my eyes without seeing flashes. So I keep staring. Hours pass. Multiple times tears pour from my eyes, running down my face. But I don't move a muscle.

On and on the night goes until the sun starts to come up.

That doesn't change anything for me. If allowed, I'd spend the rest of my life up here. Seemingly out of sight, there's nothing I need to care for. Nothing I need to watch out for.

It's mid-morning when I hear a voice from below. He's asking for me, but I don't respond. Silas finds me anyway. Pulling himself up like I did last night, he joins me.

"It wasn't easy finding you," he says. He rummages through his coat. "Here, something to eat if you get hungry."

I say nothing, and I don't take it.

"You don't need to speak. You don't need to eat," Silas tells me. "But you will need to come down at sunset. The King's funeral will be held, and Queen Mattias will take his place."

Silas doesn't expect me to respond.

"I found Peter," he tells me. "He's alive, and well enough that he's going to start building a monument for those who died yesterday."

It takes me over a minute to say it, but I finally do. "Thank you."

Hours go by. The sun rises to high noon and begins crawling across the sky. I take the food Silas offered me—a simple sandwich.

"Let's go," Silas says after a while. I look out. The sun is setting. There are wispy clouds among the orange flare of the sky. "I'm not asking. I'm here to bring you there."

I know he wouldn't be doing it if he wasn't either being told to or if he didn't think it was the right thing.

Silas pulls shadows from our bodies and has them bring us down.

The ceremonies are held where we took the stage before being transported to the Trials. By the time we get there, the funeral has already begun, and the King is carried in a casket up to the stage. I catch a glimpse of him. Someone has healed all his scars and wounds so well that it almost looks like he's sleeping.

Silas leads me up near the front, where Camila stands with her sisters. Claudius is close by, and Peter is here too, but Elder isn't. When I look at Silas, he shakes his head, telling me that Elder hasn't awoken yet. Camila squeezes my hand briefly. Looking at her sisters, I can see what Camila meant about them being prepared for something like this. While they all look solemn, none of them look like they are about to break down. There are commoners among the crowd of people who show more emotion than the family does.

A nobleman, likely the Speaker for the Royalty, reads a speech for the King, but I tune it out. I don't need to hear the typical words of praise and deeds of honor. For all royalty, it's always the same. I know this from the books I read years ago. The only difference is the accomplishments of King Mattias, such as battle victories and treaties with other kingdoms. The King also made it known worldwide that Voltar is part of the Edlyn Kingdom, which, without actually winning the land, gave Edlyn the rights to call it theirs.

I don't need to listen when the Queen takes the crown of Edlyn. When everyone chants, "Long live the queen!" I remain silent. Finally, it stops, marking the end of the crowning. But Queen Lucia Mattias breaks tradition and speaks out, addressing the crowd. I can't help but turn my attention to her.

Her hair has been done, neatly falling back and out of the way so that she may wear the crown. She has that same strength that her daughters do, the same act of solemnity, but without the sadness of loss. From this close, though, I can see the streaks that run down her cheeks. The Queen mourns the loss of her husband, but now the image of the kingdom comes first. This, for whatever reason, increases my respect for the woman.

"I will not keep you long," the Queen says. "First, I want to let you know that a memorial will be erected so that those who fell yesterday will never be forgotten."

The crowd of people shifts. No one says anything, but there is no ill will present.

"Next, I want to thank the Ash Lords for their bravery and strength, as well as Silas Thorne, without whom our kingdom may have fallen entirely."

A polite clap comes from the crowd. The Queen mentioned the Ash Lords without exclusion. I look over at Silas. I can see that he's happy to have been honored, so I say nothing. No one knows how the King died, which means everyone believes that the Ash Lords are on their side.

It's a dangerous lie.

"Lastly, I am opening Edlyn Castle to anyone who lost their home. You may stay as long as you like. In the meantime, we will work to rebuild Aeilvow." There is a pause, a moment of silence. I can feel the relief emanating from the people. There are random claps, which makes me think that most people are either still in shock or don't believe the Queen.

As people start to leave, Silas pulls me away. Camila follows us. We head west, away from Aeilvow, beyond the tower I slept in, across the land that will eventually drop thousands of feet to the ocean.

"There's been no word about Sefryn," Camila says. Silas looks at her, his eyes questioning.

"It's fine," I lie. I turn to look Camila in the eye. "I'm fine. We need to find her."

"But even when we do, what do we do?" Camila asks. "We can't kill her."

I take a deep breath. Letting out all my frustration and anger helped a lot, and while I know Sefryn needs to be stopped, I'm not ready to talk about killing her.

"I can," Silas says.

"Why don't we deal with that problem when we get there?" I suggest, wanting more than anything for the subject to change. "What's your plan?"

Camila sighs. "I don't have one. With you leaving and my father dead, all that it seems I should do is help rebuild."

"What of the war in Soulstice?" I ask.

"Still happening, apparently," Silas answers. "But nothing has begun. Honestly, there's a part of me that thinks it was all a hoax, a way to leave Edlyn defenseless."

"If it was, it worked," I say.

"I'm going to find out what I can," Camila says.

I look out to the side. The night feels lonely. Maybe I'm not as okay as I hoped I would be. I feel Camila look at me. What do we say? What do I say? Out of all those connections I made, everyone who stood by me throughout the Trials from the beginning, they're all gone. Camila is the only one left—and I'm about to leave.

"Don't worry about me," Camila tells me. "I'll be fine here. I'm worried about you."

"Why?" I ask.

"Because you're leaving. No matter what life you had on Earth, how could any of it be the same? Here, I at least have what I've always known, even if some of it is gone. But you? How can you return to an ordinary life?"

"If it would help, I'll go with you," Silas offers.

I laugh. "No, they'd never allow that."

"They who?"

I don't answer him. Everyone knows about the Shadow Realm, which means they know of Kreavlos, even if they all don't know his name or what he is. But the other Aeturnous Kitisma remain mostly secret. Camila is right. Whatever life I thought I had on Earth doesn't exist anymore.

All of a sudden, I don't want to go.

But I also don't want to stay here.

Something emerges from the sky. It doesn't produce any sense of fear. No, I recognize the presence. The giant owl, Palvadore, towers over the three of us. The Avian of the South lowers his head, looking right into Silas.

"You trust this man?"

The owl is asking me.

"I do," I answer genuinely.

Palvadore sits up straight.

"It is time," he tells me.

I turn to look at my friends. They're both shocked, that much I can tell, but they hold themselves well.

Camila gives me a hug, and I hug her tightly back. A sorrowful understanding washes over me. Arteyva is indeed my home once more. Whatever the reason the Ashen Pit has to bring me back to Earth, I must close out the life I had there so I can spend the rest of my days here.

She releases me slowly and steps away. Behind those eyes trained with emotionless strength, I can see the grief hinting at nights of tears to come.

Stepping up to me, Silas embraces me. I return the gesture, and just like that, it's as if hundreds of words are spoken between us. Despite everything I'd thought of him when we met, he quickly changed my perception of him. I wonder how our lives would have been had he been part of the Trials.

I let him go, and it's only seconds later that the darkness of the wind rushes over, tearing me away from this realm.

After the moments of what should feel like turmoil but don't, I am surprised to see blackness all around, with a single light shining down on me. I thought I was going back to Earth, so why am I in the Shadow Realm?

Without showing himself, the voice coming from all around and nowhere at all, Kreavlos says, "We need to talk."

# CHAPTER 29

# REVELATION

**Aros Caelum Hayes**

All I can do is let out a sigh. With the dark tones in his voice and the subtle tremors, I know nothing he tells me now will be good. It makes it worse when Palvadore appears, with Grisla following. The three of them stare down at me. Even with all the power I have now, I feel so insignificant facing them.

Their silence fills the well of worry inside me, drilling deeper and deeper. I already want to go back to Edlyn. Even if there will be countless nights where I lie awake, unable to sleep because of the broken memories that will inevitably play in my mind.

"The Ashen Pit is uncertain," Palvadore starts. "Sefryn's betrayal and her assassinating the King—the Ashen Pit does not know if it has chosen correctly."

"How would it have known?" I ask. "Sometimes it can be impossible to tell who someone really is, not until they show it."

Grisla shakes her head. "That is not true," she says, her tone disapproving. "There are always signs. Some hide it better than others, yes, but there are *always* signs."

"What were the signs with Sefryn?"

"Knowing who she is now, looking back, you would probably see them easily," Kreavlos answers. "But you do not want to."

He's right. I don't. I don't want to think about all the things I missed, all of the mistakes I made.

"We won't dwell on this now," the Azure Fox says, interrupting my increasing and intensifying self-deprecating thoughts. "But we have to show you something. You of all people have the right to know."

I don't get the chance to ask her what she's talking about. Palvadore lowers his head, and my vision disappears for a split second before returning to that day in Aeilvow when we fought off the Stoichea.

I can see myself, Camila, and Sefryn dealing with Ziara and her hippogriff, all the while Elder and Abigail are farther away, battling the monster of a bird. Sefryn conjures her tree from the ground, rising with it so that she can help with the Stoichea.

At that time, I couldn't see everything that was happening. I now see how Sefryn whipped out ten vines from the tree, their speed incredibly fast as they chased the bird.

Sefryn actually managed to nick the bird in the neck after it broke free from the vine it almost got tangled in. The bird's attention was drawn to the ground. The Stoichea dives, seemingly after the vine, but the extension of the tree is no longer there. Abigail is. Her eyes bulge in fear as the bird rushes toward her. She knows she can't fend it off, not without an immensely powerful and precise strike of lightning or other weather. Abigail turns to run. But like I saw before, she can't move.

Though now I can see why. Abigail looks down, and the look on her face breaks my heart. Right from the ground, barely visible to anyone, are thick roots, dark and dirty, wrapped around Abigail's ankles.

Abigail knew seconds before that she wasn't going to make it. Not because she wasn't strong enough, but because she was stabbed in the back by Sefryn, who all this time had been trying to take us out.

I don't watch to see what I've already seen.

My eyes stay open as my sight changes from a vision of the past to seeing the present.

"Why did you show me that?" My voice threatens to break.

"She was your friend, you needed to see what happened," Grisla tells me. "You wouldn't forgive us if we let you go on with your life thinking that Abigail died because she wasn't strong enough. It would be different if we didn't know, but we do. And now so do you."

"Why do you guys care if I forgive you or not?" I ask them. "Would it ever matter if I trusted or despised you? I'm strong, but I am not you."

"The only thing the Ashen Pit knows for certain is you," Palvadore says. "He knew that you had to be an Ash Lord so that our world may make it through whatever is coming."

"And what is coming?"

They don't answer me. Of course not. I'm just a pawn, a soldier, to them. I could have spent the rest of my life not knowing my true potential, but I wouldn't have the heartbreak I have now.

"Claudius is going to work with the Queen to restore Edlyn," Palvadore informs me.

"I should be there," I snap at them. "Camila needs me. Elder needs me."

"It is safe to assume that it is you who needs them. Your current state of mind, however tempered at the moment, will make you lose control. Again." The large owl doesn't look pleased and his voice even more disgruntled.

"I had to contain your power to your room in the castle," Kreavlos says. "Unchecked, you would have brought down the whole thing."

"I didn't notice."

"We know," they all answer.

"I mean, I didn't see you there," I say.

"That was the point."

Kreavlos and I stare at each other, or at least I stare at where I imagine he is. Anger begins to rise within me again. I don't know why. I want to shout at the three of them. But they haven't done anything wrong.

No, like always, it's me. If punching my reflection in a mirror would serve as all the revenge I want, all the pain I want to inflict on myself for the rage and guilt I feel, I'd break a thousand, and then a thousand more until there is nothing left for me to see or feel.

Grisla steps closer to me. "There are things that we still don't understand," she says. "Whatever change the Ashen Pit felt, it is beginning to affect us. But it is hard to act when we do not know what to do or where to go."

"Why am I going back to Earth then?"

"Because the Ashen Pit thinks you need to clear your mind."

"And Earth will help with that?"

"No," Palvadore says in his deep voice. "*Someone.*"

There's no warning. Done with our meeting, I am thrown back into the daylight, the sun beaming down on the street, full of cars and people going about their business.

It feels like I am stepping out into the daylight after months of storms and thunder. There is nothing here to fuel my rage. Even the pettiness of people like Nick doesn't compare to all that I've witnessed.

It's been what—two months? Maybe three? On Earth, time would have moved differently, but it would be similar. Before the Dark Wind called me to Arteyva, I thought about starting my life over because I felt like I had nothing here. I didn't understand how very right I was.

But then there she is, proving me wrong immediately.

That perfectly wavy and lustrous hair, always positioned so that she looks ready for a photoshoot. And those shining, pale blue eyes. She was my first true friend before I even knew what it meant to have a friend.

I don't know what to say to her. Is she going to be mad that I disappeared for so long? Or just happy to see me again? Standing in the middle of the sidewalk, several people passing right by me, I feel unable to move. Do I even want to see her again, knowing that I won't be staying here? It would almost be kinder to let her think I'm just gone. But saying goodbye—that's something she deserves. Especially after all the times she's been there for me, without judgment, without hidden motives. But how do I tell her goodbye without telling her the truth?

All that my overthinking does is eat up the time I have to make a decision. She's close now, less than ten feet away.

Olivia looks up. Her breath catches when she sees me. And then I make up my mind. There is an intense sadness inside me. I don't want her to see me; I don't want to say goodbye. It would be much easier to avoid it all and let her think that I am just some distant memory.

But that isn't what the Ashen Pit wants. It brought me here to heal. That is exactly what Olivia is going to help me do—and I am grateful for her.

# CHAPTER 30

## CALL OF THE WILD

**Ziara Belle Sandfawn**

Who is he? There's something about him that draws my attention. No, it's not his looks. Not that they're bad, but there's something else. His darker features, though, are striking... no, he looks like an asshole. That's all I will let myself think of him. But still...

Shit!

His eyes catch mine. I look away quickly, pretending to grab some food. I do and end up at the table I sat at earlier, surrounded by a bunch of people I don't know. I already ate. I was planning on going to the training grounds, but then he caught my attention.

I stand, smushed against a whole lot of other people who came here for the same purpose I did. To participate in the Trials. I hear the man named Claudius tell us about them and the different kinds of Magis that are here. He mentions what I am. Then he mentions the Maleficium. He tells us he is of a higher order of one, and that there is one other. Craning my neck, I try to follow his line of vision. Then I see him again, the same guy who caught me staring.

No, I wasn't staring. I was intrigued.

So, he is a Maleficium? Before I get caught again, I look back at Claudius.

"And the other with us is Aros Hayes."

Oh no. I've heard the stories about him. He's the strong Maleficium that Claudius was talking about? My mother told me that he would be here, but she didn't tell me what he was. She says he's the best chance at surviving the Trials but told me not to make contact. She doesn't need to tell me. There's no way I'll ever go near him.

The chaos is insane. I don't know what these creatures are, swooping down from the skies, picking people off the ground, all while imps hop off their backs to chase down those unfortunate ones who cannot outrun them.

"Move!" I'm shoved out of the way. As I fall to the ground, the grass cushioning the impact, I see a dark-haired girl run away. Her name is Lacey. I met her last night, along with several others. I thought we'd be friends or, at the very least, venture through the Trials together.

I guess not.

Oh. Yeah, definitely not. Lacey is gone. Scooped up by a flying monster, she's far out of sight.

Realizing that I need to get out of here, I call out to the skies. Seemingly a bad move, none of the monsters, airborne or grounded, seem to notice me.

A panther runs toward me. Its black fur shines brilliantly in the early morning sunlight. It comes by, and I jump on its back. Without me saying anything, it runs off into the woods, getting as far away as it can from the pandemonium.

It's been three days. Maybe four.

Five?

I've been all alone. The panther left me when it seemed safe enough to do so. And for all this time, it's been leaves and grass for meals while I melt snow in large, hollow acorns so that I have something to drink.

Wandering out into the frosted woods, I bundle up in the sweater I brought along. My mother also told me that Voltar is a mountain and that I'd better make sure I have a plan to keep warm. I am grateful for her wisdom.

Something cries out. I jerk my head toward the noise. I can't see anything except my breath in the cold air. It's quiet now.

Just when I decide it's nothing, I hear it again, but this time it's fainter. It doesn't matter. I can feel it.

I rush to where it calls me, not letting myself trip over stray roots or slick leaves. Then I see it. I can't help the loud gasp that escapes my lungs. It is absolutely beautiful.

And hurt.

The large beast lies on its side, a gash running right across it. It turns its head to look at me. He has beautiful, large, brown eyes. Scared, he rustles his wings as I approach. I offer my hand, telling him that it's going to be alright.

He lets me pet him. The cut, still bleeding, isn't as bad as it could have been. I tell him that I will be back. And then I spend the next hour foraging for herbs and leaves that will help him heal.

I stay with him for another five days before moving him. It's a slow process since he's so big, and we can't just cut through the trees like I do. We finally make it out of the thicket, but I don't know where to go from here.

We end up taking shelter under a rock ledge. Voltar looks daunting enough. Looking up, I can't even see how high the mountain goes. But for now, we have a place to rest, protected from the rain, if it even comes.

What comes instead is snow. Had the hippogriff not wrapped its wing over me, pulling me close to its body for warmth, I could freeze to death.

It takes another three days until the hippogriff is fully healed. But when he is, I see just how large he is. Out in the open, he spreads his wings. Easily twice my height and ten times my weight, the creature looks stunningly terrifying, and I love it even more for that.

He lowers his head, bending down. The hippogriff tilts his head, telling me to get on. I do. He rises slowly, looks outward to the sky, and kicks off, going airborne. We rise high. The rush of the wind in my hair, though unbearably cold, brings a thrill that fills my blood, running through my veins. I can't believe I've never done something like this before.

And...I realize that I am not scared of heights. I love this. I love flying. We shoot high into the sky, cresting over the peak of Voltar. Looking down, I can see that something has happened. I point, asking the hippogriff to go that way. It obeys.

Part of the mountain looks like it's collapsed. But even more unusual, when we get closer, it feels like we pass through something invisible. Suddenly, an entire forest that wasn't there seconds ago now is, replacing the sloping cliffs of the mountain I had just seen.

Not wanting to land here, the hippogriff flies on. We end up landing in a meadow, where we stay for a couple of hours while I get some sleep.

When I wake, my buddy has brought me some food—squirrels and a hog? He chows down on them without a care, noticeably enjoying his meal.

I can't stomach it.

We move on, the hippogriff letting me ride him again. There are storm clouds ahead. We dive right under them. I hear roaring, shrieks, and violent calls of monsters, but I can't see anything. My friend recoils slightly, doing his best to keep his balance so that I don't lose mine.

Flying further, we reach the light. There are two bridges. One spans a great length, and the other is much shorter. Soaring down, I see something that makes my heart freeze with fear. Wyverns dart up from the valley below. These things shouldn't be here. They can't be. It doesn't make any sense. We're in Arteyva, I think.

The hippogriff dodges the oncoming monsters, but he can't do much offensively himself—not with me on his back.

I throw out my arms, squeezing my legs tightly around his torso so that I don't fall off. I can feel it inside me. There's power. But what kind?

A terrible roar answers that. Making the wyverns flee, a dragon flies into the air, momentarily blocking out the sun. It dives back down into the valley, out of sight beneath the clouds that lie below. Blinking, I look around. The sun is gone. In its place rests the moon with a hundred twinkling stars.

It's nighttime. But how?

Another roar fills the air, the volume nearly deafening. But it is of a different kind. The roar, more thunderous than monstrous, comes from below. Not from the depths that sink into what surely is a void of death, but from the land of the plateaus just below us.

A stampede of animals rushes over the bridges. There are all kinds. It must be Magis, whatever the bridges are made of, to be able to sustain them all. At the front, leading the pack, is the Azure Fox. Something about her presence draws me in, and I tell the hippogriff to follow her.

We reach the far end of the bridge. Landing, I hop onto the ground. Elephants, bears, all kinds of birds, rabbits, monkeys—more kinds than I can count. They're all here, and they are all looking at me. But why are they here? I didn't call for them—not knowingly.

"Come with me," the fox says, walking by and around the tall stone in the middle of the land. "Thank you, Argett," she whispers, talking to the hippogriff. I feel rude for a moment. I never asked him what his name was, nor did I tell him mine.

"Thanks, Argett," I tell him, petting him on his face. He closes his eyes and leans into my hands. "I'm Ziara."

The hippogriff takes a last look at me before taking off. Waiting for me, the Azure Fox calls again, leading me around the oblong stone.

We descend into the ground, and I soon approach a room that ignites—but the fire is blue, keeping the room dark. What's in front of me is surely the Ashen Pit, as well as a wolf with black fur, three times the size of a bear, staring at me.

"You have passed the Trials," he says. The Azure Fox walks over to him, her large body tiny compared to his. "Congratulations. But you have not passed the Trials as I intended."

"I got sidetracked," I tell him, having no freaking clue what he's talking about. Who is he, anyway?

"I noticed," he responds. Then, terrifyingly enough, he starts to circle me. As in, walk. In. Circles. Around me, looking up and down.

Throwing my arms out, I try calling for Argett—for anyone.

"That won't work here."

Ugh, *fine*.

"Do you even want to become an Ash Lord?" the wolf asks me, still walking in circles.

I think about it for a moment.

"Answer honestly," he tells me.

"No."

"Didn't think so." I think I hear the wolf sneer. "Still, you are the first to complete the Trials. For that alone, I will keep you in my sights."

I don't even want to know what he means by that.

"Do you know Aros?"

The question surprises me, and it takes a moment before I can answer. "I know of him."

"Watch over him."

The wolf vanishes.

The Azure Fox walks up to me, a pleasantly benign look on her snout.

And I am taken out of this place and find myself in Edlyn Castle.

***

In my dreams, the Azure Fox visits me multiple times. The King and Queen were nice enough to give me my own sleeping chambers, and in one of the towers. I decided to stay on the ground floor. Argett gets to stay with me this way. But he likes to venture out into the night, which makes sense since he has always lived in the wilderness.

Despite everything I've heard about him, I am told that I must ensure Aros remains safe. And then he returns, along with one of the princesses, some girl I don't know, Sefryn—of all people—and a guy named Elder. In the next day or so, I end up talking to Camila. I don't tell her about my time in the Trials. No. No one would be happy to hear that mine were over so quickly.

And then, of course, I catch his eye again. I blame myself this time.

Later, two other volunteers return, and the Trials are closed.

On the day the Ash Lords are chosen, I do my best to avoid his gaze. I can keep watch over him from a distance, though I am unsure why I need to. From what I've heard, Aros is quite capable of protecting himself. Aros and his friends become Ash Lords.

And then the Supreme Ash does something that makes me want to get as far away as possible.

The tension and fear in the air almost feel worse than they did that first day the Trials started. I woke up to the sounds of wind-splitting shrieks. The castle is hit, the whole thing vibrating like it's about to collapse. I run out of my chambers. A large monster sticks its head into the Atrium, its body trapped behind the passageway that is too narrow for it to break through.

I help many of the servants get to safety, but there are some that I cannot help, purely based on their poor decisions.

When it seems clear, I make a run for it and head out of the atrium, onto the castle grounds and toward the forest. Argett greets me, looking around in all directions.

"Go get Aros," I hear a voice to my right. Looking over, I see the Azure Fox. She runs at me. "Get Aros and Camila. Something isn't right about this."

"What?" I ask. I don't understand anything that's happening. I must have slept through the early stages of the attack, so I don't know how far the damage has spread or what we're even up against.

"The Ashen Pit believes all this to be a distraction. The King and Queen must be protected. Without them, the strongest kingdom in this realm will fall."

In my dreams, when she speaks to me, I've learned a lot. There has been a silent war brewing for decades, and now it seems like the imminent threat to the world is growing stronger.

"Where is he?"

"Aeilvow."

I hop onto Argett, and we fly off. It takes only a couple of minutes to get to the valley. We swoop in and out, dodging all the other creatures that fly around. I take a quick look at them. There is nothing pretty about a snake with wings. Not in my book.

I see him. Aros is below, deep in the valley. What just happened? I see a rush of water farther down, disappearing quickly.

We dive. When we get close, I see Aros, Camila, and Sefryn staring at us. There's no time to explain.

"I need you to come with me."

"We're busy."

Yeah, I can see that. But why doesn't he listen to me?

Oh, right. He barely knows who I am. He probably only knows me because everyone knows the people who made it out of the Trials. He tries to get away, so I put my hand on his chest.

Damn, he's burning up.

There's a flash of lightning. I don't let it draw my attention. It gets his, though, and I have to ask Argett to stop him.

"This is all a distraction!" I shout at him, begging him to understand.

They're not listening. *He's* not listening. I need a different tactic.

"Camila! Someone very powerful is behind this, and their target isn't Aeilvow—it's Edlyn."

I think that gets her attention. But Aros doesn't seem to care.

But then something happens. I see that huge bird creature swallow up the girl I know as Abigail. I hop on Argett, and he bolts toward the creature. We catch up, and what I see makes my heart sink. Abigail is tossed inside the throat and devoured.

Then a blast of freezing air comes our way. Argett dodges it, and we return to the others.

I don't know what to say, but he has to know, so I shake my head, indicating that Abigail is gone. I can feel the anger from Aros. No, it isn't just anger. It's power.

Darkening the sky—something that shouldn't be possible—a bolt of lightning is called down, striking the monstrous beast dead. My eyes widen as I look at Aros. From the side his friends are on, he's probably friendly, reliable, and powerful. From where I stand, barely knowing him, and him knowing me even less, he's completely fear-inducing. Whatever I may do in this life, I better not get on his bad side.

But I can't let fear stop me now. We need him. The King and Queen need him.

"Aros." He doesn't hear me. I call him again.

He looks at me, and I understand now.

"I—I don't mean to be insensitive," I say, hating myself for stuttering, but I go on anyway with, "we need you back at the castle."

Camila touches his arm. Sefryn tells him to go, and the two share a moment. I can feel what they have for each other.

I can't help but think that, of course, Sefryn would go for someone like him. She's always been beautiful. And drawn to power.

We—me, Aros, and Camila—fly off on Argett toward the castle. I make sure they're okay when we land, apologizing on Argett's behalf. The Azure Fox meets us, and we end up climbing one of the towers.

And there's a tree here? A freaking tree in the middle of the tower stairwell.

Asking about it, no one answers, but the Azure Fox tells me to get Claudius. I run off, knowing exactly where he is.

When we return, Claudius immediately goes to take control of Sefryn's body, who has been behind this the whole time. Sefryn breaks free and escapes. I was too late. The King is dead.

It's been one day. I wake from my dreams, only to enter another one. But this isn't a dream—it just feels like one. I am back at the Ashen Pit, and the large wolf stares at me.

"You're it, aren't you?" I ask him.

"You already know."

He's right. The wolf is the embodiment of the Ashen Pit. I know that, but his answer strengthens my conviction. He paces, but this time not around me—just in front of me.

"Things are uncertain," he tells me. He falls silent for a moment. "Sefryn is..."

I wish with the strongest of my will that he doesn't say it.

"Hmm..."

Phew. Whatever his thoughts are, he's keeping them to himself.

But after a while, I can't take the tension.

"What's going to happen next?"

The wolf walks up to me and stares down.

"I apologize for messing with the passage of time during the Trials," he says, catching me off guard by changing the subject. "See, I saw something in you, and I had to make sure that you made it through."

I don't say anything.

"You're in a unique position."

Again, changing the subject. But what does he mean? I already know my circumstances. He and the Azure Fox are probably the only other beings who know.

"We lost a victor of the Ash Trials," he tells me. I don't need reminding. "The other victors must be kept safe."

I wholeheartedly agree with him. But he's chosen the Ash Lords. Yes, one was a mess-up. But there are still three others and the Supreme Ash. What does he care about the other victors?

Reading my mind, he tells me, "I need the victors in case any of the Ash Lords perish."

I now realize that the Ashen Pit is lost deep in thought, and I don't know if he's talking out loud or to me.

"I've seen what the Ash Lords can do," I say. "They'll be fine."

The ginormous wolf starts to walk away, deep into the depths of the darkness beyond the faintly lit Ashen Pit.

Then he speaks, the tone of his voice both certain and chilling.

"With all that is coming for the Ash Lords, it is impossible for all of them to survive."

# Acknowledgements

Writing a novel feels like a solitary activity, but it is far from it.

First, to my family, who have consistently kept up with my progress and cheered me on—you have been patient and so supportive, even when I seemed to hide away during all the time I spent writing this novel. To my mother, who somehow finds time to read all my work despite her crazy schedule, and for sharing the same love of writing. To my father, for lending an ear when I needed to vent, and for buying me coffee on multiple occasions.

To my friends, who have supported me through all aspects of life—from the typical workdays to the gym sessions, the late nights, and the long weekends spent writing. Thank you for listening to the random f*cking topics I'd bring up from the depths of my imagination, for understanding when I stayed up until lost hours writing and then needed a break the next day, and especially for getting me out of the house when I needed to be social.

To Austin Giorgio, for his song *Dangerous Hands,* of which upon listening to it, something inside me ignited so powerfully that I ended up writing the first chapter of this book in one sitting.

To Estelle, for being brave enough to read along as I wrote, chapter by chapter, and for giving me your detailed feedback. I couldn't even imagine getting this far without your encouragement and excitement.

And to you, fellow reader, for your dreams, imagination, and adventurous spirit, all of which keeps stories like mine alive.

# About the Author

Gvonni Avner spends his time between Tampa and Los Angeles. He has written five novels, but Five of Ash is the start of his first major fantasy series. After falling in love with reading at the age of ten, he knew then that he wanted to create the same kinds of words that sparked his imagination and give others the chance to escape into new worlds and possibilities.

www.ingramcontent.com/pod-product-compliance
Lightning Source LLC
Chambersburg PA
CBHW020321010826
48973CB00005B/1076